Multimillion $ Victorian Mansion Burns—Two Bodies Found

A Victorian home on Steiner Street belonging to prominent attorney Paul Hanover was engulfed in flames last night at approximately 8:00 p.m. Firefighters discovered two victims in the wreckage, each with a bullet wound to the head. Identification is pending, and police sources have not ruled out murder (continued)

Hanover Daughter-in-Law Arrested in Murder, Arson

Catherine Hanover, a daughter-in-law of slain attorney Paul Hanover, was charged yesterday with double homicide in the May 12 deaths of Hanover and his live-in lover, Missy D'Amiens. Her attorney, Dismas Hardy, had no comment on her arrest and stated that his client (continued)

continued . . .

Nothing but the Truth

"Riveting . . . one of Lescroart's best tales yet."
—*Chicago Tribune*

The Mercy Rule

"Well written, well plotted, well-done." —Nelson DeMille

Guilt

"Begin *Guilt* over a weekend. . . . If you start during the work week, you will be up very, very late, and your pleasure will be tainted with, well, guilt."
—*The Philadelphia Inquirer*

A Certain Justice

"A West Coast take on *The Bonfire of the Vanities* . . . richly satisfying."   —*Kirkus Reviews*

"A gifted writer. . . . I read him with great pleasure."
—Richard North Patterson

The 13th Juror

"Fast-paced . . . sustains interest to the very end."
—*The Wall Street Journal*

Hard Evidence

"Engrossing . . . compulsively readable, a dense and involving saga of big-city crime and punishment."
—*San Francisco Chronicle*

Dead Irish

"Full of all the things I like. Lescroart's a pro."
—Jonathan Kellerman

THE
MOTIVE

JOHN LESCROART

A SIGNET BOOK

SIGNET
Published by New American Library, a division of
Penguin Group (USA) Inc., 375 Hudson Street,
New York, New York 10014, USA
Penguin Group (Canada), 90 Eglinton Avenue East, Suite 700, Toronto,
Ontario M4P 2Y3, Canada (a division of Pearson Penguin Canada Inc.)
Penguin Books Ltd., 80 Strand, London WC2R 0RL, England
Penguin Ireland, 25 St. Stephen's Green, Dublin 2,
Ireland (a division of Penguin Books Ltd.)
Penguin Group (Australia), 250 Camberwell Road, Camberwell, Victoria 3124,
Australia (a division of Pearson Australia Group Pty. Ltd.)
Penguin Books India Pvt. Ltd., 11 Community Centre, Panchsheel Park,
New Delhi - 110 017, India
Penguin Group (NZ), cnr Airborne and Rosedale Roads, Albany,
Auckland 1310, New Zealand (a division of Pearson New Zealand Ltd.)
Penguin Books (South Africa) (Pty.) Ltd., 24 Sturdee Avenue,
Rosebank, Johannesburg 2196, South Africa

Penguin Books Ltd., Registered Offices:
80 Strand, London WC2R 0RL, England

Published by Signet, an imprint of New American Library,
a division of Penguin Group (USA) Inc. Previously published
in a Dutton edition.

First Signet Printing, January 2006
10 9 8 7 6 5 4 3 2 1

Copyright © The Lescroart Corporation, 2005
Excerpt from *The Hunt Club* copyright © The Lescroart Corporation, 2006
All rights reserved

Ⓟ REGISTERED TRADEMARK—MARCA REGISTRADA

Printed in the United States of America

PUBLISHER'S NOTE

This is a work of fiction. Names, characters, places, and incidents either are the
product of the author's imagination or are used fictitiously, and any resemblance to actual persons, living or dead, business establishments, events, or
locales is entirely coincidental.

The publisher does not have any control over and does not assume any
responsibility for author or third-party Web sites or their content.

To Lisa Sawyer
Again, and again, and again . . .

*Out of the crooked tree of humanity
no straight thing can ever be made.*
                    —Immanuel Kant

PART
ONE

1

By location alone, a block from Fillmore Street as it passes through the upwardly challenged Hayes Valley, Alamo Square would not be among the sexier neighborhoods in San Francisco. But one of the most popular and recognizable posters of the City by the Bay captures a row of beautifully restored and vibrantly painted three- and four-story Victorians that face the park on Steiner Street—the so-called "Painted Ladies." The poster created a certain cachet for the area such that the cheapest of these houses now go for three-plus. Million.

The blaze at Paul Hanover's, in the middle of this block, began around 8:00 P.M. on May 12, although the first alarm wasn't called in until nearly 8:30. Fires love old Victorians. Even though Hanover's house had been stripped to the bare bones twenty years earlier—retrofitted for earthquakes and freshly insulated with fire-resistant material—it is the nature of Victorian design to have funky interior spaces, oddly shaped rooms, crannies and closets and unusual passages. Within the walls, since heat wants to travel up, fires employ the vertical stud lines as flues, almost as chimneys, to transport themselves effortlessly and quickly up and up into the roof spaces, where billowing smoke is most often noticed first.

Even in a neighborhood of great sensitivity to the threat of fire—of old, very valuable wooden houses in wall-to-wall proximity—no one noticed anything amiss at Hanover's until the fire had progressed to the unfinished attic. The late-arriving fog camouflaged the first appearance of the smoke, and the wind blew it away. By the time one of the local residents realized that what he was actually seeing was not fog but thick clouds of smoke pouring out from under the eaves of his neighbor's roof, the fire was well advanced.

As soon as the first alarm's fire trucks arrived—three engines, two trucks, two battalion chiefs, an assistant chief and a rescue squad—the two-man aerial ladder team from the first engine began climbing to Hanover's roof, intending to ventilate it by cutting a hole into it with axes and chainsaws. Meanwhile, four men in Nomex turnout pants and coats and wearing Scott Air-Paks—the initial attack squad—got to the front door, found it unlocked and opened it right up. Although they were armed with Akron fog nozzles that could spray water over a wide angle and get them closer to the flames, in this case they were greeted by a roiling cloud of hot thick black smoke, impossible to see through. They could make no progress.

Al Daly, officer of the initial attack squad, spoke matter-of-factly into the headpiece of his walkie-talkie. "Front door is breached, Norm. We got a *working fire* here." Daly was speaking to his battalion chief, Norm Shaklee, out front in the street. The words conveyed great urgency. A working fire meant they would need at least one more alarm—four more engines, another truck, two more chiefs. In a house this size with so much exposure to the homes on either side, this working fire could go to five alarms, San Francisco's maximum.

All four stories of Hanover's home might already be—probably were—involved. Shaklee, in his white helmet, placed the next alarm call and looked up as the sound of chainsaws stopped. Over the roof, he saw a churning pillar of black smoke erupt into the sky, and spoke into his walkie-talkie. "They're through on the roof, Al. Back out a minute."

He was telling Daly that ventilation was about to start working, potentially a very dangerous moment. If the smoke inside the house was hot enough—and no one knew if it was—the addition of oxygen to it might at this time cause a tremendous and often lethal backdraft explosion. So the initial attack squad waited in a kind of suspension down the front steps out in the street until, a minute and forty seconds later, the smoke column spewing from the roof suddenly exploded into a fireball that lit the night for blocks around and rose to heights of a hundred feet and more.

By now, the first hoses had been attached to the hydrant at the corner, and eight firefighters on each of a couple of them were blasting six hundred gallons of water per minute into the open space. For all the apparent good the firefighters were doing, they might as well have been standing around spitting on the flames, but appearances in this case were deceiving. The hydrant water was lowering the temperature sufficiently so that Daly and his squad could advance again into the building.

Because of the ventilation, the smoke that filled the foyer had now begun to dissipate upward, as did the thick cloud of steam generated by the water from the hoses. Within a few seconds after the hose teams stopped soaking the entryway, Daly and his squad were back at the front door. With his night helmet's beam on and glowing, he had relatively clear sight lines through the foyer to the house beyond, to the flames still licking at the walls on all sides. Wielding his Akron, spraying in a wide arc, he advanced into the darkness, following the beam on his helmet. All around was noise and chaos—the rush of air behind him as the conflagration sucked it in, the roar of the actual fire, the creaking and splintering of wood, the hail of ax blows, disembodied voices yelling both within and outside the building.

Daly sprayed and advanced, sprayed and advanced. One foot or so at a time. The foyer was circular, high-ceilinged and quite large, perhaps fourteen feet in diameter. He could make out the shapes of burning furniture along the walls—what appeared to have been a coatrack, a sideboard, maybe an umbrella stand or wastebasket. Drapes over a pair of windows, curved to the shape of the house, were all but incinerated. One opening to Daly's right led into another open room, and directly ahead of him another doorway fed into a hall. Everywhere he looked there was flame—total involvement of the ground floor.

Despite the hose's soaking, the fire was growing again, heating up. It was excruciatingly hot, dangerously hot. Daly felt a sloshing like water in his ear, but knew that it wasn't water. It was his earwax, melting. He had to get out of here, right now. He wasn't going to be able to check for potential rescue victims until the fire died somewhat, and by then—by now, he knew—anything living in the structure would have died as well.

Still he pushed forward, forcing himself for another step or two, spraying as he went. It was full night, his only light his helmet beam. Looking down at the entrance to the hallway, he suddenly became aware of two shapes that stopped him where he stood. Leaning in for a closer look, not that he needed it, he forced himself to speak in his most neutral tone. "There's two bodies in here, Norm. In the foyer."

Out in the street, the second-alarm units had begun to arrive and Shaklee was issuing orders to nine people at once back by the rehab station, which itself was already nearly overwhelmed supplying drinks, fresh air bottles and first aid. He asked Daly to repeat what he'd just said, and he did, adding, "No ambulance needed." Which meant they were obviously dead.

Shaklee took only another second to process the information, then turned and spoke to his operator-aide, who functioned as gopher in the field. "Find Becker," he said, "and put in a call to homicide."

Arnie Becker, the forty-three-year-old lead arson investigator attached to the Bureau of Fire Investigation, arrived with the second-alarm unit. In situations like this, Becker's task was to determine the origin of the blaze. To do that, he'd have to enter the building and investigate all the indicators—"V" patterns on walls, decalcification of Sheetrock, "alligatoring" of studs, condition of electrical components and so on—and by doing so, hope to locate the spot where the fire began, and if possible determine what might have caused it.

Becker was a twenty-year veteran of the fire department. In San Francisco his whole working life, he was particularly familiar with Victorians, and he knew that this house, with all the places in which a fire could hide, would in all likelihood burn through the night and perhaps well into the next morning. He wasn't going to have an answer anytime soon.

But that didn't mean he didn't have a lot to do. A huge crowd of onlookers had coalesced on the block, and more were streaming out of houses both up and down the street and across the open space of Alamo Square behind them. This was his potential witness pool—people he and his team would need to talk to. Some percentage of them might live on the block, might have seen something suspicious.

He needed all the information he could find from a near-infinite universe of possibilities, the most tantalizing one being that if this fire was arson, if someone had started it, then that person was probably among the crowd, enjoying his handiwork, possibly even sitting in one of the cypress trees in Alamo Square getting sexual satisfaction from it. Becker had seen it before.

In San Francisco, police officers from the hit & run detail are assigned to fire investigation, so Becker had a staff of helpers and he sent them out to talk to everybody they could. They would not conduct formal interviews—not now, anyway—but he wanted names and phone numbers of everybody. If people didn't want to provide that, that could be instructive. If still others wouldn't shut up, that might tell him something as well. Becker didn't know anything, including what he didn't know. So this was his chance to start gathering information from whatever source presented itself, and he took it very seriously indeed. His men fanned out to either end of the crowd and were working it to the inside and from behind.

Becker himself was on his way to talk to the neighbor who'd called in the fire and who had waited around to help guide the trucks when they'd arrived, not that they had needed it by then. But suddenly Becker's partner in the Arson Unit, J. P. Dodd—twenty-eight years old, Army-trained, competent yet relaxed, appeared at his elbow. The night around them was a kaleidoscope of lights in the darkness—the yellow flickering fire, the red bubbles on the trucks, the white glare from the firemen's helmets, now the kleigs of the TV camera crews. Dodd's earnest face looked particularly grave. "They've found two bodies, Arn. Shaklee needs you to come on up."

The fire still raged in the back of the house and on the upper stories. The two manned fire hoses at the front door snaked across the floor of the foyer and disappeared out the right-hand doorway somewhere back into the inferno. Becker, now suited up in his turnout coat and night helmet, his Scotts down over his face, also held a wide-beam flashlight that he trained on the bodies. He squatted like a baseball catcher, having learned that to put a knee on the floor was an invitation to pain and suffering.

The clothing had been burned off where they had been exposed, but even though both figures were lying on their backs, he couldn't tell what sex either had been. One was larger, and one smaller, so they were possibly a man and a woman, but he wouldn't be sure until the coroner was finished with them. The hair and any distinguishing characteristics on the faces, likewise, were burned away.

Something in the resting attitudes struck him, though. He had seen many dead people before, the victims of fire, as well as victims of murder and/or suicide, who were at fire scenes but dead before they burned. In his experience, the bodies of people who died from fire or smoke inhalation as the blaze grew around them tended to curl protectively into a fetal position. Victims of murder or suicide most often lay as they fell, and these two bodies fit that profile. There was still the characteristic drawing up of the extremities as the flesh cooked, but it did not strongly resemble the curled-up bodies he'd seen of victims who'd died by fire and fire alone.

Suspicious by nature and now by circumstance, Becker reached for a flashlight-like device he wore on his belt— the multi-gas-detecting AIM-32/50. Turning it on, he waved it down the sides of the smaller victim—the one nearest to the front door—and wasn't exactly stunned to see that it registered the presence of gasoline.

So, Becker thought, this was probably arson. And from the attitudes of the bodies, it was quite possibly a murder, or a murder/suicide, as well.

Becker tucked in his gas detector, then trained his flashlight again on the smaller body in front of him. Directly over his head, a deafening crash shook the building and rained charcoal down over him, but he barely heard or noted it. The small and perfectly round hole high in the back of the head, above and behind where the ear should have been located—it had burned away—commanded all of his attention. Stepping over the smaller torso, Becker moved over the still-squishy rug, squatted and shone his light on the other victim. Tucked under the side of the torso, a glint of metal shone up when his beam hit it. Becker wasn't going to touch anything at this point, but he lowered his light's trajectory and saw enough to realize that he was looking at the barrel of a gun.

At a little after 11:00 P.M., Inspector Sergeant Dan Cuneo of San Francisco's homicide detail parked his unmarked car on the opposite side of Alamo Square and began to make his way through the large, awestruck, worried crowd. His immediate sense was that this fire was nowhere near to being controlled. Three houses on the block now appeared to be burning, and in the crowd he overheard snatches of panicked conversations, some from what must have been residents. People staring mesmerized, some crying, some talking in hushed tones. As he came closer, he noticed a cordoned-off command area on the steps up the street that led into the park.

Cuneo knew where he needed to go, and he made a beeline toward the white helmet that seemed to hover above the crowd. The white helmet belonged to the incident commander. Every fire scene had an IC, and his power within that setting was absolute. The president of the United States could show up at a fire, wanting to get a better look, and the IC could order him to chill for a while and that would be the end of the discussion.

Cuneo got close enough to make out some of the faces that had gathered around this IC—the name tag over his left pocket said "Shaklee." He was taller than Cuneo's own six feet. Cuneo pushed his way through the crowd, excused himself and presented his badge. Shaklee nodded distractedly, said something into his walkie-talkie, came back to Cuneo. "You need to see Becker." He pointed toward the steps. "The guy talking to the woman in the leather jacket."

Cuneo nodded his thanks and started walking over. He was an edgy man in his early forties, unable to keep still or quiet—he could not eat or listen to a witness or a colleague without humming—and this trait had kept him from retaining a regular partner in homicide. For the past year or more, he'd been working strictly solo. His fellow inspectors considered him a character, but not quite a weirdo. It was a critical distinction.

Handsome in an unusual way, Cuneo's face had an oddly misshapen character as well, almost as though it had once been broken down to its integral pieces and then imperfectly reassembled. His nose initially protruded to a ridge, then hooked left and went flat as though someone had pushed it in like a thumbtack. At times he appeared cross-eyed. He'd obviously survived a serious bout with teenage acne, but instead of scarring, the skin over his cheeks had taken on a stretched, almost shiny look—maybe too many skin peels. An inventory of the individual parts wouldn't indicate it, but somehow the mishmash came together in a way that pleased his girlfriends.

Now he was at the steps. Even here across the street and back into the shelter of the park, the fire was making it uncomfortably warm. Cuneo grabbed a Styrofoam cup of water from a table someone had set up and got himself close enough to listen to Becker and the woman in the leather coat. She wasn't a kid—maybe, Cuneo figured, about his age—but she was still very attractive. Cuneo's antennae for women were always up—he couldn't help himself and saw no reason to change. Close up, he noticed that the woman's jacket hung open, partially revealing an all-grown-up but tight-looking body in a blue silk blouse, and below a thin waist tucked into designer jeans. The woman's stylish medium-length hair picked up highlights from the flames. One of the ageless babes, he thought, as he automatically checked for a wedding ring—not that it always mattered. She wore one.

He moved a step closer, started flicking the side of his cup with his fingers.

". . . as soon as I saw it on the television," the woman was saying. "I was just over here with Paul this afternoon, so I knew exactly . . ."

Becker held up a finger, stopping her, directed a flat gaze to Cuneo. "Can I help you?"

Cuneo quickly brought his cup to his mouth and flicked free the last of the ice. Flashing his badge, he mumbled around the small cubes. "Sorry. Dan Cuneo. Homicide."

Becker stuck a hand out. "Becker. Arson. And that's what this is."

The woman turned to face Cuneo. "You're with homicide? Is somebody dead in there then?" Back to Becker. "You *know* that? God, it's got to be Paul."

Cuneo: "Paul who?"

"Paul Hanover. It's his house." She turned all the way around and stared back at what was left of the place. By this time, the fire had collapsed much of the structure. The front doorway still stood, and most of the second floor, but the third and fourth stories were all but gone. "He's in there? You've got to get him out before . . ."

Becker cut her off. "There's no reason to get him out, ma'am. He was dead a half hour ago. If you knew him, I'm sorry." Pointing toward the house, Becker said to Cuneo, "They're directing the master streams—that's those major hoses—to try and preserve as much of your crime scene as they can. But there's no telling."

Cuneo nodded. "The call said there were two of them."

"Yep."

"Oh my God," the woman said again. "That's got to be Missy, too."

Cuneo turned from the house to the woman, introduced himself again, flashed his badge. "And who are you, please?"

"Catherine Hanover. I'm Paul's daughter-in-law. Paul Hanover. He lives, lived here."

"Excuse me," Cuneo said, "are you talking about *the* Paul Hanover?"

"If you mean the lawyer, yes." She looked back to the house. "I can't believe he's in there."

"Somebody's in there," Becker said, "but we don't know it's Mr. Hanover. Or Missy."

"Who's Missy?" Cuneo asked.

"Michelle D'Amiens, Paul's girlfriend. Fiancée. Everybody called her Missy. They were getting married in the fall." Suddenly, a bolt of panic shot through her. "Can't you do anything? You can't just let them stay in there. There won't be anything left of them."

Becker's mouth was set as he shared a look with Cuneo. Both knew the awful truth, that the bodies were already unrecognizable, charred beyond any hope of recognition. Identification and forensic evidence, if any, would mostly come from a lab now. Neither they nor anyone else could do anything to change that.

"Mrs. Hanover," Becker said, "maybe you want to find a place to sit. Or go on home. Whatever happens here is going to take a long while. We can get your address and phone number and contact you in the morning."

But Cuneo wasn't quite ready to dismiss her. "Did I hear you say that you were over here at this house earlier today?"

"Yes."

"Why was that?"

"I wanted to talk to Paul about something, just some family stuff."

"Did you see him?"

She nodded. "Yes. We had some coffee." Her eyes were drawn back to the inferno. Bringing her hand up, she rubbed her forehead. "He can't be in there right now. That's just not possible. And Missy."

"Was Missy there when you talked to Paul today?" Cuneo asked.

"No. I don't know. I didn't see her, anyway."

"So what was the family stuff?"

The question stopped her and she frowned. "Why? What difference would that make?"

Cuneo looked to Becker, who shrugged. He came back to Catherine Hanover. "I don't know. If the man's dead, everything he did in his last hours is going to come under scrutiny. If this was arson, and Inspector Becker here says it is, somebody might have started the fire to kill somebody in the house. I'm going to want to know everything about his last day."

Becker butted in. "Could you please excuse us for a minute, ma'am?" Without waiting for her reply, he stepped in front of her and hooked an arm into Cuneo's to turn him. When they'd moved off half a dozen steps, he said, "Before you go too far with her, maybe you should know that there was a gun under the larger torso, probably the man, maybe this Hanover. Also what looks like a bullet hole in one of the heads. Hers. Maybe in his, too, but I didn't want to touch and turn him to find out."

"So murder/suicide?"

Again, Becker shrugged. "Maybe. That's one thing that fits, anyway. The gun was under his body."

"He did himself and fell on the gun?"

"Maybe. Could be. That works. If the whole place goes up, I've got a roll of pictures I took you can look at tomorrow, then decide. Otherwise, if they can save the foyer, we might pull a break and be able to get in again by sunrise." He glanced at the fire. "Not much before, I wouldn't think."

Cuneo nodded, found his eyes drawn back across the street, where most of the firefighting activity had now come to be centered on the houses to either side of Hanover's. Becker could be right. It looked to Cuneo as though part of the crime scene might be salvaged after all. "So where'd this woman come from?"

"She said she was home watching TV and saw it on the news and recognized the place."

"Where's the rest of her family?"

"I don't know. I didn't ask. Maybe there isn't any rest of it. I had just started talking to her when you got here."

"All right." Cuneo cast a glance over to Mrs. Hanover, who was also staring at the blaze, hypnotized by it. He came back to Becker. "But it's definitely arson?"

"There was definitely gasoline residue under the smaller body."

"Anything else?"

"That's not enough?"

"No, I didn't mean that."

They had moved out in front of Mrs. Hanover, and now both men looked back to where she stood. Her coloring was high, unwitting excitement on her face, in the look in her eyes. With the heat from the fire, she'd removed her jacket and held it by a finger over her shoulder, a posture that emphasized her already generous bosom. "That's a damn fine-looking woman," Cuneo said.

"You going to let her go home?" Becker asked.

Cuneo kept his eyes on her. "Couple more minutes," he said.

2

Fifty-five-year-old Abraham Glitsky had worked his way up through the ranks of the San Francisco Police Department and was now its deputy chief of inspectors. In his days as a homicide inspector, and then later as lieutenant in charge of the homicide detail, he was a slacks-and-flight jacket kind of cop, but since assuming his latest rank—the only step up was chief—he wore his blues every day. And though he wasn't aware of it, he cut quite a figure in them. A former tight end at San Jose State, Glitsky stood six feet two and went about 220, none of it padding. Jewish on his father's side and black on his mother's, his blue eyes were set off against light mocha skin. But a deep scar that ran between both his lips kept him from ever considering himself even remotely good-looking. If he thought about it at all, and he didn't, he'd admit that he probably looked a little scary, especially when he wasn't smiling, which was most of the time. And he wasn't all wrong.

At twelve minutes after seven on this fog-bound May morning, when Glitsky pulled his city-issued car to the curb at Alamo Square, he couldn't have dredged up a smile on a bet. He'd routinely called his office from home for messages soon after he woke up and had learned about the double homicide and the five-alarm arson. The scene wasn't much of a detour from his duplex above Lake on his route to work at the Hall of Justice, and he felt he needed to see it with his own eyes.

Getting out of his car, he stood for a moment surveying the still-smoking disaster that had occurred here last night. Before most of the city's firefighters had finally stopped the spread of flames at around 3:00 A.M., all but two of the Painted Ladies had been affected to some degree or another. The one in the center was destroyed except for its steps and a circular area on the first floor behind the front door. On either side of that structure, the adjacent homes would have to be completely rebuilt. The one on Glitsky's left as he faced the wreckage, which must have been slightly windward last night, was nothing but a burned-out skeleton. The former gingerbread house on the right was a gutted shell of broken-out windows and charred, peeling timbers. On either side of *those* houses, the adjacent homes yawned vacant and bereft—more broken windows, open front doors, obvious water and fire damage. Cleanup crews were spraying and sweeping all over the area. Teams of ax-wielding firemen jabbed and poked through the various wreckages, locating hidden hot spots for the hose crews.

Glitsky finally moved away from his car. Muted activity hummed all around him as he crossed down to the IC's car. Hoses still snaked to fire hydrants. Two engines remained parked back to back in front of the middle home. Three trucks lined the near curb. The coroner's van was double-parked by the engines near the middle of the street. Most of the onlookers had dispersed.

On the bumper of a car, a man in a white helmet sat holding a steaming cup in both hands. Glitsky, introducing himself, thought the man looked like he'd just come from a battlefield—and in a sense he supposed he had. Slack with fatigue, the IC's face was blackened everywhere with soot, his eyes shot with red.

After they shook hands, Shaklee said, "My arson guys are still in there with Strout." John Strout was the city's medical examiner. "And your guy. Cuneo?" he added.

"Dan Cuneo, yeah." Glitsky lifted his chin toward the houses. "All I got word of was fatality fire."

"You don't know who lived here?"

"No."

"You know Paul Hanover?"

"No kidding?" Glitsky looked at the house. "Was he inside?"

"Somebody was. Two people, actually. From the sizes, a man and a woman, but we won't know for sure who they were for a while." Shaklee sipped at his drink. "They're not identifiable." He paused. "You haven't heard?"

"Heard what?"

"They were dead when the fire started. Shot."

Glitsky's eyes went back to the house.

"The gun's still in there," Shaklee said. "Under the bigger torso."

"Paul Hanover."

"Probably."

"And his girlfriend?"

"That's the rumor. You can go in."

Glitsky blew a vapor trail, hesitating. Finally, he shook his head. "That's all right. I've seen enough bodies to last me. Better if I didn't step on Cuneo's toes. It's his case."

Shaklee shrugged. "Your call."

"Yeah." Another pause, a last look toward the house. If anyone else from homicide besides Cuneo had drawn the case, Glitsky would have gone inside. "I'll catch him and Strout downtown after they know a little more what they've got." After a last glance at the destruction, he met Shaklee's eye and shook his head at the waste and loss.

Crunching over broken glass and charred debris, he started walking back to his car.

The only time Abe and Treya Glitsky had ever seriously disagreed was before they got married. The issue was whether they would have children together.

Both of them had survived the deaths of their first spouses, and had raised their respective children as single parents. Treya had a teenage girl, Raney, and Abe already had two sons, Isaac and Jacob, out of the house, and Orel at the time he met Treya with only a couple of years to go. Abe, fifty-two then, figured he had already done the family thing and done it well. He didn't suppose, and really wasn't too keen about finding out, whether he'd have the energy or interest necessary to be an active and involved father again. To Treya, in her mid-thirties, this was a deal breaker, and the two broke up over it. The split had endured for eleven days before Abe changed his mind. Their baby, Rachel, was now nearly two and a half years old.

This morning—Thursday—Treya, seventeen days late, had taken the home pregnancy test, and it had been positive. Her husband invariably left their duplex by 7:00 A.M., so he'd already gone in to work when she found out. She worked in the same Hall of Justice as he did, as personal secretary to San Francisco's district attorney, Clarence Jackman, but though she'd now been at her job for the better part of three hours, she hadn't worked up the courage to call Abe and tell him.

They'd avoided pretty much all discussion of whether they'd have more children after Rachel, but Treya didn't feel as though she'd been sneaky with this latest development. They both knew they were doing nothing to prevent it. Surely that was a sign of Abe's tacit approval.

But she wasn't completely sure.

While watering the plants in Jackman's outer office, which doubled as a no-frills reception area for the DA's appointments, she caught sight of herself in the wall mirror and realized that she'd been biting her lips and had scraped her lipstick off, top and bottom. Stepping closer to the mirror, she saw traces of it on her teeth. Nerves. She had to call Abe and let him know right now. She had just finished scratching the lipstick off and was returning around the front of her desk to do just that when Dismas Hardy, Jackman's eleven o'clock and Abe's great friend, knocked at the side of the open hallway door. And the phone rang.

"If that's for me, I'm in training for a marathon and can't be disturbed," Hardy said.

Treya shot him an amused and tolerant look and reached over the desk to pick up the phone. "DA's office." She came around the desk and sat in her chair, frowning. "No," she said, "what about her?" Treya listened for another moment, then shook her head. "I haven't heard a thing, and nobody's called Clarence about anything like that. Yes, I'm sure. Do you want me to ask Diz? He's here."

Hardy looked over in some surprise.

Treya held up a finger, listened, then spoke across to him. "Kathy West"—the mayor, on her job now for about five months—"wants to see Abe. He wonders if you might have heard about anything going on at City Hall?"

"Just the rumor that she was firing him, but I don't believe it."

Treya spoke into the phone. "He hasn't heard anything

either." She listened. "Okay. Well, whatever it is, I wouldn't worry. No, I know. Good luck."

She hung up, and realizing that she hadn't told her husband her own news, *their* own news, she bit at her lip again.

"Are you all right?" Hardy asked.

"I'm fine. Just a little distracted."

"Well," Hardy copped Billy Crystal's old *Saturday Night Live* accent, "it's not how you feel but how you look, and dahling, you look mahvelous." When Treya didn't react, Hardy went sober. "Is Abe really worried? Are you?"

"I don't think so. He'd just rather be prepared whenever it's possible."

"You're kidding? Abe?" Then: "I do wonder what Kathy wants, though."

"Whatever it is, it's got to be important, don't you think? She wanted him ASAP," she said. "And in person."

Kathy West had been a city supervisor for six terms and, during the last couple of years before her election to mayor, had been a regular at Clarence Jackman's informal "kitchen cabinet" meetings, held most Tuesdays at Lou the Greek's bar and restaurant, located just across the street from the Hall of Justice. Glitsky—and Treya and Hardy, for that matter—were also members, so there was a history of goodwill and mutual respect between the deputy chief and the mayor.

Nevertheless, Glitsky did not feel free to sit down and relax in her office, but stood at ease in the center of her rug.

Nor did Kathy West come out from behind her large and ornate desk. Through the open double windows behind her, downtown San Francisco shimmered mostly white as the fog burned away. Small-boned and delicate, West's fragile packaging all but disguised a ferocious will and laser intellect. Completely at home in polite society, raised to an old standard of born-to privilege mixed with a heightened sense of civic responsibility, she was in her bones a pragmatic, skillful politician, now somewhere in her late fifties. Playing somewhat against type, she talked the good talk about believing in getting her hands dirty if that's what it would take, whatever it was. And that had gotten her elected.

This morning, Glitsky was discovering firsthand that it wasn't all talk. "I just can't accept any part of it, Abe. The Paul Hanover I knew—and I've known him for thirty-five years—did not shoot his fiancée, and then himself, and then burn down his house. That is just not what happened. *I can't accept it.*" She stabbed the open flat of her desk blotter with a bony index finger. "I don't care what the medical examiner rules."

Glitsky wasn't going to fight her. At least not yet, before he knew anything. He assumed she just needed her hand held. "I don't think John Strout is anywhere near making a ruling," he said. "It's just the usual media madness, filling that awful silence they hate so much."

West's mouth went up in a tic of appreciation that vanished quickly. "I think it's more than that. They were, and I quote, 'police sources.'"

"I heard that, too. Saying they couldn't rule out murder/suicide. Which, in all fairness, they can't. It might have been."

Glitsky reserved judgment as he always did, but if Strout eventually came to this conclusion, it wouldn't be a shock. At this stage, it certainly looked like it could have been a murder/suicide. But he wasn't going to press that argument with the mayor. "I don't blame you for being angry at the stupid reporting, but it's not like we don't see it every day. If you want, I'll see to it you're informed with every development. Then you can call the press conferences yourself and maybe even have some fun."

But fun wasn't on the mayor's agenda. Impatient, she was shaking her short bob of gray hair, a quick birdlike movement. "No," she said, "I want more than that. That's why I called you here, Abe. I want somebody I trust working on this. This cannot be what it seems. I will not have Paul Hanover's name slandered over something that he didn't do." She asked abruptly, "Do you know Dan Cuneo?"

"Sure."

"What do you know about him?"

Glitsky knew he did not like him. He guessed that the feeling was mutual. Cuneo had never worked in homicide under Glitsky, and worse, a couple of years before he'd actually accused Glitsky of collusion with Dismas Hardy for trying to deflect a murder rap from one of Hardy's clients. But West didn't need the history lesson about him and Cuneo. "Marcel Lanier says he's okay. He makes his numbers."

"My, what a ringing endorsement." West's bright eyes stayed on Glitsky, waiting.

His mouth went up a fraction of an inch—a pass at a smile—and he shrugged. "I don't know him personally. If I can ask, what about him?"

"The latest version of the news I've seen named him as the police source. He's the inspecting officer on this case. I think he's a hog for press and he's already jumping to conclusions. I think he's the wrong man."

After a minute, Glitsky nodded. "Would you like me to talk to Lanier? Maybe he can assign Cuneo a partner, although I hear he likes to work alone."

"I've heard he can't keep a partner." Kathy West scratched at her blotter. "Actually, Abe," she said quietly, "before I asked you to come up here, I called Frank Batiste." This was the chief of police, Glitsky's boss, the man who'd promoted him. West's mention of his name in this context—low-key, to be sure—marked a change in the dynamic of things. "I asked Frank who, in his opinion, was the single best homicide inspector in the city, and he said it was you."

"I don't know about that," Glitsky said, "though of course I'm flattered. But I'm not in homicide anymore, as you know. They have good people down there."

West stared at him for a long moment. "Abe, I don't want to beat around the bush. I'd consider it a personal favor if you would agree to help investigate this case. Chief Batiste has agreed to assign someone else temporarily to your administrative duties, press conferences, public appearances and so on, during the interim. You've made no secret about how little you like that stuff. You'll enjoy the break."

"And what about Cuneo?"

"That's a police matter, Abe. I'm confident that between you, Frank and Lieutenant Lanier, you'll be able to come to some resolution there."

Glitsky looked out over the mayor's shoulder to the city

beyond. Though it wasn't particularly warm in the room, he had broken a light sweat and wiped a sleeve across his forehead. "Ms. Mayor," he began.

"Abe, please." She held up a hand. "It was always Kathy at Lou the Greek's," she said. "It's still Kathy."

He had the permission, but that didn't tempt him to use it. Nodding, noncommittal, he drew a breath. "I was going to say that it's impossible to predict where an investigation is going to lead. I'm concerned that I won't find what you're looking for."

"But I'm not looking for anything," she said.

"Forgive me," he said, "but it very much sounds like you don't want me to find that Hanover killed anybody. Or himself."

"No, if that's what he did, then that's what you'll find. And I'll live with it. But what I want is somebody who'll really look. Somebody who won't go to the press on day one and say it looks like a murder/suicide, that it looks like Hanover killed his girlfriend."

Glitsky chewed at one side of his cheek. "All right, then. I need to ask you something else."

"Of course. Anything."

"What was your relationship with him? Hanover?"

The mayor's eyes closed down. "He was a friend and a donor to my campaign."

"Nothing more?"

She straightened her back. "What are you implying?"

"I'm implying nothing. I'm asking. Call it the start of my investigation."

"All right, I will, and I'll give you the same answer. He was a friend and contributor. Nothing more."

"All right."

West cocked her head to one side. "You don't believe me?"

"If you say it, I believe you, but you've got lots of friends and lots of contributors. Your interest in how one of them is remembered after his death seems a little . . . unusual."

West scratched again at her blotter. "That's not it, how people remember him," she said. "Or rather not all of it. Maybe it's a corollary." She took a minute. "What I'm getting at," she said, "is if he didn't do it, somebody else did— killed him, I mean."

"Don't you think that would probably have been the girlfriend, Missy? I'm assuming from what I've heard that she was the other body."

"If she was, then, all right. At least we'll know for sure. At least someone would have really investigated, and Paul deserves that." She lowered her voice, narrowed her eyes. "I want to be satisfied that whoever killed him is either dead or caught. Call it simple revenge, but I liked the man and I don't buy that he killed himself or anybody else. And okay, maybe it was this Missy, but if it wasn't . . ."

Glitsky jumped. "Is there any reason you think it might not have been?"

"Like what?"

"I don't know. Business problems, family issues, something you'd got wind of?"

"No. But I'd be more comfortable if the various possibilities got eliminated." She turned a palm up. "So how about it, Abe? You want to help give a tired old lady some peace of mind?"

It wasn't really a request. West seemed about as tired as a hummingbird, as old as a schoolgirl. Glitsky had no choice. He gave her a salute. "It would be my pleasure," he said.

As a deputy chief, Glitsky had a city car and a driver—Sergeant Tom Paganucci—assigned to him for his personal use. Paganucci, humorless, taciturn and loyal, suited Glitsky well. He did not make suggestions or offer opinions, and only asked questions related to his work, though he would answer them on other topics if Glitsky asked him directly. He started no conversations at all, but waited for orders that, once given, he obeyed with what seemed to be a complete commitment of his body and soul.

He was forty-three years old, heavily built, clean-shaven, prematurely gray. Because he'd asked on their first day together, Glitsky knew that his driver was married and childless, but that was the extent of his knowledge of Paganucci's personal life, except he was reasonably certain that he didn't do stand-up comedy on his nights off.

Paganucci had kept the car running where he'd left his boss off a half hour before, out in the street in front of City Hall, and now Glitsky slid into the backseat. He closed the door after him and leaned back for an instant into the comfortable black leather. He looked at his watch—11:50. "Do you think the chief's in, Tom?"

Paganucci reached for his intercom. "I'll call."

"No, wait. What am I going to say to him anyway?" Glitsky didn't want an answer from Paganucci and wasn't going to get one in any event. He let out an audible breath. "All right," he said, "let's go."

"Yes, sir. Where to?"

"Alamo Square."

Paganucci put the car in gear and they started to roll.

"He was here 'til they bagged the bodies, sir," Becker said. "Then I guess he went home to get some sleep." They were standing outside on the concrete steps, where Becker had come out in response to Glitsky's hail.

"What about you?" Glitsky asked.

"What about me?"

"And sleep."

The firefighter chortled. "Not a priority. Not 'til I'm satisfied here anyway."

"And you're not?"

"I've got a pretty good basic idea, but I'd be more comfortable if I had more answers."

"Like what?"

Becker shrugged. "Like multiple flash sights. The place went up so quick and thorough, it looks like somebody knew exactly what they were doing." He motioned behind him at the charred remains of the house. "But we've only got the one spot. You want to go in, take a look?" Without waiting for an answer, he led the way through the still-standing front doorway. Some of the ceiling above the lobby was intact, but with the fog burned off, the day was bright with sunshine and there was sufficient natural light to see clearly.

Glitsky squatted over an area of rug that appeared less scorched than its surroundings. There was another, similar spot about eight feet farther into the lobby, at the entrance to what might once have been a hallway. "This is where you found them?"

"Yeah. Plus, it's where the fire started. Get down and you can still smell the gasoline."

Glitsky leaned over and inhaled, but couldn't smell anything except fire. "You've probably gone through all this with Cuneo, but I'd be grateful if you ran it by me one more time. The mayor's personally interested. She was friends with Mr. Hanover. I'd like to sound reasonably intelligent when I brief her. I'm assuming it was Hanover?"

"That's the assumption, although Strout makes the formal call. But whoever it was—call him Hanover—he fell on his wallet so it didn't burn completely. It had Hanover's driver's license in it, so it looks good for him."

"What about the other body?"

"No way to tell. Your man Cuneo seemed to think it was probably his girlfriend."

"You don't agree?"

"I don't know. There was nothing to identify her. It could have been." Becker spoke with little inflection. He was assembling the facts and would share what he knew with any other investigating officials without any particular emphasis. "I can say it was probably a woman—we found what might be a bra strap under her—but that's all I'd be comfortable with for the time being. Again, Strout'll tell us soon enough."

"So what does it look like we have here? The news said murder/suicide."

Becker nodded. "Might have been."

"So you've seen this kind of thing before? Where somebody kills a partner, then himself, but before he does himself, he lights the place up?"

"Sure. It's not uncommon." He seemed to consider whether to say more for a moment, then shrugged as though apologizing. "The relationship goes bad, somebody wants to destroy every sign of it."

"Any sign that this relationship was going bad?"

Becker's eyes scanned the floor area. "You mean besides this? Maybe. Cuneo talked to Hanover's daughter-in-law."

"When did he do that?"

"She saw the fire on the news and came by here last night. Seems this Missy had just finished redecorating this place to the tune of maybe a million dollars of Hanover's money. Maybe he wanted to leave a message that it all meant nothing to him. But I will tell you one thing."

"What's that?"

"It wasn't her."

"What do you mean? What wasn't her?"

"She didn't do the killing. I told Cuneo, too. This might not be any kind of a proof that you could use in court, but if it's a relationship gone bad, there's two things here. First, if she does it, it goes down in the bedroom, maybe even in the bed."

"Why's that?"

"Because that's the center of the woman's life." He held up a hand. "I know, I know, it's not PC, and people will tell you it's bullshit, but you ask anybody who's spent time at this kind of scene, they'll tell you. If it's a crime of passion and it's not done in the bedroom, it's not the woman."

"Okay," Glitsky said. "What's the second thing?"

"I'm afraid it's another non-PC moment."

"I can handle it," Glitsky said. "What?"

"Women don't shoot themselves very often to begin with. And if they do, it's not in the head. They won't disfigure themselves. It just doesn't happen."

Suddenly Glitsky thought back to the suicide of Loretta Wager, the former senator from California who had been his lover and the mother of his daughter Elaine. She had shot herself in the heart. Becker was right, he thought. These were both indefensible sexist generalizations that no doubt would collapse under rigorous debate. That did not stop them, however, from being potentially—even probably—true.

"So you think it was Hanover?"

"I don't know. Cuneo seemed to take it as a working theory. The gun was kind of under him."

"What do you mean, kind of?"

"Well, here, you can see." Becker reached into his inside pocket and withdrew a stack of photographs. "My partner brought these over to the photo lab as soon as they opened. They made two copies and I gave Cuneo the other, but I've still got the negatives if you want a set." Shuffling through them, he got the one he wanted. "Here you go."

Glitsky studied the grainy picture—shadows in darkness. It was a close-up of something he couldn't recognize at first glance.

Becker helped him out, reaching over. "That's the body there along the top, and the end of the arm—the hand became disattached. But you can see there, up against the body, that's the gun."

"So not exactly under him?"

"No. Just like you see there. Kind of against the side and tucked in a little."

"And he was the one in the back here, by the hall? Beyond where the woman was?"

"Yeah," Becker said. "What are you thinking?"

"I'm just wondering, if they had hoses going in here . . ."

"For a while."

"Okay. I'm just thinking maybe the gun was on the rug and the force of the hose hitting it pushed it back against him. Tucked under, as you say."

Becker didn't seem offended by the suggestion. "No, I don't suppose we can rule that out. But it's not the most obvious explanation for how the gun got there."

Glitsky scratched at his cheek. Becker had been up front with him about his and Cuneo's investigation. Although it hadn't been his original plan, he saw no reason now to try and conceal his motive. "Well, as I said, Hanover was a friend of the mayor. She doesn't like the idea that he killed himself, to say nothing of his girlfriend. She asked me to take a look."

Bemused, Becker stood still a moment, shaking his head. Finally: "If that's what you've got to do, I wouldn't want to have your job."

Nodding, Glitsky said, "Sometimes I'm not too sure I want it either."

3

Dismas Hardy, managing partner of the law firm of Freeman, Farrell, Hardy & Roake, had his feet up on his desk. His suit coat hung over the back of his chair. His shoes were off, his tie was undone, the collar of his shirt unbuttoned. He was taking an after-lunch break from a not-very-strenuous day and reading randomly from a book he'd recently purchased, called *Schott's Original Miscellany*.

Being a fact freak, Hardy considered it one of the most fascinating books he'd come across in recent years, containing as it did all sorts of nonessential but critical information, such as the Seven Wonders of the Ancient World (the Great Pyramid of Giza, the Hanging Gardens of Babylon, the Statue of Zeus at Olympia, the Temple of Artemis at Ephesus, the Mausoleum at Halicarnassus, the Colossus of Rhodes, and the Lighthouse of Alexandria), the ten-point Mohs Scale of Mineral Hardness (from talc to diamond), the names of the Apostles, and 154 pages of other very cool stuff. He was somewhat disappointed to see that for some obscure reason it didn't include St. Dismas as the Patron Saint of Thieves and Murderers, but otherwise the diminutive tome was a pure delight, and certainly worthy of his nonbillable time.

He was poring over the Degrees of Freemasonry when the phone buzzed at his elbow. He marked his place, sighed and lifted the receiver, knowing from the blinking line button that it was his receptionist/secretary, Phyllis, the super-efficient, loyal, hardworking and absolutely trying human being who viewed her role as gatekeeper to his office as a vocation decreed by God. She'd filled the same position for Hardy's predecessor, David Freeman, and was no more replaceable as a fixture in the Sutter Street law offices than the phones themselves.

"Phyllis," he said. "Did I ask you to hold my calls?"

He loved that he could make her pause. Mostly he did this by answering with a nonlawyerly "Yo," but sometimes, for variety's sake, he'd come at her from another angle. Yahoo, living large.

"Sir?"

"I'm not accusing you. I'm just asking."

"I don't think so."

"Okay, then. What's up?"

"Deputy Chief Glitsky is here to see you."

"In person?"

"Yes, sir."

"Make a note, Phyllis, I need a back door to sneak out of here."

"Yes, sir."

"That was a pleasantry, Phyllis, a bit of a joke. You can send him in."

He mouthed "Yes, sir," as she said it, then hung up smiling. Sometimes it worried him that Phyllis was among the top sources of humor in his life. It seemed to say something truly pathetic about the person he'd become, but he couldn't deny it. Leaving his stockinged feet on the desk where they would appall his friend Abe almost as much as the sight would scandalize Phyllis, he waited for the turn of the knob and Glitsky's appearance.

One step into Hardy's office, Glitsky stopped. His expression grew pained at the socks on the desk. Hardy left his feet where they were and started right in. "I'm glad you came by. We've really got to join the Masons," he said. "You know that?"

Glitsky closed the door behind him. "You're going to wait until I ask you why, aren't you?"

"No." Hardy closed the book. "No, if you don't want to know, that's okay with me. Although I know you pretty well, and it's definitely something you'd be totally into. But I don't push my brilliant ideas. It was just a thought."

Glitsky hesitated another second or two, then sighed audibly. "What *are* the Masons anyway?"

"A secret organization. George Washington was in it, I think. But if it was that secret, how would anybody know?"

"I was just thinking the same thing."

"See? Great minds."

Glitsky moved over to the wet-bar area and felt the side of the water-heating pot that Hardy kept there. He grabbed his usual mug, picked up a tea bag from an open bowl of them and poured hot water over it. Turning, blowing over the drink, he took in the spacious office. "I should go into some kind of private business. Here you are, the middle of the afternoon, feet up, reading, no work in sight. Your life is far better than mine."

"That's because I'm a better person than you are. But I might point out that you are here, too, in the very same place as me, working about as hard, and drinking my good tea for free on top of it all. Qualitatively, there isn't much between our relative experiences at this particular moment, and one could argue that your life is in some respects as good as mine."

"If one lived to argue." Glitsky got to the armchair in front of Hardy's desk and settled in. "I still want a better office." He blew on the tea again. "Okay," he said, "why do we need to be Masons?"

"Ha!" Hardy's feet flew off the desk as he came forward. "I knew you'd ask."

Glitsky gave him the dead eye. "If I didn't ask, we'd never leave it. So why?"

Hardy opened the book to the place he'd marked. "Because if we stayed at it long enough, you could get to be the Sovereign Grand Inspector General, and I could be either Prince of the Tabernacle or Chevalier of the Brazen Serpent." He paused a moment, frowned. "Either way, though, you'd outrank me, so that couldn't be right."

"How long would all this take?" Glitsky asked.

Hardy nodded ambiguously. "You're right," he said, and closed the book with a flourish. "So what brings your sunny personality here today? What did the mayor want?"

Glitsky brought him up-to-date, keeping the punch line for last. "The original inspecting officer—the one I'm supposed to work with or replace—is Dan Cuneo."

Hardy's expression hardened, his head canted to one side. "So replace him."

"That's not a good idea. He'd see something personal in it."

"He'd be right."

"My point, exactly. Can't replace him."

Hardy drew in a breath, then let it out. "These past couple of years, I kept hoping to hear he'd been busted out of homicide."

"Not happening. If you're a certain type of cop, homicide's a terminal appointment."

"Not for you it wasn't."

"No. But unlike Cuneo, I'm born for greatness." The banter fell flat, though, and Glitsky's face reassumed its natural scowl.

"I don't like him anywhere near either of us," Hardy said after a short silence.

"Do tell. Me? I'm thrilled."

Getting up, crossing to the Sutter Street window, Hardy pulled the shades apart and looked down through them. "And you've got to work with him?"

"I don't see how I can avoid it."

Hardy kept staring out, down at the street. "You can't say a word, Abe. Not one word."

"Oh really?" A hint of anger, or frustration, breaking through.

"Hey." Hardy, catching the tone, spun around. "You work with a guy every day, you know he suspects you of something—I don't care what it is—you might get so you want to get along, try to make him understand."

"Sure, that's what I'll do. I'll say, 'Uh, Dan, about the Gerson thing . . .'" Lieutenant Barry Gerson had been Cuneo's boss, and he'd been killed at a shoot-out in the course of trying to arrest one of Hardy's clients. In the aftermath, Cuneo pushed for an investigation into the role that Hardy and Glitsky had played in Gerson's death.

"I'm just saying . . ."

"I know. That I'll be tempted to reason with him, tell him Gerson was dirty and it was pure self-defense, we had no choice." He shook his head at the absurdity of the idea. "You have my word I won't go there."

Hardy came back and boosted himself onto his desk. "Even if you don't, though, you're back on his radar. He might remember what he forgot to keep up on."

"Forget nothing. There wasn't any evidence, thank God, and he got ordered off."

"I remember, but he needs to stay off. For both our sakes. And working with you is going to bring up old memories. That's all I'm saying."

"I was aware of that even before I came in here, believe it or not. If you have any ideas, I'm listening, but otherwise the mayor's ordered me to work with the guy. What do you want me to do, quit?"

Hardy brightened. "It's a thought."

"Great. Let me just borrow your phone and I'll call Treya and let her know." He stood up and went to pull some darts from the board. Turning back with them, he shrugged. "I've kept a close eye on him, as you might guess. The plain fact—and good news for us—is that he's careless and sloppy. This morning's an example. He's at Hanover's fifteen minutes and tells the press it's murder/suicide."

"So it's not?"

"I don't know. I've got a couple of questions. I don't see Hanover burning down his house, for one big one. He just shoots the woman, stands there a minute, then does himself, okay, that flies. But Becker, the arson inspector out there, he says it looks like he did her, then in no particular order after that poured gasoline on her, wadded up a bunch of newspapers, and opened the lower-floor windows and at least one in the back on the top floor for ventilation. After all that, he goes back to where she's lying in the lobby, starts the fire, then shoots himself."

"That does sound complicated," Hardy said.

Glitsky nodded. "At least. Did you know him?"

"Hanover? Slightly, to look at. I met him a couple of times, but never faced him in court. I can't say he made a huge impression."

"Kathy West wouldn't agree."

Hardy broke a small grin. "He gave Kathy West a lot of money, Abe. If he gave me a lot of money, I'd remember him better, too." Pushing himself off his desk, he took the darts from Glitsky, threw one of them. "You know, here's a real idea, and you won't have to quit. Use the opportunity to mend fences with Cuneo. He tells the media it looks like a murder/suicide, you back him up, say he did a fine job. Everybody wins."

"Everybody but Kathy. But that's what I will do if that's what it turns out to be. In the meantime, Cuneo's going to resent me being involved at all, I guarantee it. That's my real problem. It's going to look like I'm checking up on his work."

"That's what you *are* doing."

Glitsky sat back down, elbows on his knees, hung his head and shook it from side to side. Finally, he looked back up. "I've got to talk to him," he said.

4

Glitsky got Cuneo's extension at work and, calling from his car phone, left a message that they needed to talk. He was going to make every effort to be both conciliatory and cooperative. They would be in this investigation together, and would share information both with each other and with the arson inspectors—a mini task force. But Cuneo wasn't scheduled to be back on duty until six o'clock. And Glitsky, who preferred murder investigations to all other forms of police work, thought he might spend some useful time long before that with the city's medical examiner.

John Strout worked on the ground floor behind the Hall of Justice, in the morgue and its accompanying rooms. When Glitsky got there, somebody in the outer office buzzed him inside and he crossed through the clerical desks and knocked at Strout's door. Getting no answer, he turned the knob, stuck his head in.

Behind him, one of the clerks said, "He's probably in the cold room."

Glitsky nodded his acknowledgment and kept going, closing the door behind him. The office was good-sized by city bureaucratic standards, perhaps twenty by thirty feet, with a large, wide window facing the freeway on the end behind Strout's desk. During his dozen years as head of the homicide detail, Glitsky would have occasion to come down here several times a month—certainly at least once a week. But now, struck by an unfamiliar clutter, he stopped in the middle of the office and suddenly realized that it had probably been close to five years since he'd set foot down here. Or since he'd had any substantive discussion with the good doctor.

In the interim, he noticed, Strout had continued to indulge his proclivity for the bizarre, if not to say macabre. He'd always kept a couple of shelves of unusual murder weapons—a bayonet, two different fire pokers, a baseball bat, an impact shotgun intended for sharks—and medieval torture implements out on display. But now he'd acquired what looked to Glitsky like a small museum. The center-piece was an ancient garroting chair—complete with its red silk scarf for ease of strangulation (or maximum pain) hanging from the beam in the back—that he'd given pride of place directly in front of his desk. A large glass-enclosed case featured an impressive collection of knives and other cutting and slashing implements, brass knuckles and spiked gloves. One whole side of his desk was covered with hand grenades and other apparent incendiary and explosive de-vices of different design and vintage. Strout had the obliga-tory skeleton, of course, but instead of its old place standing next to the morgue cold room entrance, the bones now sat in an easy chair, legs crossed comfortably, apparently en-joying a volume of the *Compendium of Drug Therapy*.

Suddenly the door to the cold room opened. Strout, long and lean, still in his white lab coat, albeit smudged with black and reddish brown, broke a genuine smile. "Doctuh Glitsky." He spoke with a familiar baritone drawl, bending from the waist in a courtly bow. "It's been a hound's age."

Glitsky extended a hand. "How are you, John?"

"Old and in the way, if you must know. But if they're fool enough to let me keep on doing what I do down here, I'm fool enough to let 'em." Strout was a few years on the other side of retirement age, but showed little sign of slowing. He looked Glitsky up and down. "But God, man, y'all are looking fit. Anybody tell you you're supposed to start showing your age sometime? It's like to give the rest of us a bad name."

"I've got a new young wife, John. If I get to looking old, she'll leave me, and then I'd have to go and kill her."

"Well, wouldn't want that. So what can I do for you? I'm assuming this isn't strictly a social visit."

"I'm doing some work on the fire last night."

"Paul Hanover?"

"It *is* him, then?"

Strout took a second, then nodded. "Odds are. Wallet

says he was. I can't tell from the body itself, and nobody else could neither, but I've already called his dentist and we'll know for sure by the end of the day." He went over to his desk, brushed some grenades out of the way and leaned against it.

Glitsky sat on the garrote.

"You want," Strout said, "you can move Chester." He pointed to the skeleton. "He's got the comfortable seat."

"This is fine," Glitsky said. "What about the woman?"

Strout folded his arms, lifted his shoulders. "First, it definitely was a woman. I couldn't be sure 'til I got her on the table. Crisped up terrible."

"That's what I heard. Gasoline?"

"Something hot. If they think it's gas, I believe 'em. From the damage, my guess is she was on fire a good ten, fifteen minutes longer than Hanover."

"And any ID on her?"

Strout shook his head. "Nothin' on the body. Nothin' under the body. Some witness said it might be Hanover's girlfriend. . . ." He turned and started to sort through a wire basket full of paper on the desk next to him.

Glitsky beat him to the name. "Missy D'Amiens."

"Yeah, that's it. Lived with him, right?"

"That's what I hear. Evidently they were having problems, though. She was remodeling the place, spending too much money."

"Remodeling. Well, that explains it." Strout let out a brief chuckle. "Closest my wife and me ever came to splittin' up. We redid a couple of rooms in the house back maybe ten years ago. S'posed to take two months. Went on over a year. Finally, I just moved down here—slept in Chester's spot there 'til it was finally over. If I'd stayed around, I mighta killed her, too. After I killed the contractor, of course. Son of a bitch."

"So that's your take, John? Hanover killed her?"

"No, no, no. I got no take on that, Abe. All I can tell you is they both died of gunshot wounds to the head."

"Any indication of who shot who? If it was either one of them at all."

"I'd say the man."

"Why's that?"

"The entry wound on the woman was high occipital . . ." Catching himself, he continued in layman's English. "High up on the very back. She didn't shoot herself back up there."

"What about the man?"

"Just over the right ear. Good a spot as any."

Glitsky sat still for a moment, elbows on his knees. The mayor wasn't going to like this news. "Could it have been somebody else?"

"Sure. But no way for me to tell. They would have had to have got out in a hurry, but nothin' on the bodies rules that out."

Glitsky nodded. "And I'm assuming you're getting dentals on the woman, too."

"Well, we got the teeth. Problem is, we don't know who her dentist was."

"It's funny you should ask that."

Catherine Hanover said that he hadn't awakened her with the phone call, but he wasn't sure he believed her. When he'd identified himself and asked her permission to record the call as soon as she picked up, her voice sounded hoarse, slightly groggy. Now she cleared her throat again before continuing.

"We both had the same dentist, Dr. Yamashiru. His first name is Toshio." She spelled both names out. "On Webster, between Union and Green. She had some problems with her teeth and didn't know anyone locally, so she asked me who I went to."

"So you two were close?"

"No, not really. I was the body standing nearest to her when the question came up."

"So where did she come from before here?"

"That was always a little vague. She had a French accent, but she spoke English very well. But where she came from didn't matter. She had him wrapped . . . I'm sorry, what did you say your name was?"

"Glitsky. Deputy Chief Glitsky. I'm working this case with Dan Cuneo, whom I believe you met last night."

"Yes, I remember him."

Glitsky found the response slightly off-key. "Did you have a problem with Inspector Cuneo?"

"No, not really. I told him I thought it was Missy and Paul in there."

"And about the renovation?"

"Yes." The stress in the voice was clear now. Something about Cuneo's interview with her had been troubling. "That, too," she said.

"That they were having some troubles?"

"Yes."

"About the money she spent?"

Another small silence. Then, "I'm sorry, Inspector, but did you say you'd talked to Inspector Cuneo, too?"

"No, not yet. I've got a call in to him, but the arson inspector gave me your name and I had some questions I wanted to go over. Inspector Cuneo will be back on tonight if you'd be more comfortable talking with him."

"No!"

Glitsky imagined her jumping in alarm at the suggestion. She covered her reaction with a brush of nervous laughter. "I mean, no. I don't care who I talk to. If I've got any information you might need, ask away."

"All right. You told Inspector Cuneo that Mr. Hanover and Missy had been fighting over the amount she'd spent on renovations to his house. Is that right?"

"Yes. It was obscene, really. Something like a million dollars. But that was Missy, although she fooled us at first. Well, tried to."

"Fooled you in what way?"

"In the way that attractive younger women fool older men."

"You're saying that she was after your father-in-law's money?"

"Not just after it. She got a lot of it, Inspector. You should have seen the engagement ring. The hundred-thousand-dollar trophy rock, we called it. I mean, it was just way over the top. And that didn't include the clothes and the car and . . ."

"But obviously Mr. Hanover gave her all this willingly."

"Oh yes. According to him, she was always wonderful to him. Sweet, loving, understanding. Although you should have seen her when Mary—my sister-in-law?—mentioned that maybe she was going a little overboard on the house."

Catherine Hanover paused. "Oh, listen to me. You know, I really don't want to speak ill of the dead, but it was so obvious that she was a gold digger—very subtle and very patient—although Paul wouldn't even hear of that, of course. We couldn't even bring up that he might at least consider that possibility, get a prenup, something. But he wouldn't go there. He loved her. She was the love of his life, and he was just so blessed that he'd found her. Pardon me, but puke."

"So you didn't believe her?"

"None of us did."

"And who's that, all of you?"

"The family. Paul's daughters, Mary and Beth, my husband, Will. The kids."

Taking the opportunity to get some details on the extended family, Glitsky wrote down names, addresses and telephone numbers. "But none of them came to the fire last night?"

"None of them knew about it until today, or way late. When I got back, maybe one o'clock, I called Mary and Beth but got their machines. My husband has been on a fishing trip off the coast of Mexico for the past three days—I still haven't gotten to him, though he's due back in tomorrow. He's going to be devastated about his father, although maybe a bit relieved at the same time."

Glitsky, speaking on his office telephone, shifted his weight to get more comfortable. Catherine Hanover was turning out to be the often sought but rarely encountered mother lode of witnesses, effortlessly providing him with facts, people, rumor and innuendo, context. "Why would he be relieved?" he asked.

"Well, I don't mean really relieved. That might be too strong. But it's no secret that we were all of us a little concerned about what would happen after Missy and Paul actually got married. I mean, Will is an architect and we do all right, but none of us have had Paul's incredible financial success."

"You were counting on an inheritance?"

"That sounds so cold-blooded. I don't know if saying we were counting on it is really accurate—we all loved Paul and wanted him to live forever—but let's face it, he was worth a fortune. That money had been sitting there as a possibility for us for so long, let's just say that it was a bit of an adjustment after he started talking about marrying Missy, thinking it wouldn't be there anymore. And now, suddenly, here it is again. This sounds so terrible, doesn't it? I never even thought about the money until this morning, really, but then once I realized . . ." She stopped, sighed into the receiver. "It's terrible to talk like this," she said. "I'm sorry."

Glitsky said, "It's natural enough."

But Catherine couldn't drop the topic. "It's just that there really was such a dramatic change after he started seeing her. I mean, until Missy came along, Paul used to help with all the kids' tuitions. And we'd all go to Maui for Christmas every year. All of us, the whole extended family, for a week at Napili Kai. Stuff like that. To say nothing of college coming up for all eight of the grandkids. I really shouldn't say it's a relief, but . . ." Again, she trailed off.

Glitsky wanted to keep her talking. "So Missy lived with your father-in-law full-time?"

"Mostly, I think, yes. For about the last two years."

"And do you know any of her friends from before she met him?"

"No. After she met Paul, there weren't any other friends. He was her full-time job."

Glitsky made a note that he'd need to follow up on the friends of Missy D'Amiens if the investigation widened. Although for the moment it appeared that, if anything, it had narrowed down to the obvious original theory. Certainly Catherine Hanover's breezy admission of what might under other circumstances be considered a reasonable motive for murder—a large inheritance—argued against her own involvement in any foul play. He would of course verify the whereabouts of her husband and his two sisters last night, but for the moment it looked like Kathy West would remain disappointed in her benefactor and political ally.

But that moment abruptly came to an end during the next exchange.

"Can I ask you something, Inspector?"

"Sure."

"The arson inspector thought they both might have been shot. Have you found out if that's true?"

"Yes. It is."

"So they were murdered?"

"Yes, ma'am. Or maybe one of them killed the other, and then himself."

"Or herself."

"Maybe," Glitsky said. Although he found them compelling and consistent with his own experience, he wasn't going to get into a discussion of Inspector Becker's theories on why, in a scenario like this one, it probably wasn't the woman.

"But you think it was Paul?"

"I don't know." He was silent for a minute, then realized that the details would undoubtedly be in the paper tomorrow, possibly on the television in a couple of hours. He wouldn't be giving anything away. "The location of the woman's wound indicated that she didn't kill herself. It was up behind her head. Probably not self-inflicted."

"And what about Paul's?"

Glitsky let out a breath. "About where you'd expect in a suicide. Just over the right ear."

Another short silence. Then Catherine Hanover said, "Wait a minute. The *right* ear?"

"Yes."

"You're sure?"

"The medical examiner was, and he usually gets it right."

"I think maybe you ought to go back and double-check."

"Why?"

"Because—I thought everybody knew this, but—Paul had polio back in the early fifties. His right arm was paralyzed. It was dead. He couldn't use it at all."

Glitsky caught up to Kathy West as she pursued a photo op out of the newly refurbished, utilitarian, yet lovely again Ferry Building at the bay, the eastern end of Market Street. The sun, dusk-bound, had just slipped under the blanket of coastal fog that came to cover the city at its western edge at this time of day, at this time of year. In late spring and early summer, San Francisco bore a marked climatic resemblance to Newfoundland. It was still nowhere near the evening proper, although what had only moments before been a shining, sparkling, even inspiringly welcoming downtown suddenly lost its direct sunlight and turned quite cold. Now gusts of the chill early-evening breeze flung open the jackets of businessmen, rearranged the hairstyles of women. Newspapers and food wrappers swirled in the eddies of alleyways and skyscapers.

The mayor's office told Glitsky that he'd find her somewhere along Market if he missed her at the Ferry Building, but he should try there first. He had Paganucci drop him out front and walked head down, hands deep in his pockets, until he got himself out of the wind and inside. Her honor and the press entourage surrounding her were just coming out of Book Passage, where she'd "spontaneously" picked up a couple of novels, three cookbooks, a handful of musical CDs, Don Novello's latest humor and a travel guide to Italy—all of it written and/or performed by San Franciscans.

Glitsky was standing to the side, listening with some skepticism while West talked to the assembled reporters, extolling the virtues of the city, its ongoing importance as a mecca of creativity and art, as these many eclectic works so amply illustrated. A bearded man in a wheelchair removed himself from the immediate group of a dozen or so reporters and photographers and rolled over next to him.

Glitsky knew Jeff Elliot well. A fellow alumnus, along with West and himself, of the DA's kitchen cabinet, Elliot wrote the *Chronicle*'s "CityTalk" column. He suffered from multiple sclerosis, and Glitksy knew that he had recently had to abandon his sometime use of crutches for a full-time wheelchair.

"What are you doing here?" Elliot said.

"Some business with the mayor."

"Want to talk about it? See your name in the paper?"

"It's what I live for." Glitsky almost smiled. "Maybe later, if it turns out to be anything. Don't let me keep you from getting a quote about how artist-friendly the city is. You're not going to hear too many of them."

"Or none."

"Well, the mayor just said it, so it must be true."

"If it is, it's a major scoop." Elliot looked up at him. "You know any struggling artists that actually live here?"

"I hear a couple of homeless guys are tagging every inch of the Fourth Street freeway ramp."

"I don't think she's talking about them."

"She's talking about the city supporting artists. The only way it does that is if they're homeless first and artists second."

Elliot made no response, listened to the mayor for another minute. "It must just be me," he said.

"What?"

"Finding that this city is a bit of a challenge lately to survive in, much less thrive. And I shouldn't talk. I've got a good job. What if you're trying to do art? Can you imagine?"

"No. But the mayor says we're all open arms."

"'And Brutus is an honorable man.'"

Glitsky looked down at him. "If you say so, Jeff."

"That was Shakespeare. Antony's speech after they killed Caesar."

"I thought so," Glitsky said. "I was just going to say that." He brought his attention back to the mayor. "So why are *you* here? What's this about? It can't be the poor, struggling artists."

"No. Actually, it's an interesting idea. This is the first of Kathy's scheduled walking press conferences. You haven't read about them?"

"Nope."

"I've written about them twice now. The 'Neighborhood Strolls'?"

"Still nope."

"You're letting me down here, Abe."

"I'll give myself twenty lashes when I get home, if I ever do. So what are they about, these strolls?"

"Well, it's going to be in several different neighborhoods in the next weeks, but today she's walking Market from here to Van Ness."

"That's a good walk. Lots of wildlife."

"About twenty blocks worth."

Glitsky lowered his voice. "Is she nuts? Here to Van Ness? That's derelict central."

"Yes it is. I believe she knows that."

"So she wants to see people peeing and worse in public fountains? Or selling dope on the street? And she's doing this because . . ."

"Because she wants people to know that she shares the same concerns for public safety, cleanliness and general civility as does the majority of the public."

Glitsky shook his head. "She's barking up the wrong tree, Jeff. The voters don't care about that. They care that we're compassionate and diverse and sensitive, but I don't see much sign of caring about public cleanliness."

"Well, there you go. But Kathy's idea is that by her witness to the decay in these areas, she's—and I believe I'm quoting here—'serving notice that fixing this historically blighted corridor through the heart of the city is going to become a priority for my administration, and a boon to the city in general.' "

"And how is this going to happen again? By her walking down it?"

"That's the theory. We report on the problems she encounters, awareness goes up, people see how bad some places are and stop tolerating them."

This time, Glitsky snorted quietly. "No, no. You've got it backwards. We need to tolerate them more because we don't understand them. 'The fault, dear Brutus, is not in our stars, but in ourselves.' Shakespeare again."

"Thank you, I guessed. Ah, she sees you."

Handing her shopping bag to one of her aides—she hadn't known Glitsky was going to be there, but she instinctively rose to a political moment when she saw one—she turned to the reporters, quite a decent crowd considering that there was no real story to cover. "Excuse me," she said, "I need to talk to the deputy chief."

In an instant she was at their side, greeting them both, asking Elliot if he could give them a moment. Glitsky lifted a hand in an ambiguous salute—he was either greeting Kathy or saying good-bye to Elliot. Or maybe both.

"I didn't mean to crash your party, Your Honor. If you're in the middle of something . . ."

"Abe. I told you this morning, it's Kathy. And no, this is fine. We can talk as we walk."

The two left the Ferry Building with the reporter contingent, including Jeff Elliot, hanging back a respectable distance. The first several blocks along Market, while congested with foot and automobile traffic, nevertheless were relatively clean and populated with people who worked downtown. It had very little of the urban blight that Kathy West was hoping to expose, so it left her free to talk with Glitsky as they walked. Hooking her hand in his arm, she set a brisk pace. "I'm surprised to see you so soon. I'm assuming this is about Paul Hanover. Do you have something?"

"Pretty much what you wanted," Glitsky said. "I've talked to John Strout and Hanover's daughter-in-law, and between them got convinced that there's very little chance he killed anybody, including himself." In a few words, he outlined what he'd discovered—the entry wound over the right ear, the other one in the back of the woman's head. "So really that's about it. He could only have shot himself by some awkward contortion that makes no sense, and she had the same problem. So it probably didn't happen that way."

"When the chief said you were good, Abe, he wasn't kidding, was he?"

"I'll take lucky over smart every time. I ran into the right people."

They had gotten down as far as Seventh Street, and now the mayor's eyes were flicking back and forth rapidly, scanning for the signs of urban decay that Glitsky knew would begin appearing any minute. But her mind hadn't left their topic. "So what happens now?" she asked.

"What do you mean?"

"With the investigation?"

"Well, it continues, of course. Back with Inspector Cuneo, which is where it belongs."

A few more quick steps, and then she stopped abruptly. "This would be the same Inspector Cuneo who told the press this morning that this was a murder/suicide?"

Glitsky's lips went tight for a beat before he answered. "That's what it looked like to me, too, when I first got there."

"Yes, but you didn't tell anybody about it until you had more facts, did you?"

He showed her what he hoped would pass for a smile. "I've gotten a little more used to dealing with the media than your average inspector."

"Be that as it may, Abe, the fact remains that you've made real progress in half a day, and Inspector Cuneo hasn't been any part of it."

"That's not strictly accurate. He talked to Hanover's daughter-in-law first last night. . . ."

"But managed not to learn that Paul had a withered arm."

"He didn't know where the entry wound was, so he wouldn't have known why that mattered."

"Precisely. When he could have shown some initiative and gone to the morgue with the body. Isn't that the case?"

Glitsky could only shrug. "Maybe he should have done that."

"You would have."

This was true, but Glitsky shrugged it off again. "Well, either way," he said, "we've got a good idea that Mr. Hanover didn't do anything wrong. That's what you wanted this morning."

She fixed him with that avian intensity. "But unfortunately, that's no longer the point."

Glitsky waited.

"The point, Abe, is that we now know that Paul was murdered, don't we? And you don't think it was the girlfriend, Missy. Which means they were both murdered by someone else. And that being the case, do you think I have any confidence at all that Inspector Cuneo will be more successful catching the person who killed one of my close friends and benefactors than he was identifying the cause or manner of death in the first place? You don't have to struggle with it. The answer is no."

The gaggle of reporters following them had stopped when they did, and now out of the corner of his eye, Glitsky thought he picked up an increasing awareness among some of them, including Jeff Elliot, that something significant might be transpiring here right in front of them between the deputy chief of inspectors and the mayor. He considered that the time might be propitious to try to get some mileage out of West's insistence that the two of them were really, basically, friends. He stepped closer to her, strove for a casual tone. "He couldn't keep his job in homicide if he wasn't effective, Kathy. Lanier would have lateralled him out."

"Abe." West wasn't having it. "Help me out here. I understand a little bit about politics, and I see your concerns. If it makes it easier for you, you can let Inspector Cuneo remain on the case in some capacity, but I'd count it as a personal favor if you stayed on with it, too. Whoever killed Paul Hanover isn't going to get away with it on my watch if I can help it, and you're the best man to see that he doesn't." She reached out and put a hand on his arm, looked up into his face. "Abe. Please. For me."

Glitsky glanced at the reporters, a couple of whom had already snapped some photos. This was turning into too visible a moment, laden with intrigue and import. It had to end or it would grow and become a real event, and he wanted to avoid that at all costs. At last, coming back to her, he patted West's hand in a fraternal gesture and nodded. "All right, Kathy," he said. "Let me see what I can do."

5

Cuneo lived alone on what had formerly been the grounds of the Alameda Naval Air Station, across the bay from San Francisco. The nine-hundred-square-foot stand-alone building, which back in the fifties had housed a marine engine repair shop, sat perched on a concrete slab that jutted out ten feet into the channel. All day, every day, flotillas of mostly small saltwater craft glided by his bedroom window, sometimes close enough to touch. The ferry to San Francisco passed every hour or so, too, as well as the occasional Coast Guard or naval vessel.

After six hours of fitful sleep, Cuneo—dreaming of fire—started awake at twenty minutes after four in the afternoon. Tangled up in his blankets, he was breathing hard and sweating. Throwing and kicking the covers off, he shot up to sitting and looked from side to side, getting his bearings. The smoke smell was real enough, all-pervasive in the small house. He let his breathing slow down, the tendrils of his nightmare still clutching at his psyche.

For another minute or so, he sat as he almost never did, in absolute stillness. He wore only his Jockeys, but the stench of last night's smoke still clung to his skin. At last, unconsciously, he lifted the heel of his right foot, let it fall, lifted it again. In seconds, still unaware, he was tapping a steady rhythm on the concrete floor.

Next to the bedroom on the water in the back, a tiny, low-ceilinged workroom huddled to one side of the house. Going forward, the kitchen and bathroom divided the central segment of the building two-thirds to one, and after putting some water on to boil, Cuneo stopped in at the bathroom for a shower, mostly to get the smell off him. When he was done, wearing his towel, he made some

Nescafé—two spoons of crystals, no sugar or cream, and went back to put on his clothes.

Up in the front of the house, a relatively spacious living room provided two front and two side windows that gave the space an open feel and plenty of light. A leather love seat sat against one wall, a small teak bookshelf and television stand on the other. By far the most immediately noticeable furnishing, though, was a full set of Ludwig drums in the middle of the room. Cuneo didn't have any idea where his nearest neighbor's home might be, but it was at least out of earshot. He could play all day as loud as he wanted and nobody ever complained.

Three years ago, after his fellow inspector Lincoln Russell finally couldn't take partnering with him anymore, Lieutenant Lanier had recommended that maybe he might want to see a psychologist—his insurance through the city would pay for the first three visits—and try to get some handle on why he couldn't ever sit still, or shut up. He would sing to himself driving to crime scenes, hum during interrogations, often break into unconscious song while he wrote up his reports in homicide. Maybe he had Tourette's syndrome, or Saint Vitus' dance or something, Lanier had suggested, and if he did, it would be better to at least know what he was dealing with.

As it turned out, he only saw the shrink—Adrienne Schwartz—professionally the three times that his insurance covered it, though they dated for six weeks or so after that until she started hinting that she was looking for some kind of commitment. The best thing she'd done for him was recommend that he buy the drums and take some lessons, and now he'd almost always start his day with a twenty-minute workout, getting it all moving by playing along with some CDs of the classic big band guys—Buddy Rich, Gene Krupa, Louis Bellson.

Today, though, he didn't do his full twenty. Ten minutes into it, in the middle of "Sing, Sing, Sing," he suddenly stopped, stood up, grabbed his jacket. The Hanover woman from last night was a real babe, and he'd picked up the definite sense that she and her husband weren't doing too well. She'd told him he was down in Mexico, fishing for a week, and it didn't seem to bother her too much. He didn't

think he'd have too much to do with the murder/suicide—
that appeared to be straightforward enough—but he'd
want to be thorough, find out what he could. You never
knew. The arson inspectors and their police counterparts
would have a hundred or more names they'd picked up at
the scene, and he'd want to find if any of those potential
witnesses had seen anything that might be telling, might
call the basic facts into question.

But first the Hanover woman again. See how she was
handling the tragedy. If she was lonely. Or horny.

One of the benefits of working nights was commuting
against the traffic. Cuneo checked in at the Hall of Justice
within twenty minutes of walking out his front door. Up in
the homicide detail, Lanier wasn't in his office, and the
other four inspectors still at work said hello from their
desks and then cordially ignored him. The usual assort-
ment of housekeeping and other messages cluttered his
voice mail—a snitch needing some cash to hold him over
until he testified in court; another witness sounding very
afraid about her upcoming testimony against her husband,
who was in jail for murdering their mutual lover; a friendly
notice from payroll that his overtime last pay period had
exceeded the approved hours; another call that he was behind on his credit union payments; the arson guy, Becker,
wondering how he wanted to arrange his pickup of last
night's witness list; a woman he'd stopped seeing recently.

Barely audible to the other inspectors, he was humming
the opening riff to "Satisfaction" over and over and over as
he listened to the messages, writing notes and phone numbers on the pad he carried in his back pocket. Glitsky's was
the last message and, hearing it, Cuneo went silent. He
played the message again, aware that a flush of anger was
rising to his face, but otherwise trying to keep his expression neutral. He threw a quick glance around the room,
wondering if any of his colleagues might have heard something, if they were watching for his reaction. But no one
was paying him any mind.

The recording told him that he'd finished with his last
message, to press one if he'd like to hear it again, two if
he'd like to save it, three to delete it. It told him the same

thing all the way through again. When it started to tell him for a third time, he finally heard it and slowly replaced the receiver.

What the hell did this mean? The deputy chief of inspectors didn't just call and say, "Oh, by the way, I'll be working with you on your latest case." Cuneo had never heard of anything like it. He'd been without a partner for almost three years now and didn't think much about whether he was popular or not. He was under the impression he'd been doing a good job, making triable cases on five killers in the past eight months, had gotten the collars. It was much better than the average for the detail. Certainly it was the best stretch he'd ever enjoyed professionally.

But what else could this be about except that somebody was checking up on him and his work? And on this of all cases, which on the face of it appeared very close to a slam dunk. It had to mean that they were going to begin some kind of bullshit documentation for moving him out of homicide, maybe out of the PD altogether.

And why would Lanier or anybody else want to do that?

Sitting back in his chair, he began tattooing the arms of it with a steady, rapid beat. It *couldn't* be about his work product, he thought. If it was, Lanier was straight-shooter enough to have told him, even if it was true that he and Glitsky went way back, sometimes even saw each other socially. Cuneo wondered if his lieutenant even knew about the message Glitsky had left—if he did, he certainly would have given Cuneo some warning, or at least an explanation. This kind of thing just wasn't done. It wasn't right. More, it was an insult.

And then he stopped his drumming, took in a lungful of air and let it out slowly. Suddenly, with a crystal clarity, he realized what this was really about, what it had to be about.

And it wasn't his work.

Over the months and years since he'd started in homicide, Cuneo hadn't made much of a secret of his feelings for Glitsky. When he'd been a newcomer to the detail, still partnered with Russell, one of his first cases had concerned the shooting of an old man named Sam Silverman, who ran a pawnshop a couple of blocks off Union Square. At that time, the head of homicide was Barry Gerson, and Glitsky—nominally a lieutenant—worked in a sergeant's position as supervisor of payroll. In the course of Cuneo's investigation into Silverman's death, this nobody Glitsky somehow insinuated himself into the detail's business—butting in, offering his advice, getting in the way. He'd once run homicide, and the unwelcome interference struck Cuneo, Russell and Gerson as a power play to get his old job back.

Eventually his investigation made it clear to Cuneo that Glitsky's other motive for his involvement in that case was to help out a defense attorney friend of his named Dismas Hardy, whose client, John Holiday, was the chief suspect in the killing. When Gerson finally went out to Pier 70 to arrest Holiday—Cuneo believed the event *had* to have been arranged by Hardy in some way—something went terribly wrong. Holiday, Gerson and three Patrol Specials that the lieutenant had brought with him as backup all wound up shot to death, the perpetrators never identified or, of course, apprehended.

Promoted to homicide lieutenant to fill Gerson's spot, Lanier had conducted the investigation into the incident. He had a talk with his longtime friend and colleague Glitsky and, no surprise, found nothing. Hardy had never left his office that day, either—ten witnesses there said so. There was no case against either of the men, although Cuneo in his heart of hearts continued to believe that somehow they'd both been involved. When he learned that Glitsky's alibi for the time in question was Hardy's law partner Gina Roake, his belief became near certainty.

But though he took his questions to Lanier and then, on his own and top secret, to Jerry Ranzetti with the Office of Management and Control, which investigated internal affairs, he couldn't get to anything approaching proof of wrongdoing. Ranzetti even told him that he'd run across issues—not exactly hewing strictly to the department's best interests—with both Glitsky and Hardy working together in at least one other previous case. But not only were both men extremely well connected—tight with the DA, some supervisors, the chief of police, even the mayor—but knowing the system intimately as they both did, they played it like maestros and made no mistakes. His interest piqued by Cuneo's theory, though, Ranzetti did nose around for a while on the Gerson killing—after all, this was a cop shooting, and so of the highest priority—but he hadn't been able to put either Glitsky or Hardy anywhere near the scene when the shootings had occurred.

Then, the next thing Cuneo knew, Frank Batiste became chief and Glitsky the payroll clerk got himself promoted over half the rest of the qualified lieutenants to deputy chief. He considered the appointment a travesty and wasn't particularly discreet about sharing his opinion with some of his fellow cops. Without a doubt, through Lanier or one of the other homicide people who'd heard him spouting off, Glitsky had heard of Cuneo's disapproval—to say nothing of his allegations of criminal complicity and cover-up.

Cuneo sat dead still, *The Thinker,* his elbow resting on his chair's arm, his chin in his hand. That's what Glitsky's phone message was really about—he was serving notice. Cuneo had trash-talked and then tried to backstab him, and Glitsky had found out.

Now it was payback time.

Catherine Hanover lived in a small Moorish-style two-story stucco home in the Marina District, on Beach Street a block east of the Palace of Fine Arts. As was his wont when time didn't press, Cuneo parked within sight of the address she had given him last night and sat in his car, watching and getting a feel for the place while he drummed on the steering wheel.

What he saw was a low stucco fence that bounded a well-kept property at the sidewalk. The houses on either side were both noticeably larger, outsized for their lots. The Hanovers' front yard wasn't deep by any stretch, and a brace of mature trees canopied nearly all of it. He noted the black Mercedes-Benz C-Class sedan parked in the driveway, and the lights upstairs behind what looked like a functional wooden-railed deck. This area of the city tended to get more sunshine than points farther west, and the low evening rays painted the entire neighborhood in a mellow gold.

Cuneo popped a breath mint, checked his hair in the mirror and opened the car door. A good breeze made him reach back in for his jacket.

The genes were good in the family, he thought. The teenage girl who answered the door might have been a face model. "Hi," she said. "Can I help you?" Well brought up, too.

He had his badge out, his polite smile on. "I'm Inspector Cuneo, San Francisco homicide. I was hoping to talk to your mother." He turned the wattage up on his smile. "I'm assuming Catherine Hanover is your mother?"

"You got it, every day. I'm Polly." She half turned. "Mom! There's a policeman out here to see you."

Over the young woman's shoulder, Catherine appeared from around a corner. She carried a dish towel and was wiping her hands with it. "Well, invite him in, then." As she came closer, he noticed a white streak of something high on her cheek. Her daughter saw it, too, and she took the towel and wiped off the offending stuff, whatever it was, and gave the towel back. A friendly look passed between mother and daughter, then Polly went back to wherever she'd been and Catherine, as lovely as he'd remembered, was standing in front of him. "Hello again," she said with some formality. She touched her cheek. "Flour," she said, "I'm making pasta. It gets everywhere, I'm afraid. Please, come in."

"Thank you." He was already inside, closing the door. "Did you say you were making pasta?"

"That's right."

"Not the sauce, the actual noodles?"

She favored him with a smile. "The actual noodles. Do you like homemade noodles?"

"I don't believe I've ever had them."

"You should try. They're a lot of work, but worth it, I think." In the light of day, Catherine's face was nearly as perfect as her daughter's, rescued from mere cuteness by deeply set green eyes and a strong nose. A striking, mature face. "My children are so spoiled. They won't even eat store-bought anymore. It's got to be my own. Maybe I should be flattered." She twisted the towel, took in and let out a quick breath.

Cuneo was standing next to her and reached out his hand. He touched her arm as though commiserating somehow. She backed away a step. "Anyway, you're not here for that."

"No." He stayed close to her. "We like to come by and see how everybody's holding up. The day after is often worse for next of kin. Also, frankly, maybe things occur to you that might have gone right by in the emotion of the moment, like last night."

"Like what?"

"I don't know. Anything. Something your father-in-law might have been going through, or Missy said. Why he might have had a reason to kill her."

Her eyes narrowed and she cocked her head to one side. "What do you mean?"

"About what?"

"Well, you were just talking about why Paul might have wanted to kill Missy. I thought you had decided that that couldn't have happened. You, the police, I mean. That's what the other inspector told me, anyway."

"The other inspector? Glitsky?"

"That's it. Glitsky."

"You talked to him already?"

"Yes. He called a few hours ago. We talked for about fifteen minutes. I would have thought you two would have communicated together. Haven't you talked to him?"

Cuneo showed nothing. Smiling, shrugging, he made it clear that this was normal enough. He patted her arm again. "He's on days. Sometimes we cross each other. It's all right. But how did you get to Hanover not shooting anybody? That's what you said, isn't it?"

"Right." She had backed away another step and bumped her leg against one of the room's chairs. Suddenly, she put a hand to her forehead. "What am I thinking, keeping you standing out here like this?" Without waiting for an answer, she turned and led the way, pulled out a chair for him around an oval, well-used wooden table that overlooked the backyard. Then she was moving back across the kitchen. "Can I get you some water? Coffee? Anything?"

"I'm good, thanks." He sat, half turned, kept his eyes on

her. Obviously appraising, obviously approving. He thought he was keeping it low-key, even subtle. "So," he said as his fingers started tapping on the table, "Glitsky?"

She finally tucked the dish towel into the refrigerator's handle and now, with her hands free, didn't seem to know what to do with them. Leaning up against the kitchen counter, she crossed them over her breasts. "Well, I told him about Paul's right arm being useless since the polio, so he sure didn't shoot himself over the right ear. Not with his right hand, anyway."

"No," Cuneo said, "I'd guess not."

"And then since Missy's wound was up in the back of her head—you knew that?"

He nodded, though it was news to him.

"So she probably didn't shoot herself there, either."

"So someone else was there?"

"That's what Inspector Glitsky seemed to think. It's the only thing that fit."

The sound of steps on stairs and then a tall, well-built hazel-haired teenage boy entered the kitchen. Wearing the uniform of cargo pants and a gray Cal sweatshirt, he stopped in his tracks when he saw Cuneo, looked at his mother, back to the inspector. "Hey," he said.

Cuneo nodded. "Hey."

"My son, Saul," she said. "Saul, this is Inspector Cuneo. He's investigating who might have killed your grandfather."

At the mention of it, the boy's shoulders sagged, his face rearranged itself to accommodate the grief that threatened to show. Cuneo stood up and the boy came over to shake his hand. "Nice to meet you," he said. "I hope you catch him, whoever it was."

"You got along well with your grandfather?"

He nodded. "He was great. He rocked. He really did." Looking out the windows over Cuneo's shoulder, he shook his head. "I can't believe somebody killed him."

"Maybe they really wanted to kill his girlfriend and he was just there."

"Yeah," Saul said, "maybe that." Awkward, he stood another moment, then turned to his mother. "I was just getting some food."

"All right, but save room for dinner." She pointed toward the refrigerator and he walked over, lifted a carton of milk and went to drink from it.

"Saul!"

"Oh, yeah." He grabbed a glass from the cupboard, filled it with milk, found a handful of cookies and started to leave, but then stopped at the doorway. "I hope you catch him," he said again. "Really."

"We're trying."

When Saul's steps had retreated back upstairs, Cuneo got up from his chair and crossed over to where Catherine was standing. "You've got nice kids," he said. "Is that all of them?"

"There's one more upstairs. Heather, the youngest. It's homework time, so I'm surprised you got to see any of them. This time of day, they just disappear."

"And they're just working like that on their own? You must be one heck of a good mother. What's your secret?"

"Are you kidding? It's day-to-day survival. Just so they keep talking to you and don't ever get a chance to forget that you love them more than anything. Do you have children?"

He hung his head for an instant. "Regrettably, I'm single." An apologetic smile. "Just never found the right woman, I guess." Figuring the segue was seamless, Cuneo asked, "By the way, have you had any luck contacting your husband yet?"

"No." She snapped it out, suddenly edgy. Then, covering. "He's a little late getting in is all. Probably means he caught a lot of fish." The sides of her mouth rose, although it was a sad sort of a smile and she sighed. "We'll be eating albacore 'til Christmas. I'm sure he'll call when he gets in."

Cuneo took another step toward her, looked around the warm room, again laid a brief touch on her forearm. "If I had this to come home to, I know I would," he said.

"Yes, well . . ." She crossed to the refrigerator, grabbed the dish towel, turned to face him, now twisting the towel some more. "Well," she said again, "that pasta isn't going to make itself. If there's nothing else . . ."

"I think that about covers it. I'll check in with Glitsky and get ourselves coordinated. I'm sorry about double-teaming you. That's never our intention. People get nervous around too many cops." He smiled right at her. "You're not nervous, are you?"

"No. Well, maybe a little bit."

"Don't be. Not with me, anyway. I'm harmless, really, and much sweeter than I look." Cuneo flashed a grin, then got his wallet and pulled out his business card, grabbed his pen from his shirt pocket. "Here," he said, writing on the board where she was making her pasta, "this is my home number. Work is printed on the front. If you think of anything you think might be relevant, anytime, day or night, or even if you just want to talk, if your husband goes fishing again . . ." He let it hang, half a joke, but serious enough if she wanted to take him up on it.

She *was* nervous, though, he was thinking as he drove up to Becker's fire station. Nervous the whole time. Something definitely was going wrong with her husband.

But no thoughts, not even those about his possible future conquest of Catherine Hanover, could stand up to the immediacy of his problem with Glitsky. Now not only had the man usurped his case, he'd stood it on its ear. This morning when he'd gone off duty, Cuneo was all but convinced that this seemed to be a more or less straightforward murder/suicide, with Hanover and D'Amiens the only two principals involved. Unfortunately, that's what he'd told some reporters. Now here it was barely twelve hours later, and Glitsky had gotten in behind him to *his* witnesses. To know the details about the locations of the head wounds, he must have also gone to the medical examiner. So he was *working* this case soup to nuts and already had a big jump, in spite of the fact that Cuneo was out of the gate first.

Cuneo figured that his only chance to save his job was to catch up. But the good news was that this case now looked like a righteous 187, a first-degree double murder. This was what Cuneo did and did well. And it had the added bonus that Paul Hanover was an important and well-known citizen, and Missy D'Amiens, as his fiancée, was going to have an interesting story as well.

It wasn't generally appreciated how few murders had bona fide motives. In his experience, most times people got killed for inane reasons. Some husband wouldn't let his wife change the channel. Some guy's dog shit on another guy's step. They wouldn't turn down the goddamned music. Stupid. But with someone like Hanover, or maybe even Missy, there would probably be a righteous motive—money, betrayal, extortion, jealousy. Whoever killed these people would have done it for a specific reason. Find the reason and the job was essentially done. Of course, *proving* the motive was a whole different kettle of fish than simply identifying the person who had it. You needed physical evidence. But at least, with a solid motive, you'd know where to look.

He could get this case back from Glitsky yet. He'd make another appointment with Catherine, with the rest of the family. Check out Paul Hanover's relations with past clients and partners, ex-wives if any, people to or from whom he donated or accepted money. He, Dan Cuneo, would find who benefited from these deaths and bring that person in. He'd make the arrest and *solve this case* before Glitsky knew what had hit him.

Arnie Becker was still going. His younger partner, J. P. Dodd, in a filthy, charcoal-stained T-shirt and black pants, was crashed on the cot in their little side room at the Arson Unit headquarters on Evans Street, but Becker—showered and looking freshly dressed—sat at a card table sorting through what looked to be a few hundred scraps of paper, placing them into discrete piles in front of him as though he were dealing poker. Cuneo knocked on the open door. "How you doin'?"

Becker stopped, looked up, smiled politely. "It might not have been D'Amiens," he said. He scanned the piles in front of him and put his hand on one. A thin one—two pieces of paper.

"Who? The woman in the fire?"

Becker nodded, handed the paper across. "Those two people—they're married—saw her walking from the house just before the alarm got called in."

"Saw Missy? They're sure?"

"A couple of them reasonably enough. Others not so sure."

"But if it was Missy, then who . . . ?"

"Was in the house? I don't know." His face suddenly looked much younger, invigorated by the question. "You've got to love a good mystery, though, now and again, don't you? Who's missing besides her? And if it's not her—D'Amiens—dead in the house, then where might *she* be? Huh?"

"Really." Cuneo looked at the names and addresses. "You got copies of these?"

"Already made 'em. Those are yours."

A pause. "You talk to Glitsky?"

"This morning, a little after you left."

"So he knows about this?"

Becker didn't even look up. Obviously—and why would he not?—he assumed the two cops were working together, and Cuneo saw no reason to raise a flag. The arson inspector continued sorting methodically. "I figured you'd be around sooner than he was and you could tell him. These people aren't going anywhere. They live right there on Steiner." Finally, he sat back. "I'd like to know who it was, though. In the house."

"If it wasn't Missy," Cuneo said, "then whoever she was looks pretty good for the murders."

He nodded. "If it was her that people saw leaving."

Maxine Willis lived in one of the surviving Painted Ladies, three houses down from Paul Hanover's. In her early fifties, she was a very large, handsome, well-dressed black woman with a deep and booming voice. Her living room walls were stylishly adorned with tribal African art—dark-wood masks, spears, several framed works depicting working people or animals completely rendered in butterfly wings. The sofa was zebra skin, the chairs brown leather. Out the jutting front window, enough natural light remained that they could still see the park, but it was fading fast.

"No. See? I knew it was her. And it was a little earlier than this," she said. She turned and they both glanced at the clock on the mantel—8:15. "I saw her clearly."

"Missy D'Amiens?"

She nodded. "Although I hadn't ever met her to talk to.

I didn't know her name until I read it in the paper this morning. But it was Mr. Hanover's girlfriend all right. I'd seen her here on the block a hundred times."

"Would you mind telling me exactly where you were and what you saw?" Cuneo's foot tapped a time or two, but he caught it and willed it to stop, though immediately he began to tap his notebook.

"Well, Joseph and I were having a party with some friends, Cyril and Jennifer. Just some supper and then we were going to go up to Slim's, where a friend of ours was playing, but then of course the fire put an end to all that."

"And Joseph is . . . ?"

"My husband. I expect him now any minute. He saw her, too."

"From where?"

"Right here."

"In this room?"

"Uh huh. The light is so good come evening. We like to have our cocktails out here, with the park out there across the way." She closed her eyes for a minute, then moved to the windows that looked out over the street. "I was about right here."

Cuneo came over and stood next to her. The park was deserted except for a man walking a dog on the crest of the hill. Nearer, the street in front of them yawned empty, although cars lined both sides of it. No pedestrians on the sidewalks, either. The area was still a mess due to the fire.

"Okay, and where did Ms. D'Amiens pass?"

Maxine Willis lifted the lace curtain to one side and pointed. "Just out there. She was parked by that near light post just up the street."

"So she was going to her car?"

She nodded.

"And do you know what kind of car it was? Could you tell from here?"

"I didn't have to see it from last night. I knew it from other times, too. She drove a black Mercedes. One of the smaller ones, I think, the C-types."

Cuneo looked out, then back at his witness. If this was going to be a positive identification, he wanted to eliminate any possible ambiguities, and one had occurred to him. "Were you facing the way you are now? Toward the car?"

"Yes."

"And she was on the other side of the street?"

"Right."

"So you wouldn't have seen her until she was past you, then. Walking away? Isn't that right?"

"Well, sideways maybe. Joseph saw her first. He was standing about where you are."

Cuneo again stared across into the street. After a minute: "Let me ask you this," he said. "Why would he notice?"

Her face clouded for a moment. "I'm not sure what you mean."

"Well, I mean, there's four of you—four, right?—four of you standing around having some drinks and Joseph sees some woman walk by outside. So what? Why would he comment on it? Weren't people walking by all the time?"

Striking a thoughtful pose, she crossed her arms over her chest. "I don't recall saying anybody commented about it. Man know better than act like that." She looked at him, almost challenging, maybe waiting for him to show a sign of understanding. When none appeared, she sighed. "He's standing here by the window and suddenly his eyes go wide. Poor fool don't even know he's doing it. So I look to see what he likes so much. And it's her all right. So I give him the look, you know, and he knows he's caught. Man's always been a sucker for a pretty girl, and she was pretty enough."

"So the other two, your other guests. What happened with them?"

"Cyril and Jennifer? They look to see what Joseph's making eyes about. That's all. It wasn't a big thing at the time. Nobody even mentioned it out loud until the fire happened. Then later out in the street, we heard people saying it was Missy in the house with him. This was after we told the inspector we'd seen her."

"So what did you do then? I mean after you heard that?"

She shrugged. "Nothing. What was I supposed to do? I figured I must have gotten it wrong. Until you told me just now that it might not have been her in the house after all. Which had to mean it *was* her walking by all along."

"But let me get this straight. From last night all the way until when I told you ten minutes ago that maybe it wasn't Missy in the house, maybe it was someone else, you could *not* have sworn that the woman you saw walking by out there was her?"

Maxine frowned. "No. I didn't think about that. I just figured she went back in later. Maybe went out somewhere and came back. That could explain it, am I right? I thought it was her."

Glitsky sat at his desk reviewing utilization and arrest numbers, lost in the tedium, until the telephone rang and he realized that it had grown dark outside. Surprised anew that Cuneo had apparently decided not to check in with him at all, he got the phone in the middle of the second ring.

"Glitsky."

"Abe." His wife. A sigh of relief. "Good, you're there. Is everything all right?"

He looked at his watch. "I guess not, if the time got away from me so badly. Is it really eight thirty?"

"Close enough. What have you been doing? Last I heard you had been summoned by the mayor and were running out to see her."

"And I did, too. Twice, in fact."

"What did she want?"

"It's a bit of a story. It could even be construed as good news of a sort."

"You sound like Dismas. 'Construed as good news of a sort.' You think you qualified that enough?"

"I said it was a story. It's good that she's got confidence in me, I suppose. I could tell you in person in twenty minutes."

"That'd be nice. I have something that might be construed as good news of a sort myself."

"You got a raise?"

"No, it's not money. That would be unalloyed good news."

"Unalloyed. Talk about a Hardy word. So your news isn't unalloyedly good?"

"Unalloyedly, is that even a word? This is getting too complicated for me. I'll tell you when you get home."

Glitsky lived in a smallish three-bedroom upper duplex just north of Lake Street, in a cul-de-sac that bounded the leafy southern border to the Presidio. He'd raised Isaac, Jacob and Orel there with his first wife, Flo. After the cancer claimed her, he moved a Mexican nanny/housekeeper named Rita Schultz into the living room, where she'd slept behind a screen and helped with the boys for six years. Now Glitsky had a new life, Treya's daughter and all of his sons away living theirs. Rita no longer stayed with them full-time, sleeping behind the screen, but she still came every day to care for Rachel.

If he'd come home when his shift technically ended at 5:00, Glitsky could have had Paganucci drop him at his front step. But since his promotion, he almost never left the Hall until at least 7:00, and often much later. The job didn't really have anything like regular hours, and to pretend it did was to fail in it. And failure was not on his agenda. So there were always endless meetings—with chiefs, lieutenants, civic and businesspeople, department heads—to attend, tedious yet necessary administrative duties to perform, fences to mend, people to simply visit, flesh to press and parties to attend and press conferences to hold. And all of these things happened on their own timetable, not his. So to get to and from work, he usually checked out a car from the city lot next to the Hall, and invariably had to park it at best a few blocks from his home.

Now Glitsky was on the last leg of a six-block hike from the nearest parking place that he could find. Coming up on the opposite side of the street, with the late-afternoon wind just beginning to ebb now, he stopped and looked up into the lighted front windows of the rent-controlled place where he'd long since decided he would probably die. A shadow moved across the shades and he recognized the cameo of his wife pacing in the living room. The vision stopped him. Against all of his own expectations and preconceptions, he had somehow with Treya been able to find happiness again. Sometimes, as now, the feeling all but overwhelmed him.

"*Señor* Abe?"

He'd neither seen her in the dark nor heard her on the quiet street, and he reacted, startled at the sound. Recovering, he put his hand on his heart and rolled his eyes with what was, for him, wild theatricality. "Rita," he said. "What are you still doing here?"

"Just talking to *Señora* Treya."

"What about?"

The housekeeper reached out, took his wrist and tapped on his watch. Looking up, she gave him a look of benevolent understanding. "Women things."

When he got to his front door, twelve steps up from the street, Treya was there holding it open for him. Two-and-a-half-year-old Rachel, awake way past her bedtime and finally seeing her father, broke from around Treya's legs and threw herself headlong at him. "Daddy, Daddy, Daddy, Daddy!" Catching her up, he gathered her in, smothering her with kisses while she squealed with delight. With a last kiss he pulled her close, then caught something in his wife's eye.

"Rita tells me you and she were talking about women's things. Does that have to do with your maybe good news?" Treya kissed him hello, quickly, on his cheek, then turned away and stepped back to let the two of them in. "Have you been crying?"

She kept herself turned away, shook her head no. But too fast. And she started walking toward the kitchen. Still carrying Rachel, Glitsky followed. "Trey?"

"I'm just emotional," she said. "About this possibly good news, which I so hope it is." She squared her shoulders, took a deep breath and turned to face him. "It looks like we're going to have another baby." She waited, breathless for a minute, then unloosed a torrent. "Are you okay with that? Please say you are. I know we never talked about it specifically, I mean whether we were actually trying. And I just found out this morning. I've been wanting to tell you all day, but didn't just want to leave a message, and then when you didn't call me even once during the day or come home, I thought the mayor must have done something awful, and I didn't want to bother you by calling at work if you had some crisis, but then it got so late . . ."

Glitsky closed the distance between them and put his free arm around her.

"Sandwich hug!" Rachel, in heaven between them.

"Sandwich hug," Treya repeated to her daughter, kissing her. Then she looked up at her husband through a film of tears. "Okay? It's okay, isn't it?"

"More than okay," he said. "Unalloyed."

6

The next morning, Friday, Dismas Hardy made it down-stairs at a few minutes past seven. Breakfast noises emanated from the dining room, but he walked directly across the kitchen first, to the coffeepot where he poured himself a cup. Turning right into the family room, toward the back of the house, he tapped the glass of his tropical fish tank and poured some food into it. All his dozen little fishies seemed to be in good health as they rocketed to the surface, the tank was algae-free, the pump gurgled with a quiet efficiency.

"You love those guys, don't you?" His wife, Frannie, stood in the doorway.

"Love might be a little strong, being reserved only for my mate." He crossed over and kissed her good morning. "That would be you, the mate."

"Loves wife more than goldfish," she said. "And people say the romance goes."

"Never with us. Except they're not goldfish, not at forty to sixty bucks a pop."

"Sixty dollars? And they weigh, what, one ounce?"

"That would be one of the big ones."

Frannie stared into the tank for a minute. "I'll never complain about the price of salmon again. Speaking of which, are you eating breakfast this morning? Because if you are, you'd better get in there. The lox is almost gone."

In ten seconds he was standing, glaring down at the dining room table. Both of his children were engrossed in their morning newspaper—Vincent on the comics, Rebecca with the rest of the "Datebook" section. A toasted half bagel rested in front of his regular chair at the head of the table, but there was no sign of any lox, although two small empty plates held traces of cream cheese and crumbs.

"Vincent," Frannie didn't wait to analyze, "didn't I ask you to save some lox for your father?"

The boy looked up in total affront, hands to his chest, all outraged innocence. "Hey, it's not me. I *did*." He pointed across the table. "Talk to *her*."

The Beck was a step ahead of her mother. "I didn't hear you say that." She turned to her father. "I would have, Dad, you know I would."

But Hardy didn't get a chance to answer her. This, evidently, hadn't been the first moment of friction between the women in the house this morning, and Frannie's frustration now boiled over a bit. "You were sitting right where you are now when I said it," she said. "How could you not have heard me?"

"I thought you were talking to Vincent."

"So you turned your hearing aid off? Was that it? You *know* I was talking to both of you."

"Okay, but I just didn't hear you. *I didn't think you were talking to me, okay?*"

"No, not okay. Join the rest of us in the world here, would you?"

"Uh, guys," Hardy waded in delicately. He never knew what would happen when he got between his wife and his daughter. "It's okay. I got my coffee. I'm happy."

"I'm happy for you," Frannie said, "but that's not the point, and it's not okay. She's been doing this kind of thing all the time lately. And nobody else seems to notice. Or care."

Uh oh, Hardy thought.

"All the time?" Now Rebecca's tone went up a big notch. "*All the time!* I don't even know what you're talking about. I haven't done anything except eat some stupid lox, which was right out here on the table in front of me. Okay, if I ate it, I'm sorry. But what do you want me to do, Mom? Barf it back up?" She put her finger into her mouth.

Following the action, Vincent suddenly threw his comics page down and jumped up, away from the table. "Easy, Beck. Come on."

Hardy intervened at the same instant. "Don't barf it up. I'll just go throw a couple of my tropicals on this bagel . . ."

"Don't make a joke out of it," Frannie said. "It's not funny."

"I'm not going to really barf it up." Rebecca rolled her eyes in what Hardy believed was an expression of the platonic ideal of teenage pique.

"All right then."

Frannie obviously didn't think it was even slightly all right, but the fight had gone out of her, and she turned and disappeared back into the kitchen. Hardy debated whether to follow her or not and decided they'd both be happier in the long run if he didn't. If he went to her, they'd just keep talking about the Beck and how they were losing control over her, how she didn't respect them any longer, how he didn't take an active enough role anymore. It would all escalate and somehow become all about him and Frannie. *Didn't he see the way she was getting? Didn't he care what was happening to his daughter?*

He did care. He simply didn't spend as much time with her as his wife did, didn't identify with her in a more or less absolute way, and didn't really think he needed to. His daughter was growing up, becoming independent, which he believed was her fundamental job. And doing fine at it. Better than fine, even, with her incredible grade point average, president of a couple of clubs, working a night a week this semester tutoring math.

Hardy honestly believed that she hadn't heard Frannie issue her warning about the lox. She would never have eaten it if she'd thought it was meant for her father. But Frannie would have said that was the problem—she didn't think about anybody but herself. To which his answer was, "Of course not, she's a teenager." But this wasn't a popular response.

He sat down and took a bite of his bagel, pointed to the rest of the newspaper down by his son's elbow. "Vin, could you please hand me a section?" he asked. Then, sotto voce to the Beck, "I don't think you ate my lox on purpose, but you might want to go tell your mother you're sorry you yelled at her."

"Except, you know, Dad," she whispered, "she yelled at me." But shaking her head, she got up anyway and disappeared back into the kitchen.

Vincent, back in his chair, shook his own head, rolled his eyes. Girls. Hardy nodded in understanding. In this, he and his son were allies. Then he pointed again, said, "The paper, please. If I can't eat lox, at least I can read my morning paper." Vin reached over and grabbed the front page—double-time—and went to pass it up the table, glancing at the front page as he did. "Hey," he said. "Uncle Abe." And the paper's progress halted.

"Vin." Hardy, his voice suddenly sharp, snapped a finger. "Now. Please."

The tone brooked no argument. In a second, Vincent up and over his shoulder, the two males were reading the caption under the four-column, front-page picture of Glitsky smartly saluting the mayor. "Deputy Chief of Police Abraham Glitsky gets his marching orders from Kathy West yesterday afternoon at the Ferry Building at the beginning of the mayor's first 'Neighborhood Stroll.' The new administration plans to bolster police presence as well as civic awareness in troubled areas of the city, and Glitsky's appearance, according to the mayor, underscored the spirit of cooperation between her office and the Police Department that both sides hope to build upon."

"Uncle Abe's getting famous," Vincent said.

"Just what he's always wanted."

"I always thought he hated that stuff."

"He does. He's going to hate this picture. Maybe I should call him and tell him how cute and official he looks, saluting and all. Subservient, even."

"He'd probably come over and shoot you, Dad."

"Yeah, you're right. Maybe I'll give him a day to get used to it."

Before he checked in at his office, Glitsky stopped in at the homicide detail, where Lieutenant Marcel Lanier sat behind a desk that filled most of his office, and knocked at the open door. "Permission to enter?"

Lanier snorted, said, "Denied," then waved his superior inside. "Early call, Abe. Cuneo?"

"How'd you guess?"

"Incredible psychic powers. He's not happy with things, and I can't say I blame him."

"It's the mayor."

"That's what I hear, too."

"The point," Glitsky said, "is that if we're both going to be working the case, and we are, we ought to be communicating. As it is, I don't know what he knows, and vice versa. I don't think he's even talked to Strout yet, so he might not even know that Missy couldn't have shot herself. Or that Hanover couldn't have done himself, either, for that matter. And taken together, that eliminates murder/suicide and leaves a righteous double."

"So what do you want me to do?"

"Talk to him, tell him I'm not poaching."

Lanier's face went through a subtle change of expression.

Glitsky felt a heat rise into his face. He spoke with an exaggerated calm. "Do you think I am, Marcel?"

"No. If you say the mayor put you on it, what could you do?" Lanier came forward, elbows on the desk. "But look, Abe, it's no secret that you and her honor are friends. . . ."

"That's not . . ."

Lanier held up a hand. "Please, strictly true or not, that's the perception. There's no denying it," he paused, "especially after this morning's paper, okay? Call a spade a spade. At the very least no one's going to deny you're allies, right? So one of her benefactors gets murdered and Cuneo randomly pulls the case, and next thing you know, you're on it, too, as a special assignment. Tell me if you worked here, if you were him, that wouldn't fry your ass." Lanier leaned back in his chair again, linked his fingers over his stomach. "Look, Abe, it's no secret he's not one of your fans, and I don't get the impression you're one of his. . . ."

"He all but accused me of accessory to murder, Marcel. That's pretty much kept the warm and fuzzies at bay around him."

"Okay, sure, I see that. But you've got to admit that this thing with you and the mayor might smack him as something in the line of a personal vendetta."

Glitsky took a beat. "You've already talked to him about this."

"No, but he left a message for me this morning. Relatively lengthy. He seems to think you see an opportunity here to squeeze him out. Wanted me to know about it."

"Over one case? Last I checked, inspectors had a union. I couldn't fire him if I wanted to, not without cause."

"Maybe you'd find some?"

Glitsky shook his head. "Do you believe that, Marcel?"

"No. Honestly, no, I don't." He shifted his position. "But you might want to ask yourself why Kathy West is so personally involved here. Okay, so one of her people got killed. On the face of that, you call in the deputy chief of inspectors to honcho the investigation? Why? Unless he's your friend and you want him on it for another reason entirely."

"Which would be what?"

"I don't know. But just letting it air, Abe, she could be wanting to cover something up."

Now Glitsky's voice rasped. "And you think I'd help her?"

"No. Never on purpose. But listen to me. If you're reporting to her and not to anybody in homicide . . ."

"But that's what I'm saying. I'm trying to get with Cuneo."

"Still, it's mostly you and her, not you and him. If you get close to something that she needs to be concerned about . . ."

"Wait a minute. You can't think Kathy West is involved in the murders?"

Lanier looked at the air between them for a moment, then shrugged. "Not in the sense you mean. No, not really. Though you and I both know she could be. But the real question is, Could there be some other connection between Mr. Hanover and her honor? Maybe whoever killed him meant it as some kind of a warning to her. Maybe there's an issue of, say, contribution money." At Glitsky's look, Lanier backed off, opened his hands palms out. "I'm just throwing out ideas here. But the fact remains that she might want you on this for an entirely different reason than what she's telling you, and I don't think you're naive enough—hell, you're not naive at all—to haven't considered that." Lanier was sitting back again with his arms crossed, unblinking, daring his superior to deny it.

"I don't know if I'd gotten that far," Glitsky said after a pause. "Yesterday, when it looked like a suicide, she wanted me to clear Hanover's good name. Now that it looks like somebody's killed him . . ." He stopped, let out a breath.

"I'm just saying, from a certain perspective, it looks a little squirrelly."

"Okay, grant that," Glitsky said, "but she's the mayor. And the police chief, as you may know, serves at her discretion. Batiste is already on board with this. With me on the case, I mean. You don't tell her no without some serious risk to your career opportunities." After a short silence, Glitsky went on. "Just tell Cuneo I need to talk with him, that's all. Share information. Between the two of us, we'll take it from there. You mind doing that?"

"No, that's fine. I'd be happy to, Abe. There's nothing personal here between me and you. I'm just the messenger. And the message has got some merit."

"I hear you. I even agree with you." Glitsky came off the wall, rolled his shoulders, took a breath. He reached for the doorknob, turned it, started to walk out.

Lanier stopped him. "Abe."

Glitsky turned, a question on his face. He pulled the door back to.

The homicide lieutenant took another few seconds staring at the ceiling while he decided whether or not he was going to say it. Finally, he said, "One thing you might want to know. Cuneo's call this morning? He didn't want it to get out, maybe especially not to you, but you've got to know." He let out a sigh, waited some more.

"You want to give me three guesses?"

The scathing tone made Lanier talk. "Maybe it wasn't the D'Amiens woman in the house. Some witnesses may have seen her leaving a little before the fire. Cuneo's thinking that if that's true, maybe she was the shooter."

"So who was the woman in the house?"

"No clue."

"And where's D'Amiens?"

"Nobody knows."

"*I* know where she is. She's in my locker not fifty feet from where we're resting our tired old bones, Abe," Strout said. "That's where she is for a damn pure medical certainty. And as for her doin' the shooting, well, that would have been highly unusual, if not impossible. Her bein' dead an' all at the time." The medical examiner had his feet up on his desk. Behind him through the window, the barely visible morning freeway traffic was stopped in both directions. The fog gave every indication that it was going to be around for lunch. Strout was opening and closing a switchblade as they talked. "Who's the perpetrator of this outrageous folderol? That it wasn't D'Amiens."

"Before I tell you that, John, tell me why it's folderol."

"Because I called your Dr. Toshio Yamashiru—who by the way turns out to be one of the premier forensic odontologists in the state, was called in to help identify the 9/11 victims in New York—anyway, I called him within about two minutes of getting his name from you yesterday, and he was good enough to come down here last night with her dental records and compare them to her."

"D'Amiens?"

"Well, they weren't Marilyn Monroe's." He closed the switchblade. "Same person."

"Well, wait . . ."

"Okay." The knife flicked open and closed four times. Behind Strout on the freeway, a car inched forward from one pane of his window to the next. "What are you thinking?"

"Have you talked to Dan Cuneo? About this case?"

"Sure. He was at the scene."

Glitsky shook his head. "No. Since then."

"Well," Strout drawled the word, pronouncing it as two syllables—*way-all*—" 'then' would have been only yesterday morning, Abe. But the answer's no, I haven't seen him since then. Why?"

A pause. "Nothing. Just curious."

Strout let a chuckle percolate for a few seconds. "Idle curiosity, huh? Something you're so well known for." But he held up a hand, still enjoying the moment. "But seriously, you don't have to tell me why it matters if I've seen him. Maybe it's none of my business."

"It's not that. I haven't talked to him, either, but Marcel tells me he's got witnesses who saw her leave the place and go to her car just before the fire. D'Amiens."

"Maybe she came back. Obviously she did."

"Good point."

"Shot him, then went to her car and got the gasoline, which tends to be obvious if it's sitting out in the foyer."

But Glitsky was shaking his head. "No. That's if she killed herself, which I think we agree she couldn't have."

Strout chewed on that for a moment. "So somebody who looks like her?"

"Maybe." He came forward in the folding chair. As usual, Glitsky was in full uniform, and leaning over, held his hat in his hands between his legs. "How certain was Yamashiru?"

"That it was D'Amiens? A hundred percent. We went over everything for almost an hour. Anyway, he was certain enough—and so am I—that I'm putting her name to the autopsy."

Glitsky had known Strout for thirty years, and knew that this was a point of professional pride and honor. Strout didn't call it as a matter of law unless he was completely convinced. He knew he might have to testify under oath on the witness stand, and so far as anyone in the city knew, he had never made a mistake on an autopsy—either an identification or a cause of death. He would not hesitate to decline to state when he wasn't sure. But he'd never been flat wrong. And Glitsky didn't think he was now.

Which meant that, with a slight detour, he was back where he'd been before he'd talked to Marcel Lanier this morning, or even when he'd had his discussion with the mayor yesterday afternoon. Somebody had shot Hanover and D'Amiens and then set their bodies on fire.

This, then, was a straightforward murder investigation. Cuneo was the inspecting officer, and—orders from the mayor or not—Glitsky would defer to him as long as it was practicable. Hardy's advice echoed—this might be a good opportunity to mend fences with the man, get to some kind of mutual understanding, perhaps the beginnings of respect.

Finally making it nearly to his own office, Glitsky stood frowning at the door, which sported a cutout of this morning's *Chronicle* photo. It shouldn't have amazed him, though it always did, how the news agencies—print, audio or film—all so consistently managed to convey misleading information, even in a picture. Of course, he'd seen the stupid picture first thing in the morning. It was impossible to miss. He found it odd that he had no memory of the actual moment at all, even though he appeared to be standing at formal attention and the salute was so crisp he might have been posing.

Aware that someone had come into the conference room that separated the reception area and his office, he turned around. Melissa wasn't really his private secretary—technically she was merely the gatekeeper for him and the other deputy chief within the suite, Jake Longoria—but as the highest ranking of the six clerks in the reception bay, she took a proprietary, even maternal, interest in the men whose access she protected. Now she was smiling broadly at him, clearly pleased with the reflected glory that the picture brought to her, as well as with Glitsky's obvious and growing prominence among the city's leaders. (It wouldn't be unknown for a deputy chief to take his gatekeeper with him should the promotion to chief ever come along, either.)

"You like it? That's a great picture, isn't it?"

Behind her, Glitsky saw a couple of the other clerks in the doorway, wanting to share in what would be his no-doubt positive reaction. Feeling that it would be churlish at best and negative for staff morale to follow his impulse and rip the offending thing down, he arranged his face into a bland expression and nodded. "It's nice," he said. Feeling a little more might be called for, he offered a small, stiff bow from the waist. "My thanks to you all."

Inside the blessed sanctity of his office, a low-level rage humming in his ears, he hung his hat on the rack by the door, then went to his desk and pushed the constantly blinking button that indicated he had messages in his voice mail. Thirteen of them.

Amidst the usual bureaucratic white noise, no fewer than six of the calls concerned the picture. Jeff Elliot wanted to know about the story he'd clearly missed when they'd been talking yesterday, and could they do an interview sometime soon, maybe today, for a "CityTalk" column. His friend and mentor Frank Batiste left a message tinged with the faint but unmistakable reek of jealousy. Batiste did not say it overtly, but unstated was that if there was going to be a picture typifying the mutual cooperation between the mayor's office and the PD, maybe the chief ought to have been the one on the front page, saluting. Treya, who'd slept in later than Glitsky's own six forty-five departure and saw the photo after he'd already left for work, agreed with Melissa that it was flattering and kind of cool. Dismas Hardy, on the other hand, congratulating him with heavy sarcasm on the photo op, wondered if he'd noticed that the name badge on his shirt had a typo that read "Gliktsy." (Looking down immediately, cricking his neck in the process, he checked—it didn't.) And, oh yeah, Hardy added, if Glitsky needed a campaign manager for whatever office he was running for, and though somewhat upset that his best friend hadn't included him in his original plans, Hardy was his man.

Still no callback from Cuneo, he noticed. Glitsky resolved to call him at home, wake him up if need be, after he'd gone through his voice mail. The last message, though, much to his surprise, was from Catherine Hanover, who had seen the picture and recognized his name from their conversation yesterday. Having thought about it most of the morning, she finally had worked up the nerve to call and wondered if he might get back to her. Sooner rather than later. She'd had a visit last night from Inspector Cuneo and had something a little delicate, as she put it, that she wanted to discuss.

He looked at his watch. She had placed the call less than fifteen minutes ago. He started punching numbers. "Mrs. Hanover? This is Deputy Chief Glitsky."

An audible sigh, then a rush. "Thank you for calling back so soon. I didn't know if I could just leave a message for you personally, but I . . ." She ran out of breath and, after a slight hesitation, started again in a lower key. "I didn't know who else to talk to."

"Didn't you say you'd spoken to Inspector Cuneo last night?"

"Yes." Another pause. "I just wondered," she said, "if I could arrange to talk to you, maybe, instead of Inspector Cuneo. I mean, if you need . . . if the police need to talk to me anymore about Paul or the fire or anything."

"You don't want to talk to Inspector Cuneo?"

"I think I'd prefer not."

This was tricky indeed. Especially in light of Glitsky's new information that the homicide detail—i.e., Cuneo—was in fact investigating not a murder/suicide, but a double homicide. This made Catherine Hanover not just a witness, but among the universe of possible suspects to the murders. She might not think of herself in those terms. But Glitsky had already been forced to consider them because of what she'd told him yesterday—her powerful financial incentive to see Missy D'Amiens out of Paul Hanover's will or, failing that, his life. Many people had been killed for far less money.

And now Mrs. Hanover didn't want to talk to the investigating officer. On the face of it, Glitsky couldn't even begin, and wasn't remotely inclined, to consider her request. If Cuneo's questions had rattled or upset her, or made her uncomfortable in any one of a number of ways, all the better—maybe he'd come upon something relevant to the murders she was trying to hide. She was not going to be able to avoid Cuneo. It was out of the question and he told her as much. "I'm sorry," he said in conclusion, "but witnesses don't get to choose who interrogates them."

"All right," she said, her voice thick with regret. "I tried." Then, almost as an afterthought, added, "I might have known that you'd stick together."

"That who would stick together?"

"You. The police."

"Well, in this case, yes we do. It's a general rule, for obvious reasons, that suspects are rarely anxious to talk to inspecting officers."

He heard an intake of breath. She whispered. "Suspects? Did you say suspects?"

"Yes, ma'am."

"So now I'm a suspect? I thought I was a witness." Her voice went up in pitch and volume. "I *volunteered* everything I told Inspector Cuneo, both at the fire and then here at my house. How can I . . . how can you think I had anything to do with this?"

"I don't think that."

"But you just said I was a suspect."

His hand tight on the receiver, Glitsky threw a glance at

the ceiling. This had gone far beyond where it should have already, and now he felt he needed to explain himself and his position, always a situation he'd rather avoid. "No," he said. "I said that suspects often didn't want to talk to their inspecting officer."

"But the inference was there, that I was one of them."

Glitsky spoke with an exaggerated precision. "Mrs. Hanover, since we have no suspects at all that I'm aware of, everyone is technically a potential suspect. That includes you, though it doesn't move you to the head of the pack. You asked if you could somehow avoid talking again to Inspector Cuneo, and I was telling you why that wasn't allowed."

Some steel now in her tone, she pressed him. "All right, then, what if I were to make a complaint about him? Who would I go to for that? What would happen then?"

"What kind of complaint?"

She hesitated for a minute. "Inappropriateness."

"In what sense? What kind of inappropriateness?"

Another breath, another pause. "Sexual, I would say."

Now it was Glitsky's turn to go quiet. The silence hung with import. Finally, treading carefully, he said, "There is an Office of Management and Control in the department that investigates these kind of allegations. I could put you through to them right now."

But this time she jumped in quickly. "I don't want to go there. Not yet, anyway."

"Why not? If Inspector Cuneo assaulted you . . ."

"He didn't *assault* me. It's just, I mean, it was clear he was coming on to me, and I'd just prefer if I didn't have to see him again. He makes me uncomfortable. I'm not trying to get anybody in trouble here. I'm willing to talk to anybody else you send out, but Inspector Cuneo makes me nervous. That's all I'm saying."

"Did he touch you?"

"Several times. Then he squeezed my arm before he left, said I could call him at home anytime, gave me his number. It was definitely . . . inappropriate. He was hitting on me."

"But you don't want to lodge a complaint?"

"That just seems a little strong for what it was. I don't want to overreact. I don't really want to get him into trouble. . . ."

"He may already be."

"No! I really don't want that. But look," she said, intensity now bleeding through the line. "Really. I just didn't want to see him, that's all. You could come out if you need to talk to me, or anybody else. I'm not trying to avoid anything with the police, and he didn't do anything so blatant that I feel like I need to file a complaint."

"All right, but if you don't file a complaint, then officially nothing happened," Glitsky said. "That'll be the story."

"But nothing really *did* happen."

"He didn't touch you?"

"Yes. I already said that."

"Well, that's something. It's grounds for a complaint." He wanted to add that if she wanted to know what he'd do if he were in a similar position, he would file immediately. But he couldn't say that. It was completely her decision, and couldn't be any of his.

"Well, maybe, but even so . . . I'll think about it."

7

Hardy and Glitsky were at the counter of the Swan Oyster Depot on Polk Street, way in the back, eating fried oysters and iceberg lettuce salad with Louie dressing. Hardy nursed a beer while Glitsky, incognito without his hat on and with his old flight jacket covering the uniform, stuck with his standard iced tea. "And of course," Hardy was saying, "if you get the message through to him in any official way at all, he'll either accuse her of lying or you of making it up." He sipped his beer. "It just gets better and better, doesn't it?"

"I've got to tell him. I can't *not* tell him."

"I thought that was why you needed to see me so urgently. So I could advise you how not to do just that."

"But I've got to."

"Okay, then. Now maybe we can enjoy this fine lunch."

"If she—Hanover, I mean—doesn't file a complaint, it didn't happen."

"I thought we were done with the discussion."

"So it's really not a department matter."

"If you say so. On-duty cop hits on pretty witness—I'm assuming she's pretty. . . ."

"I haven't seen her, but it doesn't matter."

"Of course not. I jest. But pretty or not, witness gets hit on . . ."

"*Possible suspect* gets hit on."

"That, too. But whatever, she gets hit on, maybe even assaulted, depending on your definition of the term, by an on-duty officer. You're saying that it's not a department matter?"

Glitsky chewed ice from his tea.

"I'm hoping you've already written a memo to file, at

least." Reading Glitsky's face, he went on. "Okay, and this is your legal adviser talking, do that first, as soon as you get back to your office. Then at least you're covered if it gets bigger or, God forbid, Cuneo rapes her or kills her or something." He wiped some dressing around the plate with a crust of sourdough. "It's got to get official in some way. Don't tell Cuneo directly. Take it to Batiste, man to man. He'll support you."

"Maybe not. He's none too pleased with me at this exact moment—the *Chronicle* picture. Besides which, he won't want to be bothered. It's my problem."

"No. Your problem is that you *think* it's your problem. We've already determined by the process of rigorous debate that this is a police department matter, and Frank's the chief of police. So it's his problem more than yours. He'll probably fire Cuneo, in fact."

"Not without a complaint he won't."

"Call Hanover back. Convince her to file one."

"Good idea. Except what if she's the killer?"

"That would be bad luck, I admit."

"More than that."

"And how likely is that anyway? That she's the killer?"

"I don't have any idea. I'm completely out of the loop on Cuneo's suspects or anything else, for that matter. She sang me a long song about money that gives her plenty of motive, but it sounded like everybody else in the family knew the same tune. And you know a guy like Paul Hanover always had some deals going on. You see the profile on him Channel Four did last night? He had his hands in a dozen pots, and not just here in the city. Or Missy. Nobody knows squat about her either, except that she spent a lot of money on the house."

"Well, there you go."

"What?"

"Who'd she spend the money with?"

"I don't know. The contractor, I'd guess." He put down his tea, wrote a note to himself on his memo pad. "But that's not your worst idea."

"Thank you. But back to Cuneo . . ."

"Always back to Cuneo."

"Well, yeah. You blame me?"

Glitsky considered the question for a long minute. "No," he said at last. He chewed more ice. "I could just finesse it."

"How could you do that?"

"I just block his access to her. He's on nights, right? I make it a point to take her statements during the days. He doesn't have a reason to see her again."

"Maybe he doesn't need one."

But Glitsky shook his head. "No, he won't take it further if he doesn't see her on duty."

"You know this for a fact?"

"I've heard rumors. It's a pattern."

"So he's done this kind of thing before?"

A shrug, then a nod. "And they don't all resent it, either. The magic of the uniform, even if he doesn't wear one. Marcel told me he had a thing with his shrink after she stopped seeing him professionally."

"You're shitting me."

"Would that I were. Apparently he thinks there's no harm in asking, or letting a witness know you think she's hot."

"Any of these documented?"

"You mean as assault or harassment? Nope. They said yes."

"So he's just a dick? Pardon the pun."

"At least that."

The two men took a break to eat. Glitsky finished first and was chewing ice again when he said, "I'm going right to him, cop to cop. Tell him what she said, say he might want to be a little discreet."

"Be his friend."

"Exactly. Keep him close."

Hardy swallowed his last oyster, tipped his beer up. "I've heard worse plans," he said. "But do yourself a favor first."

"What's that?"

"Memo to file."

Two o'clock, and Cuneo was blasting away with the Beach Boys. Not that Dennis Wilson was a rock drummer in the league of, say, Charlie Watts of the Stones, or any of the big band guys, but he beat the living hell out of his skins, and sometimes Cuneo just wanted to play loud and hard, not good. He was letting the cymbals ring at the end of "Help Me, Rhonda" when he heard the knock on his front door.

"Hold on!" Barefoot, drenched with sweat, he was wearing a tank top over a pair of lime-green swim trunks. Because of his location he didn't get a lot of action at his front door, so the knock was a little unusual in itself. And he'd been a cop long enough—thirteen years—that he carried the standard load of paranoia around with him wherever he went. His gun and shoulder holster hung from the back of one of the chairs in his kitchen, and he skipped the three steps over to it and had the weapon in his hand within about two seconds. "Just a sec," he said. "Coming."

But first he parted the gauzy white living room drapes and looked out. On the concrete apron that comprised his front yard was a city-issue car with a uniformed driver behind the wheel. Pulling the curtains further apart, he put his eye against the window and saw Glitsky standing at ease on his stoop, so he set the gun on top of his television set, went to the door and opened it.

Glitsky began in an amiable way, with a grotesque but perhaps sincere attempt at a smile. "Sorry to bother you, Inspector, but I didn't know if my messages were getting through, and we need to get on the same page with this Hanover thing. It's heating up pretty fast. You mind?"

"No. Sure. Good idea." Cuneo, thrown off-balance, half turned back to his room. "I was just doing my workout. I haven't got to my messages yet. I think we must have just missed each other last night. I stopped by your office."

"That's all right. I was in and out." Glitsky cast a quick glance over Cuneo's shoulder. "I'm not interrupting anything, am I? You got company?"

"No. Just me." Cuneo backed up a bit and said, "You want to come in? We can sit."

"Thanks." A step into the room, Glitsky stopped. "Cool place, great location." He pointed at the drums. "How long have you been playing?"

"A couple of years now. It blows off energy."

"I hear you," Glitsky said. "I haven't had that since I gave up football. If you don't include a baby. They can wear you out pretty good." He scanned the room, apparently relaxed. "One of my boys, Jacob, is a musician. A singer, actually. Opera, believe it or not." Cuneo had no reaction to all the chatter, but Glitsky went on anyway. "We didn't exactly play a lot of opera around the house when he was growing up, so I don't know how he got the taste for it, but he's pretty good. The downside is, he lives in Italy and I never get to see him."

Glitsky sat himself on the edge of the love seat. He let a silence build, then broke it. "So I'm guessing you're pissed I'm involved in this. I know I would be."

Cuneo sat down at the drum kit, hit the kick drum. "Sure, a little, but what am I gonna do? Nobody asked me. But it's my case."

"Nobody's saying it isn't."

"Well, pardon me, sir, but that's just bullshit."

Glitsky frowned at the profanity, the insubordination, although he'd invited it to some degree by coming to Cuneo's home unannounced. "Actually, it's not. As I thought I explained in my message, the mayor had a personal connection to Hanover. She wanted to be in on it."

"And Lanier couldn't get it from me, then let her know?"

Glitsky shrugged. "She knows me better."

"Lucky for you."

"Maybe. Some people might think that's debatable. But the point is, as far as I'm concerned, you're still the investigating officer."

"And you're what? My supervisor?"

"I was thinking, for this case, partner."

Cuneo started a light but quick tattooing on the snare drum. Caught himself and stopped. Started again. "I've had most of my luck working alone," he said.

"So have I." Thinking this was about as far as this topic could take them, Glitsky decided to break the stalemate and move along to the facts of the case. "I talked to Becker and he told me some of your witnesses thought they saw Missy leave the house before the fire."

The drumming stopped.

Glitsky continued. "So I'm assuming first thing this afternoon you were going to put out a net on her. Obvious, right? She was the shooter."

"So?"

"So have you gotten with Strout yet?" He raised a hand, cutting off the reply. "That's not a criticism, in case you haven't. It's a question."

"I was planning on seeing him right after I saw you this afternoon."

"Well, maybe I can save you a trip. I went by the morgue this morning. He ran dental records last night. It was Missy."

The news finally sparked a show of interest. Cuneo's whole body came forward, forearms on his knees, his eyes sharp now, focused. "How sure was he?"

Glitsky's mouth turned up a half inch. "It was Strout." Meaning that if he said it at all, he meant it completely.

Nodding in understanding, Cuneo asked. "So she went back inside?"

"That's one theory."

"She did him, went out to get the gasoline, spent a few minutes pouring it around, then lit it and did herself?"

"Except she didn't."

Cuneo cocked his head to one side, then remembered. "That's right. She was shot pretty far around in the back of the head, wasn't she?"

"Right. Physically possible, maybe, but not likely. More likely somebody else did both of them." He spread his palms. "That's where we are."

Cuneo tapped his hands on his thighs. "So who did my witnesses see that they thought was Missy?"

"Maybe it *was* her. Who were your witnesses?"

"Neighbors."

"So your take is maybe she went someplace and happened to come back in at the wrong time?"

"I don't really have a take. Do you think it was about Hanover?"

"I don't know. The mayor thinks it, though."

"She give you any other information?"

"Nope."

"So she might be someone to talk to?"

Nodding, Glitsky said, "Maybe. I intend to ask."

"And then you'll tell me what she says?"

"That's the plan. We're working together. And that being the case, I wanted to pass something along. I got a call from Catherine Hanover this morning. The daughter-in-law?"

"Sure. I talked to her twice already. She called you?"

"She did. It seems we've been doubling up on her. I talked to her yesterday, and then evidently you came by to visit her after we'd talked, she and I?"

He answered warily. "Right. She told me you'd called her."

"Well," Glitsky said, "you won't like this, but she said you came on to her."

Cuneo's face hardened down in an instant. "She said *what*? How did I do that?"

"You touched her."

"I *touched* her. Where? Did she say?"

"Arm and shoulder."

"Arm and shoulder. As if I'd remember arm and shoulder. And that was *coming on* to her?" Then, a different tone. "Is she filing a complaint?"

"No."

"She says I came on to her, but she's not filing a complaint? What's that about?"

"That doesn't matter," Glitsky said. "Did you touch her?"

Cuneo paused for a second. "I really don't remember."

"It would be better if you did, one way or the other."

"Okay then. No, I didn't."

"You're sure?"

"Positive. If I did, maybe passing by her, it was so innocent I didn't even notice."

"So if you did that, maybe by mistake, you're saying she must have overreacted?"

"Either that or just flat lied. It's been known to happen."

"And why would she do that?"

"That's what I'm asking myself, especially if she's not filing a complaint." His fingers tapped a steady beat on the snare drum. Ta da dum, ta da dum, ta da dum. "Maybe I was getting close to something she didn't want to talk about."

Glitsky leaned forward. "Do you remember what that might have been?"

Cuneo drummed some more, thinking about it. "Nothing specific."

"What did you go to see her about?"

"She was a witness who might have remembered something. You know how that is."

"Okay."

The fingers stopped. The silence this time thicker. "Okay what?"

Glitsky hesitated. "If you weren't asking her about anything specific, and didn't call on her for a specific reason—something she said the night before that bothered you, something like that—people might wonder why you went to see her in the first place." He held up a hand again. "Just an observation if the topic comes up again."

Cuneo threw him a long, flat stare. "So what did you call her about, then?"

"I called her because I was hoping somebody in the extended family might know who worked on Missy's teeth, and she was the only contact I had. I lucked out." Glitsky kept his voice calm against Cuneo's clear rage. "Listen, I'm not accusing you of anything. If you say you didn't touch her, you didn't touch her. If you felt you had to talk to her a second time without a specific reason, that's good enough for me. Good cops have good instincts."

The kick drum went *thud*.

Glitsky continued. "After she gave me the dentist's name, she talked about her family and money. Things are going to be better for them all after Paul's death."

"How much better?"

"A lot."

Glitsky offered his opinion that Catherine's ingenuous and offhand cataloguing of the benefits of Paul's death mitigated considering her a suspect. So Cuneo would probably be well advised to stay away from her. If any further direct interrogation of her were necessary, Glitsky ought to do it. Cuneo didn't buy the argument. But he wasn't going to argue with the deputy chief, whose visit here had to be intimidation pure and simple.

Instead he said, "If it's my case, how about if I work it and keep you informed?"

"We could do that, but it might be awkward for me with the mayor. She asked me to stay involved. I'm asking you how I can do that and still let you do your job."

"I just told you. How about if I work it and let you know what I get?"

Glitsky put his notepad down. "I'll ask you one more time. Either you tell me how you want to do this or I'll tell you how we *will* do it. Is that about clear enough?"

After a minute, Cuneo nodded. "All right." He got out his own notepad, flipped a few pages. "You said the mayor might know something she's not telling you. Ask her what she really knows about Hanover."

"All right."

"Then you might see if you run across anything about Missy while you're at it."

"You think she might have been the primary target?"

"She's just as dead as Hanover. And Catherine said the two of them had been fighting."

"About the remodel? Catherine said . . ."

Cuneo interrupted. "Catherine, Catherine, Catherine."

"Yeah, I know."

"I didn't touch her."

"I never said you did."

A stretch of silence. Then Glitsky pulled a page of newspaper from inside his notebook, unfolded it and handed it across to Cuneo. "That's Paul and Missy three months ago at a party. It's the only picture of her I could find, which I thought was a little weird since Paul's picture was in the paper every couple of weeks. The *Chron*'s even got a head shot of him on file. But nothing on her except this."

"She didn't like to have her picture taken."

"Apparently not."

"Why not?"

"No idea."

Cuneo finally looked at the photograph. "Somebody looks like her, you'd think she'd love to get photographed." He stared another second, emitted a low whistle. "Definite trophy material." Still, he kept his eyes on the picture.

"You see something?" Glitsky asked.

Almost as though startled out of a reverie, he said, "No. Nothing. Just a hell of a waste."

8

Cuneo left his house about a half hour after Glitsky had gone, and this put him in the city at around 3:30, long before his shift was scheduled to begin. But he figured he wasn't going to be on the clock for a while anyway, not if he wanted to break this case before Glitsky could claim any credit for it.

The Arson Unit had for years worked out of one of the station houses close to downtown. But that station didn't have toilets and changing areas for female firefighters, so to make room for these improvements, the Arson Unit had been transferred to its present location in a barricaded storage warehouse on Evans Street in the less-than-centrally-located, gang-infested Bayview District, far, far south of Market. Inside the cavernous main room downstairs they kept the arson van as well as spare engines and trucks and miles of hoses and other equipment. There was also the odd historical goody, such as an engine that had been used in the 1906 earthquake and fire, with an eight-hundred-pound, five-story ladder it had taken twenty men to lift.

Becker sat upstairs at a small conference table in a common room outside of his small office. When Cuneo entered, he was turning the oversize pages of some computer printout. Looking up, and without preamble, he said, "Valero gasoline."

"What about it?"

"That's the accelerant." He tapped the pages in front of him. "We had a good-enough sample from the rug under her. We ran a mass spectrometer on it. Valero."

Cuneo drew up a chair. "They're different? I thought all gas was the same."

"Not exactly." He put a finger on the paper. "This was Valero's formulation."

"So what does that tell us?"

"Unfortunately, not a whole hell of a lot. Valero's the biggest gas producer in the country. However—the good news—it's nowhere near the market leader here in the city. And there's a Valero station not three blocks from Alamo Square. Not that our man necessarily bought the gas there, but somebody bought almost exactly two gallons on Wednesday morning. The sales get automatically recorded and we checked."

"Did anybody notice who bought it?"

"Nobody's asked yet."

Cuneo clucked. "I'll go by. I've got a picture of Missy. Maybe it'll spark something." He pulled out his notepad, unfolded the picture and passed it across. "Can you say 'babe'?"

Becker stared at it for a long moment. "This is Missy? She looks a little familiar."

"You know, I thought that, too. You heard it *was* her, by the way, didn't you?"

"Yeah. I called Strout, keeping up."

Cuneo drummed on his chair for a few seconds, staring into the air between them. Suddenly he snapped his fingers. "That's it. I knew there was something else. You just said something about 'our man' when you were telling me about the gas. You got anything that narrows it down to a guy?"

"No," Becker said. "I've just always assumed it was a guy. I told this to Glitsky."

"And what did he say?"

"Nothing, really. He just took it in. Why? Is something pointing you toward a woman?"

"Maybe," Cuneo said. "I'll let you know."

Glitsky figured that if he didn't want to ask the mayor directly, and he didn't, then his best source of information on her perhaps-hidden connection to Paul Hanover was likely to be found in the basement of the *Chronicle* building at Fifth and Mission. Despite the receptionist calling Jeff Elliot to tell him Glitsky was upstairs wanting to see him, when Glitsky got buzzed down and got to Jeff's small, glass-enclosed cubicle, the reporter/columnist was in his wheelchair at his desk, typing up a storm at his computer terminal, apparently lost to the world until he suddenly stopped typing and looked over. "This is my Pulitzer," he said. "You mind waiting for two more 'graphs?" He motioned to a chair just inside the cubicle.

Glitsky nodded and took the seat.

The office was small and cluttered. It sported an old metal desk that held Elliot's computer and a telephone, a waist-high oak bookshelf crammed to overflowing, and another metal shelf contraption stacked with about a year's worth of newspapers, and against which leaned a set of crutches. A bunch of *New Yorker* and other cartoons were taped on the glass wall by Glitsky's head. Next to the phone on the desk was a picture of his wife with their daughters.

Elliot stopped typing and stared at his screen, then raised his right hand over the keyboard and brought it down with a triumphant flourish. The screen cleared. He turned his head toward Glitsky. "Sorry about that, but it's brilliant. You'll see tomorrow. So to what do I owe the personal appearance?"

"You said you wanted to talk to me, remember? About the picture of me and the mayor? The scoop I was hiding from you?"

"I was giving you grief, I think. Now you're telling me there was one?"

"If there was, I thought maybe between us we might find it."

Elliot pushed his wheelchair back from the desk and around to face him. "You're losing me."

"I don't mean to. What do you know about Paul Hanover?"

"Other than the fact that he's dead? This is going to have to do with the mayor?"

"It might. And we're off the record, okay? It'll be worth it in the long run."

Elliot nodded with some reluctance. "All right. What do you have?"

"I don't know if it's anything, but you remember yester-

day at the Ferry Building when I told you I had business
with Kathy. The business was that she had asked me to get
involved, personally, with Hanover."

"Why would she want you to do that?"

"That's unclear. Maybe she thinks we've got a relationship."

"So you'll control what gets out?"

"I don't want to think she thinks that."

"But you suspect it?"

"Maybe that's putting it too strongly. I know nothing
about Hanover other than the fact that he gave her campaign money. I thought you might have heard a little
more."

Elliot took his hands off the armrests of his wheelchair
and linked them on his lap. His eyes went to the cartoons
on the partition by Glitsky's head, but he wasn't looking at
them. Finally, he drew a breath and let it out. "First," he
said, "he didn't just give her *some* money. He threw the
fund-raising dinner that kicked off her campaign last summer, where they raised I think it was about six hundred
grand. You might have read about that, since the story appeared in the general newspaper and not my column." He
grinned at his little joke. "But Hanover, I guess you'd say,
was catholic in his political contributions. Kathy, of course,
is a Dem, but he was also the Republican go-to guy."

"When did we start allowing Republicans in San Francisco?"

"You'd be surprised. Last time the president came out
here to raise some money, guess who hosted the party?"

"So what were his politics? Hanover's."

"He didn't have politics so much, per se. He had clients.
But wait a minute." Jeff went back to his terminal, hit a few
keys, then sat back in satisfaction. "There you go. When
memory fails . . ."

Glitsky came forward in his chair. "What'd you get?"

Donnell White, a mid-thirties black man with an upbeat
demeanor, managed the Valero station on Oak and Webster. He wasn't the owner, but he worked afternoons six
days a week. He took one look at Cuneo's picture of Missy
D'Amiens and nodded. "Yeah, she in here all the time,
every week or two. She must live nearby."

"Not anymore." Cuneo told him the news, then went on. "But the question is whether you saw her come in on Wednesday and fill up a portable gas container."

"Not if she come in the morning." He looked down again at the picture, scratched his short stubble. "But hold on a sec."

They were standing out in front by the gas islands, and now he turned and yelled back into the garage area, where some rap music emanated. "Jeffie, come on out here, will you?"

When there was no response, White disappeared back into the station. After a few seconds, the music stopped and White and Jeffie emerged back into the late-afternoon sun. Jeffie was young, as sullen as White was effusive. Apparently bored to death, his eyes rolled upward as he slouched with his hands in his pockets, listening to why the cop was here. Finally they got to the picture and he nodded. "Yeah," he said. "Could have been her."

Something about the phrase struck Cuneo. "What do you mean, could have been? It either was or it wasn't."

He shrugged. "Hey, some woman get some gas." He looked to his coworker. "Who you said you lookin' for?"

Cuneo jumped in. "It might not have been this woman?"

He shrugged. "I'm eating lunch inside. She fills the thing and not her car. Put it in the trunk."

"She put the portable container in her trunk?"

He fixed Cuneo with a flat stare. "What'd I just say, man? Yeah, she put the container in her trunk."

"What kind of car was it?"

Again, the eye roll. "Maybe a Mercedes? I don't know. Coulda been. Something like that."

Cuneo held the photograph out again. "And would you say it was this woman or not?"

Jeffie looked more carefully this time, took it in his hands and brought it closer to his face. "I seen her . . . this woman, before, I think." He kept looking. "Mighta been her, but if it was, she had her hair different. But I don't really know, 'cept she was white and fine-lookin'. Big jugs, no fat. Nice butt."

"You remember what she was wearing?"

The young mechanic cast his eyes to the sky again, then closed them. "Maybe a blue shirt, kind of shiny. Oh yeah, and sunglasses. She never took the shades off." He pointed at the picture again. "It could have been her, now I look at it. It's hard to say. But maybe not."

This time, cocktail hour Friday night, Maxine and Joseph Willis were both home at their place a few houses down from where Paul Hanover's used to be. They were drinking manhattans in stem glasses and going out to meet some friends for dinner in a while, but Cuneo didn't pick up any sense that they resented his visit. They invited him in, offered him a drink, which he declined, and then Maxine explained to Joseph again about what she'd told Cuneo the night before. As she talked, the three of them drifted back over to the space by the front window.

"I'm here about the same thing again, I'm afraid." Cuneo took out the picture and handed it across to her. "We want to be sure that Missy D'Amiens was who you saw. I wondered if you'd mind looking at this?"

Maxine put her drink on a side table, then took the newspaper cutout. Looking out the window for a second—revisiting the moment—she came back to the picture and nodded her head one time briskly. "Yep," she said, "that's her all right."

Joseph, maybe forty-five years old, was physically much smaller than his wife. Short and very thin, he probably didn't weigh 150 pounds. His shoulders barely seemed sufficient to hold up his head. What hair he had, and it wasn't much, he wore in a buzz. He was wearing rimless eyeglasses, a red bow tie over a starched white shirt, red paisley-print suspenders and brown tweed pants. But in a quiet way he managed to project a sense of confidence and inner strength.

He placed his drink carefully next to his wife's, then peered at the picture over Maxine's arm and shook his head, speaking with absolute certainty. "That's Missy D'Amiens, certainly, but I can't swear she was the woman we saw the other night."

Maxine frowned deeply, looking over and down at him. "What are you saying, Joseph? That sure was who she was."

Joseph put a hand lightly on her arm. "Could I please see the picture myself?" He was the soul of mildness, holding out his other hand. When she gave it to him, he crossed over to the window and stood where the light was better, studying it for the better part of a minute. Finally, he raised his eyes, looked directly at Cuneo and shook his head. "I'm not sure."

Cuneo emitted a long, low, single-note deep in his throat. Maxine crossed over to Joseph and pulled the picture from his hand, holding it up close to her face. While she was looking, Cuneo asked Joseph, "Where was her car, again, exactly?"

Pointing out the window, he indicated the same place that Maxine had shown Cuneo the night before. "Just across the street over there, five or six cars down, by the light post."

"And what kind of car was it? Do you remember?"

"I'm not sure. Dark, certainly. Black."

"It was a black Mercedes," Maxine said, "C-type."

Joseph turned to her, placed his hand on her arm again and said, "It might have been that, after all. I didn't pay too much attention."

"You weren't looking at the car, were you?"

He gave his wife a tolerant smile. "Perhaps that, too." Back to Cuneo. "In any event, she went to the car and we all went back to our drinks. Speaking of which . . ." He picked up both drinks and gave his wife hers.

"Did you see her do anything at the car?" Cuneo asked.

Joseph silently consulted with his wife, then shook his head. "No. She just went to the door."

"Not the trunk?"

"Not that I saw. Maxine?"

"No. She just got in and drove off."

Cuneo's low hum had developed a melody, but the song remained unidentifiable. "Let's get back for a minute, if you don't mind, to whether or not it was Missy D'Amiens. Mrs. Willis, you say it was?"

"I thought it was."

"But do you remember last night, when we talked, you said you thought you might have been mistaken? Do you remember that?"

She didn't like the question and straightened up to her full height. "That was when I heard that she'd died in the house."

"Right. So you reasoned that she must not have left. So maybe it was someone else out on the street here."

"Or she left and came back later."

"Sure, which is what she must have done, if she was in the house when it burned. But your husband now says he's not sure it was her at all."

The husband spoke up. "It might have been. But there was something . . ." He moved back a couple of steps, so he was standing in the jutting alcove of the front bay window. "I saw her as she came out of Hanover's place and I remember first thinking, 'Oh, there's Missy.' But then, something about her walk . . ."

"Her *shake*, more like," Maxine said.

He shrugged. "I don't know what it was exactly, but something made me form the impression that it wasn't Missy."

"You knew her, then? Missy?" Cuneo asked.

"We'd spoken on the street a few times. We're neighbors, after all. I can't say we had a real relationship of any kind. But I knew who she was."

"Okay. So you're standing here and she comes out of Hanover's . . ."

Joseph sipped at his cocktail, broke a small smile. "I must have kept looking a bit too long out of the corner of my eye."

"Only the corner, Joseph?"

"Well." He touched her arm gently and continued. "In any event, my dear bride must have seen me looking at something, because she turned to see what it was."

"But," Cuneo wanted it crystal clear, "by this time the woman from Hanover's had come down as far as this window. Isn't that when you told me you first saw her, Maxine?"

A nod. "She was right there."

"Okay. Do either of you remember what she was wearing?"

"Blue," Joseph said.

"Black." Maxine turned on her husband. "A jacket. Leather. Now, *come on*, Joseph. I *know* what I saw, and I saw that."

Joseph explained the apparent contradiction. "From the side you saw only the jacket. When she first came out, the jacket was open, and she was wearing a bright blue blouse, shiny. It caught the sun."

"Skirt or pants?"

They looked at each other. "Pants." They agreed.

"So pants, a blue shirt, a leather jacket. Driving a black Mercedes."

"That sounds about right," Joseph said.

It sounded about right to Cuneo, too. But he wasn't thinking it sounded like Missy D'Amiens.

9

Glitsky in shirtsleeves came out of Dismas Hardy's back door and stopped on the top step that led down to the backyard. He had just left Treya and Frannie and his baby in the kitchen. He looked up at cerulean blue. The sun hadn't yet set behind him, and the shade the house threw carried all the way across Hardy's deep, narrow back lawn and halfway up the fence, to about the height where Frannie had trimmed the riot of blooming roses—white, red, yellow, purple, flame.

Hardy's home stood on the top of a small rise, and from his vantage Glitsky could look over the sun-splashed roofs of the Richmond District all the way to downtown four miles east. The top of the Transamerica Pyramid peeked somewhat ludicrously above the rust-red dome of the synagogue on Arguello. Slightly to his right, he could just make out the shining whiteness of St. Ignatius Church on the USF campus. Here and there, a window would reflect the sinking sun's light and cast it back, little diamonds sprinkled across the panorama. There was no sign of fog, only the barest of breezes, and the evening was completely without chill.

Just up against the house below him, Hardy the purist was arranging charcoal over newspaper in a chimney-flue-lighting device. Glitsky watched him counting out some no-doubt mystical exact number of briquettes. When Hardy held a match to the paper underneath, the smoke started to rise up toward where Glitsky sat.

"You're safe," Hardy said. "Smoke follows beauty."

With a grunt, Glitsky took that as his cue to move. "You know," he said, coming down the stairs, "you can buy a propane barbecue for about a hundred bucks. Turn on the gas, press a button, you get heat. It got invented a few years ago, you might not have heard."

Hardy drank from his beer bottle. "The starters always break. They don't work."

"And that chimney thing does?"

"You wait."

"That's my point. What if I don't want to wait? Or get smoked out?"

"Then you don't elect to barbecue, which, my friend, presupposes a lack of hurry and, you might have noticed, some likelihood of smoke. When things cook, especially over a fire, they often smoke. You could look it up. Besides, I don't like the idea of a bomb in my backyard."

"A bomb?"

"Those propane tanks. One of 'em blows up, it can level a building."

"And this happens a lot in your experience?"

Hardy sipped his beer and shrugged. "Only takes once."

"I'm not going to change your mind, am I? On propane or anything else."

"But you so enjoy trying. And I think you did once on something. Change my mind, I mean. I know it wasn't getting me to try Spam. I would never do that."

"I know I got you to wear better shoes when we walked the beat."

"See? There you go. Even if that was twenty years ago."

"It was thirty years ago."

"Thirty?" Hardy said. "Don't say thirty. It *couldn't* have been thirty. That would mean I'm old now."

"You are *way* old." Glitsky walked over to the grill, put his hand flat over the chimney starter. "And this isn't hot yet."

"You're not supposed to monitor it by the second. It gets hot eventually."

"So does pavement on a sunny day, but people generally don't try to cook on it. Here's another one."

"Another what?"

"Time I got you to change your mind. I got you to apply back to the DA's office after God knows how many years of wandering in the desert."

"Only about a decade. And it wasn't the desert. It was the Shamrock." This was the bar that Hardy owned a quarter of. "Jews like yourself wander in the desert. Good Irish stock like me achieve spiritual peace in a wetter environment. Guinness comes to mind, the occasional black and tan, if you recall."

"I probably remember better than you do. But the fact remains. The reason you're back practicing law and getting rich is because I changed your mind lo these many years ago."

Hardy raised his beer bottle. "For which I salute you."

Glitsky pulled a chair around to sit at the patio table. Hardy tinkered with the chimney thing, lifting it up, blowing into the bottom of it, putting it back on its grill. Now he, too, sat down. "Thank God for a warm night," he said.

Glitsky didn't respond right away. When he did, he said, "Do you ever wish you could just stop?"

"Stop what?"

"Everything. Change, new and exciting experiences, whatever comes next."

"Then you're dead," Hardy said.

Glitsky shook his head. "I'm not talking forever."

"But if you're stopped, there's no time, so it is forever."

"Let's pretend it isn't, okay? But you know those books I love, Patrick O'Brian? *Master and Commander,* the movie. Those books."

"What about them?"

"They make a toast all the time in them. 'May nothing new happen.' That's how I'm feeling. That it would be nice to just stop for a while. When things are good."

Hardy threw his friend a sideways glance over the table. This wasn't a typical Glitsky conversation. "They *are* good," he said. "Knock on wood, may they stay that way." He rapped his knuckles on the table, lowered his voice. "You thinking about Cuneo?"

Glitsky was tracing the grain in the patio table's surface. "A little."

"A little bit, but all the time?"

Glitsky nodded. "Pretty much."

"Me, too."

"Waiting for the other shoe to drop."

"That, too, but maybe it won't." Hardy looked over at his friend. "You all right?"

"Right now, this minute, yeah. But things are going to change because they always do."

"With Cuneo, you mean?"

"Him, yeah, but other stuff, too." He indicated the house. "The pregnancy . . ."

"I thought everything was good with that."

"It is." Glitsky let out a heavy breath. "I keep telling myself," he said, "that you can acknowledge a happy moment once in a while and it doesn't necessarily curse you for eternity."

"When things are good, the only way they can go from there is bad?"

"Maybe."

"The other option is maybe they could get better."

"Not too often."

"Well, of course your ever-cheerful self would say that. But it could happen. Sometimes it does." He twirled his beer bottle on the table. "I wasn't particularly gung-ho when Frannie and I were deciding whether we were going to try to get pregnant with Vincent. I figured we'd already hit the jackpot with the Beck, we got a healthy little girl, we win. We should count our blessings and just stop there. But then we got Vinnie, and he's been icing on the cake."

"Maybe it's that," Glitsky said. "The second kid thing. Maybe it won't be all right. The baby."

"Why wouldn't it be? Rachel's fine. Your other kids have been fine. You and Treya have good genes. What's the problem?"

"Nothing, except that, as you say, my kids have always been fine."

"So you're pushing your luck?"

A nod. "There's that element."

"And a miserable guy like you doesn't deserve a happy life?"

"Some of that, too."

"Why not?"

"I don't know. Guilt, I suppose."

"Over what?"

Glitsky paused. "Maybe what we did."

Hardy took a beat, then whispered. "We had no choice. We never had a choice. They would have killed us."

"I know."

"That's the truth, Abe."

"I know," he repeated. "I know."

"So? What's to be guilty about?"

"Nothing. You're right. Maybe it's just general guilt. Original sin. Maybe we don't get to be happy. I mean, the human condition isn't one of happiness."

"Except when it is."

"Which is why," Glitsky said, "right now, tonight, everything could just stay the way it is and it would be fine with me."

"You realize you're dangerously close to admitting that you're happy right now?"

"Marginally, I suppose I am. Comparatively."

"Whoa, rein it in, Abe," Hardy said. "All that enthusiasm might give you a hernia."

"What I can't believe," Glitsky was saying to his dinner mates at the table an hour later, "is that Hanover was such a player and so few people knew."

"Probably what made him good at it," Hardy said. "I mean, who follows the ins and outs of the city's contract for its towing business, fascinating though I'm sure it must be?"

Frannie put down her fork. "You don't really think somebody might have killed him over that, do you?"

"The city's towing business," Abe said, "is worth fifty million dollars. Ten mil a year for five years. I might kill Diz here for half that."

Hardy nodded, acknowledging the compliment. "But then who's the suspect?" he asked.

The men were at the opposite ends of the table, the women on the sides. They'd finished their halibut steaks and green beans, and nobody seemed inclined to start cleaning up. At the mention of the concept of a possible murder suspect, Glitsky couldn't help himself—he came forward with a real show of excitement. "That's where it gets interesting. Tow/Hold's had the contract now for twenty years. Anybody want to guess how many complaints it's gotten in the past two years alone? And I'm not talking complaints like people upset that they got towed. I'm talking criminal complaints. Stealing money and CDs and radios and stuff out of the vehicles, selling parts, losing the car itself. How many?"

"How many cars does it tow?" Hardy asked.

"About eighty thousand a year."

This made Frannie come alive. "No. That can't be right. In the city alone?"

Glitsky nodded. "That's per year. It's a big number."

"Wait a minute," Hardy said. He drummed the table, eyes closed, for a minute. "That's fifteen hundred or so a week. I guess it's doable. Two hundred a day."

"A little more." Glitsky loved the details. "Okay, so back to how many criminal complaints has the city received?"

"One a day?" Treya said.

"More."

"A hundred and six?" Frannie asked.

"If you're going to be silly." Glitsky spread his palms. "Try three and a half average. Every single day."

"And these are the people," Hardy said, "that the city in its wisdom has awarded its towing contract to for how long?"

"A mere twenty years," Glitsky said. "At, remember, ten mil a year."

"Not including what they steal, I presume," Treya said.

"Right. Not including that."

Treya stiffened her back, turned to her husband. "Does Clarence know those figures?"

Glitsky shook his head. "The DA generally doesn't get involved. Maybe with some individual complaints, but not the whole picture."

"Why not?" Frannie asked. "I mean, somebody official must know about this stuff. You found it out in one day, Abe."

"That's only because I happened to be looking for anything on Hanover, and he turned up in this article."

"Which said what?" Hardy asked.

"Well, ironically enough, it wasn't even about him, not mostly. It was about Tow/Hold. The *Chronicle* did an investigation last year, although the story was kind of buried in the back of the Metro section. The way they wrote it, it came out like Tow/Hold had hired a few bad eggs, that was all. They were all fired long ago. It wasn't anything systemic in the way they did business. It certainly wasn't the leadership of the company."

"No," Treya said with heavy irony, "it couldn't have been that."

"So what happened?" Frannie asked. "I mean, where is Hanover involved?"

Glitsky paused and sipped some water, relishing the moment. "It seems that Tow/Hold has ties to our recently departed ex-mayor, Mr. Washington."

"Why did I see this coming?" Hardy asked.

"Because you're an astute judge of how this city works. It turns out that Washington started to feel some heat around these complaints. So when the last contract expired, he didn't automatically extend it as he had the last time it had come due."

"Without putting it up for bid?" Hardy asked.

"Right. It's sole source. We do lots of them here. Tow/Hold hasn't bid on the job for fifteen years, through four administrations."

"Imagine that," Frannie said. "They must have just been doing a terrific job."

"Only modestly terrific, as we've seen," Glitsky said. "But not so terrific that Washington didn't put them on notice."

"So what did he do?" Treya asked.

"Went month-to-month, which really straightened 'em out, as evidenced by the complaints. Those numbers we were talking about? They were *after* they cleaned up their act."

Hardy put his wineglass down. "So why didn't Washington just fire them?"

Glitsky actually smiled. "Ahh. Now we're getting to it. He didn't fire them because his campaign manager—we all know Nils Granat, do we not?—well, Mr. Granat's day job is he's a lobbyist, and Tow/Hold just happened to be one of his biggest clients."

"How big?" Treya asked.

"A quarter million a year retainer. Ever since they went month-to-month."

Hardy whistled. "I need more clients like that."

"So Granat," Treya said, "basically made excuses for Tow/Hold to the mayor."

Glitsky nodded. "That would be the kindest interpretation. The cynical among us think Granat just funneled some of his fees through to Washington somehow. There are rumors of actual briefcases of cash."

"You're shocking me," Hardy said. "Graft out of city hall?"

But Frannie said to Glitsky, "Did I miss where Hanover came in?"

Glitsky reached out and touched her hand gently. "Your patience shall be rewarded, my dear. Here he comes. Hanover's day job, it turns out, was pretty much like Granat's, though maybe on a bigger scale nationally. He wasn't Kathy West's campaign manager, but between money and contacts, he helped her campaign in a big way."

"He represents another tow company," Hardy said.

"Excellent, Diz!" Glitsky sat back and spread his arms out. "Ladies and gentlemen, may I present Bayshore Autotow, which until last Wednesday was a client of Paul Hanover's."

A small silence ensued, which Frannie broke by asking, "And you really think this had something to do with his murder?"

Glitsky shook his head. "I don't know if I actually *think* it yet, but it's definitely the kind of connection I'd more or less expected and hoped to find."

"So now that Hanover's gone," Hardy asked, "what happens with Bayshore?"

"That's the question," Glitsky said. "Parking and Traffic"—the city's department that controlled the towing contract—"has already recommended them to replace Tow/Hold, but first it's got to be approved—the meeting's in ten days—by something called the Municipal Transportation Agency, which has seven members, four of whom are reportedly in the pocket of guess who?" Glitsky turned to his wife in expectation.

She didn't let him down. "Kathy West."

Frannie said, "So Kathy controls the appointment of the contract."

Glitsky nodded all around. "And it goes to Bayshore. Except of course if the murder of Bayshore's lobbyist makes her decide to rethink her priorities."

"It would explain her personal interest," Hardy said, "and going outside of channels, wouldn't it?"

"That thought," Glitsky said, "did occur to me."

10

Paul Hanover's first wife, Theresa, was a dominating and still very handsome woman of seventy-four years. Good cheekbones and a face-lift kept the lines from her face, and her confident carriage and stylish clothes made her appear more like a sister than the mother of her three adult children in the room. She had taken pride of place in the large and comfortable reading chair with ottoman by the picture window as she looked around her family, gathered in her son's now-crowded living room.

Will, finally back from his fishing trip, sat noticeably apart from Catherine over by the fireplace, while his wife kept flitting in and out of the kitchen as she did (to avoid mother-in-law interaction, Theresa always felt), supplying drinks, coffee and dessert. Carlos and Mary Rodman sat together holding hands on the couch. Beth and Aaron Jacobs took the folding chairs that Catherine had set up next to one another just to Theresa's right, and she could hear them discussing their eldest daughter Sophie's schoolwork, as usual.

Theresa thought they should have called this family meeting at her daughter Mary's home, which was much larger. At least there they could have all eaten at the same table instead of catch-as-catch-can wherever there was a flat surface—kitchen counter, breakfast nook, dining room table—anywhere big enough to accommodate a chair and a dinner plate. Theresa almost wound up in the living room with a TV tray, and would have if Beth hadn't noticed and given up her own place in the dining room.

Still, the catered (though self-serve) dinner in the small-ish house had been agreeable enough, considering that

Catherine had organized it. It was better than most of her other efforts with the family. Now the older kids had vanished on their Friday night out while the younger ones had been banished upstairs with a video.

Catherine brought out a piece of cherry pie and gave it to Carlos, then sat in the chair she'd pulled around to the kitchen entrance, apart from all of them, as always. Gradually, the hum of conversation died away, and Theresa cleared her throat, a signal that she was going to take the floor. "I didn't think it would be like this," she said. "I never wanted anything like this to happen."

Next to her, Beth reached out and took her hand. "We know you didn't, Mom. Nobody thinks anything like that."

"Still, I think it's important that I say it. It's no secret I had some bitter words with your father about . . ." She exhaled heavily. "About his responsibilities to all of his grandchildren. You all know how he felt."

Will had come forward in his chair, elbows on his knees. "He didn't think he owed them anything, Mom. Or us, either. He'd made it on his own and we should all do the same. That's just who he was and how he thought."

"Okay," Mary Rodman said. The youngest of Paul and Theresa's three children, she had been crying off and on since she'd learned of her father's death. Her eyes were red and swollen. "But giving it all to *her* . . ."

"We don't know for sure that he was going to do that," Will said.

"Yes we do," Catherine snapped at him. "He told me explicitly when I went there . . ."

"Hold it, hold it, hold it." Aaron, an attorney in jacket and tie, put his hands out in front of him. "That whole question is moot now. She's dead. The question is what he did with his will. Catherine. When you talked to him Wednesday, did he tell you he'd already changed it?"

"No. But he'd made the decision. He was coy about whether he'd already done it."

Theresa asked. "But he didn't say he hadn't done it, either, did he?"

"He said he had scheduled a meeting with his partner—what's his name . . ."

"Bob Townshend," her husband said.

"Right. Bob. They had an appointment for next week, to talk over some of the issues, he said. He just kept saying that the main thing was that he was going to marry her. He loved her. She loved him."

A chorus of muttered negative reaction stopped her. When it died down, she went on. "Whether or not we believed any of it, of what they had together, he told me we weren't going to talk him out of it, or into some kind of prenup, either. And when he married her, she would become his heir. She'd had a very hard life, and he was going to make it up to her. We buzzards could stop circling. That's really all he said."

This brought more tears to Mary's eyes. "Did he really say that?" She looked around at her family. "But he was our *dad*, you guys. It wasn't all about his money."

Theresa wasn't having that. "Your children, my grandchildren, deserve that money more than Missy did, Mary, even if you didn't care about it." She threw her imperious gaze around the room, daring anyone to contradict her. "All of your children, my grandchildren," she repeated, "absolutely deserve the benefit of his wealth—for college, or medical care if any of them get really sick. Or housing. If they need a down payment on their first home, who's going to be able to help them?"

Into the small silence, Beth said, "So we still don't know?"

"Not until we see the will, we don't," Will said.

"In the meantime," Theresa said, "I think for my grandchildren's sake that it's critical, absolutely critical, that we consider possible scenarios and come to unanimous agreement about our response to each of them."

"Well," Aaron the lawyer spoke up. "It's pretty straightforward, Theresa, really. If Paul didn't change his will yet in favor of Missy, then the last we heard the estate goes in equal thirds to the three kids. Anybody have an estimate of what ballpark we're talking about?"

Catherine Hanover spoke up. "Fourteen million dollars."

Beth snorted. "Is that before or after the renovation?"

"That's as of Wednesday, so after."

Carlos sat forward on the couch, looked across to Catherine. "It sounds like you two had a pretty substantive talk."

Catherine gave him a flat look. "I was motivated," she said, then turned quickly to her other brother-in-law. "You were outlining options, Aaron. First was thirds to the three kids, if nothing had changed. But what if he'd already rewritten it in favor of Missy?"

"Well, then we don't know for sure until we see it, but I'd say the most likely scenario is that he'd just move her up in front of the kids. His kids, not the grandkids. In which case the secondary beneficiaries would be Will, Beth and Mary anyway, and everything would go back to being the same as it was before he met Missy. That's assuming they died at the same time, Paul and Missy."

"But what if he died first?" Mary asked.

Aaron shook his head. "That won't be an issue, even if the coroner concludes that one of them killed the other, which I gather they've ruled out."

But Mary wasn't convinced. "How can you know it won't be a problem, Aaron? What if, just hypothetically, she lived after he did, even for a minute, then wouldn't her heirs inherit?"

"No, because Paul never would have left his will vague on that point. Any good estate lawyer—and fourteen mil buys good help, trust me—covers it. Usually it's ninety days."

"What is?" his wife asked.

Aaron sighed. "The amount of time a beneficiary—Missy—needs to survive after Paul before her heirs get the inheritance."

"Who are they anyway?" Will asked. "Her heirs?"

Everybody looked at each other, and then Aaron said, "I don't think anybody knows, but I promise it won't be an issue."

"If there's a ruling that she died after him," Theresa put in, "we'll find out who they are soon enough, believe me. Cousins and uncles and siblings she didn't even know she had."

"Well, maybe," Aaron said. "But the greater possible concern for us, I think, and what we should be prepared to litigate if necessary, is if he changed the will in favor of Missy . . ."

Theresa turned on him angrily. "*Must* you keep using her nickname, Aaron?"

He shrugged. "It's nothing personal, Theresa. It makes it clearer for everyone. But if he changed the will in her favor, then it's likely he changed the rest of it, too, maybe in favor of some charity, or to the kids, and I mean *our* kids. Your grandkids, Theresa. That's what we ought to be prepared for."

"That would be fine with me," Theresa said. "That's who I'm in this for."

"We're all in it for them, too, Mom," Will said with some asperity.

"Well, he didn't mention any of those other possibilities to me, Aaron." Catherine sat rigidly in her chair. "He told me it was going to Missy. That's what he wanted. It really wasn't any of the family's business."

"That's so ridiculous and just so like him," Theresa said.

"Easy, Mom, okay?" Will said.

"Well," she shot back, "you tell me. How could it be any more the family's business? We were certainly all well enough aware that it was before . . . well, before this week."

"Okay," Will said, "but it's still Dad."

"I'm sure it was mostly her," Beth said, "not him. She had him so fooled. I can't believe he intended to cut us out completely."

"You can believe anything you want, Beth," Catherine said, "but the fact of the matter is that once the marriage happened, the whole financial picture was going to be different. And we all know what that was going to mean in practice, even if they hadn't died."

"But they didn't just die," Mary said. "Somebody killed them."

"Well," Theresa said, "of course I'm sorry about your father, but all I can say about Missy is good riddance."

"Mom!" Mary exploded. "God!"

"What?" Theresa said. "If you're honest, I know you're all saying the same thing inside yourselves. Thank heaven that woman is out of the picture." The matriarch threw her gaze around the room, daring anyone to disagree with her. "I've heard all of us say one time or another that we wished she would either go away or just die."

Catherine spoke up. "If we did, of course we were joking, Theresa. What do you think?"

"No. Obviously. I was just making the point that we knew what a danger that woman was to all of us."

"Well, she's not now," Aaron said.

And at that truth, the family went silent.

Will was forty-five years old, with an athletic frame and a conventionally handsome face that had not yet gone to slack or jowl. Still wearing his Dockers and short-sleeved Tommy Bahama shirt, he was sitting on the bed as his wife came into the room carrying a load of folded laundry. "Hey," he said.

"Hey," she answered with an uninflected, mechanical precision.

"How are you doing?"

"I'm doing fine, Will. How are you doing?"

"Good."

She stood still for a moment, looking at him. Then she exhaled and went over to the dresser, put the pile of laundry on the chair next to it, and opened the top drawer. She wasn't facing him. "So," she said, "no fish?"

"None. No keepers anyway. Isn't that weird? We're out two hundred miles, feels like halfway to the Galápagos, and there are no fish. I've never been completely skunked before on one of these trips."

"How many of you were there?"

"On the boat? Just three of us, plus the captain and crew."

"Nice guys?"

"Okay, I guess," he said. "The usual. Good 'ol boys. Tim and Tom."

"Easy to remember."

"What does that mean?"

"Nothing. Never mind." She closed the top drawer, opened the next one down. "I wish you'd have called, though. Not being able to reach you was terrifically frustrating."

"I'm sorry about that. Next time I'll remember." He pushed himself back against the headboard. "What was that motivation you talked about tonight?"

"When?"

"When Aaron asked why you'd gone to see Dad that day."

She stopped moving, let out a long breath, still facing away from him. Slowly she turned full around, holding one of his folded T-shirts. Finally, she shook her head slightly from side to side. "I guess I just got tired of not knowing where we were going to stand. Saul starts college in a little over a year, and he's the first of the grandkids. I'd talked to Beth and Mary and both had asked if I'd heard anything from your dad, what with Sophie and Pablo right behind Saul. So I just thought I'd go get it from the horse's mouth." She was wringing the T-shirt between her hands. "Then, as you heard, we got on to other things."

"Missy."

"Among others."

"Did you have words?"

"Some. Nothing worse than usual. We just talked, maybe argued a little. But it was all his decision, and there was really nothing to fight about. Besides, your father, as opposed to your mother, likes me. Or should I say liked."

Will shrugged. "He liked attractive women. So does his son." He patted the bed next to him. "Speaking of which, you're looking good tonight, especially to a man who's just spent five days at sea. Are you planning on coming to bed?"

"Eventually," she said. "I usually do."

"I've missed you," he said.

Biting her lip, nodding to herself, she turned back to the dresser, dropped the crumpled T-shirt into the open drawer. Clearing her throat, she said, "Let me go check on the kids," then left the room.

The assistant district attorney who handled arson cases was Chris Rosen. He'd been a prosecutor for nine years now, after first serving a year fresh out of law school as a clerk for Superior Court Judge Leo Chomorro. So he'd lived his entire legal life in the Hall of Justice at Seventh and Bryant. Rosen thrived in the environment.

An old-fashioned, hard-on-crime professional prosecutor, he didn't believe that he'd ever seen an innocent person in custody. "You don't get all the way to arrested—and believe me, that is a long, long way—unless you did it," he liked to say. "That's the truth, it always has been and always will be nothing but the truth, so help me God."

Unmarried and slightly unkempt, with an easygoing personal style, he often grew a day or two's stubble when he wasn't due in court. His dark hair licked at the top of his collar. The conscious image he projected was borderline blue collar, a guy with no special passion for prosecuting his fellow citizens. He was just a regular working dog going about his business, doing his job. Nobody to worry about. Attorneys who hadn't already faced him in court found out the truth soon enough, and often found themselves on the defensive from the get-go, blindsided by his cold passion.

"No law says you can't come across out of court as sympathetic, you know, a little . . . sensitive," he was saying over midnight drinks to Dan Cuneo as they sat at the bar at Lou the Greek's. "Then you get 'em in court, suddenly I'm the iceman and whop 'em upside the head. They don't know what hit 'em."

Rosen's experience had taught him that he needed every advantage he could get in San Francisco, where juries tended to see their main role as finding some reason, almost *any* reason—stress, hardship, bad luck, unfortunate upbringing—to let defendants off. There always lurked some mitigating factor, some reason for juries to forgive.

"Hey, but enough about me." Rosen sipped at his single malt. It wasn't anywhere near his working hours on a Friday night. He was out here now with his Oban on the rocks as a favor to his main-man arson inspector Arnie Becker, and also because the recent double-homicide fire was going to be the biggest case he'd tried to date. "Becker says you got a lead on Hanover."

Cuneo, on duty, drank Cherry Coke, no ice. "You know the basics?"

"Not much beyond Hanover and his girlfriend."

"All right." Cuneo tapped his fingers on the bar. "There was this couple, Maxine and Joseph Willis . . ." Drinking more Cherry Coke, fidgeting in his chair, continuing his percussion on the bar top, Cuneo laid out for Rosen the originally conflicting stories of the Willises—how Maxine had seen Missy D'Amiens leave the Hanover house within minutes of when the fire must have started, how Joseph had been uncertain—it might have been somebody else. Then there was Jeffie at the Valero station who *volunteered* that someone who looked something like her, but had different hair, had bought gasoline in a container and put it into her trunk.

"I'm still listening," Rosen said. "So you've got a woman who resembled this Missy."

"Well, wait. More than that. I've got a true fox, middle-aged . . ."

"Which one?" Rosen asked. "A fox or middle-aged?"

"Both." At Rosen's skeptical look, Cuneo said, "It happens. You'd seen her, you'd believe it. Anyway, she's in jeans and a shiny blue shirt, black leather jacket, driving a Mercedes, buying a container of gasoline and then coming out of Hanover's house a few minutes before it goes up."

"If it's all the same woman."

"Right. Of course. It was."

"Which means?"

"Which means, what if she had a motive?" Cuneo waited, but Rosen didn't bite. "Which she did."

"So you're telling me you've got a suspect."

"Not quite yet. I'm close. Light on physical evidence, but loaded with probable cause."

"You want a warrant," Rosen said.

"Yep, yep, yep." Cuneo bobbed his head, tattooed the bar with a final paradiddle. "Becker says you're tight with some judges."

Rosen shrugged. "The question is, can we make the case. I don't want to bring anybody in front of a grand jury and have nothing to talk about." He cast his eyes around. "I need a narrative. If I buy it, I can sell it to whoever's signing warrants."

Cuneo willed himself still, met Rosen's eye. "Grand jury's Tuesday, right?"

"Every week. You're thinking that soon?"

"I can do the search tomorrow if we can get a warrant now. We'll know by Sunday. Is that enough time for you?"

Rosen swirled the last of his Scotch and drank it off. "Plenty," he said.

11

Glitsky used police magic to find the address he wanted. Now, just before ten o'clock on Saturday morning, he was walking up Russian Hill in bright sunshine to the door of an enormous three-story brown box of a building on the corner of Green and Larkin. He stood in the covered entryway for a minute, trying to imagine what a place this big, in this neighborhood, would cost. Decided it didn't bear reflection. From his perspective, it was all the money in the world.

He rang the doorbell and listened as chimes sounded behind the double doors—etched glass in carved dark wood. After a long, silent moment, a short female figure appeared behind the glass and opened the door. In a black uniform with a white apron, she smiled formally and, seeing that Glitsky was a man of color in casual clothes said, "Deliveries are in the back."

Producing his wallet, Glitsky displayed his badge. "I'm Deputy Chief of Inspectors Abe Glitsky. I wonder if I might have a word with Mr. Granat."

"Do you have an appointment?"

"No, ma'am. I was hoping to catch him in."

"Is this, then, official police business?"

"I'd just like to talk to him, if he can spare a minute."

"Certainly," she said. "I'll see if he's available." She turned, had a thought and turned again. "Would you care to wait inside?"

Glitsky crossed the threshold into the house and watched the maid walk down the long hallway and then somewhere off to her left. She'd left him standing on a burgundy Oriental carpet that was larger than Glitsky's living room, yet still did not quite reach the walls around the grand foyer. Even with the sunshine outside and the windows behind him, even with the six-foot chandelier and its fifty bulbs lit above him, the space was dim. No sound came from the rest of the house, and only gradually did Glitsky become aware of the ticking of a clock, although he couldn't locate its source. His eyes went to the art—dark oils in large burnished gilt frames—hung in the spaces between doorways. They were frankly—he thought purposefully—disturbing, all blacks and reds, flesh and blooded browns. Erotic overtones, sexually ambiguous— hints of nakedness amid industrial waste, a pack of dogs gathered over something not quite identifiable in a graffitied doorway.

"You like my paintings?"

Surprised—where had the man come from?—Glitsky whirled and found out. A door on the left wall stood open, blessedly light and even inviting. "I can't really say they speak to me."

"Yes, I do suppose it's an acquired taste. The tension of whether something terrible has just happened, or whether it's about to."

Glitsky shook his head. "I get enough of that in my job."

"Yes, of course. I suppose you do." He extended his hand, revealing a mouthful of perfect teeth under a crisp gray mustache. He was about Glitsky's size, a bit thinner. His hair was thick, silver. Even here in his home on the weekend, he was well turned out—black merino sweater, tan slacks, expensive-looking loafers. A handsome, confident man. "Nils Granat," he said, gripping Glitsky's hand hard, meeting his eyes. "We've met before, haven't we?"

"Yes, sir, a couple of times at City Hall. I wasn't sure you'd remember."

Granat turned his mouth up slightly, touched his forehead. "I remember people. It's almost what I do best. So what can I do for you, Chief? Is 'Chief' all right?"

"Fine."

"You want to sit in the library?" He jerked a finger behind him. "Right here." Without waiting for Glitsky to respond, he was already through the door and into the large, airy, pleasant adjoining room. "That foyer is a little gloomy, isn't it?" he said over his shoulder. "I should probably leave the side doors open, brighten it up. But then, I wasn't expecting anybody, especially this early on a weekend morning." He turned, confident that Glitsky would be there, and when he was, motioned him to the red leather couch. Granat himself pulled an Empire chair around and sat on it, crossing one leg over the other. "So how can I help you?" he asked. If he had any sense that this no-warning, early-morning visit by a high-ranking policeman meant that he was in trouble, he showed no sign of it.

Glitsky came forward to the front edge of the couch, and came right to the point. "I'm investigating the murder of Paul Hanover."

"God. Wasn't that a tragedy!"

"Yes, sir. But it was more than that. Somebody killed him."

Granat nodded. "That's what they're saying."

"You don't believe it?"

"Oh no, not that. Of course I believe it. I mean, he was shot, wasn't he, before the fire? I just meant I hadn't heard that anyone had determined he'd been the primary target."

"You mean the woman?"

"Yes. Didn't she have some . . . well, maybe I shouldn't say."

"No. Say anything you want. At this point, I'm interested in anything you might know."

"Well, I can't say that I know anything. It's just that . . . Missy, wasn't it? You know that she just sort of *appeared* one day, and after that she was with Paul—a fait accompli, if you will. Not that she wasn't beautiful, but she didn't seem to be quite . . . one of us in some way. I may not be saying anything very coherent."

"So you think somebody in her past might have . . ."

Granat shook his head. "I can't say I've gotten so far as to actually *think* anything. Maybe it was just that she was foreign. French, I think. In any event, when I heard about the killings, I wondered about her background first, her enemies, not Paul's. I mean, Paul was extremely well liked, very respected by everyone. And not just here, but in Washington, everywhere. He put people together, did immense good work on many, many fronts. I knew him pretty well, as you may know, and I can't imagine anyone wanting to hurt him, much less kill him. It just doesn't make any sense."

"So your initial feeling was that it had something to do with Missy?"

"More than with Paul. Yes."

Glitsky sat back. "That's interesting."

"Do you know anything about her? Not that it's any of my business."

"Not too much," Glitsky admitted.

"Well." Granat lifted his hands palms up. "But you came to see me? About Paul? It must be about the towing, then?"

Glitsky halfway apologized. "It was someplace to start."

"Sure, I understand. It would be." Granat sat back, his arm outstretched along the row of books behind him. "Well, I'd be the first to admit that for the most part, the towing industry is a bit of a tough crowd, although that's still a long way from saying that violence is a common negotiating tool."

"But not necessarily unheard of."

Granat shook his head. "As a matter of fact, I'm not aware of any time recently that Tow/Hold has resorted to anything like strong-arm tactics. It's one of the reasons they retain me. To get things done a different way."

"But now with Mayor Washington gone . . ."

The lobbyist smiled. "We still have a mayor, and the city still needs an experienced company to handle its towing. And in spite of what you might have heard, no final decision has been reached."

"No, I realize that. In fact, it's kind of my point. Now, with Hanover out of the picture, it leaves Bayshore rudderless. . . ."

Granat's dry chortle cut him off. "I wouldn't say 'rudderless.' These people are not rudderless. They're a very sophisticated bunch of venture capitalists who are trying to buy their way into a business they believe to be profitable but don't completely understand."

"As Tow/Hold does."

Another nod. "I believe the mayor might come to see it that way, yes."

"Or one of the members of the Municipal Transportation Agency?"

"Or one of them, that's true. Three, I believe, are already inclined to retain Tow/Hold."

"I've heard that, too."

"So from my perspective the decision is still very much a matter of the merits. Three of the MTA people obviously think that we—Tow/Hold—should stay on because we're doing a pretty good job, in spite of some of the problems we've had." Granat leaned forward in his chair. "You've got to understand, Chief, that whoever gets the contract, they're going to have the same problems. Fact is, they're going to have to hire the very same folks that we use to run the lots and patrol the streets. That's the reality. And they're not going to pay those people any more than we do—they can't and make a profit. So they've got the same labor pool doing the same work for the same price. The only change is the employer's name and a few guys at the top of the food chain. At least Tow/Hold has identified a lot of the bad eggs and knows to keep them off the payroll. Under Bayshore, it'll be the same thing we've got now, only worse because of the learning curve on top of everything else. I'll be telling that to the folks at MTA next week, and I wouldn't be at all surprised if I convince at least one of them with the simple logic of it."

"Especially now that Hanover won't be rebutting you."

For an instant, Glitsky thought he saw a spark in Granat's eyes, but if he had, it disappeared immediately. "I liked Paul a lot, Chief. I really did. As you can see, I'm pretty comfortable here financially, so are the top guys at Tow/Hold. If we lose the contract, of course we'll be disappointed, but nobody's going under. I promise. We do twelve other cities in the nine-county area. Nobody took Paul out to keep him from influencing Kathy West, which seems to be what you're implying."

Glitsky shook his head. "I haven't implied anything. I was just wondering what you'd have to say about all this. Have you talked to the mayor since Wednesday?"

A tepid smile. "I called and had a small talk with her right after I heard about Paul."

"And since then?"

"Well, I'm afraid her honor doesn't return many of my calls."

"So you've tried, then?"

"Of course. But it's all about access. And I don't have

it. Not yet, anyway." He sat back, seemed to gather himself. "Look, I'm not going to bullshit you and pretend we don't want to keep the contract. It's a huge deal. But it's business."

"Yes, but if Bayshore can stop you in San Francisco, they're in a better position to poach in your other territories."

"That, too, I'm afraid, is just business. But, yes, of course, we'd like to stop them here. And I think we've still got a very good chance."

"Well, actually," Jeff Elliot said, "they don't." Glitsky was in his city-issue Taurus, talking on his cell phone with the reporter. "West's taken a potful of Bayshore's money to get elected, and she's not likely to forget that Tow/Hold's people came in large for Washington. It's payback time. She's not going to fold, and neither are her MTA members."

"Why not?"

"Because if one of them votes to retain Tow/Hold, she'll just fire him, replace him with a new warm body, keep the contract on monthly extension, go back again in thirty days and get Bayshore approved. So one of her MTA people going sideways, it's not going to happen."

"Except if she takes Hanover as a warning."

"You see any sign of that?"

"She called to get me involved in this within a very short time of talking to Granat. In any case, I'm going to ask her directly."

"What, though, exactly?"

"If Granat's call made her feel physically threatened. If this tow thing is playing on her mind at all. Why she really wants me on this case."

"I've got that one. She trusts you. She doesn't know much about Cuneo, and what she does know she has no confidence in. I think it's legitimate that she wants to get whoever killed Hanover. Whoever it was. He was politically important to her, plus she just plain liked him from everything I hear. She just wants to make sure it doesn't get screwed up."

"Okay."

"You don't believe that?"

"No. It makes sense. It's a little odd, that's all."

"Well, you'll find out."

"I know," Glitsky said. "I'm just not completely sure that I want to."

"Why not?"

Glitsky hesitated. "Cuneo," he said. "If I wind up taking the lead here, he's not going to like it. I'd rather he gets on to something and I come along afterward and say, 'yeah, looks good, nice job.' "

"So what's he looking at?"

"I don't know. He won't answer my page."

At that moment, Cuneo stood in the driveway of the Hanovers' stucco home on Beach Street, sniffing into the trunk space of their black Mercedes.

He'd arrived at a little after eight along with his former homicide partner, Lincoln Russell, whom he'd asked along to help with the search, as well as to serve as a witness that he was not sexually harassing Catherine Hanover. They'd sat, waiting outside, Cuneo driving Russell nuts with his drumming on the steering wheel, until Catherine Hanover came outside in her bathrobe to pick up the newspaper on her driveway—a bit of luck since Cuneo hadn't really known for sure how he would get a picture of her, which he badly wanted. And got.

A few minutes later, Catherine, her husband and all three kids had been shocked and startled by the appearance of the two policemen with a search warrant at their front door (*"What's this about?" "You mean I'm some kind of a suspect or something? Of what?" "Do we have to let you in to do this?"*). But then, perhaps because of the inspectors' assurances that it wouldn't take too long, they had all become reasonably cooperative, or at least acquiescent, waiting around the kitchen table while Cuneo and Russell went upstairs in search of the clothes that Cuneo remembered Catherine had been wearing on the night of the fire. In no time at all they'd found the blue silken blouse, black leather jacket, faded blue jeans. All were in her closet, the jeans still faintly smelling of smoke. They wrapped them all up, told Catherine that they would return them after the lab was through with them.

"What's the lab going to do with them?"

"Test for blood spatter. Traces of gasoline."

"This is ridiculous. Go ahead and look for that."

"We intend to, ma'am. We intend to."

The two daughters started crying.

When they had finished inside and announced their intention to inspect the car, the family broke up, the kids chattering nervously, upset about the weirdness of having their house searched. Everyone then went their various ways—the husband and wife uncommunicative, formally distant with one another, Cuneo noticed.

Will drank coffee and read the morning paper at the kitchen table, and Catherine announced that she would like to go outside with the inspectors. She couldn't imagine what they might be looking for. Now Cuneo was straightening up, and he turned to her. "Smells like you've got a gas leak. Did you know about that?"

She came closer, careful to keep her distance, leaned over the trunk and sniffed. "I do smell it. I ought to take it in for service."

"Have you noticed that smell before?" he asked.

"Not really," she said. "I don't use the trunk very often."

But Russell was feeling the rug on the trunk's floor. "This isn't a leak, Dan. Gas got spilled in here."

"No! That's not . . ." Then Catherine stopped herself. "Oh," she said. Her hand went to her mouth.

"What?" Cuneo was standing straight up in front of her, inside her comfort zone and knowing it, squinting in the sun. "Oh, what?" he repeated.

"That was a couple of weeks ago," she said.

"What was?" Cuneo's features were somehow expectant. On both hands, his fingers opened and closed.

Russell stood next to his ex-partner, paying attention to this development. Catherine Hanover, perhaps seeking some kind of support, directed her words over Cuneo's shoulder to him. "It was a few weeks ago," she said, beginning again.

"A few or a couple?" Cuneo asked.

"What?"

"First time you said 'a couple.' Then you said 'a few.' Which is it?"

"I don't know. I could probably remember."

"Take your time," Russell said. He was a black man with a pleasant face, and he had put on a patient expression. "We've got all day if you want."

Catherine looked from one of them to the other. "I should probably call a lawyer, shouldn't I?"

"If you think you need one," Cuneo said.

"That's your absolute right," Russell agreed.

"Are you two thinking about arresting me? For Paul's murder? I didn't have anything to do with that. I don't know anything about it at all, except that I saw him that day. That's all."

"We're just executing a search warrant, ma'am," Russell said. "If you were under arrest, we'd be reading you your rights."

"So I'm not?"

"No, ma'am."

"But," Cuneo put in, "you were starting to tell us about the gas smell in your car, two or maybe more weeks ago."

"Let me think," Catherine said. "I'm sure I can remember. Okay, it was . . . today's Saturday . . . it was the week before last. Monday, I think."

"So more like ten days?" Russell, being helpful, wanted to nail down the day.

"Something like that. I was going to pick up Polly for something after school, I don't remember exactly what it was now—her orthodontist appointment maybe. And I passed a car parked off the road—it was in the Presidio. Anyway, there was a young woman, a girl really, standing beside it, kind of looking like she hoped someone would help her, but maybe not wanting to actually flag somebody over. So I stopped and asked if she was all right, and she said she was out of gas."

Catherine looked into Russell's face, then Cuneo's. Sighing, she went on. "She had one of those containers in her trunk, you know, so we got in my car and I took her to a gas station, where we filled it up and put it in my trunk, and then I took her back to her car, but when we got there, the container had fallen over and leaked out a little."

"A little," Cuneo said.

"It seemed like a little."

He leaned over and ran his hand along the rug. As Russell had, he smelled his hand. Russell, meanwhile, moved up a step. "What kind of car was it?" he asked.

"Whose? Oh, hers? White."

Russell said, "That's the color, ma'am, not the kind. What kind of car was it?"

Catherine closed her eyes, crinkled up her face, came back to him. "I think some kind of SUV. I'm pretty sure."

"Any memory of the license plate?"

"No. I don't know if I ever looked at it."

"Did you get the young woman's name? First name, even?"

"No. We just . . ." Her expression had grown helpless. She shook her head. "No."

Russell nodded. "You're going to go with that story?"

"It's not a story," she said. "That's what happened."

Cuneo had removed a Swiss Army knife from his pocket and was back inside the trunk, cutting fibers from the rug that he then placed in a small Ziploc bag. "Well, okay, then," he said, turning to Russell. "I think we're through here for now."

The law firm of Arron Hanover Pells had a recorded message that provided a number clients could call if they had a weekend emergency. When Glitsky called that number, he reached one of the associates, who agreed to call Paul Hanover's secretary and ask her to call him back. Glitsky pulled up to a mini-mart just off Columbus in North Beach, double-parked and got a cup of hot water with a tea bag, then went back to his car to wait. The tea hadn't yet cooled enough for him to sip it when his cell phone rang. "Glitsky."

"Hello? Is this the police?"

"Yes it is. This is Deputy Chief Glitsky. Who am I speaking with?"

"Lori Cho. Paul Hanover's secretary."

"Thanks for getting back to me so fast."

"That's all right. I wasn't doing anything anyway except staring at his files. I can't get used to the idea that he's not coming back in."

"So you're at your office now? Would you mind if I came by for a few minutes?"

"If you'd like. We're in the Bank of America building, twentieth floor. There's a guard downstairs who's got to let you up. I'll tell him I'm expecting you. Could you give me your name again?"

Lori Cho met him at the elevators. She appeared to be in her mid-thirties, small-boned, fragile-looking, close to anorexic, with a haunted, weary look about her eyes. Or perhaps it was simply fatigue and sorrow over the loss of her boss. Here at the office on Saturday she was dressed for work in a no-nonsense black skirt with matching sweater, tennis shoes and white socks. Her hair softened the general gaunt impression somehow—shoulder-length, thick and shining black, it might still have been damp.

Glitsky followed her in silence down a carpeted hallway, through a set of wide double doors, then across an ornate lobby and into a large corner office. Hanover's panoramic view was mostly to the east, down over the rooftops of lesser high-rises to the Bay, across the bridge to Yerba Buena and Treasure Island, with Berkeley and Richmond off in the distance.

"You can just sit anywhere," Cho said. She seated herself behind the highly polished dark-wood desk, swallowed up by the black leather swivel chair that must have been Hanover's. Flattened sheets of cardboard, which Glitsky realized were unassembled boxes, were stacked by the file cabinets against one of the internal walls. The other wall featured framed photographs of Hanover with a couple of dozen politicians and celebrities, among them several San Francisco mayors, including Kathy West, and three of California's governors, one of them Arnold. At a quick glance, here was Paul Hanover, shaking hands with both Bill Clinton and George Bush; on a boat somewhere with Larry Ellison, in a Giants uniform with Willie Mays. Evidently he'd been to the wedding of Michael Douglas and Catherine Zeta-Jones.

A showcase office. Nothing in the way of law books.

Glitsky came back to Cho, who hadn't moved since she sat down. She was so still she might have been in a trance. Her eyes were open, but she wasn't looking at anything. "How long had you worked for him?" Glitsky asked.

Her surface attention came to him. "Fourteen years."

"I'm sorry."

She nodded absently.

"I wanted to ask you if there was anything in his work that you were aware of that might have played some kind of a role in his death. Was he upset about something? Was some deal going wrong? Anything like that?"

Her eyes went to her faraway place again, then returned to him. "Nothing I can think of. There was no crisis. He was doing what he always did."

"Which was what?"

Again, it took her a second or two to formulate her response. "He put people together. He was very good with people." She gestured at the photo gallery. "As you can see. He genuinely liked people."

"Did he like Nils Granat?"

The question surprised her. "I think so. They had lunch together every month or so. Why? Did Mr. Granat say there was a problem?"

"No. He said they were friends."

"I think they were."

"Even with this conflict over the city's towing?"

She nodded. "Yes. It wasn't a conflict between the two of them. Mr. Granat had his clients, and Mr. Hanover had his. He had dozens of similar relationships."

"But he never mentioned to you that he was worried about Mr. Granat's clients. The company Tow/Hold?"

"Worried in what way?"

"Physically afraid."

She shook her head no. "He wasn't physically afraid of anybody. Did you know him?"

"I never did, no."

She seemed to take this news with some disappointment. "He was a good man."

"Yes, ma'am. Everybody seems to think so." Glitsky sat back, crossed a leg. "Did you know Ms. D'Amiens very well?"

Cho's jaw went up a half inch, her eyes came into sharp focus. "Not too well, no. I shouldn't say anything bad about her. She seemed to make Mr. Hanover happy. And she was always nice to me."

"But you didn't believe her?"

Cho hesitated. "You know how some people can just seem *too* nice? It was almost like some trick she'd learned how to do. Maybe she was just trying too hard because she wanted Mr. Hanover's friends to like her. And his family, too. But they weren't going to like her, no matter how she acted. They thought she was in it for his money."

"Did you think that?"

She bit at her cheek. "As I said, I didn't really know her. Mr. Hanover didn't think it, and he was nobody's fool. He might have been right."

"But you disagreed with him?"

"A little bit. With no real basis in fact, though. Just a feeling."

"Feelings generally are based on something."

She sighed. "She just seemed calculating. It made me feel she was . . . not very genuine. I suppose you want an example."

Glitsky didn't push. "If you've got one."

"Well." She paused. "Okay. When Paul first met her, one of her big things was she volunteered once a week at Glide Memorial, the soup kitchens?"

"Okay."

"The message, of course, being that she had this big heart and cared about the homeless and all that. But once she and Paul . . . once they got together, that pretty much stopped."

"So you think it was a ploy to make her seem somehow more attractive?"

"I don't know. I hate to say that. Maybe she was sincere and just got busier with Paul, you know. But it struck me wrong. And then, you know, she really did come from nowhere and then suddenly was going to marry him. So quickly, it seemed."

"So Mr. Hanover never talked to you about her background?"

"Not too much. Evidently she had had a husband who died of cancer about five years ago. . . ."

"Do you know where?"

"No. I'm sorry. I never even asked. But she wanted to start over and she'd always dreamed of living in America.

In San Francisco. So she came here." She let out a breath. "It really wasn't mysterious. She had a few connections here with people she'd met overseas and then met Paul, and then . . . well, you know. If he wasn't rich, no one would have thought anything about it. But of course, he was." Though the admission seemed to cost her, she shrugged and said, "They just got along. She made him happy. He seemed to make her happy."

"So they weren't fighting?"

"Why do you ask that?"

"The rumor is there was some tension between them. The expense of the remodel, maybe? I heard she'd spent something like a million dollars."

Cho allowed a small, sad smile. "That's about what he told me. But he thought it was funny."

"Funny?"

"Amusing. I mean, after all, he was going to be living there. He had the money, and if she spent it to make a nicer house for him, what was he going to complain about?" Cho stared for a second into the space in front of her. "If there was any tension at all, it was about the appointment."

"The appointment?"

She nodded. "This wasn't public yet, but the administration had gotten in touch with him and told him he'd been short-listed for assistant secretary of the interior, a reward for all the fund-raising he'd done for the president. But Missy wasn't happy about it. She didn't want to move to Washington, uproot her life again, especially after all the work she'd done on the house." Cho's face clouded over. "But even so, so what? Didn't I read that it wasn't murder and suicide? Even if they were fighting, somebody killed them. So would it even matter if they'd been fighting about something?"

"No, you're right, it wouldn't," Glitsky said. "I'm sorry to have taken so much of your time. I'm just trying to get a handle on this whole thing. Who might've wanted to kill them."

"Well, I hate to say this . . ."

"Go ahead."

"Well, just . . . have you talked to his family? They were really unhappy about him and her. And he was unhappy about them."

"His kids, you mean?"

She nodded. "All the time on him. Missy wanted his money. He should be careful, make sure she signed a prenup, some worse things about her. He said he might change his will before the wedding if they kept it up."

"Did he tell them that?"

"I don't know. I think so. Told them, I mean—maybe not actually done it."

Before Glitsky left Cho, just being thorough and believing that at this early stage in the investigation he needed facts even if they later proved to be irrelevant, he found out that before he'd handed the build phase of the remodel over to Missy, Hanover had paid the first few contractor bills himself during the design phase. The company, James Leymar Construction, was in the phone book, and so was Mr. Leymar himself. Glitsky called, and the man being home made his hat trick for the day.

A half hour later, he pulled up in front of a good-size two-story stucco house on Quintara Street, out in the residential avenues of the Sunset District. A shirtless man was working with lengths of PVC pipe in the earth up close against the house, the sweat on his broad back glinting in the sun. At the sound of Glitsky's car door closing, he looked around and stood up, slapping his hands together, then wiping them on his well-worn blue jeans. "Glitsky?"

"Yes, sir."

Leymar was a big, handsome balding man with a well-developed torso, big arms and a shoulder tattoo of a heart and the word "Maggie." Squinting against the brightness, he took a few steps over the torn-up landscape of his front yard and stuck out his dirty hand. "Jim Leymar. How you doin'?"

"Good. You're putting in a sprinkler system?"

"I know. Ridiculous, isn't it?" He turned back to survey the trenches he'd dug. "Like the foggiest damn real estate in America needs more water. But the wife decided for God knows what reason, so that's the end of that discussion." He swiped at his forehead, leaving a streak of dirt. "But you said you had some questions about the Hanover job?"

"If you don't mind."

"No, I don't mind, but I've got to say it breaks my heart to think about the work we put in on that house only to have it all go up in smoke. It was a beautiful job. And the people, too, of course. A tragedy."

"You knew them pretty well?"

"Well, they were clients, you know. I'd done some work for him before, rebuilt his kitchen, maybe three years ago, and it went okay. So we got together again."

"But this time was mostly her?"

"More than mostly. She wrote the checks, so she was the client."

Glitsky filed that bit of information. "And how was she to work with?" he asked.

"Uncompromising, but without a personal edge to it. She wanted things a certain way, and if you didn't give her what she wanted, she'd have us do it again, down to the floorboards if need be. But she was just firm, that was all. Give me that anytime over somebody who changes her mind seventeen times."

Something about Leymar's phrase stopped Glitsky. "So you're saying she did not make lots of changes as you went along?"

"No." He thought about it for another minute. "If you want to see, I've got all the change orders . . ."

"That's all right. I'd just heard somewhere that she kept adding to the job."

"No more than anybody else. Less than some folks. No, what happened was we got a good design and went ahead and built it."

"So the initial bid was for a million dollars?"

Leymar laughed out loud. "*A million dollars?* You think I make a million dollars a job and I'm laying my own sprinkler system?" He shook his head, still chuckling. "A million dollars. Jesus Christ. A million is nearly the gross on my best year ever. The gross. Hanover was a good job—hell, a great job, I'll give you that—but it went out for five hundred, maybe a little less. And that's what we brought it in for, too. Give or take. Where did you ever hear a million?"

"Several sources," he said.

"Well, I'd go back to them and tell 'em they've got

their heads up their asses. You want, I'll show you my books on it."

"I won't need to do that." Glitsky wiped his own brow. The sun was directly overhead now, the temperature nearing eighty, about as hot as it ever got in San Francisco. "Okay, let's leave the money. I'd like to eliminate the possibility that *she* was the target instead of him, so I'm hoping to find somebody who might have known her a little bit, see if she had enemies."

"Who wanted to kill her?"

"Maybe."

He shook his head. "That'd be a stretch, I'd say." He thought another minute. "Except maybe if there was some other guy before Hanover."

"Did you get a feeling that there had been?"

"No. It's just that she was . . ."—he glanced over his shoulder—"I don't want Maggie to hear me, but she was an unbelievably attractive hunk of woman. My crews would trade off with each other so they could work on her place and get a glimpse of her. If she'd dumped some guy for Hanover, I could see him maybe taking it out on both of them."

"Did she or Hanover ever say anything to make you think that?"

"No. We didn't talk personal. They were clients, that was all. We didn't hang with the same social crowd." He gestured around him. "As you probably figured anyway, huh?"

Dismas Hardy came down the stairs from a rare Saturday afternoon nap to find Abe Glitsky in his kitchen, helping Vincent cut up vegetables on a cutting board on the counter, the two of them working silently next to a rapidly diminishing pile of tomatoes, onions, peppers, okra. When he stopped in the doorway, Glitsky glanced his way and, just loud enough to be heard, said, "Here he is now, Vin, I'll tell you later."

Hardy crossed to his boy and put a hand on his shoulder. "Have I ever told you your Uncle Abe's Indian name, Vin?"

"His Indian name?"

"You know, Dances with Wolves, like that? A phrase that captures a person's essence. Abe's is People Not

Laughing. Why? Because every time you see him he's surrounded by people who are not laughing. But I do think
that actually crying real tears is taking it a little far."

"It's the onions," Vincent said.

"That's what they all say." Hardy threw a chunk of
tomato into his mouth. "What are you guys making?"

"Gumbo," Vin said. "I need it for school on Monday and
wanted to make a test batch."

Hardy squeezed his son's shoulder. "I love this boy. Make
it hot," he said.

"I'm thinking of calling Treya, inviting her over, too,"
Glitsky said.

"That would be swell, and I love your wife even more
than I like you, but weren't you guys just here? It seems
like only yesterday."

"It *was* yesterday. Maybe we should all just move in
since we're spending so much time here anyway. We'd save
a bundle on rent. And Vin, you could get in time with that
critical small-child experience you're going to need when
you have your own kids."

"I'm not having kids."

"Sure you are."

"No, I'm not. I'm going to be a rich bachelor."

"There's a noble calling," Hardy said. "How are you
going to do the rich part?"

"I'm thinking the lottery."

"He got that from you," Hardy shot at Glitsky. "The
adults in this house don't play the lottery. And you know
why? Because we're good at numbers, and the lottery is the
tax for the math-challenged. I believe I've even mentioned
this to you before."

"Don't listen to your father, Vin. Somebody wins the lottery every few weeks, and you've got as good a chance as
anybody else."

Withering Glitsky with a glance, he said, "Pathetic," and
looked at his son. "You got a backup? Plan, I mean, to get
rich."

"I guess if things got tight I could always be a movie star
for a while."

"There you go," Glitsky said proudly. "Plan B, ready
to go."

"Although traditionally," Hardy said, "doesn't the movie star come from within the ranks of the supremely attractive?"

Vin looked at Glitsky, sniffed theatrically. "He cuts me deep."

"I heard it."

"It happens all the time. My self-esteem's in the toilet."

Hardy stopped in the middle of a bite of red pepper. "You'll live, I promise. I didn't even *know* the word 'self-esteem' when I was a kid."

"Isn't it two words?" Glitsky asked.

"It's hyphenated," Vinnie said. "And Dad didn't hear of it as a kid 'cause it wasn't invented until after the Renaissance."

Hardy deadpanned his son for a minute, said, "Too bad Abe's Indian name is already taken." He turned his attention to Glitsky. "But callously leaving for a moment the discussion of my son's future plans for wealth and world domination, what really brings you here?"

Glitsky laid his knife down. "This morning I talked to Nils Granat about the towing business. As I was in the neighborhood anyway, I thought I'd stop by since you seemed interested last night. He says nobody he knows would ever consider using strong-arm tactics to accomplish their business goals. Those may have been his exact words."

"Well, what did you expect? He's not going to tell you they've got a team of hit men out whacking people who get in their way. I still think it's a pretty good theory."

"Well, I'm going to have a few conversations with Tow/Hold management, see if any of them get nervous. Meanwhile, though, I also talked to Hanover's secretary, who seems to think it's probably somebody in the family who stood to lose the inheritance."

"You already had that one. What was her name again, the daughter-in-law?"

"Catherine Hanover, but I don't think so. I can't believe she would have spelled her motive out so clearly if she'd had any part in it. Still, the family connection's on the table. But you know the most interesting thing?"

"The uncertainty principle?"

"What?"

"The most interesting thing. The uncertainty principle. Actually, quantum mechanics in general, in fact. All of it damned interesting, although I'm not sure I get most of it."

Glitsky picked up his knife again, went back to the cutting board, shaking his head. "Why do I talk to your father, Vinnie?"

"It feels so good when you stop?"

"That must be it."

"Okay, okay," Hardy said. "I'm sorry if I hurt all the dainty feelings in this kitchen. I give up, Abe. What's the most interesting thing?"

He put his knife down again. "Missy D'Amiens didn't spend a million dollars fixing up her house."

Hardy leaned back against the counter, crossed his arms. "Few of us do, Abe. Why is that interesting?"

"Because everybody I talked to up 'til now said she had. Hanover's secretary, the daughter-in-law, Cuneo. That was the number."

"And this means?"

"If it's true, it means half a million dollars cash has gone missing."

"With who? Where'd it go?"

"That's the question."

The Beck was in the honor society at her high school, and one of the requirements of that organization was doing some nonschool community service, in this case cleaning up selected city parks and other public amenities in a "graffiti abatement" program, which had begun in a bit of controversy.

Hardy and Frannie both thought it was a nice "only in San Francisco" touch that the program—created to clean up the worst of the obscene tagging that desecrated nearly every square inch of wall space in certain neighborhoods—had been hotly debated and nearly disallowed by the school district on the grounds that the cleanup represented an authoritarian stifling of artistic expression among the city's troubled youth. A number of adult San Francisco residents and parents, and nearly half of the school board, held to the belief that spraying "FUCK" and other such creative epithets in Day-Glo on billboards and benches at bus stops and anywhere else the spirit moved one was apparently therapeutic and good for a child's self-esteem. That word again.

With a growing sense of outrage, Frannie had eventually joined the debate and for the past few weekends, in support of the kids' efforts, she had been going out with her daughter and her friends, all of them armed with buckets and detergent, to help with the cleanup. And now they were home.

The guys were still making the gumbo—Hardy, with a just-opened bottle of Anchor Steam next to him, peeling shrimp over the sink, Glitsky cutting up the andouille, Vincent seeding and chopping the jalapeños.

"What's cooking?" Rebecca yelled from the front door. "It smells great!" Footsteps broke into a run in the hallway, and in a second, she burst into the kitchen. Hugs all around. "Uncle Abe! Two days in a row! Hey, Dad! What are you guys making?" She was at the stove, wooden spoon in hand. "What is this stuff?"

Vin flew across the room. "No, no, no, no, no! No tastes, no bites. That's dinner."

Frannie showed up a few steps behind her daughter. Her windblown red hair, which she'd been growing long for some months now, fell below her shoulders, and her color was high after all day in the sun. She was wearing khaki shorts and a pink tank top, and her green eyes were sparkling.

Hardy found himself struck by a sudden contentment so acute that it felt for a moment like a hot blade through his heart.

The sun was low enough in the late afternoon that it made it through the picture window in the front of the house, spraying the hardwood in the dining room with an amber glow that reflected all the way up and into the kitchen. Behind him, over the sink, the window was open and a still unseasonably warm breeze tickled the back of his neck. The smell of the gumbo was intoxicating, both of the women in his family were smiling and almost too lovely to believe, and his son and best friend were working with him to make something everybody would love to eat.

Everything dear to him was close, safe and protected in this room, on a perfect day.

He closed his eyes for an instant against the rush of emotion.

"Are you okay, babe?"

Frannie was in front of him, her hand on his arm, a worried look on her face.

Blinking a couple of times, Hardy leaned down and planted a quick kiss on her forehead. The moment passed unnoticed by everyone else—still bickering over the gumbo—but Frannie gave him a last concerned glance before he said, "Too good, really. That's all. Too good." He pulled her to him for a second, and squeezed, as the words of Abe's toast came back to him. May nothing ever change.

On the counter by Vincent's cutting board, the telephone rang.

"Let it go," Hardy said. "I don't want to talk to anybody."

But Vincent had already grabbed it on the first ring, said hello and was listening. "Just a second," he said. "Can I tell him who's calling?" He passed the phone over to his father. "Catherine Hanover."

Glitsky gave him a startled look. Hardy looked back at him, shrugged, took the phone and said hello.

12

"Dismas?"

Hardy was moving with the phone on the steps toward his bedroom upstairs. His face took on a quizzical expression at this unknown woman's use of his first name. But he had no doubt that she was a potential client, and didn't even stop to consider the unusual familiarity. Still, there was a question in his voice. "This is Dismas Hardy, yes."

"Dismas," she said again. "It's Catherine Rusk."

Halfway up the stairs, he stopped still. "Catherine . . . ?"

"Hanover. Now."

Hardy found that he couldn't frame a response. The two or three seconds before he could speak felt like a very long time. "Catherine," he said. "How are you?" Then, still struggling for something to say. "How have you been?"

He heard a throaty chuckle that vibrated in some distant region of his psyche. "You mean this last thirty-seven years? I've been okay, although right at this moment I'm not too good, I'm afraid. I hate to contact you for the first time under these conditions, but I didn't know who else to call. I've thought about it a lot over the years, you know, calling you, but always thought that maybe we'd just run into each other again somewhere. It's not that big a city."

"No it isn't. You've lived here all along?"

"Mostly, after college and then a couple of years back in Boston. I know you've been living here. I've seen you in the papers." He heard her sigh. "Anyway. I called you because I think I need a lawyer. Apparently I'm some kind of a suspect in a murder case."

"Yes, I know that."

"You *know*? Already?"

"I mean, I'd heard about Catherine Hanover, the name,

but I didn't know she was you." The next words slipped out before he could stop them. "I thought you weren't ever going to change your name."

"I wasn't, but it seemed important to Will, so I guess when push came to shove, I abandoned my high principles and sold out my old feminist beliefs. And how about you? I thought you weren't ever going to work nine to five."

"Touché," he said. "I'm sorry."

"It's all right. You sounded just like your old self."

"Well . . . I'm still sorry. I have no idea where that came from or why it came out."

"It's okay, really." Again he heard the oddly mnemonic throaty chuckle. "You're probably still feeling guilty about how you dumped me."

"Maybe," he admitted, and again before he could think added, "that could be it." He wasn't quite sure what he was saying, since he hadn't consciously thought of her in years.

Frannie appeared below him at the flight of the stairs, looking up with some concern, mouthed, "Is everything all right?"

Nodding, Hardy gave his wife a smile, then turned and started up the steps again. "But now you're in trouble?"

"I think I must be. The police came by this morning with a search warrant and looked through my house and my car."

Hardy sat down in the reading chair in his bedroom. This was a new development that hadn't yet made the news. If they'd already served a search warrant on her, the case had progressed far beyond a casual suspicion based on a possible motive. Somebody in the investigation was already into evidence and causality. And it was not Abe, who surely would have mentioned this to him either last night or downstairs just a few minutes ago. That left only Cuneo, and the realization made Hardy's stomach go tight. "So you've talked to the police?"

"Several times."

"Without a lawyer?"

"I didn't think I needed one. I didn't know I was a suspect. The first time was down at the fire . . ."

"You were at the fire?"

"Yes."

"Why?"

"Because it was my father-in-law's house and I saw it on the news and ran down to see what was happening and if I could help."

"And you talked to cops down there?"

"Yes, somebody Cuneo. And an arson inspector, too. And since then a deputy chief. Glitsky. But they just wanted to know about Paul. My father-in-law. Paul Hanover."

"I know that, too."

"How can you know all this?"

"It's a big case, Catherine. Everybody in town knows about it."

In the phone, her voice grew smaller. "That's right, of course. But are you saying I shouldn't have talked to the police? I was trying to cooperate."

Hardy, one hand rubbing his forehead, said, "No. Cooperation's okay. I'm just being a lawyer. Sometimes it's bad luck to say anything to the police."

"But I didn't think I was a suspect."

"No. I know. That's their favorite."

"So I'm in bigger trouble than I thought?"

He didn't want her to panic and spouted out a white lie. "Maybe not. I don't know. What were they looking for at your house?"

"The clothes I was wearing when I was at the fire. They were in my closet and I think the hamper."

"So you hadn't washed them yet?"

"I guess not." Then, on a higher note, the worry clear in her voice. "Is that a problem, too?"

"I don't know about 'too.' I don't know what the problems are yet, Catherine. What did they do with the clothes?"

"They took them away. They said they'd bring them back. They were going to analyze them for . . . I don't know what. Something."

"Did they take anything else?"

A silence.

"Catherine?"

Now he heard a definite strain in the pitch of her voice. "Some cuttings of the fabric from the trunk of my car. It had some gasoline on it. See, a couple of weeks ago I helped this woman who'd run out of gas . . ."

"Catherine?"

A sob broke over the line.

Hardy stopped to lift the lid and stir the gumbo, then went and stood in the entrance to the dining room. Glitsky was sitting at the table, apparently content to wait for Hardy's descent after his business call and pass the time with Frannie, who had poured herself a glass of Chardonnay. The kids were nowhere to be found. Hardy stood in the door to the dining area, hands in his pockets, leaning against the jamb.

"So Abe," he said, "you searched her house this morning and just didn't get around to telling me because . . . ?"

Glitsky's face clouded. "What are you talking about?"

"I'm talking about a search warrant for Catherine Hanover's clothes and her car. They found gasoline in her trunk."

"Who did? I didn't . . ." He stopped. "Cuneo. Why didn't he . . . ?"

Hardy knew the answer. "He didn't want your input in the first place, and now he's proving he didn't need it. He wants the collar himself."

"But . . ." Glitsky was reduced to sputtering. "We haven't . . ."

"Obviously, he's not interested. He's got his suspect and he's in a hurry."

Glitsky's mouth was tight, his scar in high relief through his lips, his blue eyes flat and hard. "She under arrest?"

"Not yet. Apparently. Though she might be anytime."

"Did she say that?"

"No. But she's got herself worked into a pretty good panic right about now. I don't know what she's going to do."

"She wants you to represent her, then?" Glitsky asked.

"That's what she called for."

"And you wisely suggested she get somebody else, right?"

"Not exactly." Hardy took a deep breath.

Frannie said, "Why would he do that, Abe?"

Glitsky looked across the table. "Because your husband

doesn't want to have anything to do with Catherine Hanover." Back over to Hardy. "I'm correct here, am I not?"

Before Hardy could reply, Frannie asked, "Why not?"

"Because of Dan Cuneo, that's why not. He's already got Diz and me together in his brain. Now if Diz gets involved in this case . . ." Suddenly he turned his head. "What's 'not exactly' mean, Diz? This really wouldn't be a good idea."

"No, I know that. But there are other issues."

"Such as."

"Such as I know her." His eyes went to Frannie. "Catherine Hanover is Catherine Rusk," he said.

"And Catherine Rusk is?" Glitsky asked.

"His first girlfriend." Frannie assayed a brave smile that didn't quite work.

"Well, I'm happy for her," Glitsky said, "but she's not his girlfriend now. You are." Again he looked at Hardy. "Tell her, Diz."

Hardy broke his own tired smile. "I'm pretty sure she knows, but for the record"—he walked up behind where Frannie sat and placed a kiss on the top of her head—"you're still my girlfriend."

She patted his hand where it rested on her shoulder. "I'm so glad."

"Okay," Glitsky said, "that's settled. Now you've got to let Catherine go."

"That's my intention."

"Good. You had me worried there for a minute."

"Well, I don't mean to worry you some more, either of you"—he squeezed Frannie's shoulder again—"but I think I'm going to have to see her tonight. She needs some help and she needs it now." He sat down next to Frannie. "She's a wreck, hon. Crying on the phone. She didn't know who else to call. I've got to go see her this one time. She was desperate."

"You don't have to go see her," Glitsky said. "Send one of your minions."

"Did you ever try to find a minion on Saturday night, Abe? Besides, she called me. Maybe I can calm her down. I knew her."

"You *knew* her," Glitsky snapped. "You don't know her anymore." He turned to Frannie. "You tell him. This is dumb."

"He makes his own decisions, Abe. You may have noticed."

Hardy kissed her cheek and stood up. "Sorry. I know it's Saturday night, but she's really in a bad way, Fran. I won't be too long."

She patted his hand. "I'll deal with it. We were just vegging with a video anyway."

Glitsky was getting up, too. "Don't let her hire you."

"That's not my plan. I'll get her calmed down and give her some tips to get her through the weekend, like don't talk to any more cops, then we'll see where we are."

Hardy couldn't help but notice that Catherine hadn't conceded much to the passage of the years. His first reaction on seeing her was that it was nearly unfair. She'd kept her body in terrific shape, and her face, always her best feature, was if anything more interesting and attractive than it had been when she was eighteen. A couple of lines around the eyes gave her a sense of experience, humor and maybe even a hint of wisdom. Smooth skin, a strong chin, well-defined cheekbones and an assertive nose would make her face at home on a magazine cover. She looked Frannie's age, although he knew she had twelve years on his wife.

She opened the door and he consciously had to stop himself from commenting on her attractiveness, a compliment that for all its truth would not have been appropriate.

And she wasn't alone. "This is my husband Will, our boy Saul, Polly and Heather. This is Mr. Hardy." She explained to the children, "He's going to be my lawyer for a while until all this with the police gets sorted out. I hope not too long."

Not even inside the door and Hardy felt blindsided, confronted with two of the character traits that he suddenly remembered had led to them breaking up so long ago. The first manifested itself by the presence of her family. On the phone, Hardy had gotten an impression so strong that it was a conviction that Catherine was alone at home, in a panic. She had no one else to turn to, certainly not a husband, a nuclear family gathered around. Now here she was in their bosom, and Hardy felt a bit abused that he'd been coerced into leaving his own family on a Saturday night, thinking it was an emergency, when it was really just Catherine being overly histrionic, and being not entirely truthful because of omission—the coward's lie.

And then the comment in her first breath about him being her lawyer. He remembered all too well—she used to make assumptions and jump to conclusions based on the belief that whatever it might be, people wanted to do it for her. And she'd been so desirable that usually it wasn't an issue. Doing what she wanted instead of what you wanted was a small enough price to pay because when you were with her, in her presence you felt that life was good.

"We weren't going to the game, Dismas. I said I wanted to go to the movies, remember? I just assumed . . ."

And here—he hadn't told her he was going to be her lawyer, although obviously she now assumed he was. *Why wouldn't he be?* When in fact, he'd rather consciously avoided making any kind of overture or commitment in that direction.

But Polly, chirping up, brushed away the thoughts. "Were you really my mom's boyfriend?" she asked.

Hardy downplayed it. "A long time ago in high school. We were good friends." He glanced at her to verify that this was her version of events as well and got an infinitesimal nod of acknowledgment.

Next, her husband Will stepped up and shook hands. "Thanks for coming by. After this search this morning, we didn't know what to do. Obviously things are further along than we thought, but how they could think Catherine . . ." Shaking his head, he abruptly stopped.

Will was a step or two above conventionally handsome. Tanned and trim, he had a boyish face. His handshake was not strong, and the smile left a strange impression of distance, if not outright discomfort. "But you know more about all this than we do," he concluded.

Hardy took the opportunity to clarify things. "I really don't know too much beyond what I've read in the papers. After you catch me up, we'll have to see how bad things are. You may not need a lawyer at all."

But Catherine didn't let him off. "No, I need a lawyer, Dismas. I'm sure of that. After this morning . . . the search was just so, so *weird,* in a way. This Inspector Cuneo, he must be thinking . . ."

Will shook his head, his voice with an edge to it. "Let's not go there yet. We don't know what he's thinking. He's not going to find anything on Catherine's clothes, but if he does . . ."

Catherine turned on him. "There's nothing to find, Will. He's harassing me, pure and simple."

Hardy, drawn in, had to ask. "Who is? Cuneo?"

She nodded. "Who else? But here you are standing in the open door. Please come in, Dismas. I'm not thinking. This has got us all so upset."

"I don't blame you. It's upsetting." He looked at the assembled children. "How are you guys doing? Holding up?"

Saul said, "My mom didn't kill Grandpa."

"No," Hardy replied, "I'm sure she didn't."

"It's bullshit!"

"Saul!" But Catherine's rebuke had no teeth. "Mr. Hardy's here because he knows I couldn't have done anything like that. That's why I called him. And it's why we need to talk."

Will spoke up. "Mom's right, kids. It's adult time. We'll be right out front here if you need us."

Saul didn't particularly like it, but the girls went without hesitation and, in a moment, so did he. Hardy took the moment to look around the room, then at Catherine. "At least they didn't tear the place up down here, did they?" he said to her.

"No, it was all upstairs," Will said.

Catherine's tone brooked no objection. "I think he asked me, Will, if you don't mind."

"No," Hardy said, "that's all right."

A hard look passed between husband and wife. "She's right," Will said. "It's her problem, really. You two work it out." And with that he was gone.

Hardy and Catherine remained in the living room, sitting facing one another at the far end by the fireplace. Their eyes met and held for an instant. Catherine drew a breath, made an attempt at a smile, another one. "I don't know where to begin," she said at last, "except to tell you that . . ."

"Wait," Hardy said, "Catherine, please. Just one second." Now that he had her alone, he was going to set the record straight. "I came over here to talk to you because you sounded like you were in trouble and you needed some emergency legal advice. I'm prepared to give that to you, free and for nothing, because I do feel like I know who you are, and of course there's our history."

She seemed to be suppressing some amusement. "You do sound like a lawyer."

"That's because I am a lawyer, Catherine. And I don't know if there's even a case here, much less if I'm prepared to take it on. If they discover some evidence and you become a legitimate suspect . . ."

She shook her head, stopping him. "It's not about the evidence, Dismas. It's about Inspector Cuneo."

"How's that?"

"I made him mad and now he's out to show me I wasn't going to get away with it."

"With what?"

An hour later, Hardy had the whole story from Catherine's point of view, as well as she could piece it together. She believed that her accusation of Cuneo's sexual advances was at the base of everything that had happened up to now, and took the position that the search wasn't so much about evidence as an example of pure police hassle. She had no idea why her clothes might be important. Readily admitting her concerns about the family's future finances, especially if Paul and Missy were to marry, she also told him about her conversations with Glitsky. Finally, they'd exhausted everything she'd brought up and decided to take a break.

Without any conscious decision, Hardy had spent the hour asking questions, giving answers and generally acting as though he was already, de facto, taking the case.

In the kitchen, she brewed up a pot of decaf and they crossed over to the table in the breakfast nook. Hardy slid in on the bench and sipped at his coffee as she lowered herself onto one of the chairs. "This is just so strange," she said quietly. "How many times do you think we sat like this either at your place or mine and drank coffee and did homework together while it was dark outside?"

"A lot. But I'm not sure I remember much about the homework."

"No. We always did homework before." Hardy felt the "before" hanging in the air between them. Then she said, "That was the rule. Don't you remember? We were such serious students."

"We were?"

"Listen to you. Mister never got a 'B'?"

Hardy shrugged. "I got some 'B's. Especially in college. But grades weren't what I put my energy into, anyway."

"I know. I remember where you put your energy."

Hardy's mouth twitched and his eyes flicked across at her, then away. "They were good times." He brought his cup to his mouth and sipped. "Do you realize that my daughter's as old now as you were then? Is that possible?"

"What's her name?"

"Rebecca."

"I love that name. Does she have a boyfriend?"

"Going on two years. Darren. Nice kid."

"Are they serious?"

"Probably. They'd say they were, anyway, first true love and all that."

"You sound cynical."

"I'm not. They just don't really have a clue yet."

"Like we did?"

"No. We didn't either."

"I thought we did." She scratched at the table with a fingernail. "I thought we had it all."

"Maybe you did. I didn't."

"I think you did, even then. You were always so good with who you were, so together."

He snorted. "Together. There's a word you don't hear a lot of anymore. If I was so together, how did I fall so completely apart?"

"How about your parents being in a plane crash? You think that could have been a life-changing event?"

"I guess it was."

"You guess?"

Hardy shrugged. "Well," he said quietly, "whatever it was. In any case, I'm sorry. I was a shit to you."

"You weren't really. You just dumped me, that's all."

But it was the only way Hardy had been able to do it. He had had the excuse of his parents' death so that he could keep at bay his own guilt over wanting to end it with Catherine. He was sorting out his life and had no time for a relationship, especially such a demanding one as theirs. The truth was that he had simply grown tired of the dramatics, the narcissism, the omissions. (*"I never said I wouldn't see anybody else when you went to college."*) But he also knew that if he allowed himself to get back into her presence, the physical connect might make him weaken. So without a word he'd just dropped out of her life. In retrospect he knew that she was what he'd had to abandon to get to where he'd come now, to where he needed to go.

But now, a salve to his conscience, he said, "After three years, a decent person maybe shouldn't just disappear without some explanation."

"Sometimes maybe the decent person needs to. Maybe he needs something else."

"Still."

She reached across the table and briefly touched his hand. "Okay," her voice was gentle, "you were a shit. But you're here now because I called and said I needed you. So let's call it even."

Hardy nodded. "Even it is." He put his mug down and reached into his briefcase for a yellow legal pad and a couple of pens. "Now, at the risk of ruining our new and hard-won equilibrium, I've got to ask you a few more questions."

She backed her chair away from the table and crossed her legs, holding her mug in her lap. She wore shorts that flattered her legs and a salmon-colored, sleeveless pullover. "Does this mean you're my lawyer?"

"Not yet," he said. "Maybe not ever, if they never charge you. But either way, I'm going to clear it with my wife first. It's one of our rules. Murder cases can be hell on family time."

Catherine sat back and crossed her arms. "You've really changed, haven't you?"

"Most of us do, Catherine."

"I don't know how much I have."

"I'll bet more than you think. You've got a family, and after kids the whole world is different."

"With the kids, yes." Hardy noted the omission of Will and wondered exactly what it meant in this context, but this wasn't going to be the time to pursue it. "But assuming that your wife . . ."

"Frannie."

"Okay, assuming Frannie agrees, and if I become a suspect . . ."

Hardy shook his head. "Too many ifs, Catherine. Let's get specific. Why did you go and visit your father-in-law that day?"

"I told you. I was worried about the college money for the kids."

"I'm sure you were, but why that particular day? Had something changed? Did Paul and Missy move up their wedding day or anything like that?"

She twirled the mug before looking up at him. "Maybe it had just been building up and suddenly I needed to know for sure. And . . ."

"And you're trying out how that answer sounds on me?"

The tone—unexpectedly sharp—stopped her. She shot a glance at him and took in a quick breath. "No. No, I'm not doing that."

"So there was no reason? Nothing different that day from any other?"

"Like what?"

Hardy lowered his voice. "Well, for example, your husband was out of town."

"He was fishing down south."

"That's what you said on the phone earlier. So maybe you had a little more time to yourself to think about all these money issues?"

"Right."

"And you suddenly needed to know Paul's plans?"

"Right." She thrust out her chin. "You don't believe me?"

"I'm just asking you questions and listening to how you answer them, Catherine. How are you and your husband doing?"

"Fine." The defensiveness unmistakable now. "We're fine."

"No problems?"

A pause, then. "Everybody has problems, Dismas. Nobody's perfect."

"I didn't say anybody was. I asked about you and Will."

Her eyes went to the doorway, then looked Hardy full in the face. "We're not great."

He leaned in toward her, his voice barely audible. "Catherine, nobody's indicted you yet. Maybe they never will. And maybe you're completely, factually innocent . . ."

"I am. I didn't do any . . ."

He raised a palm. "But if they do arrest you, if you wind up going on trial for these murders, you won't have any secrets. Everything comes out. And getting surprised in the courtroom is the worst bad luck you can imagine."

He drank coffee. When he spoke again, his tone was more conversational. "But as I say, there's no indictment yet. We're just covering some possible contingencies here tonight. So we'll leave you and Will for the moment. Let's talk about Paul Hanover. Did you know he owned a gun?"

"Sure. We all knew that."

"And where he kept it?"

"In the headboard of his bed."

"Loaded?"

"Yes. He mentioned it more than a few times over the years. He got a kick out of riling up his daughters, who think weapons are dangerous."

"They're right," Hardy said. "But you did know where Paul kept his gun? And people knew it and would testify to it?"

"It wasn't a family secret."

"So, family members?"

"Yes."

"And you think they'd testify against you, if it came to that?"

This obviously brought her up short. She took in the familiar kitchen surroundings as if suddenly seeing them in a different light for the first time. "Well, no. I mean, Mary wouldn't. We're fairly close. I can't imagine Beth or even Theresa . . ."

"Beth and Theresa?"

"Will's older sister and my mother-in-law. Not my favorite people and probably vice versa, but I mean, there's nothing inherently negative about knowing where Paul kept his gun, is there? They knew where it was, too."

Hardy looked up from his note taking. "Yes, but they weren't at his house a few hours before he was shot. Were they?"

"No. No they weren't. I mean, I don't know that for sure, but . . ."

He waved it away. "Don't worry about that. If they don't have alibis, the police will know soon enough. But was there somebody else?"

"Who?"

"I don't know. You said Mary wouldn't testify against you. I got the feeling you were going to say Beth or Theresa might."

"I didn't say that!"

"No, I know you didn't."

"I wasn't going to say it!"

"All right."

He waited while she worked through her emotions. "This is not about the family," she said at last. "It's about Cuneo."

"Well, no," Hardy said, "it's about everything." He came forward and spoke quietly but with some urgency. "You might not want to talk about it now, but everybody else in your family has the same motive that you do, and if someone among them doesn't like you and you get charged, they might find themselves in an unusually good position to do you damage and at the same time protect themselves. If this is about Paul's money, which seems likely, then it's about *their* money, too. Okay?"

"Okay. I'm sorry."

"You don't need to be sorry. You're allowed to feel defensive about your family. If you didn't, in fact," he broke a small smile, "I might think something was fishy about that."

The jab of lightness broke some of her tension. "So I can't win no matter what?"

"Essentially right. But all I'm after now is basic, general information." He sat back. "I believe we were on Theresa."

Something went out of Catherine's shoulders. Hardy

stole a glance at his watch—quarter to ten—and realized he should wrap this up pretty soon. If the investigation truly came to settle on her, and if he took it on, they'd have all the time in the world. But her relationship with her mother-in-law was already on the table and he wanted to hear what else she had to say about it.

"She doesn't approve of me and never has."

"Why not?"

"I wish I knew. God knows, I've tried to be a good wife and mother and even daughter-in-law, but she's ... well, she's a very difficult woman. She's got this one rock-solid vision of how all women should be, and I'm not it."

"And what's that vision?"

"Well, first, they should work. She works. Beth and Mary both work." Catherine stopped and shook her head. "But that's not really it because when Will and I were first together, I *did* work, and if anything she was more negative about me then than she is now, which is kind of hard to imagine." She sighed again. "I just wasn't good enough for her baby."

"That would be Will?"

She nodded. "The golden boy. He should have married someone with more ... I don't know what ... ambition. Who maybe would have pushed him harder to get to his true potential. I just weighed him down with a family and stayed at home instead of bringing in an income, so he constantly had to struggle just to make ends meet. Which is why he's never ... he's never been as successful as his father."

"And that's your fault?"

"Absolutely. How could it not be? How can you even ask? It couldn't be Will, so that left me, right?" Catherine suddenly looked over at the kitchen door, got up and swung it shut, then sat back down. The color had come up again in her cheeks.

"But the real fun didn't start until we had the children. I, of course, was a terrible mother. I spoiled them, then I was too hard on them. I let them get away with murder, then wouldn't let them have any fun. I fed them the wrong food and made them wear awful clothes. I was ruining the girls because I didn't give them the example of a strong working woman, and ruining Saul because I was too soft on him. Except when I was too hard on him and squished his sensitive soul." She brushed her hair back from her forehead, drew a breath. "Well, we're getting into it now, aren't we?"

"It's all right."

"I know. I know." She paused. "Anyway, finally it got bad enough—Saul was about five at the time—that I told Theresa she couldn't come by anymore. She was relentless, poisoning the kids against me. I got Will to agree. So you know what she did then?"

"What?"

"Filed a petition for grandparents' visitation rights. Against *us*! By this time, she and Paul were divorced and she had nothing else in her life except her job and her grandkids. She just went off the deep end. Lord, what a time."

"So what happened?"

"So finally Paul got involved and made us all sit around and talk it out. Theresa really didn't want to break the family up, did she? And we didn't want the kids not to know their only grandma. Bottom line, she could come and visit whenever she wanted within reason, as long as she agreed not to criticize me anymore, especially in front of the kids."

"And how did that work out?"

"Surprisingly, pretty well. Although I still think she considers all eight grandchildren ultimately her responsibility because none of the families have done as well as Paul did. She's always double-checking us on how much we've saved for their colleges and the down payments on their starter homes. Down payments! I love that." A last sigh, and she offered an apologetic shrug. "Anyway, that's Theresa."

"Sounds charming." Hardy again consulted his watch, came back to her. "Do you feel like stopping? We've covered a lot. How are you holding up?"

A sudden warm expression transformed her face. "You know," she said, "I'm really okay." She paused. "Do you find it a little bit surreal that we're sitting here doing this?"

He smiled at her. "To be honest, yes."

"Okay. So it's not just me. Maybe you really haven't changed all that much after all."

"Except in every fiber of my being."

"Well, that, of course. The life thing."

"The life thing," he repeated, and a short silence settled between them.

She reached over and squeezed his hand. "I'm so glad I called you."

He nodded, blew out some air, tapped his pen against the legal pad. "So. Let's talk about after you left Paul's that night."

"All right," Catherine said, "what about it?"

"Everything," Hardy said, "beginning with what time it was."

She sat back, an elbow on the table. "A little after four, I'd say, four thirty."

"And what did you do then? After you left?"

She met his eyes, then looked quickly away and swallowed. She paused another moment. "I drove home, Dismas. Here. Straight here."

Hardy suddenly flashed on a time that she'd gone out with another guy. She'd looked him right in the eye and even swallowed the same as she did now as she denied it—and then she broke down in an admission, begging his forgiveness.

He almost expected her to have the same reaction now as he waited for her to retract the obvious lie. But she kept her composure this time, meeting his gaze. He made a mental note to return to this point—where had she gone after leaving Hanover's?—and pressed on. "Were your kids here when you got home?" He gave her a somewhat sheepish smile. "I'm really hoping you're going to say yes right about now."

"I wish I could, but they weren't."

Hardy hated that answer and must have shown it, because she hastened to explain. "I could show you in my calendar. It's really nothing sinister. Wednesdays they've all got something at school until five or six. Saul's got band. Polly's in the school play and Heather has yearbook. She's the editor. And since we all knew Will would be gone that night, I told them I could use a night off from cooking and to catch up on my bills. So I said why didn't they all rendezvous at school and go out for a pizza."

"Which they did?"

"Right. I assume so. I didn't ask."

Hardy took in a breath. "So you were home alone, paying bills and watching television until you saw the fire on TV?"

"That's right." She came forward. "I wasn't there, Dismas, at Paul's. I really was right here. All night before I went out."

"Okay, then," he said. "Although it would be a plus if we had any way to prove it. Did you call anybody? Go out to borrow some sugar?"

She brightened for a beat. "I called Mary, my sister-in-law. I wanted to tell her what Paul had said."

"That's good. And when was that?"

"As soon as I got home. I had to tell somebody."

"Okay, what about later?"

"Like when?"

"Five, six, seven?"

She shook her head. "I was just here, puttering around, having something to eat. One of the neighbors might have seen me pull in, or the car in the driveway."

"That would be helpful," Hardy said, "but let's not hold our breath." He thought for a beat. "So you don't really have an alibi."

"I was watching television. I've got the dish. Maybe there's some way they can verify that I was using it."

Hardy made a note, decided to leave the topic for one that was potentially even more explosive. "Okay, Catherine. This one you're really not going to like. Did you come on in any way to Inspector Cuneo?"

Her jaw clamped down tight. "No, I did not."

"Because he's going to say you did."

"Yes, I suppose he will."

"And you did nothing that he might have construed as some kind of sexual advance?"

"Dismas, please."

He held up his hands. "I've got to ask. It wouldn't be very much fun if he had something that he dropped at trial."

"Let's not say 'trial' yet, all right?" She shook her head. "But no. There was nothing."

"Because from what I'm hearing tonight, he can't have

much of a case. Unless he finds something like gasoline or gunshot residue on your clothes, which isn't going to happen, is it?"

"No."

"Okay, then. So what's probably happening is exactly what you said. That he heard about your accusation of sexual harassment . . ."

"But I didn't file anything! I didn't do anything with it."

"Yes you did. You told his boss. Cuneo looks like a horse's ass and maybe worse. So now he serves the search warrant on you as a pure hassle, telling you that in spite of you going over his head, he hasn't been pulled from the case, he's still got his mojo working and you'd better not say anything else against him."

She considered that for a long moment. "Well, in a way it's almost good news, I suppose," she said. "It means they don't really think I killed Paul. They're just mad at me."

"That may be true," Hardy said. "But don't underestimate how unpleasant cops can make your life if they're mad at you."

"Well, I'm not going to talk about the harassment anymore. He'll see he made his point and just leave me alone."

"Let's hope," Hardy said. "Let's hope."

13

At a little after nine the next morning, the extended Glitsky family was sitting in bright sunshine at one of the six outdoor tables on the sidewalk in front of Leo's Beans & Leaves, a thirty-year-old family-run tea and coffee shop/delicatessen at the highest point of Fillmore Street, just before it fell precipitously down to the Marina. Abe and Treya were splitting a smoked salmon quiche, drinking tea, while Rachel was happily consumed with negotiating a toasted bagel and some slices of lox from the knee of her grandfather Nat.

Who was trying to lecture his son. "Abraham, listen to what you say yourself, and you have your answer. You are the deputy chief of inspectors. This Cuneo putz is an inspector, which puts him under you. Am I right?"

"Technically."

Nat was closing in on eighty years old, but his mind was sharp enough that already this morning he had completed the Sunday *New York Times* crossword puzzle. He gave Treya a conspiratorial glance. "So 'technically' he gives me." Then, to Abe. "What's to be technical about? Take him off the case."

"How am I supposed to do that, Dad?"

"What, this is a mystery? You've got rank and the mayor on your side. You just do it."

"And why? Because I don't like him?"

A shrug. "There's worse reasons, I can tell you. If all else fails . . ."

Treya jumped in to her husband's defense. "But Abe can't do it without cause, Nat," she said. "He'd have to bring charges of obstruction or even of insubordination against him. . . ."

"Or the sex stuff. How about that?"

"That, too," she said, "if he had any proof."

"Although since our witness—or should I now say suspect?—declined to file a complaint," Glitsky put in, "proof is not forthcoming." He took a bite of quiche and washed it down. "Anyway, even saying that I do show cause and try to get him busted off the case, he'll just grieve it with the P.O.A."—the policemen's union—"and probably win, seeing that it was his case to begin with and I'm the interloper. That's how the union's going to see it, I guarantee. Here's a good cop minding his own business, doing his job according to the book, and suddenly the brass shows up, no doubt going political . . ." He shrugged. "You see where this is going."

"But it makes no sense," Nat said.

"Okay," Treya said, "and your point is?"

"That *was* my point. It's all backwards."

"Dad, you've got to catch up with the times. Making sense is a low-priority item. The city's got way more important things to worry about than making sense."

Nat came back at his son. "So you're saying you've got to work with him? Cuneo."

"No, not really. I've tried that. He seems to have rejected it."

"So what's that leave? You quit the case?"

"Can't do that either."

"So?"

"So I play his game."

"Which is?"

"Ignore the other guy. I go about my business. I gather evidence, pursue leads. I *investigate*. Maybe find something he missed."

"I wouldn't be surprised," Treya said, "if he's missing the boat entirely."

Glitsky drank tea and nodded. "That would be sweet and wouldn't shock me either. But he obviously got a warrant pulled, so he got enough to convince a judge. In any event, he's in a hurry to cut me out, moving fast and maybe loose, and the evidence might not back him up.

"As far as I know, he's not even aware of Tow/Hold or Hanover's other business. Or even the other family members. There's just a lot out there and Cuneo's only looking at one part of it, and one that just more or less fell into his hands on top of that. Usually, it doesn't work that way."

It was Glitsky's first time in the mayor's private residence, an East Coast–style four-story brownstone a few blocks down from the crest of Nob Hill, in the neighborhood of Grace Cathedral, the Fairmont and Mark Hopkins hotels.

He'd called Kathy West and asked if he could drop by for a few minutes, so she was expecting him and answered the door herself. She wore a light yellow no-nonsense blouse and a skirt of stylish brown tweed and low heels, and Glitsky had the impression that she was planning to go out shortly to another of the endless appearances that seemed to make up her life. After greeting him cordially, she led him through the house and outside to a nice-sized garden and patio of red brick, with a circular table and umbrella, a small fountain bubbling up out of a well-tended flower bed, a hot tub and a large, built-in barbecue. Surrounding homes, the same height as the mayor's, lent to the place a refined feeling of privacy, while a corridor through the adjacent backyards let the sunshine in.

The mayor took a chair at the table and motioned for Glitsky to do the same, which he'd barely accomplished before she flashed a professional smile and began. "I must say, Abe, I was surprised and impressed to get your call on a Sunday morning. You're not taking a day of rest?"

"Well, some things have come up." He started in with Cuneo, with Catherine Hanover's allegation of his sexual harassment, the search warrant. When he finished, West came forward in her crisp manner, her legs crossed, her hands tightly clasped in her lap. "Why wouldn't this woman file a complaint? Do you think he did harass her?"

"I have no way of knowing. He's been known to hit on witnesses in other cases, but that's not necessarily proof of anything in this one."

She cocked her head to one side. "It isn't?"

"Unfortunately, technically, legally, no."

"That's funny. A history like that seems somewhat . . . persuasive to me."

Glitsky allowed a ghost of a smile. "Well, the Hanover woman isn't pursuing it, so it's a nonissue. My concern, and what I wanted to talk to you about, is that I don't step on his investigation if he is in fact on to something."

"And how would you do that?"

"A dozen ways, really. Closing in on a suspect is kind of a carefully orchestrated ballet, and I don't want to spook his witnesses if he's already got them talking."

"So basically, what you're saying is he's cutting you out?"

He nodded. "Of course I could make a stink, pull rank, all that nonsense. But all that would do is stop the investigation." Now Glitsky shrugged. "It's entirely possible he's got her, and she did it, which is what you wanted. My question is: How hard do you want me to push to stay in?"

West frowned, scratched at the fabric of her skirt. "I'd just like to be sure," she said.

Glitsky moved his chair slightly, into the shade of the umbrella, then sat back in a casual attitude, which was nothing like how he felt. It was time to call the mayor's bluff. "Do you want to tell me why again? The real reason."

Her chin came up. She blinked rapidly three or four times. "What do you mean?"

He held her gaze. "I think you know what I mean." He used her name on purpose. "Kathy."

She looked away, staring into some empty space over his shoulder. "No, I don't. Really, I don't."

"Okay, maybe I can help you." Glitsky spoke quietly, his face locked down. "You're afraid that Paul Hanover might have been a warning to you. And if he was, you don't want to misconstrue it."

She sat stock still for a long moment, then some tension went out of her. She almost seemed to smile. "Frank Batiste was right," she said, "you *are* good." She drew in a breath. "It started just after I got elected, with Harlan." She didn't have to explain to Glitsky whom she meant. Harlan Fisk was her nephew, an overweight, often jovial, supremely political animal who'd worked for a time as an inspector under Glitsky in homicide, and who now was one of the city's eleven supervisors.

"Harlan's connected to this?"

"No. Not directly, anyway. But when Tow/Hold saw how

the wind was blowing with me, they offered him a job. Security director."

Glitsky almost laughed, but he didn't think this was funny. "Because he'd been a cop?"

"Partly. Mostly, I think, because we're related and they thought he could influence me."

"What does the security director of Tow/Hold do, exactly?" Glitsky asked.

This brought a prim smile to the mayor's mouth. "In theory, he coordinates the off-duty regular city officers and the rent-a-cop staff that guard the lots. In practice, not much. In spite of which it pays pretty well." The smile was gone. "In case you were wondering, a hundred and forty thousand dollars. It was a bribe, plain and simple," West went on. "Harlan turned them down flat, said he didn't want any part of it."

"So then they went to Hanover?"

West nodded. "He—I'm talking about Paul now—Paul told me he'd had threats, but that he didn't put any stock in them. They came with the territory, he said. Happened all the time, nothing to worry about. Then when ..." She wound down and stopped. "I didn't know how to handle it, Abe. I'm sorry. I didn't mean to be underhanded or duplicitous with you. But I didn't know what to do. I still don't. I'm afraid, if you must know the truth. And you know, a mayor—particularly a woman mayor—can't appear to be afraid. Venal, petty, selfish, arrogant, anything else, but not that."

Glitsky clipped off his words. "You could have just asked me directly."

"I didn't know how to do that. You're rather famously nonpolitical and I didn't want to contaminate you." She held a hand up. "I'm not flattering you. You wouldn't have even started if you'd thought this was all just about politics. If it's any consolation, I didn't know myself exactly what I expected you to do."

He hesitated, then said, "You should know that I've already talked to Nils Granat."

Even in the warm morning, she suppressed a shiver. "It's all so nebulous," she said. "On the one hand, I can't imagine it's real, that someone would kill a wonderful man like

Paul Hanover over a business deal. On the other, if they could do that . . ."

Glitsky had spent a lot of time and energy on this already, all of it under false pretenses, and realizing that put him in a cold fury. His patience—always thin under the best conditions—was gone. He wasn't in the mood for her conjectures. He cut off her. "Excuse me," he said, "but what do you want me to do now? That's the question. Leave it to Cuneo?"

West's eyes went up. She drew a quick breath. "That's the other thing."

"What is?"

"Inspector Cuneo. You know that hundred-and-forty-thousand-dollar job I told you about with Tow/Hold?"

Hardly able to credit what he was hearing, Glitsky squinted into the sun. "Cuneo's up for it," he said. His voice rang hollow in his ears.

West's shoulders sagged. "It's a lot more than cops make, even inspectors, as you know," she said. "When Harlan turned it down, word got out that the position was there, and several policemen applied. I've seen the list and Cuneo's one of them. Of course, there'll be no job for anyone if Bayshore gets the contract, but . . ."

"But Cuneo's not going to investigate them for these murders, no matter what. That's your point."

"That's right."

"So you want me to keep looking?"

"I think it's the only way we may get to the truth, don't you think?"

"Unless it comes out at the trial."

"What trial?"

"Catherine Hanover's."

West sighed again. "I don't believe it will come to that, Abe, and certainly not if she's innocent."

"Certainly not? Why not?"

West's expression of surprise was, he thought, like the MasterCard commercial—priceless. "Well, they'll find out before they get that far, I'm sure."

There was no point in arguing. Glitsky stood up. "In the event they don't, though?"

West stood, too, moved a step toward him, put a hand on

his arm. "Whatever you can do, Abe," she said with great, if unintentional, ambiguity. "I'd really appreciate it if you stayed involved."

He bit back his first three responses, all inappropriate. This was, after all, the political leader of San Francisco. He mustered a salute. Unintentionally, if anything is truly un-intentional, his words came out as ambiguous as hers had been. "I'll see what I can do," he said.

The picture of Catherine Hanover that Cuneo had snapped when she'd gone out to get her newspaper on Saturday morning turned out to be a good likeness. He'd used his 35mm Canon with an excellent close-up lens and good color film and had snapped seven shots in rapid succession, then printed them out in eight-by-ten format. In the one he liked the most, she was looking directly at him, so much so that he wondered if she'd in fact seen him, but her reaction of absolute shock when he'd knocked at her door fifteen minutes later with the warrant had been, he was sure, completely genuine. She'd had no clue.

What he liked about the picture wasn't merely how good she looked—no surprise, since Catherine Hanover seemed to get more attractive with every sighting—but that the angle was so very close to the one in the newspaper picture of Missy D'Amiens that he'd been showing around. Not only that, Missy's hair had been up in an elegant coif, and Catherine, obviously and recently post-shower, had hers wrapped in a towel. So nothing blocked the contours of ei-ther face. The biggest difference was that Missy was smil-ing, at a party, and Catherine's expression was inward. She was nearly frowning.

When he had first put the two pictures together, they confirmed what he'd noticed from the first time he'd seen the Missy photo. The two women weren't close enough in looks to be identical twins, of course, but the similarity be-tween them was marked. They could easily have been sis-ters. Both had high, broad foreheads, strong chins and noses, well-defined cheekbones. Both had a near-identical widow's peak at the hairline.

Maxine and Joseph Willis sat with Cuneo at around noon at the back of their house, this time, under the strong light in the kitchen. They were looking at both of the pictures now, side by side, in silence. After a half minute or so, Maxine raised her head and said to Cuneo, "You're bouncing the table, Inspector. If you're impatient, maybe you'd like to walk around while we look."

The identification issue, and the couple's disagreements over it, sat at the table with them all like an unwelcome guest. Cuneo was inclined to let them take whatever time they needed, but it was difficult for him not to move while he waited. After Maxine spoke to him, he asked if he could get a glass of water, and so he was over by the sink when Joseph turned in his chair and said, "If I had to swear, I'd say it was Missy."

This was not what Cuneo had been hoping to hear, but now Maxine—who'd at first been so certain that the woman she'd seen had been Missy—was shaking her head from side to side.

"You don't agree, Mrs. Willis?" Cuneo asked. He was back at the table with his glass of water, pulling up his chair again. She reached out and put her index finger on the color picture of Catherine. "I *know* I've seen this girl before," she said. "You look again, Joseph!"

The small man drew the photo back directly in front of him and stared down at it. Joseph clearly didn't want to discuss this with his wife any longer. Now she was saying—wasn't she?—that it had *not* been Missy D'Amiens on last Wednesday. And more, that the person they'd both seen had been the woman in this other picture.

Joseph, in his heart, wasn't completely certain that it had been either of them. If the truth be known, Joseph hadn't been looking too carefully at the woman's face at all. He'd assumed it was his attractive neighbor, whose walk he'd often admired, but this time he'd been more drawn to the woman's generous bosom. That, and not her face at all, was the reason he'd entertained his doubts over whether the woman had been Missy D'Amiens. She'd just seemed, well, *bigger*. As for the face, he couldn't swear that he'd even glanced at it.

Now he looked up at Cuneo. "I'm going to let my bride here make the call on this one, Inspector. She knows very well who she saw. If she says it's this woman in the color picture that we saw last Wednesday, then that's who it was."

As advertised, Jeffie from the Valero station was working on Sunday, manning the cash register. Cuneo had learned from his earlier experience with the Willises and this time only brought the picture of Catherine Hanover in with him.

Jeffie didn't have to look for very long. "Yep," he said. "She the one."

Coming out to the living room from the back half of the duplex, Treya Glitsky sagged against the doorway to the kitchen. "Okay, she's down."

Finally getting around to reading the Sunday *Chronicle*, Glitsky sat sideways in the leather love seat by their front windows, which he'd opened to let in the fresh air. It was early afternoon and sunlight spilled over him. The tone in his wife's voice sparked concern, and he put his section down, started to rise. "Are you all right?"

She nodded wearily, then barely lifted a hand, motioning for him to stay seated. "Thank God she still takes her nap."

"I hear you. But you don't look too good."

"I don't feel too good." She closed her eyes for a moment. "I know it's unusual, but would you mind terribly if I just took a minute and lay down for a while? I don't mean to be boring, but it's like somebody suddenly just pulled the plug. I don't know what it is."

"I can guess."

"You think? The pregnancy?"

He shrugged. "It's pretty normal, isn't it?"

She let out a deep breath, fatigue all over her. "Not for me. I never got any kind of morning sickness or anything with Raney or Rachel. Neither of them."

"So this one's different." He pointed. "Go, sleep."

She dropped her head and sighed, but didn't move. "Wake me up when she does."

"No promises. Do you want me to carry you in?"

"No, really. I just need a couple of minutes."

"Okay. Go, then."

He got up and walked across to her. She was standing

with her eyes closed, all but asleep on her feet. Peeling her off the doorpost, he put his arm around her. "I'm sorry," she mumbled, "I'm just so tired."

Five minutes later, she was covered up in their darkened bedroom. Glitsky closed the door to the hallway and returned to the living room. There he took a few steps toward his paper, but stopped as though some physical force had restrained his movement. He stood in the center of the room, hands at his sides. Closing his eyes, he let out a stream of air and realized that he'd been holding his breath. He wasn't aware of any noise, even from the street through the open windows. He drew another deep breath. Another. Closed his eyes again.

Perhaps a minute passed. In the house, all was Sunday-afternoon stillness.

When he opened his eyes, the rectangle of sunlight had grown and it now covered the whole love seat and a few inches of floor. He realized that, incredibly for San Francisco, it was almost uncomfortably warm in the room. He walked to the front door and opened it for some cross-ventilation, then went to the refrigerator, took out a bottle of iced tea and drank half of it down in a gulp.

What had been his sons' rooms when they'd lived with him were down a hall behind the kitchen on the opposite side of the duplex from his own bedroom. Now his youngest boy Orel's old room was Rachel's, and at her door Glitsky turned the knob gently and went to stand over her bed—still a crib, really, with the bars up. She was sleeping soundly, sprawled on her back, her breathing regular and deep, and he couldn't resist putting his palm down flat over her chest. She didn't stir. He felt a vibration at his belt, someone paging him. The number wasn't immediately familiar and his initial reaction was to ignore it, go finish reading the Sunday paper, maybe let himself doze off like the rest of the world.

Instead, in the kitchen, he picked up the wall phone's receiver and punched in the number.

"Hello."

"This is Abe Glitsky. You just paged me. Who is this?"

"Dan Cuneo. We need to talk about Catherine Hanover."

* * *

Assistant DA Chris Rosen didn't mind being bothered about work at home on a Sunday night, least of all by a homicide inspector with a big case. He lived in a small, stand-alone bungalow in the flats of Emeryville, across the bay from San Francisco, not more than six miles from Cuneo's place in Alameda. The inspector's long day in the city had come to an end, and the two men decided they'd meet up at the bar of Spenger's Fish Grotto, just off the freeway in Berkeley.

They arrived almost simultaneously. By the time they got their drinks—the place was packed and it took a while—Cuneo had brought him pretty much up-to-date. Three witnesses had definitely identified Catherine Hanover from her picture as the woman who'd 1) purchased the Valero gasoline in a portable container and 2) left the Hanover house about a half hour before the fire. Cuneo had taken the rug sample from the back of Catherine Hanover's car directly to Arnie Becker, since the regular police lab probably wouldn't be able to get to it within a week. Becker had ready access to the fire department's own mass spectrometer, and yes, in fact, the gasoline in her trunk was Valero, the same brand that had started the fire. He'd luminoled the pants from her closet himself, and though he'd found no evidence of blood spatter, he'd dropped the clothes at the police lab and was hoping they'd find something useful.

Throughout this recital, Rosen sipped his Scotch and said nothing. After Cuneo stopped, he signaled the waitress for another round for both of them and said, "Don't get me wrong, Dan. There's nothing I'd like more than to be able to move on this. But you've got to admit that you don't have much in the way of evidence."

Cuneo was ready for this. "I didn't expect much. The fire burned it all up. But she denies being near Hanover's house when one of my witnesses put her there. Same day she got the gas around the corner. She did it, Chris, I swear to God."

"I'm not saying I don't believe you." He centered his empty glass on his napkin. "Last time you mentioned a motive, but we didn't get to it."

Cuneo spent a little time spinning it out. Aside from his work on the warrant and this morning's identifications, in the past two days, he'd spoken to all the other members of Paul Hanover's nuclear family except Catherine's husband, and no one denied that his coming marriage to Missy D'Amiens and the possible change to the inheritance was a very big concern to all of them.

What set Catherine apart from her other relatives was the fact that she'd gone to Paul's *that day* to "have it out" with him. "Her own words from the first night I talked to her at the fire—'have it out.' One sister and the mother-in-law both had heard her say it. And now we know she was at the house not just in the afternoon when she admitted it, but later, just before the fire."

"Anybody see her walk in there, with the gas?"

"Not yet, no."

"Or walk out with it?"

"She left it in the house. Arnie Becker's got the container with the other stuff from the house down at the station." One of an arson inspector's most tedious yet most important jobs after a fire was to go through the ash and debris in a three- or four-foot radius around a body and sort *everything*—the burned and destroyed remains of furniture, floors, walls, clothing, appliances, knickknacks, jewelry—until they had identified every item down to the size of a match head, to see if any of it might be relevant to their investigation. "No prints, if that's what you were thinking."

"Hoping." Rosen frowned. "Anything else?"

"Yeah. The day after the fire, after we'd had this talk at the scene . . ."

"Wait a minute. She was at the fire itself? I'm not sure I realized that."

"That's when I first talked to her."

"Okay, go on."

"So she tells me—this is at the fire now—that she'd heard that Paul and Missy had been fighting, setting it up for the murder/suicide story. Then, next day, I go to talk to her at her house, and by now she realizes that we've ruled that out. Not only that, the other stuff she told me, she's implicated herself and she knows I know it. So what does she do?"

"Tell me."

"Calls Glitsky—you know Glitsky? Deputy chief?— anyway, she calls him and says I sexually harassed her." He held up a hand. "The answer is no, not a chance. But she told Glitsky she didn't want to talk to me anymore."

"So after Glitsky stopped laughing, what did he tell her?"

"Well, wait, this is getting to the good part." Their drinks arrived and both men lifted their glasses. "Glitsky comes and tells *me* that from now on, he's on the case with me. . . ."

"What, you mean personally?"

"Personally. The mayor asked him."

Now Cuneo had Rosen's complete attention. "What? Why?"

A nod. "It gives one pause, doesn't it? So he says from now on he'll be questioning Catherine Hanover. He's trying to protect me from the sex charge."

"So she filed?"

"Funny thing. She decided not to." Cuneo drank again. "Wait, it gets better. We've got Glitsky and Kathy West somehow connected to Catherine, right? So now I'm starting to wonder. They're pulling me off when she looks good to me. I come to you on Friday, get the warrant this weekend, do some digging. Finally, couple of hours ago, I call Glitsky to keep him in the loop as he's requested. I tell him what I got, the fucking gasoline, the motive, two positive IDs, Catherine's lying about where she was and when. She's it. I say we ought to bring it to you and get her in the grand jury before she blows town."

"And what was his response?"

"Bad idea, he says. Too soon. We really don't have anything on her. He says there's still a lot of questions. We don't want to rush to judgment. Plus, and we should know this, this is really my favorite . . ."

"What?"

"She hired herself a lawyer. You know Dismas Hardy?"

"The name, yeah."

"Well, guess what? He's Glitsky's pal. They used to be cops together." He finished his drink and leaned back in satisfaction, tapping his toes to beat the band. "What we've got here, Chris, isn't just a sweet little double murder. There's some major conspiracy going on with these guys, going all the way up to the mayor. This city is lousy with politics, and these guys are smack-dab in the middle of it. And you want my opinion? Just between us. It doesn't start here, with Hanover. I'm betting it started back before Barry Gerson got killed."

"You mean *Lieutenant* Gerson?"

"My old boss, yeah. And a great guy."

"I thought ... wasn't he killed at some shoot-out? I thought it was some Russian gang thing."

"Maybe. That's what they want you to believe. But the whole mess wasn't ever really investigated, not carefully enough anyway. And here's a factoid for you—one of the guys killed in the shoot-out with Gerson was a guy named John Holiday, wanted for murder at the time. And guess who his attorney was?"

"Got to be Hardy."

Cuneo made a gun with his fingers, pointed it at Rosen and pulled the trigger. "He and Glitsky both were all over that Holiday case. It's ugly as shit, Chris."

"So how does Catherine Hanover fit in? Or Paul?"

"I don't know yet, but I'll tell you one thing. She did him." He tipped up his glass and drank off the whole thing. Eyes shining, he came forward in his chair. "This is the biggest case you're ever going to be part of, and we've got to get this damned woman locked up before the whole thing blows away in the dust. Because believe me, these people can make it happen."

14

As soon as Hardy's children were out the door to school on Monday morning, he and Frannie unplugged the main telephone jack, turned off their own cell phones and repaired upstairs to their bedroom.

An hour later, Hardy climbed the stairs again, this time bearing two fresh cups of coffee. "It occurs to me," he said, "that carrying hot coffee in a state of undress might not be wise."

"No risk, no reward," Frannie said. "Besides, it's a good fantasy moment. Being waited on by a naked slave and all."

He bowed from the waist. "Your servant, madam." Handing her a mug, he slid in beside her, pulled a sheet over himself. "Your fantasy slave looks like me?"

"Who else would he look like?"

"I don't know. Brad Pitt, maybe. Who's that new guy Rebecca loves?"

"Orlando Bloom?"

"Yeah, him."

"He's not that new, but why would I want either of them?"

"Well, we're talking fantasy, right? Your average fifty-something lawyer isn't exactly fantasy material."

"Who's talking average?" She lifted the sheet away, looked him up and down. "Yep. Works for me. Just did, in fact. Plus, the coffee's perfect, thank you. Brad and Orlando, those other guys, they'd probably burn it or something." She took another sip. "So speaking of fantasies . . ."

"What?"

She gave him a don't-kid-me look. "Have you decided what you're going to do with Catherine?"

"Well, first, Catherine is not my fantasy. You're my fantasy."

"All right, but you have to say that."

"I don't have to say anything like that."

"But I just did, so if you didn't, you'd be in trouble."

"That doesn't mean I don't mean it. Seriously. You don't think this is a fantasy? Monday morning, nobody home but us up here alone? Taking time out on a workday to make love? Do you know what we'd have done for this moment even a couple of years ago?"

"Probably killed small cute furry animals."

"At least."

"But you still haven't told me about Catherine."

"That's because, truly, I haven't decided. The main thing is, I don't think it's likely they're going to charge her. Cuneo's just rattling her cage."

"But if they do?"

"Charge her?" He turned to her. "I wouldn't take it if it would make you uncomfortable."

"It's not just me. There's this whole Cuneo thing. I know Abe's definitely worried. . . ."

"But Abe worries for a hobby."

"Okay, but he's got a reason this time. Cuneo could make a big mess for both of you. If anything about that day ever comes out . . ."

"Actually," Hardy said, "that's one of the reasons the nasty side of me is almost hoping they go ahead and charge her and try to make a case with this lousy evidence."

"What reason is that?"

"Cuneo. Unless he strikes gold—or Hanover's blood on Catherine's stuff—he's got a weak case he's rushing in on. Abe says he's a sloppy investigator. That's just who he is. So depending on how fast and loose he decides to play, give me a chance to get him on a witness stand and I'll bet I can do some serious damage to his basic credibility as a cop. At least enough so nobody would be inclined to go on a wild goose chase after me and Abe on his say-so. I'd almost look forward to the chance."

Frannie sipped at her coffee. "If you turned her down, how much would it cost the firm?"

Hardy considered for a minute. "High-profile murder

trial? Three to five hundred thousand, maybe more. Plus, maybe, referrals."

"So do you want to do it?"

"We're not there yet. Maybe we won't get there. But really, as I said, if you've got a problem with it . . ."

"Then I'm an insecure bitch."

"Not at all. It's completely legitimate that you'd be uncomfortable. Me and Catherine went together for four *years*. That's a significant chunk of time. Obviously, as I've already told you, there's still a connection. There'll always be some connection."

"And she's still attractive." Not a question.

He nodded. "She's very good-looking. But, you know, we've already done the fantasy thing with you and me this morning. I'm yours, you're mine. Like that."

"Yes, but here's a case where you can help someone you care about who you think is probably innocent and make half a million or more dollars in the bargain, and at the same time you'd get to professionally destroy someone who's out to get you and Abe. How can I ask you *not* to take it?"

Hardy put his coffee cup down, reached over and pulled his wife close against him. "You say, 'Diz, I'd just prefer you let someone else take this one.'"

"I'm not going to do that."

"Well, that is your decision, Flaversham." Hardy quoting a longtime household favorite line from Disney's *The Great Mouse Detective*. "And I haven't made my own decision yet, either."

"You can't turn her down if she needs you."

"Somebody else could defend her."

"But who as well as you?"

"Well . . ."

"But between us," Frannie added, cutting him off, "it is a little scary."

Just off the main lobby in Hardy's Sutter Street offices, the Solarium conference room contained a profusion of greenery—rubber trees, ferns, dieffenbachia. One of the associates had even brought a redwood tree in a two-hundred-gallon pot; thriving, its trunk was a foot thick and its boughs scraped the glass ceiling.

Now, after he and Frannie had continued their morning date with an early lunch, cell phones off, at Petit Robert, Hardy sat in one of the sixteen chairs that surrounded the immense mahogany table in the center of the room. Waiting for him on his arrival at the office were three urgent calls from Catherine Hanover—the first when the police had come early in the morning to serve a subpoena for her to appear *tomorrow* to testify in front of the grand jury, the second when Cuneo had arrived personally to deliver another search warrant at her house, and the third in a barely controlled, *I need help right now* hysteria, similar in tone to the first call he'd gotten from her on Saturday night. He called her right back and told her to get down to the office as soon as she could. She was barely coherent. Her voice had been choked and hoarse—"I'm sorry. I can't seem to stop crying."

Hanging up, he put in a call to Abe's pager. He wondered what, if anything, had happened on Sunday, or maybe Saturday, with the results of the first search warrant. Had the lab in fact uncovered significant evidence?

Clear on what he next wanted to do, Hardy forced himself to take a moment before he did it. Every action he took now as Catherine's de facto lawyer moved him closer to the decision he hadn't yet consciously made. But at each small incremental step, he didn't seem to be able to stop himself. *Of course* he would call Catherine back after her three urgent calls. What else could he do? *Of course* he would page Glitsky and try to discover what the police had come up with. On some level, he felt he didn't really have a choice. But up until now, his moves had been small and personal. What he contemplated next was larger and more public. He wanted more certainty about his commitment before he moved.

Whether it was more hangover from the guilt he'd felt at the way he'd had to drop her so long ago or a testament to the bond they'd once forged together, he couldn't deny that between him and Catherine there remained a strong personal connection. They'd come of age in the same culture—it had been immediately clear to Hardy on Saturday night at her house, when they'd easily fallen into a comfortable familiarity, even with the hard questions. The plain fact was that she'd been his first love, and the person he'd become could not bring himself to abandon her when she needed him so badly. Even as he recognized that she might—he told himself it was an infinitesimally small chance—even now be playing him.

Because she knew she could.

But that, he told himself, was *her* fate, *her* karma. Hardy himself had no choice but to be true to his own character, and to trust that she would not betray him.

Finally, telling Phyllis to interrupt him if Glitsky called, he rang up the district attorney's office, where he talked to the relatively new chief assistant district attorney, Craig Bellarios, about the grand jury subpoena. There was really only one question Hardy needed to have answered, and that was whether his client—*his client!*—was considered a "target" of the investigation, i.e., a suspect, as opposed to a witness.

Bellarios, who didn't know Hardy very well, wasn't the most forthcoming man on the planet. He told Hardy that he couldn't predict what the grand jury would do, and that it was always wise to be prepared for any eventuality. Thanking him for nothing, Hardy asked and did learn the name of the presenting prosecutor—Chris Rosen—and called him next, but he was out.

He sensed a stonewall and it tightened his stomach. If things had gotten to this juncture already, he had no choice but to tell Catherine to plead the Fifth Amendment before the grand jury and to refuse to talk anymore to the police. And in the terrible catch-22 of the legal game, once she adopted that strategy, though technically she'd still be a witness, in the eyes of the prosecution she would have moved a long way toward becoming the target of the investigation.

Now, with his legal pad and another cup of coffee on the table in front of him, Hardy was cramming with a single-minded attention, reviewing all the notes he'd taken at Catherine's on Saturday night. Feeling her presence as soon as she entered the lobby, he looked up, stood and walked over to the Solarium door. "Catherine."

If she'd been crying, there was no sign of it anymore, other than maybe an added luminosity to her eyes. She wore a well-tailored khaki-colored pantsuit. Hardy was thinking that he was glad she'd chosen demure even as she turned toward him to reveal a light tangerine garment with a lace top, a sweep of décolletage underneath the jacket. An elegant chain of malachite beads encircled her neck and rested in the deep hollow of her chest. He realized that she'd had her breasts enlarged.

But he'd hardly digested these impressions when she stepped into his arms. Vaguely aware of the stares of Phyllis and Norma, the office manager, and a pair of paralegals who had stopped at the reception area for something, Hardy held her against him for the briefest of seconds, then turned to the gathered multitudes and introduced her, all business, as an old friend and new client.

A new client.

Back in the Solarium, they got seated and Hardy asked if he could see the subpoena. "You got this this morning?"

"Seven o'clock. I was hardly out of bed."

"They're still hassling you."

"I thought so, too. And they're doing another search. Is that unusual?"

He didn't answer that one. Instead, he asked, "When did they do this, the search? At seven, too?"

"No. Nine or so. They were separate. Cuneo was with the second bunch. I called you again."

"I had business this morning," Hardy said. "I called back as soon as I got in. Was Glitsky with the search team this time?"

"I don't think so. I've never met him, but I'm sure that wasn't the other name. I would have remembered."

"So what were they looking for this time?"

"I don't know. Everything, I think. They went upstairs and just started in."

Hiding his exasperation, Hardy smiled helpfully. "They list specifics on the warrant. Did they show that to you?"

"No."

"What about your husband? Wasn't he there? Did he ask to see the warrant, by any chance?"

She looked down, scratched at the fabric of her pants. "Will's taken a . . ." She stopped. "He's not home right now."

Hardy waited.

After a minute, she wiped an eye with her finger, then the other one. Reaching down, she opened her purse and removed a small package of Kleenex, brought one of the tissues up to her face. "This is anger, not sadness." She dabbed at her eyes some more, sniffed once, clenched the Kleenex in her fist. "He started having another affair," she said without looking at him. "The son of a bitch."

Hardy said the first thing that came to his mind. "So he wasn't fishing last Wednesday?"

She kept her eyes straight in front of her. "He was in Southern California, though. That's where they met up. On the same goddamn boat as the last one." Finally, she cast a sidelong glance at him. "I'm sorry about the language, and I didn't mean to lie to you about Will and me the other night." Again, a labored breath. "Anyway, after you left on Saturday, it blew up. He made some smart-ass remark about you and me. . . ."

"You and me?"

"All the time we spent talking, just making it sound sleazy."

"I was there as your *lawyer*, Catherine." Hardy didn't like being cast as the wedge between wife and husband, but he immediately regretted referring to himself as her lawyer. It seemed to be another irrevocable step.

"Of course you were. What else could you be? But you have to know Will. As though he needed a real reason to pick a fight. Anyway, he was slandering you, too, and I just thought, 'How dare he?' and lost it. I threw him out."

"He thought you didn't know about the affair?"

"He must have thought I was an idiot. He even wanted to . . . to have sex with me when he got home, maybe so I wouldn't suspect he'd been rutting around for four days. The bastard." A bitter little sound escaped. "I thought if I could avoid bringing it up, it might stay hidden from the kids. I used to hope I could hold out until Heather went to college, then I could file for divorce. The kids wouldn't really be in our lives as much, so it would be easier. This last time, though, last week, I realized I couldn't do that anymore. I couldn't go on that way. But I still hadn't really *decided*, you know?"

"Decided what, exactly?"

"When I'd call him on it. Move out or have him do it. Bring it to a head. I didn't want it to just *happen* the way it did. I wanted to control the timing, at least. Now I'm just feeling so ashamed of myself."

"For what?"

She turned in her chair and faced him. "Don't you see? For ruining our home life. Bringing it out into the open." She shrugged. "But something just snapped. Maybe it's all this being a suspect."

"If your husband was having an affair, how was it that *you* ruined your home life?"

"I know, it's stupid, but it's how I feel. If I were a stronger person, I could have kept pretending"—she motioned around the room ambiguously—"except for all this. And seeing you, in some way. Remembering how good you were, how sweet a relationship could be. It all broke me down."

"I'm sorry if I had a role in it. I wouldn't have come over if . . ."

"No, no. It was going to happen sometime."

Hardy let a moment pass. Then said, "So that's why you went to your father-in-law's? To talk about this? Will's affair."

She couldn't hide her startled expression. "Why do you assume that?"

"Because that's what changed, Catherine. You're going about your normal life and your husband goes off with another woman. You're going to do *something*. I'm glad you didn't decide to follow him down and kill him."

"The thought crossed my mind."

"Let's keep that between us, okay?"

She found half a smile. "I wouldn't have killed him, Dismas. Or his father, either."

Hardy's antennae were all the way up. Without a conscious thought, he noted her use of the subjunctive and wondered if she'd done it on purpose. *She wouldn't have killed Paul, except for . . .*

And then something happened, and she'd had to. It was only a small feat of mental legerdemain. A child, Hardy thought, could do it. And they often did.

At the same time, part of him hated himself for realizing the fundamental truth that while what she'd just said *sounded* like an absolute denial of her guilt, in fact it was not. As a good, Jesuit-trained former Catholic, Hardy was often able to argue himself into a state of tolerable comfort in the outer reaches of moral ambiguity, and he knew that Catherine's education with the Mercy nuns had trained her in the same way. Hell, she'd been the acknowledged master—it was the thing he could never beat her at. And so now he also knew enough not to ask her for clarification; it would only complicate things down the line.

All this in the blink of an eye.

He asked her, "So what did you want to ask him? Paul, I mean?"

"The same thing I said last time, Dismas. I wanted to know what was going to happen to the money." She threw him a glance that he couldn't read. "He was going to marry Missy in the fall and change his will to make her his beneficiary. Maybe he'd leave a few thousand dollars to each of his grandchildren. That was it. They weren't doing a prenup."

"Why not? Did he say?"

"Because Missy wasn't out for his money, and Paul resented the hell out of his family for implying that she was. In fact, before the family had started the campaign, as he called it, he'd been inclined to set up trusts for the kids and all that. But then Will and Beth and Theresa, especially, wouldn't let it go. And the blind greed of it, he said, made him sick. His kids and their families were getting along just fine. And Missy had had a tremendously difficult life, we had no idea. Now it was her turn for comfort and security and he was going to give it to her. And too bad if we didn't like it."

"That sounds harsh."

She lifted her shoulders. "It didn't when he said it, though. He was a straight shooter. He'd worked hard to get his kids set on their way. Now they should do the same with theirs."

"So where did that leave you? Did you tell him about Will?"

"I didn't need to." She looked away. "He seemed to know, yes. To have known."

"You mean about Will's other affairs?"

She nodded. "Anyway, he gave me what I'd come to find out."

"And what did that mean to you?"

She worried her lower lip. "I wanted to know where I stood. I know it sounds mercenary, but I'd already endured more than a few rather difficult years with Will. If it looked like he was going to inherit several million dollars . . ." She stopped, unwilling to enunciate it.

"You might try to endure a few more?"

She scratched at her pants again. "I admit it sounds awful." She raised her eyes to his. "But if there wasn't ever going to be a windfall, if he signed it all over to her . . ."

"You might as well leave him now."

She bowed her head in tacit agreement. "I needed to know my options, Dismas." Then, "I hate him."

Outside the Solarium's glass walls, a tiny parklike area, a hundred or so square feet of open space tucked between the buildings, held a concrete bench that the associates had chipped in for in memory of David Freeman. Hardy spent a minute watching a few sparrows pecking around in the decomposed granite. Finally, he came back to her. "Had he changed his will?"

"He was going to . . . oh my God!" Her hand went to her mouth. "The will!"

"What?"

"That's today!"

Bob Townshend's office was on the same twentieth floor as Paul Hanover's in the Bank of America building. Its great windows afforded a stunning view of the city spread out below, with the sunlight glinting on the bay, far off the Golden Gate Bridge standing sentinel over the entrance to the harbor, and closer in the spires of the churches in North Beach. None of the Hanover relatives seated in front of Townshend's ultramodern chrome-and-glass desk paid it the slightest attention.

Theresa Hanover sat in the third chair from the right in the row of seven that Townshend had set up for the reading of the will. Will Hanover sat in the center chair, next to his mother. The chair next to him was empty, and beyond that to his left sat Mary and Carlos. On the other side of Theresa were Beth and her attorney husband, Aaron.

Townshend had finally put down his coffee cup and saucer at the service table against the inside wall and had come around to claim his seat behind the desk. Florid and overweight, Townshend—unlike his partner Paul Hanover—had never been comfortable interacting with actual living people. He enjoyed numbers and games and legal puzzles. He was also an excellent legal writer and a whiz at business strategy, which made him an invaluable partner to Hanover, but dealing with humans in the flesh was for him always a bit of a strain.

And never more than at a moment like this one, when things weren't going according to protocol. He'd scheduled the reading of Paul Hanover's will for one o'clock, and now it was nearly two, and still no sign—not even a phone call—from Catherine Hanover. Neither had she returned any of the several calls he'd made to her home, or to her cell phone. There was nothing absolutely critical about her attendance, of course. Her husband was here representing the family and that was enough, but even with his limited sensitivity to human emotions, Townshend sensed a tension in the group—especially between Will and his mother—that in turn made him nervous.

Now he checked his watch for the twentieth time, ran a finger under his very tight shirt collar, cleared his throat. Over an hour ago, he'd gone to his safe and removed the sealed Last Will & Testament of Paul Hanover, and placed it exactly in the center of his desk. Now he pulled the package toward him. "Well, then, if we're all in agreement . . ."

"Lord, Bob, we've waited long enough," Theresa said. "For some reason that I can't fathom or imagine, Catherine has decided she isn't coming. But her presence one way or the other doesn't make any difference anyway, so let's get this show on the road."

Mary, holding her silent Carlos's hand, spoke up in her timid voice. "Isn't anybody else worried about her?"

Will shot a glance across his mother at his younger sister. "I'm sure it's something with school and the kids," he said easily. "It's always school and the kids. You know that. More important than anything else."

"But you'd think this . . ." Aaron began.

Will cut him off. "She knows it's going to be what it's going to be. Her being here isn't going to change anything."

"Bob." Theresa, at the end of patience, used her most dismissive tone. "Either you open that damned folder or I'm going to take it from you and read it myself."

"Mom!" Beth said. "You don't have to be so difficult."

Theresa whirled on her elder daughter, her tone sharp and angry. "Don't you talk to me about difficult, young lady. I'm the one who knows how difficult it can be going it alone in this world. And I'm the one who wants to be sure that my grandchildren don't have to find out what that's like. That's why I'm here, and that's the only reason I'm here. I doubt if your father left me a dime." She came back front to Townshend. "Bob? Now. Please."

With a last look at Catherine's empty chair, he sighed and carefully unsealed the envelope.

"She called from here," Hardy said, "and they'd just read it."

"And he stops," Glitsky grumbled, half to himself. "You're going to make me guess?" He stood by one of the windows in Hardy's office, studying the traffic patterns—unmoving—on Sutter Street below. It was five thirty, still light out, still sunny.

"Of course not. I'll tell you." Hardy had his feet up on his desk. "If you just ask me politely, I'll tell you."

"All right." Glitsky took his hand off the window shade, half turned to face his friend. "I'm asking."

"Come on, Abe. Just say, 'Tell me about the will.'"

Glitsky threw his eyes to the ceiling, summoning all of his endurance. He sighed heavily. "Okay," he said, "tell me about the will."

Hardy shot back. "Say 'please.'"

"I don't think so." Shaking his head in disgust, Glitsky started walking over to the cherry cabinet where Hardy kept his darts. Glitsky hadn't stolen Hardy's darts in nearly six months now, and when he'd come in he'd been thinking that it was getting to be about that time again. If his friend happened to leave the room.

"If you just say 'please,' " Hardy was grinning broadly, "I promise I'll tell you."

Glitsky got to the cabinet and opened up the side doors to reveal the black, yellow, red and green "professional" dartboard within. Hardy's three custom tungsten darts were hanging in their little holders, blue flights attached. Glitsky pulled them and without a glance at Hardy walked to the dark-wood line in the light hardwood floor that had been inset seven feet, nine and one-quarter inches from the face of the board. Turning, he fired the first dart and hit a double bull's-eye, smack in the center of the board. He turned around again and put the two other darts on Hardy's desk.

"All right," Hardy said. "Bull's-eye counts as a 'please.' " He eyed the darts, looked up at Glitsky. "Hanover hadn't changed the will. Missy wasn't mentioned. All the money went to the family."

"How much?"

"Well." Hardy pulled his feet off the desk and grabbed the darts. "It's complicated, with the property and investments and various other liquidatable assets . . ."

"Liquidatable. Good word," Abe said.

"Thank you." Hardy was now around the desk and standing at the throw line. "But the best ballpark estimate looks like it's going to come out at something like seventeen, eighteen million." He threw the dart, then the next one in rapid succession. Two twenties. He leaned back against his desk. "Which of course isn't the best news in the world for Catherine."

"Or any of them," Glitsky said, "if they didn't all have alibis, which Cuneo says they do. Except the ex-wife, Theresa."

"Maybe it's nobody in the family. Are you getting anything on Tow/Hold?"

Glitsky shook his head. "I talked to a lot of people. Harlan Fisk, Granat again, went down to the corporate office in San Bruno. Swell group of folks. Nothing." Now he pushed himself against the back cushion and ran both hands over his buzz cut. "I know I'm a cop and ought to be glad we've got a suspect, but I don't want to think Cuneo has got this one right. Catherine doesn't *feel* right. Hasn't from the beginning."

"I love when you say that," Hardy said. In truth, though, he was far from sanguine. He flatly didn't believe, despite her low-key and self-effacing protestations to the contrary—*"I am so scattered lately. I think all this stress must be eating my brain cells."*—that Catherine had simply *forgotten* that the reading of the will was going to be today. She could have told him she didn't want to be in the same room as her husband, and okay, he could have possibly accepted that. But even with the distractions of a spouse's affair, a subpoena to testify before the grand jury and a police search of her house in progress, Hardy had to believe that your average person would probably remember that this was the day you found out if you were a millionaire or not. Sitting on his desk, the darts stuck in the board and forgotten, Hardy laid all of this out. "She didn't forget that today was the reading of the will, I promise you."

Glitsky, who'd settled on the first couple of inches of the couch, listened without interruption and when Hardy had finished said, "I admit it's improbable. So why would she pretend?"

"The drama of it. She didn't really need to be at the reading, did she? Her attendance wouldn't change anything. But she could make me feel her urgency, hook me into it."

"So call her on it and let her go."

"I know. I know. I'm tempted. Except what if she really did forget?"

"You just made a pretty good case that *that* wasn't likely."

"No, not likely, but not impossible, either." Absently, he pulled the darts from the board again. "This is the kind of thing she always did to me. It used to drive me crazy, but at least it was never dull."

"Dull gets a bad rap. Give me dull anytime."

Hardy broke a smile. "That's why you went into police work, right? For the slow times."

Glitsky shrugged. "I was younger."

"So was I. I loved the mystery."

"I thought it drove you crazy."

"That, too. It was complicated. In fact, it was too complicated. It was fucking exhausting, which was why I gave it up."

"You miss it?"

"Not at all."

"But here you are, taking her on."

"Yeah." A small silence settled. At last Hardy said, "She's not stupid, Abe. There's no reason she would have given you her own motive."

"Except if she knew that that's exactly what I'd think."

"The old double-reverse, huh?"

A shrug. "It happens. And in the same general vein, why wouldn't she file a complaint against Cuneo? If she'd have filed the first time I talked to her . . ."

"I know."

But Glitsky went ahead. "If she'd done that, end of story. He was off the investigation against her. But now it looks like she was trying to run him off with a bluff. And why had she wanted to run him off? Because he was getting close, and because she was guilty."

But Hardy said, "I don't know why she didn't file. A million reasons. Fear, mostly, then maybe embarrassment, finally just hoping it would go away. You know as well as I do."

Glitsky had come forward to the front of the couch again, elbows on his knees and hands clasped. He let out a heavy breath. "You want my advice?"

"No. You'll just tell me I don't want to do this."

"Right."

"So how do you propose I get out of it? Give her to somebody else?"

"It's possible."

Hardy shook his head. "Not in real life, it isn't. I believe I can help her. I know her. I *want* to help her."

Glitsky narrowed his eyes. "You believe her?"

"I think so. I'm not sure."

"Which one?"

"Right." Hardy shrugged. "I know. On the basic question— is she a killer?—I'm with her. Other than that . . ." He let the sentence hang. "Here's some good news, though. At least now I know she's got the money to pay me."

"You're billing her, then?"

"Double homicide, special circumstances. I'm billing her, trust me."

This seemed to give Glitsky a little relief. "Just making sure," he said.

PART
TWO

15

Hardy awoke with a start, sweat pouring off him.

Not that it was warm. In fact, if anything, it was unusually cold, not only inside his bedroom but out in the terrible night. It was the third week of January, and the second full day of the Arctic storm that was pounding at the bedroom windows, shaking them with a low rumble.

He threw the covers off and sat up, trying at once to remember and to banish the dream that had shaken him from his sleep. Reflexively, he checked the clock on his nightstand. 2:53. The trial would start in under seven hours. He had to get back to sleep. He couldn't show up on the first day wiped out with fatigue. There would be the gauntlet of reporters, first of all. Not only the local channels, but stringers for every station and cable outlet in the country had been parked in the back lot of the Hall of Justice for each of the motion hearings—to quash the warrant, to exclude Catherine's statements to the cops, admissibility, 995 for dismissal—they'd been there for all of them. And they'd be there this morning, too. The judge had forbidden any communication with them, but they could be relentless and he had to be sharp, get back to sleep.

Now.

The dream had been sexual, that much he remembered. He dreamed almost every night now, and they were all sexual, all mouths and legs, switched identities, all frustration and guilt and deception—his subconscious working overtime to process the conflicts and unacknowledged tensions to which he would give no assent in his daily life.

He wasn't in love with Catherine Hanover, but there was no point in trying to deny the attraction. He also ached at her plight, at where her life had gotten to. The physical chemistry between them had always been palpable. As teenagers, to their mutual pride, confusion, horror and shame, they'd gone from untried virgins to lovers without any commitment or discussion on their third date. The care they both took to avoid even the most innocuous and casual physical contact over the past months had been such a constant companion that it felt like a living thing in the visiting room with them.

She'd been in jail for nearly eight months for a crime that with all his heart he wanted to believe she'd not committed. In that time, the weak, circumstantial case against her—which nonetheless had been strong enough to persuade the grand jury to indict her for special circumstances double murder—had only grown stronger. It hadn't helped, either, that with all the fanfare, Chris Rosen had succumbed to his ambition and was now a widely rumored, though unannounced, candidate for district attorney in the next citywide election.

Catherine's own mother-in-law, Theresa, had become the witness from hell. Dan Cuneo had interviewed her for the better part of a week in the first flush of the indictment last May, and she'd done all she could to braid the rope that would hang her daughter-in-law. According to Theresa, Catherine had threatened to kill Paul Hanover and Missy D'Amiens not just once or twice. It had been a running theme. The threats were often given in front of her children and other members of the extended family.

Catherine's position was that this was just the way she talked when the family was gathered together—she tended to be histrionic, to exaggerate for effect, and this Hardy certainly knew to be true from his own experience. From the beginning, she knew she was unwelcome in the Hanover family. Catherine felt that the only path to even modest acceptance within the family was to be entertaining, a personality. Without a pedigree, a past, a bloodline, it was all she had.

So yes, she'd often joked that they all really needed to get together and kill Missy before the wedding, though of course she'd never meant it. They'd all laughed. They couldn't have believed she ever meant it. (Beth thought the repetition ominous enough, though; all the kids considered it unimportant, a joke.)

Her husband piled on as well. In his statements to the police, Will denied that he'd ever had an affair with anyone. He had time cards from his secretary, Karyn Harris, the "other woman" Catherine had suspected, for the days when he'd been fishing, and the records showed that she'd been at the office every one of those four days. Moreover, the captain of the *Kingfisher*, Morgan Bayley, swore that he'd been out on the ocean the whole time with Will, but that their radio had been on the blink. He had the radio repair records to prove it. They'd also been out of the cellphone reception zone and hadn't been able to call anyone on shore.

Will told Hardy that his wife had always been jealous. In the past couple of years, she'd become dangerously unstable in a number of ways—accusing him of adultery being just one of them. She'd also, he said, conceived either an affection for his father or a mania for his money. There was a strong and in some ways almost uncanny resemblance between Catherine and Missy D'Amiens—remarked on by anyone who knew them both—and Catherine seemed to believe that if Missy could snag her very wealthy and charismatic father-in-law, she could and should have done it herself. She imagined that Paul had propositioned her when she'd first been married. She should have gone with his father when she had the chance. At the end, Will said that Paul had told him that she'd even come on to him, and he'd had to rebuff her. Finally, she constantly berated Will for his business "failures," his inability to adequately provide for his children's education, for his general lack of acumen and drive—this when he made what he called "strong six figures per year."

Hardy subpoenaed his tax records—his top grossing year was 1999, when he had earned $123,000. Last year he'd earned $91,000.

Catherine's response to all of these claims? A curt dismissal, a refusal to even discuss it. "He's delusional."

For the record, the kids more or less sided with her. But she was in jail and their dad was home full-time, paying her legal bills (out of his four-million-dollar inheritance), peddling the line that he was on Catherine's side, he wanted to help her, he felt sorry for her. She was sick, but a good woman. He would still love her and take her back if she ever got "better." He never, not once, came to visit her in jail.

Then there was Hanover's partner Bob Townshend, who got a call from Paul on the afternoon of the very day that he was killed. Catherine had just come to visit him and he'd felt threatened. She was near hysteria over the imagined infidelity of her husband. She freaked when Paul had told her that he was going to change his will in Missy's favor sooner rather than later. Townshend told Hardy that Paul had made an appointment for the following week to do just that.

Hardy had fought the good fight to keep much of this testimony out of the trial, but Judge Marian Braun had taken it under submission and Hardy couldn't shake the suspicion that she would let some, if not most, of it in. Braun herself was one of the worst possible choices of trial judge from Hardy's perspective (only Leo Chomorro would have been worse). As soon as she'd been assigned, he considered using his 170.6 peremptory challenge—for which no reason need be given and which can't be denied—to get Braun off the case. But then he stood the risk of drawing Chomorro. In fact, he wouldn't put it past the Master Calendar to arrange to assign Chomorro to punish him for his arrogance. In the end, he'd kept her on.

There was more. Catherine's alibi for the night of the murders had been blown by none other than her own youngest daughter, Heather, who kept a diary that Cuneo had discovered during his interview with her. Supposedly out having fast food for dinner with her brother and sister, in fact she'd had "a ton" of homework and she'd had Saul drop her off at the house and "scrounged" something to eat since neither her mom nor dad were home, which was "like, getting to be the norm lately."

Called on this, Catherine admitted to Hardy that she'd lied to him about that. A low point, to say the least. Catherine was sorry. She'd been trying to save face with him. She didn't want him to know that she could be the kind of insecure, snooping bitch who would actually go by the house of Will's illicit paramour, Karyn Harris, to make sure she was still not home. Every day for four days! And Ms. Harris hadn't once been there.

Hardy had subpoenaed the flight manifests of every airline that flew from any Bay Area airport to any Southern California airport on the days in question. No Karyn Harris. The plain truth was that whether or not her husband had been having this alleged affair, Catherine's alibi crashed.

Further, Glitsky, looking under rocks for other scenarios, both because of his own agenda vis-à-vis Cuneo and because of his work at the mayor's request, had come up empty. The "other dude" play, the argument that some mysterious other person had committed the crime, was ever popular among defense attorneys. Indeed, Hardy had used it to good effect during other trials. But if there was another dude in this case, Glitsky with the full weight of his position hadn't been able to unearth him. The Tow/Hold people had lost their contract with the city in June and nobody else had died, or had even caught a cold, as far as Hardy could tell. The mayor abandoned personal interest in the investigation.

With new evidence against Catherine appearing regularly, even Glitsky grudgingly came to consider the possibility that Cuneo had been right. For his own reasons, Glitsky still seemed ready to jump up at the slightest scent of another lead, but they had been scarce to begin with, and dwindled to none. And that left only one alternative—that Paul Hanover's death, and Missy's, had come at the hands of Hardy's client.

There were days Hardy considered the possibility himself.

Now, with his breathing under control, he got up and went into the bathroom where he drank a few handfuls of water and threw some more in his face, then toweled himself dry. Back in bed, he lay on his back, uncovered.

Silent up to now, apparently sleeping, Frannie reached out and put a hand over his hand in the night. "Are you all right?"

"Just nerves," he said, "the trial."

"I guessed."

"No flies on you."

"Can I do anything?"

"It's okay. I'll get back to sleep in a minute." He squeezed her hand. "I couldn't find the car," he said as though the words made any sense.

"The car?"

"In my dream. Missy's car." The one he and Catherine were going to go and make out in, in the dream, as soon as they could find it, but he left that part out.

"What about it?"

"I don't know where it is. I mean, I still don't know where it is."

"You know everything that's possible to know about this case, Dismas. You've lived and breathed it for most of the past year. How many binders do you have?" These were his black, three-ring binders for testimony, evidence, motions, police reports, everything that comprised his records on the case.

"Twenty-six."

"Is that a new record?"

"Close anyway. But I know there's nothing about the car. How could I have forgotten that?"

"I don't know. Is it important?"

"No. I mean, I don't know why it would be. It's just a question I can't answer. We start in a few hours, Fran. I can't have questions I don't know the answers to. Not now."

Frannie turned onto her side, moved over against him. "If it's important, you'll have it when you need it. But right now, what you need is sleep."

He let out a long breath. "I'm a mess."

"You're fine."

"I can't believe Marian didn't recuse herself."

"That's good news, remember. Grounds for appeal. You told me yourself."

"Or venue? How could she leave the damn trial here? The jury's tainted. I can feel it."

"I've got a question for you."

"What?"

"Are you going to play this whole thing over in your mind before morning?"

"No. I hope not." Then, "You're right, I've got to stop."

"Okay. So stop then. Go easy on yourself."

He put his arm around her. "Did I just say you were right?"

"Yep."

"You are."

"I know." She kissed the side of his face. "Let's say we go to sleep, okay?"

"Okay." Then, as sleep approached, "I love you, you know."

"I know," she said. "Me, too." And kissed his cheek again.

Within two minutes, Hardy's breathing was deep and even.

Frannie, it took longer.

Hardy was dressed in a dark blue suit with a white shirt and red and blue rep tie. It was 6:42 by the clock on his stove. He had poured his coffee first thing as always, taken a drink, then realized that if Treya hadn't gone into labor during the night, Glitsky would be awake and at home.

He answered on the second ring with a cheerful, "This better be important."

Hardy didn't waste time with chitchat, either. "Where's Missy's car?"

"I don't know. Bolivia?"

"Why do you say that?"

"Are we a little wound up this morning? Oh, that's right. The trial . . ."

Hardy cut him off. "Do you know that? Is the car really in Bolivia?"

"Do I have any idea? I'd be surprised. Bolivia just seemed like a good answer at the time. What's this about?"

"Last night I had a dream and realized I didn't know anything about her car."

"So what?"

"So I don't know what that means. Why did I dream about it if it doesn't mean anything?"

"I give up," Glitsky said. "Because dreams are random?"

"Not as often as you'd think. I realized it's something I've never looked at. I wondered if you had."

"No."

"You know anything about it? She owned her own car, right?"

"Right." Glitsky's ongoing frustration with finding another suspect and his futile investigation to this point made him Hardy's go-to guy for all facts related to the Hanover case. "She drove a black Mercedes," he said, "like Catherine Hanover's."

"Okay, so where is it?"

"Real guess this time? It's parked in a garage somewhere. Where are you going here?"

Hardy took in another slug of coffee. "She comes home from wherever she's been. Where's she been? She doesn't work."

"Is this twenty questions? She was shopping, or hanging out with a friend of hers."

"Anyway," Hardy running with it, "that doesn't matter. What matters is she gets home and parks . . ."

"Maybe she took a cab. Or even the Muni."

"I doubt it, but either way her car had to be somewhere around Alamo Square. The Willises both talked about her car."

"Okay. So she had a car parked around Alamo Square."

"Then she's killed in the house. Paul's car is in the garage. There's no second car. So where did it go?"

"If it was on the street, it's towed or stolen," Glitsky said. "Mystery solved. Nice talking to you." Glitsky's voice changed, softened. "I've got a pretty little thing pulling on my leg that needs her breakfast, don't you, baby?"

"You don't think it's anything?" Hardy asked.

"Yeah, I do. I think it's first-day-of-trial jitters."

"You'd have the jitters, too, if your client was innocent and you knew it."

A lengthy pause. "Well, Diz," he said, "that's why they have trials. You can prove it there."

"I don't have to prove anything! That's the thing. *They've* got to prove she did it. The burden of proof is always on the prosecution."

Glitsky's voice was surprisingly gentle. "Oh, that's right, I forgot for a minute there."

Jacked up for the day and realizing he'd overstepped, Hardy started to apologize. "Sorry, Abe, it's just . . ."

"Hey." Still low-key. "Shut up. I'll find the car for you. Now say, 'Thanks, Abe' and hang up."

"Thanks, Abe."

"Don't mention it."

Treya had been off work for the week since her due date. In theory she could sleep in every day, but that didn't seem to be in her nature. Hardy's phone call this morning hadn't helped, either.

Glitsky was sharing ketchup with some scrambled eggs, as opposed to scrambled eggs with a little ketchup, with Rachel—"one big spoonful for Daddy, one biggest spoonful for Rachel"—when his wife appeared in the door to the kitchen. "Who was that, this early?"

"Diz. He's having a breakdown."

"Catherine Hanover?"

A nod. "He says she's innocent."

"So do you."

"Yes, but only in the privacy of my own home. I actually think it might be tougher on Diz."

"Why is that?"

"It's got to be easier if he thinks his client's guilty, wouldn't you think? That way, they get convicted, on some level you've got to know they deserve it, so how bad can you feel? They don't convict, you win, so you feel good about that. But if you think they're really not guilty . . . I think it's eating him up."

"Just like with you."

"Well, maybe not eating me up exactly. But somebody's walking around free who shouldn't be."

"You really want him, don't you?"

"Or her. Whoever. Yeah, I want 'em."

Glitsky's face wore a sober expression, and with some reason. After Cuneo and Chris Rosen had ramrodded the grand jury into returning an indictment against Catherine Hanover late last spring, the two of them got wind of the onetime personal connection between Hardy and his client. To the homicide inspector and the assistant DA, this relationship was anything but innocent—not that they cared about sexual involvement (which in the tabloid environment of the San Francisco political scene they both assumed without discussion). Working together on the case, Cuneo and Rosen both immediately took Hardy and Catherine's involvement as another level in their conspiracy theory. Now it wasn't just Glitsky and Hardy and Kathy West. All of those three were now neatly connected to the defendant in a sensational and highly political double-murder trial. They had to be colluding in some kind of cover-up.

Meanwhile, Glitsky had been continuing on his own semi-parallel investigations into Tow/Hold and Paul Hanover's other business and political endeavors when, early one evening in his office, he got an unannounced visit from an FBI field agent named Bill Schuyler.

Field officers with the FBI didn't drop in at the office of the deputy chief of inspectors every day, or even every month, so clearly Schuyler had come with a specific purpose. The fact that he'd come after normal business hours was interesting, too. Though they'd always had an easy and collegial acquaintance, neither man wasted any time with pleasantries before getting to it. "I thought you'd want to know," Schuyler began, "that I got a call from Chris Rosen—one of your DAs here—a couple of days ago. He was asking questions about you."

Glitsky, at his desk in the amber twilight, sat deeply back in his chair, fingers templed at his lips. He'd been in a tense state of waiting for the appearance of this discussion for the better part of two years, and now that it was here, it was almost a relief. But he feigned complete ignorance. "What did he want to know?"

"He was following up on a report filed by Lieutenant Lanier, who interviewed you on the day that Barry Gerson got shot," Schuyler said. "You remember that?"

"Pretty well. What did you have to do with that?"

"Nothing directly. But you mentioned me to Lanier, said you'd called me earlier in the day."

"That's because I did, Bill."

"I know. I remember. You wanted me to round up some of my troops and help you with an arrest. Your friend Hardy's client, if memory serves. But there wasn't enough time."

"That's right. That's what happened. So what's the problem?" Glitsky asked.

"I'm not sure, Abe." Schuyler was a broad-shouldered, always well-dressed athlete with a bullet head covered with a blond fuzz. Now he leaned forward in his chair. "Rosen wouldn't say, of course. But he asked me if I'd followed up with you. With what you'd done that day. If I knew whether you'd gone ahead, anyway, without my guys."

"That would have been stupid and indefensible."

Schuyler nodded. "That's what I told him. But the real answer was no, I hadn't followed up afterward with you. I didn't know what you'd done."

In the darkening room, Glitsky blew on his templed hands.

Schuyler continued. "Your alibi was that . . ."

Glitsky sat bolt upright. "Whoa! Alibi? He said the word 'alibi'?"

"Your alibi is that you spent the day with Gina Roake, Hardy's law partner, at her apartment."

"That's because I did. Her fiancée had just died. We're friends, Bill, Gina and I. She needed the company. I was with her." This was strictly true, although he hadn't been with Roake at her apartment, but out on Pier 70, where both of them had taken part in the gunfight that had killed Gerson and five others. So what he was telling Schuyler was the truth, but it was also a lie. "What do you want me to say, Bill?"

Schuyler held his palms out in front of him. "Nothing, Abe. You've got nothing to prove to me. But I thought you'd want to know they're asking around."

"They? Who's they, besides Rosen?"

"He mentioned this homicide cop, I don't know him, Cuneo. This case you're on now, evidently Hardy's in it and you've been working with him again and the mayor, too, to undercut him—Cuneo, I mean—since their suspect is Hardy's girlfriend . . ."

"So we're somehow in this grand conspiracy?"

"He seemed to be thinking that way, yeah."

Glitsky kept his voice low, under tight control. "And what exactly are we or were we conspiring to do? Did he say?"

Schuyler shrugged. "All I'm saying is, he's building a

case. I don't know what it's about, but the smart bet is somebody wants to tie you to Gerson."

"I had nothing to do with Gerson. Although I heard he was dirty."

"Cuneo didn't think he was."

"Yeah, and he thinks he's got the right suspect here, too."

"You don't think he does?"

"That's why I'm still looking."

Schuyler digested that for a minute. "Well, you want some free advice?"

"Always. Not that I always take it, but I'll listen."

"Bail on this case, the one you're still working on. Cuneo's got a suspect in custody, Rosen's got an indictment, so what the hell are you still looking for? What message are you sending out about these two clowns? They're jerk-offs, that's what. You don't believe they made their case?"

"I don't think they did."

Schuyler shook his head with impatience. "Doesn't matter, Abe. If their suspect didn't do it, odds are she'll walk, right? Your man Hardy's pretty good."

"He's not my man, Bill. He's a friend of mine, that's all."

"Whatever. Doesn't change the fact. The girl's not guilty, she's off. If not . . ." He shrugged again. If not, Glitsky was wrong looking for another suspect in the first place and he'd be well advised to be rid of the case sooner rather than later. "The point is you take the heat off yourself right now. If Cuneo wants this collar so bad, maybe he fucked up the investigation. *Not your problem, Abe.* The trial goes south, maybe you get involved again later, low-key, point out where they fucked it up. But this guy's got a hard-on for you, both of them do. They don't think you're looking for an alternate suspect, they think the real story is that you and Hardy and Kathy West are covering something up, maybe going all the way back to Gerson. That's what I read."

Glitsky simmered for a long moment. By now the room was frankly dark. "Let them look," he said. "There's nothing to find."

"Don't kid yourself." Schuyler lowered his voice.

"There's always something to find, Abe. Maybe not what they started looking for, but if you let them get a foothold, start talking to the whole world, get the accountants involved, they'll find a time card you filled in wrong, or a company car you went to the beach in, or some secretary says you felt her up, something. And if it gets to the politicos sniping at West, once they got the climate established and you're all in some conspiracy together, then the pro liars will just use what Rosen's got and make up other shit. Unless you got a righteous somebody else for the murders . . . ?"

"No. Nobody. Not a hint."

"Then drop it."

But he hadn't dropped it.

He couldn't do that, not while he was a cop and not while he believed that Cuneo had arrested the wrong suspect. Which meant that the real killer was still on the streets, and now—if not for Glitsky—with no one in pursuit. On top of that, Glitsky wasn't about to be chased off by the fear that Cuneo would expose him in some way. Once he let that happen, he might as well resign. He would be useless. No, the most effective way to neutralize Cuneo would be to discover what he'd missed—to be more thorough, more organized, a better cop.

He realized that in fact it would not hurt at all if Cuneo and Rosen believed that he was dropping out of the case. He could use the power of his office as a cover to pursue his own leads under their noses—if he played it right, and he would, he might actually be aided in his interrogations by his witnesses' perception that the police already had a suspect in custody, so Glitsky couldn't possibly be focusing on them.

He did not want this to become a political liability for Kathy West, however. There was no point in that, so he went to her and convinced her that he had to drop the case. He had nothing going anyway, no real leads. Then he told her a little about Schuyler's theories, Cuneo and Rosen, which she'd considered ridiculous and infuriating, but in the end didn't want to pursue. Obviously, the men lived in an alternate universe, but a witch hunt with her as the central figure in an undefined conspiracy theory was something she'd prefer to avoid.

Finally, Glitsky went to Lanier and gave him the news, too, that he was off the case. It was all Cuneo's from here on out. The homicide inspector had done a good job of identifying the defendant, and Catherine Hanover's arrest took Glitsky out of the loop.

So whatever conspiracy he'd been involved in around this case became moot to both Cuneo and Rosen, and he hadn't heard another word about it since.

It was still there, though.

Now, holding Treya's hand, he scratched at the kitchen table. "Maybe I should just call back and tell Diz no."

"I don't think so, hon. This thing has been sticking in your rather well-developed craw for months. If you want to help Diz, just acknowledge what you're doing so you're ready when the shit hits the fan, which it will, I promise." She smiled in her teasing way. "For the record, I apologize for the use of profanity in front of our daughter, too." She looked down at Rachel and said, "We don't say 'shit' in this house, little girl."

Rachel returned her gaze with a questioning, open expression. "What shit?" she asked.

Glitsky hung his head and shook it from side to side. "Wonderful."

But Treya suddenly sat up straighter. "Oh." Her hand went to her stomach and she blew out a long breath.

Glitsky squeezed her hand. "Trey?"

She held up her index finger, telling him to be patient a minute. Breathing deeply and slowly, she looked up and found the clock on the wall. "We're there," she said.

"Where we?" Rachel asked.

"We're in labor, sweetie," Treya answered gently. "You know the little brother we've been waiting for all this time? He's telling me he's on his way."

16

Hardy parked under his office, in the managing partner's spot next to the elevator. His mind elsewhere, he got in the elevator and rode upward, not realizing that out of force of some long-buried habit, he'd pushed "3." Before he'd become managing partner, this was where he'd worked. Now, his partner, Wes Farrell, worked out of his old office. The elevator door opened and Hardy stepped out into the hall and stood for a minute, wondering where he was.

"Brilliant," he said to himself.

Knocking on Farrell's door and getting no answer as he passed, he descended the steps to the main lobby—Phyllis's station, the Solarium, David's old office—hermetically preserved—next to his own and then Norma, the office manager's. Off to his right ran a long hallway at the end of which was the lair of the firm's third name partner, Gina Roake. Behind the doors and their secretaries' cubicles, the eight current associates now toiled. Hardy assumed most if not all of them were working already, although it was still a few minutes shy of eight o'clock. You didn't bill 2,200 hours a year if you didn't put in a very full day every day. Phyllis wasn't at her station yet—she came on at eight thirty—so Hardy crossed directly to his own ornate door and was surprised to see Wes Farrell, coat- and tie-less, throwing darts.

"I know what you're going to say," Farrell began.

"You do?"

"I do. You're going to say you're busy and you don't have time for any childish games. Your trial starts today."

Hardy brought a hand to his forehead. "That's *today*? Yikes!" He crossed around to behind his desk, lugged his triple-thick briefcase up and onto the blotter. "Actually, I knew it was today." He snapped open the clasps, started removing folders. He broke a brittle smile—not very convincing. He liked Wes a lot, but he didn't always work the way Hardy did, and sometimes his presence was more distraction than help. "So what's up, in ten words or less?"

"Today's shirt." He'd thrown the last dart of the round as Hardy had entered and had turned to follow his progress. Now, his grin on, Wes held open his unbuttoned dress shirt. Actually, this was an almost-daily ritual, and Hardy found himself breaking into a genuine smile. Wes prided himself on having one of the world's most complete, ever-growing collections of epigrammatic T-shirts, which he wore under his lawyer's disguise. Today's shirt read: GROW YOUR OWN DOPE/PLANT A MAN.

"Sam gave it to me," he said, "and that goes a long way toward explaining why I love that woman." He was buttoning up. "Anyway, I thought you might need a little humor running around in your system before you hit the Hall."

"I might at that," Hardy conceded. "Did you drive by there on your way in?"

"No. You?"

Hardy nodded. "Thirty-seven mobile units, if you can believe it. You can't even get onto Bryant. They're diverting traffic around before you get within three blocks." Hardy glanced at his watch. "And we don't even start for an hour and a half. It's going to be a circus."

Farrell sat on the couch, doing up his tie. "You probably shouldn't have dated her. I mean, if you wanted to keep all these scurrilous lies out of the paper."

"Where were you when I was seventeen?"

"I didn't date until I was much older than that, so I couldn't have advised you very well."

"Funny. Frannie says the same thing."

A quick glance. Serious. "She okay with it?"

"Great. Peachy." He settled into his chair. "Although I can't say she's been totally thrilled with the Romeo lawyer angle everybody in the news seems to like so much. But the news jocks don't like it as much as my kids. Vincent's even taken to calling me Romeo in private, which of course just cracks me up. And then if the Beck hears him, she goes ballistic. It's a great time. Or how about last week, our 'Passion Pit' in the jail? Did you see that?"

"I thought it was pretty cool, an old guy like you."

"Yeah. Those *Enquirer* guys are talented."

"I wondered where that was exactly, the Passion Pit, to tell you the truth. But I was afraid you'd had so many intimate moments there that you didn't want to talk about it. Too private."

"So many. So many. Actually, it's the visiting room downstairs at the jail," Hardy said, referring to the antiseptic, brightly lit, glass-block-enclosed bullpen off the admitting area where lawyers got to meet with their incarcerated clients. "That's where we've 'consummated our love.' But to get to feeling really passionate in there, you've got to use some serious imagination, believe me. More than the *Enquirer* guys, even."

Wes had his tie on now and stood up, grabbing his coat. "And now it begins in earnest, huh? Can I do anything to help at home? Maybe Sam . . ."

Hardy shook his head. "No, I told you, we're fine. In fact, it's added a whole new dimension to our marriage, where she pretends it doesn't bother her and I pretend that I appreciate her understanding. It's special, but what am I supposed to do? It's a little late now."

"You could pray for a short trial."

"Prayer is always a solace," Hardy said. "I might go for that."

Twenty minutes later, he left his office to a gaggle of well-wishers in the lobby. This was a major case for the firm, and everyone was aware of its importance. It was still bitter cold outside, but Hardy was damned if he was going to hassle first with the impossible parking around the Hall of Justice, which for twenty-some bucks a day would not get him appreciably closer to the courtroom than he was in his office, and then with the gauntlet of the TV cameras and Minicams. No, wrapped in his long heavy coat and wearing gloves, he would walk the twelve blocks carrying his twenty-pound briefcase and sneak in past at least most of the jackals through the back door by the jail.

First though, there was the jail itself, and the pretrial

meeting with his client. Over the months, he'd grown accustomed to seeing Catherine in the familiar orange jumpsuit that was her garb in the lockup, so this morning when she entered the "Passion Pit" in low heels, a stylish green skirt and complementary blouse, earrings, eye shadow and lipstick, he boosted himself off the table where he'd been sitting. He met her eyes and nodded in appreciation. "Okay, then," he said, "that works."

The female guard who'd escorted Catherine from the changing room closed the door behind her. Now the client took a step or two into the room, toward him, and stopped. There was something in her stillness that struck him as a falsely brave front, but she summoned what passed for a smile. "You ever get tired of being a lawyer," she said, "I think you've got a career in women's fashion."

Hardy had pulled a bit of a break with the judge when she'd allowed Catherine the dignity of changing into normal clothes upstairs instead of in a holding cell next to the courtroom. Hardy had contacted the good husband, Will, and he'd sent over three boxes of clothes and underwear, none of which fit her anymore because she'd lost so much weight in jail. So Hardy had her take her measurements and write down her sizes, then had spent the better part of a day a few weeks before buying a wardrobe for her at Neiman Marcus.

As it turned out, this straightforward and practical move had backfired in a number of ways. First off, Hardy really didn't know all that much about women's fashion, but his ex-wife, Jane Fowler, happened to still work in the field—she'd been a buyer at I. Magnin for years. The two weren't exactly close anymore, but they had lunch together a couple of times a year just to keep up. When he asked if she would do him a favor and accompany him on the shopping expedition, she'd agreed.

What happened next he might have guessed if he'd thought about it. But he really wasn't sufficiently paranoid yet, and maybe never would be, to fully appreciate what appeared to be happening around this case. Several tabloid reporters shadowed him on this shopping trip. Not only did someone snap a picture of him holding up a sexy bra, but the article followed up with the news that Hardy had bought the clothes with the firm's credit card, implying that he was paying for it. Although of course he'd just be listing the clothes in his regular bill to Will Hanover for his hours and expenses, the article made the purchase look suspect.

And the icing on the cake was that Jane appeared behind him in the bra picture. The Romeo not just fooling around with his client, but now caught with his ex-wife. Frannie liked that part almost as much as the picture of *her*—wearing formless jogging clothes, with her hair in disarray and a somehow distracted and worried look on her face as she carried a couple of bags of groceries. The caption under that one: "Brave But Clueless."

Hardy shook his head to clear the memory. In front of him, Catherine did a little self-conscious pirouette. "I really look okay?"

"Better than okay."

She sighed, then threw a second sigh at the ceiling. When she came back to him, she was blinking. "I'm not going to cry and ruin these eyes today."

"No. Don't do that. That would be wrong."

Nixon's famous line from the Watergate era brought a smile, enough to stem the immediate threat of tears. "It's just," she sighed, "I thought I'd never wear anything like this again."

"You'll do that all the time, Catherine. You wait."

"Do you really think so?"

With more conviction than he felt, Hardy nodded. "You didn't do this. The jury won't convict you. You'll see. The system really does work."

"I want to believe that, but if that's the case, I keep wondering how it got me to here?"

Now Hardy feigned his own brave smile. "One little teeny tiny design flaw. A bad cop. This is the version where he gets edited out. You ready?"

"I'm ready."

"All right. I've got to remind you that the next time I see you, we're in front of the jury. Some of them are going to think you and I have something going on, courtesy of our ever-vigilant media. So it's important that you and I appear to have a professional distance. Frannie's going to be out there. So is Will . . . no, don't look like that. He's got to be there. It's critical that the jury sees that your husband is supporting you through all this, that in spite of everything, he *must* believe that you're innocent."

"In spite of everything he's said about me. And what he's done."

Hardy nodded. "In spite of all that, he's *our* witness. He's got nothing to say about the crime itself. He's your husband. They can't make him testify against you."

"I hate him."

"I believe you've mentioned that, but it doesn't matter. He's out there, and it's good for the jury to see him and see that you're with him."

"But I'm not."

"Right. But that doesn't matter."

She closed her eyes and for a breath her structure seemed to crumble. Then she straightened up, opened her eyes, lifted her jaw and flashed a high-octane smile. "I'm innocent," she said. "I've got nothing to be afraid of."

"Correct. Let's go get 'em. I'll see you out there."

They'd been standing a foot apart and now Catherine stepped forward. "Dismas, I just want to say that I know how hard this has been for you. I mean personally. I never meant . . ."

"It's not you," he said. "It's all right."

She moved closer and leaned her head against his chest, the weight of it against him. Carefully, delicately, he put his arms around her and held her lightly. It was the first time they'd embraced. Catherine brought her arms around his back and tightened her hold on him. Again, her composure broke.

He patted her back, gradually easing her away, kissing her chastely on the cheek. Without another word, he picked up his briefcase, went to the door and knocked for the guard, and was gone.

The courtroom was Department 21 on the third floor of the Hall of Justice. Hardy had been in it on many occasions by now, but never failed to be disappointed by its lack of grandeur. More than twenty years ago, the city had installed extra security for the trial of Dan White, who'd shot Mayor Moscone and Supervisor Harvey Milk in their offices at City Hall. Now heavy doors and bulletproof glass separated the gallery from the well of the courtroom in Department 21. Except for these amenities, the room might have been a typical classroom in a marginally funded school district.

In front of the bar, Hardy sat at a plain blond library desk on the left-hand side of the nondescript, windowless, fluorescent-lit room. His counterpart with the prosecution—Rosen, with case inspector Dan Cuneo next to him—sat at an identical table about ten feet to his right. Beyond them was the varnished plywood jury box.

They'd finished jury selection yesterday, and now the box was filled with four men and eight women; with three African Americans, two Asians, two Hispanics, five Caucasians; one dentist, one high school teacher, three housewives, a city employee, a computer repairperson, two salesmen, three between jobs. Hardy had been living with the endless calculations of the crapshoot of the makeup of the eventual panel for nine working days. Now here they were and he'd done all he could. He even felt pretty good about some of the people; but he still wished he could start again. But it was always like this—something you just couldn't know or predict.

He'd entered the courtroom through the back door, coming up the hallway by the judge's chambers, to avoid the reporters and the general madness, and now at his table he ventured a half-turn to catch his wife's eye. Frannie was in the first row, the first seat by the center aisle, next to their friend, the "CityTalk" columnist Jeff Elliot. Frannie didn't often come to court with Hardy, but for his big trials she tried to be there for his opening and closing statements. He caught her eye and put his hand over his heart and patted it twice, the secret signal. She did the same.

Behind her and Elliot, it was bedlam.

Every one of the twelve rows, eight wooden, theater-style seats to a side, was completely filled, mostly with media people. Hardy also recognized not just a few people from his office who had come down to cheer him on, but several other attorneys from the building, as well as what appeared to be quite a sizable sampling of regular folks and trial junkies. And now, before the entrance of the judge, everyone was talking all at once.

On Hardy's side, Will Hanover sat with the other adult members of his extended family who would not be called as witnesses for the prosecution—Catherine's two sisters-in-law and their husbands. Unbelievably, Hardy thought, given the testimony they'd supplied to Cuneo, Beth and Aaron, like Will, still considered themselves to be on Catherine's side. Despite their comments in police reports to the contrary, none of them actually seemed to believe that Catherine was guilty. Yes, she'd known where Paul kept his gun. Yes, she'd been worried about the inheritance. Yes, she'd repeated many times that somebody would have to kill Paul and Missy. Either they didn't believe in causality or they didn't understand the gravity of their statements, but nonetheless, by their very presence on Catherine's "side" of the gallery, they would be living and breathing testimony to the fact that they still cared about her—and in the great nebulous unknown that was the collective mind of the jury, this might not be a bad thing.

Cuneo, of course, was turned around at the prosecutor's table and sat jittering nonstop, talking to a couple of assistant DAs from upstairs in the front row, down for the show. But then suddenly the bailiff was standing up to the left of the judge's utilitarian desk. "All rise. Department Twenty-One of the Superior Court of the State of California is now in session. Her Honor Judge Marian Braun presiding. Please turn off all cell phones and pagers, be seated and come to order."

Without any fanfare, Braun was seated almost before the bailiff had concluded his introduction. She scowled out at the gallery, as though surprised at its size, then faced the clerk and nodded. The clerk nodded back, then looked over to the second bailiff, who was standing by the back door to the courtroom, on Hardy's right. They'd already called the case number and read the indictment for special circumstances double murder when they'd begun jury selection so long ago. So now, today, there was little of that earlier formality—the defendant merely needed to be in the courtroom so that she could face her accusers.

The back door opened and Catherine Hanover appeared to a slight electric buzz from the gallery. The loss of the fifteen pounds hadn't hurt her looks. Neither had the light makeup, the subtle lipstick, the tailored clothing. In the brassy fluorescence of the courtroom, she seemed to shine, and Hardy was not at all sure that this was a positive. Good looks could backfire. He glanced at the jury for reactions and suddenly wished there were at least eight men on it and four women, instead of the other way around. Or even twelve men, all of them older and self-made.

During jury selection, he'd convinced himself that the women he'd accepted were of a traditional bent, and hence would be deeply suspicious of Missy D'Amiens and her unknown and thus arguably colorful and potentially dangerous past. On the other hand, he suddenly realized—and Catherine's appearance today underscored this—that these same women might have a great deal of trouble identifying with this attractive woman whose husband's six-figure income wasn't enough to support her lifestyle. In the end, he'd gone along with impaneling all the women because women, at least the sort he hoped he had left on the jury, tended to believe that sexual harassment happened. But he shuddered inwardly now, suddenly afraid that he might have outright miscalculated.

He tore his eyes away from the jury and brought them back to his client. He stood and pulled out the chair next to him for her, glad to see that she had apparently found her husband and in-laws in the gallery and acknowledged them.

Then she was seated. Hardy whispered to her. "How are you doing?"

"Fine."

The judge tapped her gavel to still the continuing buzz, then turned to the prosecution table. "Mr. Rosen, ready for the people?"

Rosen got out of his chair. "Yes, Your Honor."

"Mr. Hardy?"

"Yes, Your Honor."

"All right, Mr. Rosen, you may begin."

Chris Rosen was a professional trial attorney with nine years of experience and a specialization in arson cases.

He'd prosecuted three homicides and a dozen arsons in that time, winning four of them outright and getting lesser convictions with substantial prison time on the others. So he could say with absolute truth that he'd never lost a case, which in this most liberal city was an enviable, almost unheard of, record. Maybe Rosen hadn't always gotten a clear win, either, but Hardy knew the truth of the defense bias in San Francisco—indeed, it was one of the factors involved in this case for which he was most grateful—but this was cold comfort as he watched his young, good-looking opposite number rise with a quiet confidence and a friendly demeanor to match it.

"Ladies and gentlemen," he began. "Good morning. We're here today and for the next few days or weeks—let's hope it won't be too many weeks—to hear evidence about the murders of two people, Paul Hanover, a lawyer here in San Francisco, and his fiancée, Missy D'Amiens." Hardy noticed that Rosen came as advertised—he was playing it smooth. He didn't refer to the dead impersonally as "the deceased" or even "the victims." Rather, they had been real, live people until they had been "murdered." He continued to the jury in his serious, amiable voice. "On Wednesday, May the twelfth of last year, someone set a fire at the home that Mr. Hanover shared with Missy D'Amiens. Firemen coming to fight the blaze found the bodies of a man and woman, burned beyond recognition, in the foyer of the house. Wedged under one of the bodies was a gun. Both victims had been shot in the head. The evidence will show beyond a reasonable doubt that neither wound was self-inflicted. Neither victim killed the other and then him- or herself. These people were murdered in their home, and the murderer lit a fire in the hope of destroying the evidence that would connect him or her to the crime."

Rosen paused to collect himself, as these grisly and dramatic events would obviously upset the psyche of any reasonably sensitive person. Clearing his throat, excusing himself to the jurors "for just a moment," he took a few steps over to this desk, where Cuneo pushed his glass of water to the front edge of the desk. Rosen took a sip, cleared his throat again and turned back to the jurors.

"We will prove to you, ladies and gentlemen, and prove beyond a reasonable doubt, that the person who fired those shots into the heads of each of these victims was the defendant in this case, Mr. Hanover's daughter-in-law, Catherine Hanover. She did it for a common and mundane reason—Mr. Hanover was going to change his will and name Missy D'Amiens his beneficiary. When he did that, his inheritance of nearly fifteen million dollars would go to Missy, and the defendant would get no share of it.

"On the very day that he died, according to the defendant's own statement to police, Mr. Hanover told her that he was thinking of changing his will in favor of Missy before the wedding date, possibly as early as the following week. Spurred by this confession of his plans, the defendant resolved to kill Mr. Hanover before he could change his will."

Here Rosen turned and faced Catherine, his body language as well as his tone suggesting that it pained him to make these accusations against a fellow human being. But she had brought it on herself; he so wished that she hadn't. He raised an almost reluctant hand until his arm was fully outstretched, his index finger wavering in controlled indignation. "And shoot him she did. At point-blank range, in the head. And shot Missy D'Amiens, too, because she'd had the bad fortune to come home and be in the house."

Recounting the tale was imposing a great burden on Rosen, and he needed another sip of water. Hardy thought this was overdoing the sensitivity a bit, and he was glad to see something about which he could—privately, at least—be critical. He knew that juries had a way of sniffing out a phony, tactical interruption, and they might resent it. Otherwise, Rosen was presenting a textbook opening statement—recounting the facts the prosecution had and would prove, without any editorializing. He had even avoided the potential minefield of Missy's presence in the house—clearly the killer had intended the scene to look like a murder/suicide, which would have ended the investigation before it began. But Rosen didn't accuse Catherine of that. He steered clear altogether. Hardy, with a grudging admiration, had to let him continue unchallenged.

"The relevant events of this tragic day are relatively

straightforward and really began around noon. We will prove to you that the defendant, Catherine Hanover, stopped at a Valero gas station on the corner of Oak and Webster, about three blocks from Paul Hanover's home on Alamo Square. A worker at that gas station will testify that he saw the defendant get out of her car, a black Mercedes-Benz C240, and fill a portable container with gasoline and put it into her trunk.

"According to the defendant's own statement, she went to visit her father-in-law later that same afternoon to discuss the finances of her immediate and extended family. We will show you that the defendant came back to Mr. Hanover's home later in the day. You will hear two witnesses testify that she left Mr. Hanover's home a few moments before the fire broke out. You will discover that the defendant lied to the police about her actions at this time. She said that she was at home alone during these critical hours. But her own daughter's diary disproves her story."

Hardy covered his mouth with his hand, hiding from the jury his displeasure. Heather's diary was perhaps the biggest issue he'd lost in pretrial. Although Hardy had argued bitterly against its inclusion, there was no question of the importance and relevance of the diary entry. So one way or another, it was going in. And in the normal course of events, that evidence couldn't have been admitted—it wouldn't have had a foundation—if Heather as a prosecution witness against her own mother didn't testify in court that she'd written it. Understandably, this was a scenario that Catherine, in a genuine display of motherly protectiveness, wanted to avoid at all costs. The psychological damage to her daughter could be incalculable. But Rosen needed the evidence, which meant he needed Heather. And no one could stop him from forcing her to testify. The only solution had been for Hardy to cut a deal to allow the diary entry without the foundation. But even without Heather's testimony, it was a bitter pill, and potentially devastating for his client.

Meanwhile, Rosen was gliding easily over the last of the evidence. "Finally, you will learn that the same type of gasoline used as an accelerant to start the fire in Mr. Hanover's home exactly matches that found in fibers of rug from the trunk of the defendant's black Mercedes-Benz C240." He paused for one last sip of water.

"As I said at the outset, this is a straightforward story, and I'm nearly through with it. On May the twelfth of last year, Paul Hanover himself told the defendant that within days, she and her entire family would be written out of her father-in-law's will. That they would lose millions of dollars. She decided to kill him to keep that from happening, and to use his own gun that she knew he kept loaded in the headboard of his bed. She bought gasoline to set Paul Hanover's house on fire to cover her tracks. She had the means. By her own admission, she'd been at the house during the afternoon, and you will hear witnesses place her there again just before the fire broke out. Opportunity."

Rosen let out a little air. "We will show you, and prove beyond a reasonable doubt, that Catherine Hanover killed her father-in-law, Paul Hanover, and Missy D'Amiens for money by shooting them both in the head. This is first-degree murder with special circumstances under the law of the State of California, and that is the verdict I will ask for. Thank you very much."

In a California murder trial, the defense attorney has an option. He can either deliver his opening statement directly after that of the prosecuting attorney, as a sort of instant rebuttal, or he can deliver his statement at the conclusion of the state's case in full. Hardy was a big fan of the former, believing as he did that the jury made up a great deal of its collective mind—impressions of the players, general believability of the state's narrative, strength or likely strength of the evidence to be presented—in the very opening stages of a trial.

Hardy's experience was that by the time the jury members had heard and seen all the state's evidence, even if the veracity and provenance of every bit of it had been questioned, denied and demeaned by a vigilant defense lawyer, the weight of all of it often just got to be too much to lift. So despite being the defense attorney, Hardy didn't want to fall into a defensive posture. The last thing he wanted was to be passive, parrying the thrusts of his opponent without striking any blows of his own.

No, a trial was a war, and the goal was to win, not simply to defend. And if you wanted to win, you had to attack.

Hardy knew the book on Rosen was that he never objected during open, believing, as did most lawyers, that it ticked off the jury. So he had a hunch he could mix a little argument into a straight recitation of his facts—in fact, his plan was to find out exactly how much argument his counterpart could tolerate.

So after his own low-key and affably gracious greeting to the jurors, Hardy wasted no time bringing out his own guns. "Well, we've all now heard Mr. Rosen's account of the murders of Paul Hanover and Missy D'Amiens, and I couldn't help but be struck by his use of the phrase, 'we will show, and prove to you beyond a reasonable doubt.' Just hearing him use those words creates a powerful impression, doesn't it? He's telling you he's got evidence to support his theory of Paul and Missy's deaths that is so persuasive that it will leave you in a state of virtual certainty, beyond a reasonable doubt, that Catherine Hanover killed them both.

"But let me tell you something. He doesn't have any such thing. He has, in fact, *no physical evidence* at all that places Catherine at Paul Hanover's house at or near the time of the murders." He stopped as though struck nearly mute for a second by the enormity of what he'd just said. "Can that be right? You must be thinking, How can the State of California have arrested and charged Catherine Hanover with this heinous double murder of her father-in-law and his fiancée if there is simply no physical evidence tying her to the crime?"

A flummoxed look on his face, he turned first to the prosecution table as though he expected an answer to this very reasonable question. When none was forthcoming, he came back to the panel. "That, ladies and gentlemen of the jury, is a very good question. Because the pure fact is that Mr. Rosen does not have so much as a single fingerprint of Catherine Hanover on any part of the murder weapon. He does not have anything tying Catherine Hanover to the gasoline container that Mr. Hanover's killer used to start the fire at his house. He has, let me repeat this one more time, *no physical evidence*. Remarkable."

Hardy took a casual stroll of his own now across to the defense table where Catherine sat. Borrowing from Rosen's bag of tricks, he, too, raised his arm and pointed a finger at his client. "This woman is innocent, completely innocent of these crimes. She is guilty of nothing at all, in fact, except for drawing the attention and incurring the wrath of the lead investigating officer on this case, Sergeant Dan Cuneo, by resisting his inappropriate sexual advances and reporting them to his superior."

Out in the gallery, a low roar erupted. This was what all the reporters had come for! Sex and scandal. Salacious accusations and powder-keg secrets.

Hardy took a beat's quiet pleasure in the sight of Cuneo's startled fury, of Chris Rosen's jaw, visibly drooping. Startled and disconcerted, though he must have known that the issue would arise, he simply didn't seem prepared for the accusation so early in open court. Welcome to the big leagues, Hardy thought. He had drawn first blood.

It got better. Cuneo whispered something to Rosen, who belatedly rose to his feet. "Objection, Your Honor. Argument."

"The objection is overruled. He's not arguing, Mr. Rosen. He's telling his version of events, as you did. That's what opening statements are for. Go on, Mr. Hardy."

Hardy nodded respectfully. This was wholly unexpected. Not only had Braun ruled for him, but she'd thrown Rosen a backhanded rebuke in front of the jury. Hardy had to like it, but couldn't dare show any of it. "Thank you, Your Honor," he said.

He moved to the center of the courtroom. Again he turned and looked back over at the defense table. "I said a minute ago that there was no physical evidence tying Catherine to this crime. But more than that, there is no convincing evidence of any kind, physical or otherwise, that she is guilty." The adrenaline was definitely running now, and he was aware of a keen pleasure—almost a thrill—knowing that he was going to let it take him as far as it would.

"The critical prosecution witnesses are inconsistent and contradict one another. My client's statements have been twisted and taken out of context. The so-called motive has been exaggerated and distorted, and the whole foul-smelling mass has been coaxed into the feeble semblance of a case by an overhasty and careless investigation.

"Two people are dead here. And the evidence will show they were shot to death. The prosecution evidence beyond this is simply not clear enough, clean enough, convincing enough to convict Catherine of murder." He paused for a beat, confident now that he'd be able to slip in a last bit of argument. "At the beginning of your service," he said to the jury, "you swore an oath. As Catherine sits there now under your gaze," he said, "you must presume that what I have told you is the truth. You must presume that she is innocent. That is where this trial begins.

"Mr. Rosen would have you believe that she is not innocent. That she plotted and executed this double murder for financial gain. That she is guilty as charged. But no amount of political ambition, no desire to close a high-profile case can make her so. The law of this country presumes the innocence of the accused. It is on that presumption and upon your oath that we will rely."

He met the eyes of several jurors, every one rapt. Up to now, at least, he had them with him.

17

The only witness before the lunch break was John Strout, an ageless and usually uncontroversial figure at every murder trial that Hardy had ever attended in San Francisco. Prosaic as it might seem, usually one of the first orders of business for the prosecution was to establish that a murder had, in fact, taken place. Or, in this case, two murders.

Hardy had studied the forensics and the autopsy until he'd gone cross-eyed trying to find some wedge to cast doubt on the causes of death or, more specifically, to reintroduce the idea of murder/suicide. It certainly didn't look good, knowing all the facts as he did; in fact, the possibility was so remote as to be an impossibility. Still, he didn't see how it could hurt to give the jury a nugget of doubt about that point.

So when Rosen finished his none-too-rigorous direct on what had been the obvious causes of death of the two victims, Hardy stood and walked up to where Dr. Strout sat with consummate ease in the witness box. As some people grow to look like their dogs, Strout the coroner had over time come to resemble a cadaver. Nearly six and a half feet tall, gaunt and sallow, Strout's many-lined cheeks were covered with a crepe-paper skin that sank into the hollows of his face. A prominent Adam's apple bobbed with every frequent swallow. But for all that, he somehow managed to retain something of a youthful air—a shock of unruly white hair, pale blue eyes that had seen it all and laughed at a lot of it. When he spoke, a Southern drawl cast much of what he said in a sardonic light. Although here, of course—on the witness stand under oath—he would strive to be nothing but professional.

Hardy had known the man for thirty years and greeted

him cordially, then got down to the business at hand. "You've testified that both Mr. Hanover and Missy D'Amiens died from gunshot wounds to the head, is that correct?"

"Yes, it is." Strout was sitting back in his seat, arms resting on the arms of his chair, his long legs crossed in the cramped witness box, an ankle on its opposite knee.

In the kindergarten simplicity of the courtroom, Rosen had presented a drawing, mounted on a portable tripod, of the two victims' heads, showing the entry and exit wounds of the bullets and their trajectories. Hardy went first to the location of the wound on Missy's head—verifying that it was in the upper back. "Let me ask you then, Doctor, could this wound have been self-inflicted?"

Strout's initial reaction, covered quickly, was a twinkle in those pale eyes. He knew Hardy well, and the question was so stupid on its face that he almost didn't know how to respond except with sarcasm. But it stirred him from his complacent lethargy. He uncrossed his legs and pulled himself up straight. "In my opinion"—*"In ma 'pinion"*—"it would have been well nigh impossible to inflict this wound on herself."

"*Im*-possible, you say?"

"That's right."

"All right. And turning now to Mr. Hanover's wound. Same question."

"Could he have shot himself there, over his right ear?"

"Right," Hardy said.

"Well, no. I don't rightly think so."

"But unlike the case with Missy D'Amiens, it might not have been impossible?"

"Well, no. If he'd used his left hand, but even so, the trajectory . . ." He stopped, shook his head with some decision. "I'd have to say no. No."

"No, Doctor? And why is that?"

"Because he had polio when he'd been younger, and his right arm was useless."

Hardy nodded at this fascinating discovery, brought in the jury with his eyes. "So he couldn't have lifted the gun with his right hand to where it needed to be to have fired the shot that killed him? Is that your testimony?"

Strout's eyes were narrowed down now to slits. He famously did not like his medical opinions challenged, either in or out of court. "That's my understanding. Correct."

"Your understanding, Doctor? I take it then that you did not have a chance to examine Mr. Hanover while he was alive, did you?"

"No. Of course not."

"No. Well, then, in your examination of the body after his death, did you find the muscles in Mr. Hanover's right arm to be atrophied or useless?"

"No, I did not."

"No? Why not?"

"Because there was essentially nothing left of the right arm. It had cooked away."

This macabre recital brought a hum to the gallery that made Braun lift her gavel, but it died away before she could bring it down.

"So, Doctor," Hardy continued, "there is nothing about your examination that precludes the possibility that Mr. Hanover shot Ms. D'Amiens and then himself. Is that correct?"

A glint of humor showed again in Strout's eyes. So this was where the apparently stupid questions were leading. He nodded. "That's right."

"In other words, according to your personal examination of Mr. Hanover after his death, you found nothing that would rule out the possibility of a self-inflicted wound?"

"Correct."

"And of course, Mr. Hanover, before he took his own life, could have shot Ms. D'Amiens. Isn't that true?"

"Yes," Strout replied.

"Thank you, Doctor," Hardy said. "No further questions."

As soon as Braun called the lunch recess, Hardy gave his client a small pat on the hand before she was led away to her holding cell just behind the courtroom for her own jail-time meal. Most days, Hardy would probably be back there with her, going over issues with sandwiches or sometimes with food phoned in by Phyllis from any one of a number of terrific local eateries. But today—and Hardy had told Catherine beforehand—he had a point to make.

So he gathered his notes and binders into a neat pile in front of his place, then got up and pushed his way through the swinging gate to the gallery. Frannie stood waiting for him, and he slung an arm around her shoulders, drew her to him, kissed the top of her head—the picture of a happily married man casually meeting up with his spouse. He then leaned over to say hi to Jeff Elliot, who'd wheeled himself up next to Frannie before the proceedings began. "I love this woman," he said, "and you can quote me." Then, sotto voce, he added, "In fact, I wish you would."

"It's not exactly news," Elliot said. "Man loves wife. You know what I mean?" He knew what Hardy was talking about, however, and said, "But I'll see what I can do."

The three of them stood chatting in the press of people as the courtroom slowly emptied, the jury first. Hardy noticed Cuneo, who'd nearly bolted from the prosecution table, drumming the back of a chair in front of him. His face was a black mask as he tried to keep his cool, or rather not to show his self-evident fury, as the other people in his row (four rows away from Hardy) patiently awaited their turn to file out. There was only the one center aisle in Department 21, so exiting this courtroom was always a bit like leaving an airplane—slow, slow, slow. While the people in front of you struggled to get their luggage out of the overhead bins, or helped their children or older parents, or just talked and talked and talked, unaware that they needed to keep the *goddamn line moving*.

And then at last Cuneo was on his way up the aisle, his back to them after a few furtive and angry glances. When Elliot, Hardy and Frannie at last got out into the hallway, there was Cuneo again, in a heated discussion with Rosen. And again, as he saw Hardy, a flash of pure hatred.

"Who's that?" Even through the milling crowd, breaking up in various permutations as people went to lunch, Frannie noticed the directed glare.

Hardy still had his arm over her shoulder, and turned her away. "Cuneo."

"That would be *Inspector* Cuneo to you." Elliot was wheeling himself along next to them. "He seems a little perturbed."

Frannie turned for another look back. "I'd say scary."

"He's just a cop," Hardy said dismissively, "and not a particularly good one." They were waiting with several other citizens for the elevator on the second floor to open. "And speaking of cops, did either of you see Abe around this morning before my brilliant opening?"

"You had a flash of brilliance? When was that?" Elliot asked. "Darn, I must have missed it."

"Come on, Jeff," Frannie said. "He was." She looked up at him, amusement in her eyes. "Or at least, as David used to say, he was 'fairly competent.'"

"You're both too kind, really," Hardy said. "But Abe?"

Frannie shook her head no. So did Jeff Elliot. "Haven't seen him."

John Strout shambled over while the three of them were eating their lunch at Lou the Greek's. The medical examiner hovered over the table like a smiling ghost. "Y'all havin' the Special?" An unnecessary question, since Lou's only served one meal every day—the Special—always some more or less bizarre commingling of Asian and Greek foodstuffs. Today the Special came under less bizarre, although still passing strange—a "lamburger," with a bright red sweet-and-sour pineapple sauce over rice.

Strout peered down at the plates through his bifocals. "As a medical man, I'd recommend caution. You mind, Jeff?" He slid into the booth next to Elliot, shot an appreciative glance at Frannie, then held out his hand. "I don't believe I've had the pleasure."

In the middle of a bite, Hardy swallowed. "I'm sorry. John, my wife, Frannie. Frannie, John Strout, who gave such a fine performance this morning."

"Thank you," he said. But the smile faded. "Though I must tell you, Diz, that little primrose path you led me down in there don't lead nowhere."

Hardy put down his fork. "Never said it did, John. But now Mr. Rosen is going to have to talk about it. Might put him off his feed, that's all."

"My husband has a cruel streak," Frannie said. "It's well documented."

"I've seen it in action myself." Strout was all amiability. "You going after my forensic colleagues, too?"

"And who would they be?" Hardy asked.

"You know, the teeth people."

"Whoever's up next, John. I'm equal opportunity at skewering prosecution witnesses. But I'm saving the big show for later."

"Who's that?"

Hardy smiled. "You'll have to wait around and find out. Maybe I can get you a special pass to let you back in the courtroom."

"Put me on your witness list."

"That might do it." Hardy's fork had stopped in midair. He chewed thoughtfully for a second or two.

"He's thinking cruel thoughts again," Frannie said. "I can tell."

"Dr. McInerny," Hardy began his cross-examination of Hanover's dentist. "For how long was Paul Hanover your patient?"

"Twenty-seven years, give or take."

"And in that time, how many X-rays of his mouth did you take?"

"I don't know exactly. Usually we do one a year, but if a tooth cracks or . . . well, really any number of other reasons, we'll do another."

"So it's not a complicated process?"

"No, not at all."

"Would you describe the X-ray process for the court, please?"

Rosen spoke from behind him. "Objection. Three fifty-two, Your Honor." This was a common objection raised when the relevance of the testimony and its probative value was substantially outweighed by the time consumption, prejudicial effect, or by the likelihood of confusing the jury. "We all know how X-rays work."

Braun nodded. "Any particular reason to do this, Mr. Hardy?"

"Yes, Your Honor, but I'm trying to draw a distinction between how X-rays get taken in a dentist's office and how he took the X-rays of the male victim's mouth at the morgue."

"To what end?"

"What I'm getting at, Your Honor, is that if the picture is taken from a different angle in the morgue, or with a different technique, it will look different than a typical office X-ray, and the identification of the victim might then not be as certain."

McInerny, apparently in his late fifties or early sixties, carried twenty or so extra pounds on a midsize body. Pattern baldness was well advanced, and what remained of his hair was snow white. But his face looked like it spent a lot of time outdoors—open, intelligent, expressive. Now he spoke up, helpful, but out of turn. "Really, though, that's not a concern."

Braun, surprised at his intrusion, swung her head to look at him. "Doctor," she said mildly, "just a moment, please." She looked out at the still-standing Rosen, then came back to Hardy. "I'll overrule the objection at this time. Go ahead, Mr. Hardy."

"Thank you, Your Honor. So Doctor, those X-rays. Is there a difference in the way you take standard diagnostic X-rays at your office, and the way you took them to help identify the victim in this case at the morgue?"

In his element now, enjoying this chance to explain the intricacies of his work, McInerny first walked through the familiar procedure that took place in his office—the film in the mouth, the big machine, the lead-lined sheet. "But of course in a forensic laboratory setting, such as a morgue, we typically don't take a picture at all."

"Why is that?"

"Well, because we can simply look at what's there and compare it to our known sample. Let's say, for example, you look in a victim's mouth and have seven fillings, a crown, and a root canal or extraction site, and they're just where they are in your sample. Well, then, you've got a match."

Hardy, sensing an opportunity, jumped at it. "So you can get a match with only, say, a few matching teeth? Less than a whole mouthful?"

"Sometimes, of course. Sometimes you don't have a whole mouthful. But you work with everything you have. In the case of Mr. Hanover, I compared all of the teeth. There was a one hundred percent correlation."

"And so you positively identified the victim as Mr. Hanover?"

But McInerny was shaking his head. "Not precisely," he said.

"No? Could you explain."

"Sure. I simply verify the match. My dental records match the victim's. And in this case they did."

Hardy, having wasted twenty minutes of the court's time on this dry well of a cross-examination, realized that he let himself succumb to the luxury of fishing. He'd gotten an unexpected and gratuitous, entirely minor victory of sorts from Strout during the morning session and he'd let it go to his head. He was going to alienate the jury if he kept barking up this kind of tree, to no effect.

Acknowledging defeat, he tipped his head to Dr. McInerny, thanked him for his time, and excused him.

The afternoon passed in a haze of redundancy.

Toshio Yamashiru was, as Rosen took pains to point out, not only the dentist of Missy D'Amiens, but one of the top forensic odontologists in the country. As Strout had told Glitsky so long ago, he had assisted in the identification of the 9/11 victims. He had twenty-plus years of experience not only in general dentistry, but in advanced forensics.

No doubt prompted by Hardy's aggressive cross-examination of Dr. McInerny, Rosen went to great lengths not only to establish Yamashiru's credentials, but also the techniques that he'd used in the morgue and then in his own lab to exactly correlate the various fissures, faults and striations of each tooth in the skull he examined with the dental records of Missy D'Amiens.

After an hour and forty-one minutes of this excruciatingly boring detail, he finally asked, "Doctor Yamashiru, what was the correlation between the teeth you examined at the morgue and that of the woman whose records are in court, Missy D'Amiens?"

"One hundred percent."

"You're certain?"

"Completely."

"Thank you, Doctor." Rosen turned to Hardy. "Your witness."

Hardy blinked himself to a marginally higher state of awareness and stood up. "Your Honor, I have no questions for this witness."

With ill-concealed relief, Braun turned to Yamashiru. "Thank you, Doctor, you may step down." She then looked up, bringing in the jury, and raised her voice. "I think we've had enough for today. We'll adjourn until tomorrow morning at nine thirty."

In the holding cell just behind the back door of the courtoom, Catherine, caged, paced like a leopard.

Hardy, who'd endured complaints—many justified, he'd admit—about the family since Catherine had gone to jail, felt compelled to try and tolerate another round. Even if he were wrung out and ready to go home—or really, back to the office for a minimum of a couple of hours where he would check his mail and e-mail, answer urgent calls from other clients and deal with any other outstanding firm business that needed his input—he had to let her get some of her frustration out. Because if she didn't blow off steam back here, out of sight, she might do it in front of the jurors, and that would be disastrous. So he let her go on, unaware that with the tensions of the day his own string was near breaking. "I was just so conscious of them all day long, sitting there in the gallery, watching my back, my every breath, I think, and all of them believing I could have done anything like this. How could they even think that?"

"I don't think they do."

"Ha. You don't know."

"No, I don't. That's true."

She got to one end of her twelve-foot journey, grasped the bars for a moment, then pushed off in the other direction. "Shit shit shit."

"What?"

"Just shit, that's what." She opened her mouth and let out something between a scream and a growl.

"Hey, come on, Catherine, calm down."

"I can't calm down. I don't want to calm down. I'm *locked up*, for Christ's sake. I might be locked up forever. Don't you see that?"

She reached the other end, turned again.

"Catherine, stop walking. Please. Just for a second." He patted the concrete bench next to him. "Come on. Sit. You'll feel better."

She didn't stop walking. "I've been sitting all day."

He sighed, let the words out under his breath. "Christ, you can be a difficult woman!"

She stopped and looked at him. "You're not mad at me, are you?"

"No, Catherine. How could I be mad at you? I make a simple request for you to sit down so *you'll* feel better and, because I've been working all day every day for eight months already on your behalf, of course you completely ignore what I want and continue to pace. This makes me happy, not mad. And why? Because I need the abuse. I thrive on abuse, if you haven't noticed."

"I'm not abusing you."

Hardy had to chuckle. "And I'm not mad at you. So we're even. You continue pacing and I'll just sit here, not being mad, how's that?"

She stared down at him. "Why are you being this way?"

"What way? Calling you on your behavior? Maybe it's because how you behave in the courtroom is going to have an effect on the jury."

"Okay, but we're not in the courtroom now." Some real anger crept into her tone. "I've been behaving well in there all day and now, if it's all the same to you, Dismas Hardy, I'm a little bit frustrated."

"Well, take it out on me, then. I'm a glutton for it. Here." He got to his feet. "I'll stand up, be your punching bag. Go on, hit me."

She squared around on him as though she actually might. Hardy brought a finger up to his chin, touched it a few times. "Right here."

"God, you're being awful."

"I'm not. I'm facilitating getting you in touch with your inner child who wants to hit me. You'll really feel better. I swear. This is a real technique they teach in law school."

In spite of herself, she chuckled, the anger bleaching out of her, her face softening. "I don't want to hit you, Dismas. We can sit down."

"You're sure? I don't want to stem your free expression."

She lowered herself to the concrete bench. "It's just been a long day," she said.

He looked down at her. "I hate to say that it's only the first one of many, but that's the truth. We ought to try to keep from fighting. I'm sorry if I pushed you there."

"No. I deserved it. I pushed you."

"Well, either way." Hardy put his hands in his pockets, leaned against the bars behind him. "This is worse for you, and I'm sorry."

They were in a cell in an otherwise open hallway that ran behind all of the courtrooms. Every minute or so, a uniformed bailiff or two would walk by with another defendant, or sometimes an orange-suited line of them, in tow. The place was lit, of course, but in some fashion Hardy was dimly aware that outside it was close to dark out and still cold. Down the way somewhere, quite possibly in an exact double of the cell in which they sat, but invisible to them, they both could hear someone crying.

"She sounds so sad," Catherine said. "It could be one of my daughters. That's what I'm missing the most. The kids." She took a deep breath. "It's bad enough now, with them having to deal with all that high school nastiness, with their mother in jail, what they must be going through day to day. But what I really agonize about is how it's going to affect them in the long run, if I wind up . . ." She stared at her hands in her lap.

"That's not going to happen," Hardy said. "I'm not going to let that happen."

Down the hall, they heard the crying voice suddenly change pitch and scream, "No! No! No!" and then the clank of metal on metal. From out of nowhere, at the same instant, their bailiff opened the courtroom door at the mouth of their cage. "You want dinner, we better get you changed," he said.

Wordless, Catherine hesitated, let out a long sigh. Then, resigned, she nodded, stood up and held out her hands for the cuffs.

18

The pediatric heart specialist at Kaiser, Dr. Aaron True-blood, was a short, slightly hunchbacked, soft-spoken man in his mid- to late sixties. Now he was sitting across a table from Glitsky in a small featureless room in the maternity wing, his hands folded in front of him, his kindly face fraught with concern.

Treya had been a trouper. They got to the hospital well before nine o'clock that morning, and after eight hours of labor, Glitsky breathing with her throughout the ordeal, she delivered an eight-pound, two-ounce boy they would call Zachary. Crying lustily after his first breath, he looked perfectly formed in all his parts. Glitsky cut the umbilical cord. Treya's ob-gyn, Joyce Gavelin, gave him Apgar scores of eight and nine, about as good as it gets.

In a bit under an hour, though, the euphoria of the successful delivery gave way to a suddenly urgent concern. Dr. Gavelin had the usual postpartum duties—the episiotomy, delivering the placenta and so on—during all of which time Zachary lay cuddled against his mother's stomach in the delivery room. The doctor released mother and baby down to her room in the maternity ward, and Glitsky walked beside the gurney in the hallway while they went and checked into the private room they'd requested, where the hospital would provide a special dinner and where he hoped to spend the night. After making sure that Treya and Zachary were settled—the boy took right to breast-feeding—Glitsky went down the hall to call his father, Nat, to tell him the good news and check up on Rachel, who was staying with him. Everything was as it should have been.

When he came back to Treya's room, though, she was crying and Zachary was gone. Dr. Gavelin had come in for a more formal secondary examination of the newborn. But what began as a routine and cursory procedure changed as soon as she pressed her stethoscope to the baby's chest. Immediately, her normally upbeat, cheerleader demeanor underwent a transformation. "What is it? Joyce, talk to me. Is everything all right?"

But Dr. Gavelin, frowning now, held up a hand to quiet Treya and moved the stethoscope to another location on the baby's chest, then another, another, around to his back. She let out a long breath and closed her eyes briefly, perhaps against the pain she was about to inflict. "I don't want to worry you, Treya, but your little boy's got a heart murmur," she said. "I'd like to have one of my colleagues give a listen and maybe run a couple of tests on him. We'll need to take Zachary away for a while."

"Take him away! What for?"

The doctor put what she might have hoped was a comforting hand on Treya's arm. "As I said, to run a few tests, shoot some X-rays. Maybe get a little better sense of the cause of the murmur. We've got a terrific pediatric cardiologist. . . ."

"Couldn't you just do it here? Have somebody come down . . . ?"

"I don't think so. We'll want to do an X-ray and an echocardiogram at least. And then maybe some other testing."

"What kind of testing?"

"To get a handle on what we might be dealing with, Treya."

"But you just said it was a murmur. Aren't murmurs fairly common?"

"Some kinds, yes."

"But not this kind?"

Dr. Gavelin hadn't moved her hand, and now she squeezed Treya's arm. "I don't know," she said gently. "That's why I want to have a specialist look at him."

And then, somehow, by the time Glitsky got back from his phone call, Zachary was gone.

Sometime later, the volunteer maternity staff people wheeled in the special dinner that had been ordered for this room and seemed confused that the baby wasn't with the parents, who were both on the bed, silent, clearly distraught, each holding the other's hands. They didn't even look at the food. Finally, when the orderlies came back to remove the untouched trays, Glitsky decided he had to move. He didn't have any idea how long he and Treya had been sitting together waiting, but suddenly he had to get proactive. He needed to get information. Like, first, where was his son? And what exactly was wrong with him?

He told Treya that he'd be back when he'd learned something, and walked out into the hallway. He at once had recognized Gavelin and an older man approaching, heads down in consultation. One of them must have looked up and seen him, because without exchanging too many words, it seems that they decided that Joyce would go back in to talk to Treya, and the other doctor—the stooped, sad and kind-looking one—would break the news to Glitsky.

Too worried to argue the logistics—why weren't they seeing him and Treya together?—he followed Trueblood into the tiny room, but they weren't even seated when Glitsky said, "When can I see my son?"

"I can't tell you that exactly." Glitsky recognized something in Trueblood's voice—the same sympathetic but oddly disembodied tone he'd used numerous times before, when he had to inform relatives about the death of someone in their family. He knew that your words had to be clear and carefully chosen to forestall denial. You were recounting an objective fact that could not be undone, painful as it was to hear. At that tone—by itself—Glitsky felt his heart contract in panic's grip. Trueblood's next words, even more gently expressed, were a depth charge in his psyche. "I'm sorry, but this may be very serious."

"You mean he might die?"

Trueblood hesitated, then nodded. "It's not impossible. We're still not sure exactly what we're dealing with."

Arguing, as though it would change anything, Glitsky said, "But my wife said it was just a murmur."

Trueblood's red-rimmed, exhausted, unfathomably cheerless eyes held Glitsky's. His hands were folded in front of him on the table and he spoke with an exaggerated care. "Yes, but there are different kinds of murmurs. Your son's, Zachary's, is a very loud murmur," he said. "Now this can mean one of two things—the first not very good and the second very bad."

"So not very good is the best that we're talking about?"

Trueblood nodded. He piled the words up as Glitsky struggled to comprehend. "It could be, and this is the not very good option, that it's just a hole in his heart. . . ."

"Just?"

A matter-of-fact nod. "It's called a VSD, a ventricular septal defect. It's a very small, pinhole-sized hole that can produce a murmur of this volume. Sometimes."

"So the very bad option is more likely?"

"Statistically, with this type of murmur, perhaps slightly."

Glitsky couldn't hold his head up anymore. They shouldn't have tried for this baby. He shouldn't have let Treya talk him into it. She was already in love with it, with *him*, with Zachary, as was Glitsky himself. After the long wait to welcome him, in only a couple of hours Zachary had moved into their hearts and minds. And not just the thought of him. The presence, the person.

But Trueblood was going on. "In any event, the other option is called aortic stenosis, which in a newborn can be very difficult to correct." He let the statement hang between them for a second. "But that's what we're testing to see now. We've X-rayed the heart already, and it doesn't seem to be enlarged, which is the most obvious sign of aortic stenosis."

Glitsky, grasping at anything resembling hope, said, "And you're saying it doesn't seem enlarged?"

"No. But at his age, we'll need to analyze the X-rays more closely. A heart that size, we're talking millimeters of difference between healthy and damaged. We'll need to have a radiologist give us a definitive read on it."

"And when will that be?"

"We've got a call in for someone right now, but he may not get his messages until morning. In any case, it won't be for a few hours at best. And the echocardiogram couldn't be scheduled until tomorrow. We felt we had to talk to you and your wife before then."

Glitsky met the doctor's eyes again. "What if it's the VSD, the hole in the heart? The better option."

"Well, if it's a big hole, we operate, but I don't think it's a big one."

"Why not?"

"The murmur is too loud. It's either a tiny, tiny hole or . . . or aortic stenosis."

"A death sentence."

"Not necessarily, not always."

"But most of the time?"

"Not infrequently."

"So what about this tiny hole? What do you do with that?"

"We just let it alone as long as we can. Sometimes they close up by themselves. Sometimes they never do, but they don't affect the person's life. But if the hole does cause . . . problems, we can operate."

"On the heart?"

"Yes."

"Open-heart surgery?"

"Yes. That's what it is. And it's successful a vast majority of the time."

Glitsky was trying to analyze it all, fit it in somewhere. "So best case, we're looking at heart surgery. Is that what you're saying?"

"No. Best case is a tiny hole that closes by itself."

"And how often does that happen?"

Trueblood paused. "About one out of eight. We'll have a better idea by the morning."

Glitsky spoke half to himself. "What are we supposed to do until then?"

The doctor knew the bitter truth of his suggestion, but it was the only thing he could bring himself to say. "You might pray that it's only a hole in his heart."

"*Only* a hole in his heart? That's the best we can hope for?"

"Considering the alternative, that would be good news, yes."

It was eight thirty and Hardy told himself that he should close the shop and go home. He reached up and turned the switch on the green banker's lamp that he'd been reading under. His office and the lobby through his open door were now dark. A wash of indirect light from down the associates' hallway kept the place from utter blackness, but he felt effectively isolated and alone. It wasn't a bad way to feel. He knew he could call Yet Wah and have his shrimp lo mein order waiting for him by the time he got there, but something rendered him immobile, and he'd learned over the years to trust these intuitive inclinations, especially when he was in trial.

The primary reality in a trial like this is that there was just too much to remember. You could have pretty damned close to a photographic memory, as Hardy did, and still find yourself struggling to remember a fact, a detail, a snatch of conflicting testimony. The big picture, the individual witness strategies, the evidence trail, the alternative theories—to keep all these straight and reasonably accessible, some unconscious process prompted him to shut down from time to time—to let his mind go empty and see what claimed his attention. It was almost always something he'd once known and then forgotten, or dismissed as unimportant before he'd had all the facts, and which a new fact or previously unseen connection had suddenly rendered critical.

Once in a while, he'd use the irrational downtime to leaf through his wall of binders, pulling a few down at random and turning pages for snatches of a police report, witness testimony, photographs. Other times, he'd throw darts—no particular game, just the back and forth from his throw line to the board and back again. Tonight, he backed his chair away from his desk and simply sat in the dark, waiting for inspiration or enlightenment.

He hadn't noticed her approach, but a female figure was suddenly standing in the doorway. She reached for the doorknob and started to pull the door closed.

"Hello?" Hardy said.

"Oh, sorry." The voice of Gina Roake, his other partner. "Diz, is that you? I saw your door open, I thought you'd left and forgotten to close it."

"Nope. Still here."

A pause. "Are you all right?"

"First day of trial."

"I hear you. How'd it go?"

"You can flip on the light if you want. I'm not coming up with anything. It went okay, I think. I hope. I even got a little bonus from Strout's testimony, so maybe I should declare victory and go home."

But Roake didn't turn on the room lights. Her silhouette leaned against the doorpost, arms crossed over her chest. "Except?"

"Except . . . I don't know. I was waiting for a lightning bolt or something."

"To illuminate the darkness?"

"Right, but not happening."

"It's the first day," Roake said. "It's too soon. It never happens on the first day."

"You're probably right," Hardy admitted. "I just thought it might this time."

"And why would that be?"

"Because Catherine didn't . . ." He stopped.

"Didn't what?"

"That's it."

"Okay, I give up. What?"

"I told her she wouldn't spend the rest of her life in jail. Spontaneously. That I wouldn't let that happen."

Silent, Roake shifted at the doorpost.

"I don't think she did it, Gina. That's why I said that. She didn't do it."

But Gina had been in more than a few trials herself. "Well, you'd better defend her as though you think she did."

"Sure. Of course. That's about all I've been thinking about all these months. How to get her off."

"There you go."

"But it's all been strategy. Get the jury to go for murder/suicide. Play up the harassment angle with Cuneo. Hammer the weak evidence."

"Right. All of the above."

"But the bottom line is, somebody else did it."

She snorted. "The famous other dude."

"No, not him. A specific human being that I've stopped trying to find."

Roake was silent for a long moment. "A little free advice?"

"Sure. Always."

"Defend her as if you believed with all your heart that she's guilty as hell. You'll feel better later. I promise."

But driving home, he couldn't get the idea out of his mind. So basic, so simple and yet he'd been ignoring it for months, lost to strategy and the other minutiae of trial preparation. If Catherine didn't kill them, someone else did. He had to get that message into the courtroom, in front of the jurors. In his career, he'd found nothing else that approached an alternative suspect as a vehicle for doubt. It struck him that Glitsky's failure to get an alternative lead to pursue—another plausible suspect—had derailed him from any kind of reliance on the "soddit," or "some other dude did it," defense. He never had come back to it, and he should have, because in this case some other dude *had* done it.

It wasn't his client. It wasn't Catherine. Somehow, from the earliest weeks, and without any overt admission or even discussion of the question of her objective guilt, Hardy had become certain of that. This was a woman he'd known as a girl, whom he'd loved. They'd met nearly every day for months and months now, and even with all the life changes for both of them, every instinct he had told him that Catherine was the same person she'd been before. He'd been with her when she sobbed her way through *The Sound of Music*. One time the two of them had rescued a rabbit that had been hit by a car. She'd been a candy striper at Sequoia Hospital because she wanted to help people who were in pain. This woman did not plan and execute a cold-blooded killing of her father-in-law and his girlfriend and then set the house on fire. It just did not happen. He couldn't accept the thought of it as any kind of reality.

Every night as he sought parking near his home he would drive up Geary and turn north on 34th Avenue, the block where he lived. He never knew—once or twice a year he'd find a spot. His house was a two-story, stand-alone Victorian wedged between two four-story apartment buildings. With a postage-stamp lawn and a white picket fence in front, and dwarfed by its neighbors, it projected a quaintness and vulnerability that, to Hardy, gave it great curb appeal. Not that he'd ever consider selling it. He'd owned the place for more than thirty years, since just after his divorce from Jane, and now he'd raised his family here. He felt that its boards were as much a part of who he was as were his own bones.

And tonight—a sign from the heaven he didn't really believe in—twenty feet of unoccupied curb space lay exposed directly in front of his gate. Automatically assigning to the vision the status of mirage, he almost drove right by it before he hit his brakes and backed in.

He checked his watch, saw with some surprise that it was ten after nine, realized that he hadn't eaten since his lunchtime lamburger. In his home, welcoming lights were on in the living room and over the small front porch. When he got out of the car, he smelled oak logs burning and looked up to see a clean plume of white coming out of the chimney.

Home.

Cuneo didn't hear the telephone ring because he was playing his drums along with "Wipeout" turned up loud. He had the CD on repeat and lost track of how many times he'd heard the distinctive hyena laugh at the beginning of the track. The song was a workout, essentially three minutes of fast timekeeping punctuated by solos on the tom-toms. Midway his sixth or seventh time through the tune, Cuneo abruptly stopped. Shirtless, shoeless, wearing only his gray sweatpants, he sat on the stool, breathing heavily. Sweat streaked his torso, ran down his face, beads of it dropping to the floor.

In the kitchen, he grabbed a can of beer, popped the top and drank half of it off in a gulp. Noticing the blinking light on his phone, he crossed over to it and pressed the button.

"Dan? Dan, you there? Pick up if you're there, would you. It's Chris Rosen. Okay, you're not there. Call me when you get in. Anytime. I'm up late."

Cuneo finished his beer, went in to take a shower, came out afterward wrapped in a towel. Armed with another cold one, he sat at his kitchen table and punched up Rosen's numbers. "Hey, it's me. You called."

"Yeah, I did. I just wanted to make sure you were still cool about this Glitsky thing."

"Totally."

"I mean, today, earlier . . ."

"It just pissed me off, that's all. It still does. But what am I gonna do?"

"Well, that's what I wanted to talk to you about. What you're going to do."

"Nothing. That's what you said, right?"

"It's what I said, yes, but I've been reconsidering. Maybe we can spin this sexual thing back at them. I mean, everybody already believes Hardy's poking her, right? So she's the loose one, she's easy, get it?" Rosen gave Cuneo a moment to let the idea sink in. "I mean, isn't she the kind of woman who would have made the first move? We didn't want to bring it up before because, well, I mean, what would be the point? Try her on the evidence, not on innuendo or her personal habits. More professional. Blah blah blah. We didn't want to embarrass her. But once they introduce the whole question, the jury needs to hear the truth. I mean, only if it is the truth, of course—I'm not trying to put words into your mouth. But if she did come on to you first, and you rejected her . . . it's your word against hers. And you're a cop with an unblemished record and she's a murder suspect. If we bring it up first as soon as I get you on the stand . . . you know what I'm saying?"

Cuneo brought the ice-cold can of beer to his lips. His internal motor suddenly shifted into a higher gear, accelerating now on the straightaway instead of straining up a steep grade. He'd never done anything to harass Catherine Hanover. He knew it. Whatever it was had been her imagination and her lies. Not him. He was sure of that.

Let's see how she liked it.

For the first couple of Hardy's murder trials, Frannie had tried to have some kind of dinner waiting for him when he got home. She went to some lengths to try to time his arrival at home to coincide with dinner being done so that they could sit down as a family together—the sacred ritual, especially when the kids had been younger. But the effort turned out to be more a source of frustration than anything else. Try as he might, Hardy couldn't predict when he'd get home with any regularity. It was another of the many things in their daily lives that was out of their control. Aspects not as ideal as they had once imagined it, and yet were part and parcel of this constantly evolving thing called a marriage. Tonight, as Hardy stood at the stove and Frannie, in jeans and a white sweater and tennis shoes, sat on the kitchen counter with her ankles crossed, watching him, neither of them remembered the growing pains of the dinner issue that had led them here. Hardy was in trial, so he was responsible for his own meals. That was the deal because it was the only thing that made any sense.

From Frannie's perspective, the best thing about Hardy's cooking was that it was all one-pot—or, more specifically, one-pan. He never messed up the kitchen, or created a sinkful of dishes. This was because he was genetically predisposed to cook everything he ate in the ten-inch, gleaming-black cast-iron frying pan that had been the one item he'd taken from his parents' house when he'd gone away to college. Ignoring his own admonition to keep the iron from the barest kiss of water lest it rust, she noticed that he was steaming rice as the basis of his current masterpiece, covering the pan with a wok lid that was slightly too small.

Talking about the usual daily kid and home trivia, interspersed with trial talk, and then some more trial talk, and once in a while a word about the trial, she'd watched him add a can of tuna to the rice, then a lot of pepper and salt, a few shakes of dried onions, a small jar of pimentos, a spoonful of mayonnaise, some green olives, a shot of tequila. Finally, she could take it no more. "What are you making?" she said.

He half turned. "I haven't named it yet. I could make you immortal and call it 'Frannie's Delight' or something if you want."

"Let's go with 'something.' *Now* what are you putting in there?"

"Anchovy sauce."

"Since when do we have anchovy sauce?"

"Since I bought it. Last summer I think. Maybe two summers ago."

"What does it taste like?"

"I don't know. I just opened it."

"And yet you just poured about a quarter cup of it into what you're making?"

"It's the wild man in me."

"You've never even really tasted it?"

"Nope. Not until just . . ." Hardy put a dab on his finger, brought it to his mouth. "Now."

"Well? What?"

"Primarily," he said, "it smacks of anchovy." Hardy dipped a spoon and tasted the cooking mixture. "Close. We're very close." He opened the refrigerator, nosing around, moving a few items.

"I know," she said, teasing, coming over next to him. "Banana yogurt."

"Good idea, but maybe not." He closed the refrigerator and opened the cupboard, from which he pulled down a large bottle of Tabasco sauce. "When in doubt," he said, and shook it vigorously several times over his concoction. He then replaced the cover. "And now, simmer gently."

"Are you taking a conversation break while you eat this," she said, "or do you have more work?"

"If you're offering to sit with me if I don't open binders, I'll take a break."

She put a hand on his arm and looked up at him. "We're okay, right?"

"Perfect." He leaned down and kissed her. "We're perfect," he said.

19

Arson inspector Arnie Becker took the oath and sat down in the witness box. In a sport coat and dark blue tie over a light blue shirt, he looked very much the professional, completely at home in the courtroom. He canted forward slightly, and from Hardy's perspective, this made him appear perhaps eager. But this was neither a good nor a bad thing.

Chris Rosen stood and took a few steps forward around his table, until he was close to the center of the courtroom. After establishing Becker's credentials and general experience, the prosecutor began to get specific. "Inspector Becker, in general, can you describe your duties to the court?"

"Yes, sir. In the simplest terms, I am responsible for determining the cause of fires. Basically where and how they started. If there's a determination that it's a case of arson—that is, a fire that's deliberately set—then my duties extend to other aspects of the crime as well. Who might have set the fire, the development of forensic evidence from sifting the scene, that kind of thing."

"Do you remember the fire in Alamo Square at the home of Paul Hanover on May the twelfth of last year?"

"I do. I was called to it right away. Very early on, it looked like an obvious arson."

"What was obvious about it?"

"There were two dead bodies in the foyer. They appeared to have been victims of homicide, rather than overcome by the fire. The assumption was that someone started the fire to hide the evidence they'd left."

Hardy raised a hand. "Your Honor, objection. Speculation."

Braun impatiently shook her head. "Overruled," she said.

Rosen ignored the interruption. "Would you please tell us about the bodies?"

"Well, as I say, there were two of them. They looked like a man and a woman, although it was difficult to tell for certain. The burning was extensive, and the clothes on the tops of their bodies had burned away. Under them, later, though, we found a few scraps of clothing."

Rosen gave the jury a few seconds to contemplate this visual, a common prosecutorial technique to spark outrage and revulsion for the crime in the minds of the panel. "Anything else about the bodies, Inspector?"

"Well, yes. Each had a bullet hole in the head, and what appeared to be the barrel of a gun was barely visible under the side of the man. So that being the case, I decided to try to preserve the scene of the crime—the foyer just inside the front door—as carefully as possible, and asked the fire-fighting teams to try to work around that area."

"And were they able to do that?"

"Pretty much. Yes, sir."

After producing another easel upon which he showed the jury a succession of drawings and sketches of the lobby, the position of the bodies, the location of the wounds—the prosecutor definitely favored the show-and-tell approach—Rosen took a while walking Becker step-by-step through the investigative process, and the jury sat spellbound. According to the witness, the blaze began in the foyer itself. The means of combustion, in his expert opinion, was one of the most effective ones ever invented—ordinary newspaper wadded up into a ball about the size of a basketball. Even without accelerants of any kind, a ball of newspaper this size in an average-size room—and the foyer of Hanover's would qualify as that—would create enough heat to incinerate nearly everything in it, and leave no trace of its source.

"You used the term 'accelerant,' Inspector. Can you tell us what you mean by that?"

And Becker gave a short course, finishing with gasoline, the accelerant used in this particular fire.

"But with all these other accelerants, Inspector, surely

they would burn up in the blaze? How can you be sure that this one was gasoline?"

Becker loved the question. "That's the funny thing," he said, "that people always seem to find difficult to understand."

"Maybe you can help us, then, Inspector."

Hardy longed to get up and do or say something to put a damper on the lovefest between these two. Earlier, Hardy had interviewed Becker himself and had found him to be forthcoming and amiable. Rosen's charming act played beautifully here—the jurors were hearing interesting stuff talked about by two really nice guys. Not only were they giving him nothing to work with, if they did get on something worth objecting to, and Hardy rose to it, he would look like he was trying to keep from the jury what this earnest and obviously believable investigator wanted to tell them. So he sat there, hands folded in front of him, his face consciously bland and benign, and let Becker go on.

"All these accelerants, in fact everything, needs oxygen to burn, so whatever burns has to be in contact with the air. But there is only one part of a liquid that can be in contact with the air, and that is its surface. So what you can have, and actually *do* have in a case like this, is the gasoline running over the floor, sometimes slightly downhill, pooling in places. But no matter what it's doing, the only part of it that's burning is its surface. Maybe the stuff that isn't burning underneath, the liquid, soaks into some clothing fabric, or into a rug. Both of those things happened here, so we were able to tell exactly what kind of accelerant it was."

"And it was?"

"Gasoline."

"Inspector, you used the word 'exactly.' Surely you don't mean you can tell what type of gasoline it was?"

Hardy and Catherine were of course both intimately familiar with every nuance of this testimony. Unable to bear his own silence any longer, he leaned over and whispered to her. "Surely he doesn't mean that?" A wisp of a smile played at Catherine's mouth.

"That's exactly what I mean." Becker gushed on, explaining the mass-spectrometer reading, the chemical analysis (more charts) of Valero gasoline, the point-by-point comparison. Finally, Rosen, having established murder and arson—although no absolute causal relationship between the two—changed the topic. "Now, Inspector, if we could go back to the night of the fire for a while. After you told the firefighters to preserve the crime scene as best you could, what did you do then?"

"I went outside to direct the arson team." He went on to describe the members of this team—another arson inspector, the police personnel—and their various functions, concluding with getting the names and contacts of possible witnesses from people gathered at the scene. "And why do you want to do that?"

Becker seemed to have some trouble understanding the question. Suddenly his eyes shifted to Hardy, but he braved a reply. "Well, lots of people tend to come to a fire, and you never know which of them might have seen something that could prove important. Sometimes a spectator might not recognize the importance of something they've seen. We just like to have a record of everybody who was there so inspectors can go back and talk to them later."

The reason for Becker's sudden edginess soon revealed itself. Rosen had obviously rehearsed this part of the testimony to get to this: "Inspector, isn't it true that, in your experience, when arson is involved, the arsonist, the person who set the fire, often comes back to admire his or her handiwork?"

Hardy shot up. "Objection, Your Honor. No foundation. The witness is not a psychologist." This was kind of a lame objection, since the question was more about what arson inspectors observed than what was in the mind of arson suspects, but it sounded good, and the judge went for it.

"Sustained."

Rosen tried again. "Inspector Becker, among arson inspectors is it common knowledge that a person who sets a fire . . . ?"

Hardy wouldn't let him finish. "Objection! Hearsay and speculation."

"Sustained. Mr. Rosen, ask a specific question or drop this line."

"All right, Your Honor." Rosen stood still, all but mouthing his words first to make sure he got them right. "Inspector, in your own experience, have you personally ever identified and/or arrested an arsonist who had returned to a fire he or she had created?"

Hardy was on his feet. "Your Honor, I'm sorry, but I must object again."

But Rosen, this time, had made it narrow enough for the judge to accept. "Objection overruled. Go ahead, Mr. Rosen."

"Thank you, Your Honor."

Hardy caught a bit of a smirk in the prosecutor's face and, suddenly realizing his own blunder, he tightened down on the muscles in his jaw. By objecting time and again to Rosen's questions, he'd fallen for the prosecutor's bait, thus calling the jury's attention to an item they might otherwise have overlooked as unimportant. Now no one in the courtroom thought it was unimportant, and Hardy had no one to blame for that but himself.

Rosen asked the reporter to read back the question, which she did as Hardy lowered himself to his chair.

The answer, of course, was yes. Becker himself had personally had cases where arsonists had returned to or remained at the fire scene at least a dozen times.

"So now you were outside, across the street from the fire? Can you tell the jury what happened next?"

Hardy had seen this coming. He might have objected on relevance with some chance of being sustained this time, but he had a use in mind for the information.

Becker answered. "Yes, a woman saw that I was in a command position and she approached me and told me that she was related to the man who owned the burning house."

"Do you recognize that woman in this courtroom?"

"I do."

"Would you point her out for the jury, please?"

"Yes." He held out his hand. "Right there, at the table."

"Let the record show that Inspector Becker has identified the defendant, Catherine Hanover." Rosen gave his little bow. "Thank you, sir." Turning to Hardy. "Your witness."

"Inspector Becker," Hardy said. "In your testimony, you used the word 'sifted' when you talked about recovering evidence from the scene of the fire. What did you mean by that?"

In spite of the time he'd already been on the stand, Becker remained fresh and enthusiastic. "Well, it's not a very high-tech procedure, but what we do is kind of sweep up and bag everything around a body and then try to identify everything that was at the scene, down to pretty small items."

"And you used this technique after the Hanover fire?"

"Yes, we did."

"Were you looking for anything specific?"

"To some extent, yes. I hoped to find the bullet casings, for example."

Hardy feigned surprise. "You mean you could locate and sift out something that small?"

"Sure, and even smaller than that. By the time we're through, we're pretty much down to ash and nothing else."

"And did you in fact find the bullet casings?"

"Yes."

"Two of them?"

"Yes."

"Were there any fingerprints or any other identifying marks on either of the casings?"

"Yes. Mr. Hanover's."

"*Mr.* Hanover's?" Hardy said. "Not Catherine Hanover's?"

"No."

"What about the gun itself? Were there fingerprints on the gun?"

"Yes. Mr. Hanover's and some others."

"Some others? How many others?"

"It's hard to say. There was nothing to compare them with. It might have been one person, or maybe two or more."

"But did you try to compare them to Catherine Hanover's fingerprints?"

"Yes. Of course."

"And did you get a match?"

"No. And the other stuff in the house was all burned up."

"In other words, Inspector Becker, there is no physical evidence to indicate that Catherine Hanover had ever touched either the gun that has been identified as the murder weapon or the bullets that were used on the victims? Is that correct?"

"Yes."

"No evidence she was ever even near the gun at any time? Ever?"

"None."

"In fact, Inspector, isn't it true that in your careful sifting of all the evidence found in the house after the fire, you did not discover any physical evidence that linked Catherine Hanover either to these murders or, for that matter, to the fire itself?"

Becker answered with a professional calm. "Yes, that's true."

Hardy took the cue and half turned to face the jury. "Yes," he repeated, driving the answer home. But he came right back to Becker. "I'd like to ask you a few questions now about the first time you saw Catherine Hanover on the night of the fire. Did you question her?"

"Not really. She came up to me and said she was related to the home's owner. That was about it. There was really nothing to question her about at that time."

"Nothing to question her about. Did anyone else join the two of you at about this time?"

"Yes. Sergeant Inspector Cuneo arrived from the homicide department, which we'd called as soon as we discovered the bodies."

"And did Inspector Cuneo question Mrs. Hanover?"

"A little bit. Yes."

"Just a little bit?"

"A few minutes. As I said, there was no real reason to question her."

"Yes, you did say that. And yet Inspector Cuneo chose to question her?"

"Your Honor!" Rosen said. "Objection. Where's this

going? Sergeant Cuneo was a homicide inspector called to a crime scene. He can talk to anybody he wants for any reason."

"I assume," Braun said stiffly, "that your objection, then, is for relevance. In which case, I'll overrule it."

Hardy took a beat. He'd gotten in the inference he'd wanted—that Cuneo basically just wanted to chat up Catherine, and now he was almost finished. "Inspector Becker, on that first night that he'd seen her, did Sergeant Cuneo express to you any thoughts about Catherine Hanover's physical appearance?"

As a bonus, Rosen reacted, snorting, objecting again.

Braun spoke sharply. "Overruled. Inspector, you may answer the question. Do you need Mr. Hardy to repeat it?"

Hardy, with a second chance to put it in front of the jury, wasted no time. "Did Sergeant Cuneo express to you any thoughts about Catherine Hanover's physical appearance?"

"Yes, he did."

"What did he say?"

"He said she was a damn fine-looking woman."

"Those were his exact words?"

"Pretty close."

When Hardy got back to his table, Catherine leaned over and urgently whispered to him, "What about the ring?"

"What ring?"

"Missy's. Paul gave her an enormous rock. If they swept up everything in the room down small enough to find a bullet casing, they must have found the ring, too. Right?"

"Maybe it was still on her finger."

"Oh, okay. You're right. I'd just assumed . . ."

"No. It's worth asking," Hardy said, although he couldn't have elucidated exactly why he thought so. "I'll go back and ask Strout."

"Mr. Hardy." Braun stared down over her lenses. "If we're not keeping you . . ."

"No. Sorry, Your Honor."

Braun shifted her gaze to the other table. "Mr. Rosen, call your next witness."

Rosen got to his feet. "The people call Sergeant Inspector Daniel Cuneo."

Hardy put a hand over his client's hand on the defense table, gave what he hoped was a reassuring squeeze. "Get ready," he whispered. "This is where it gets ugly."

20

Glitsky's prayers were answered. It appeared that it was "only" a hole in Zachary's heart after all. It was so small that the doctor thought it might eventually close up on its own, although Glitsky and Treya shouldn't count on that since it was equally possible that it might not. But whether it eventually closed up on its own or not, Zachary's condition required no further immediate medical intervention, and neither doctor—Gavelin nor Trueblood—suggested an increased stay in the hospital for either mother or child.

So Paganucci had come out to the hospital with Glitsky's car, and Abe and Treya were back to their duplex by noon, both of them completely wrung out with the stress and uncertainty of the previous twenty-four hours. Neither had slept for more than an hour or two. And they were nowhere near out of the woods yet with their boy. There was still some likelihood that he'd need open-heart surgery in the very near term—the doctors and his parents would have to keep a close eye on his overall development, heart size, energy level, skin color—turning bluish would be a bad sign, for example. But what had seemed a bad-odds bet yesterday—that Zachary might be the one child in eight born with this condition able to live a normal life without surgery—now seemed at least possible, and that was something to hang on to, albeit precariously. At least it was not the probable death sentence of aortic stenosis.

Rachel was staying another day with her grandfather Nat. By pretending that he was going to take a much-needed nap with her, Glitsky got Treya to lie down in the bedroom with Zachary blessedly sleeping in the crib beside her. Within minutes she, too, was asleep.

Glitsky got out of bed, went into the kitchen, turned in a full circle, then walked down the hallway by Rachel's room. He checked the back door to make sure it was locked, deadbolt in place, and came back out to the living room. Outside, a bleak drizzle dotted his picture window, but he went to it anyway and stared unseeing at the view of his cul-de-sac below. Eventually, he found himself back in the kitchen. Apparently he'd eaten some crackers and cheese—the crumbs littered the table in front of him. He scooped them into his hand, dropped them in the sink, and punched the message light on his telephone.

The only call was from Dismas Hardy, wondering where he was, telling him that suddenly he had many questions, all of them more critical than the location of Missy D'Amiens's car. They needed to talk. There'd already been a few developments in the first day of the trial that would affect him. But more than that, he needed to revisit what Abe had done to date.

Glitsky looked at the clock on his stove. Ten after one. There was some chance that Hardy wouldn't yet be back in court after lunch. In some obscure way, and despite his pure fatigue, Glitsky all at once became aware of a sharp spike in his motivation. Maybe the sense of impotence he'd experienced while unseen doctors performed tests on his newborn had upset his equilibrium. Or was it the fact that now there appeared to be a reasonable chance that his son would be all right? That sometimes a cause might appear lost, and that this appearance of hopelessness could be a stage on the route to success, or even redemption? All he knew was that it all seemed of a piece somehow. It was time to get back in this game.

And, a critical point, he could do it from his home. And in a way, conducting an investigation from his home would give him another advantage. There would be no reporters, nobody to witness what he was doing, to question who he might talk to. Rosen and Cuneo, busy in trial mode, would certainly never take any notice. Everything he did would remain under the radar, where he wanted it.

He reached for the telephone.

Hardy's pager told him to leave a number. He did that,

then immediately placed another call to his own office. If and when Hardy called back, they'd coordinate their actions. In the meantime, Missy's car was a question even Glitsky had failed to ask. In fact, he realized, every strand of his failed investigation up until now had emanated from Paul Hanover—his business dealings, his politics, his personal life. To Glitsky's knowledge, neither he nor Hardy nor Cuneo nor anyone else involved in the case had given the time of day to Missy D'Amiens. She was just the mistress, then the fiancée, unimportant in her own right.

But what if . . . ?

At the very least it was somewhere he hadn't looked. And nowhere else had yielded any results.

"Deputy Chief Glitsky's office."

"Melissa, it's me."

"Abe." His secretary lowered her voice. "How are you? And Treya?"

"Both of us are pretty tired, but all right."

A pause. "And the baby? Tom"—Paganucci—"Tom said . . ."

Glitsky cut her off. "Zack's going to be fine."

"Zack? Of course, Tom didn't know what you called him." She was obviously spreading the news to the rest of his administrative staff. "His name is Zachary." Now she was back with him. "Thank God he's all right. We've all been sick here wondering."

"Well . . ." To avoid going into any more detail at the moment, Glitsky switched to business. "Listen, though, the reason I called . . ."

"You're not working, are you?"

"I'm trying to, Melissa. But you've got the computer. I'd like you to run a name and vehicle R.O."—registered owner—"for me. On a Michelle D'Amiens. D apostrophe . . ."

Hardy felt the vibration of the pager in his belt, but he was in the middle of an uncomfortable discussion with Catherine's husband. Hardy had originally intended to huddle with Catherine in the holding cell during the lunch recess, but had noticed that Mary and Will were the only family members who'd made it to the courtroom today, and he needed to talk to both of them. Separately. And sooner rather than later.

So he cut his time with Catherine short and was waiting at the defense table when the brother and sister got back from their lunch together. They had nearly a half hour before court would be back in session, so he walked back and said hello and asked Will if he could spare a minute, then Mary when he and Will were finished, if there was time. So, although obviously unhappy about this unexpected ambush—Will thought he knew what it was about, money, and he was right—he accompanied Hardy back up to his table inside the bullpen. Both men sat down.

"So," Will began with a not entirely convincing show of sincerity, "how can I help you?"

He'd given Hardy a retainer of one hundred and fifty thousand dollars eight months before. Between Hardy's hourly rate, the billable time his associates and paralegals had spent drafting motions and preparing briefs, the large and long-running newspaper advertisements to try and locate the girl who'd run out of gas in the Presidio, the fees for filings and his jury consultant and the private investigator Hardy had hired to find out the truth about Will and his secretary (an irony Will would certainly not have appreciated, had he known), the retainer was long gone. Now Will was past due on his last two monthly invoices, nearly forty thousand dollars.

"The point is," Hardy said, after a short recap and overview, "I don't want this billing issue to interfere with my defense, but we discussed this, you remember, when I first signed on. How it was going to get more expensive when it got to the trial."

"Not that it's exactly been cheap up until now."

"No. Granted. Murder trials are expensive. Even at the family-and-friends rates you're enjoying."

Will chuckled. "Enjoying. I like that."

Hardy shrugged. "I'd hope so, since it's saved you nearly sixty thousand dollars so far. But even so, I wanted to ask you if there was a financial problem. Frankly, it makes me uncomfortable to be here in the first days of the trial and have my client so far behind in payments."

"It's not that far, is it?"

"Sixty days." Hardy waved that off. "But that's not the issue. The issue is that I know you've come into quite a large sum of money recently. I'm assuming you've got significant cash flow, so that's not the problem. And meanwhile, I'm going ahead with my defense of your wife and you're not paying your legal bills."

"Well, I . . ."

"Please let me finish. I find this conversation as difficult as you do, believe me. But I told you coming in that my trial day fees are three times my normal billing rates, and at the time you said that sounded reasonable. It's still reasonable. But I want to tell you, you're going to get whiplash from sticker shock next month if you don't keep up on these monthly payments."

"Are you saying you're raising your rates now?"

"Not at all. It's all in the contract we signed last June. But the trial has started and that changes everything." Hardy leaned in closer and lowered his voice. "You may not realize it, Will, but it's standard practice among criminal attorneys to get the entire cost of the defense up front. You know why that is? Because a client who gets convicted often loses his motivation to pay his lawyer anymore. Now I didn't make that demand with you and Catherine because of the personal connection, but I'm beginning to wonder if maybe I should have."

Will Hanover's eyes were flashing around the courtroom, and when they came back to Hardy, he'd obviously decided to be shocked and outraged. "You've got some balls trying to shake me down at a time like this. I've paid you a hundred and fifty thousand dollars already. Up front. If that's not good faith, I don't know what is."

"It was. Then," Hardy said. "This is now. And I wanted to put you on notice that it's becoming a big issue."

"Or what? You'll quit? You'd abandon Catherine over a late payment? You've got to be kidding me?"

Hardy didn't rise to the question. Instead, he said, "What might be easiest is if you provide another retainer like the first one . . ."

"You're out of your mind."

Hardy didn't pause. ". . . like the first one, to cover what you owe and get us through this month, if the trial goes on that long. And then to begin the appeals process, if we need it."

"If we need an appeal! In other words, if you lose."

"That's right." Hardy's voice was calm. "We won't need to appeal if we win."

"Well, I'm not writing you a check for another hundred and fifty thousand dollars on that off chance, I'll tell you that. And you can take that to the bank."

Hardy pushed himself away from the table, draped an arm over the back of his chair, and looked into the callow and handsome face. With an air of sadness, he came forward again. "Will. I know that you're through with Catherine, however this comes out. I appreciate you coming down here to trial and putting on the face of the good husband. But I also think I know why you're really doing it, and that's because you don't want to lose the respect of your kids."

Will shook his head in disgust. "I've had enough of this. You don't know what you're talking about." He started to stand up.

"I'm talking about Karyn Harris, Will. Your secretary."

Sitting back down, he said, "There's nothing between me and Karyn Harris."

Hardy nodded. "That's been the party line, anyway, that you've worked so hard to keep from your kids. You weren't having an affair. It was just Catherine who was crazed, right?"

"Right." Defiant still.

"And so to your kids, you're still the good guy, aren't you? The dad they can trust, who's holding the whole thing together?"

"That's right."

"But what if they found out you've been lying to them the whole time, too? How would they feel about that? About you?"

"I haven't been lying to them. There was no affair."

Hardy stared at him for several seconds. When he spoke, there was no threat to his voice or in his manner. It was more the measured tones of disappointment that things between them had come to this pass. "Will," he said. "Do yourself a favor. Take a look at the statements I've sent you over the past months. You're going to notice payments totaling about five grand to an entity called The Hunt Club. You know what that is? No? It's a private-investigator service."

Will's initial expression of disdain turned to disbelief and then a distillate of fear itself.

Hardy went on. "If you weren't having an affair, one of the things I considered early on was that you had the same motive to kill your father as Catherine did. You'd gone to some lengths to create an airtight alibi. You would have been perfect. So I had to know, you see, if you were really in San Francisco on May twelfth, or down south."

He let the words hang in the air between them. "Understand that I don't have to bring up any of this for Catherine's sake, and really never planned to. For my purposes, it's enough that Catherine believed you were being unfaithful, and suddenly she needed to go see Paul to find out where a divorce would leave her. But if you in fact *were* having this affair, and the jury knew it, they might view Catherine in a more sympathetic light. And all other things being equal, that's always to the good."

Will's hands were shaking, his color had gone gray. "You're blackmailing me," he said.

"I've had this for four months. If I was blackmailing you, I would have started then."

Will glanced back at the gallery, which had started to fill for the afternoon session. In the bullpen, the popular court reporter Jan Saunders was sharing a laugh with a bailiff. Several of the jurors had wandered back in and taken their seats. "Where is all this stuff?" he asked.

"Locked away," Hardy said. "No one ever has to see it. No one ever will."

Hardy kept his poker face straight. No one would ever see the documentation of Will's affair with his secretary because it didn't exist. The Hunt Club had come to the conclusion that Will and Karyn had spent their four days aboard the *Kingfisher*. The captain of that boat, Morgan Bayley, wasn't talking—Hardy's private investigator was of the opinion that the newly wealthy Will Hanover had sent him a quiet bundle of cash to keep his mouth shut. And had given Karyn a nice raise.

Hardy was running a pure bluff, and wasn't one hundred percent sure he was right until Will stood up and growled down at him, "You'll get your fucking check by the weekend."

21

"Sergeant Cuneo, did you have a specific reason to question the defendant on the night of the fire?"

"Yes I did."

"And what was that?"

"Well, I was called to the scene to investigate a double homicide. The defendant said that she was related to the owner of the house. That alone justified talking to her. But she also admitted that she'd been to the house that afternoon and had talked to Mr. Hanover."

"Did she say what they'd talked about?"

"At first, yes. She said they'd talked about family matters. But when I asked her if she could be more specific, she became evasive."

"Evasive?"

Hardy stood up with an objection. "Objection. Witness is offering a conclusion."

Braun overruled him, and Rosen barely noticed the interruption. "When you asked the defendant to be more specific about these family matters, what did she say?"

"She asked why I wanted to know."

"And what did you tell her?"

"I said I was going to need to know everything that happened in Paul Hanover's last hours, which included what she'd talked to him about."

"And did she then go into the substance of her discussion with Mr. Hanover?"

"No. She did not."

"Did you specifically ask her about this?"

"Yes. Probably half a dozen different ways."

"And she did not answer?"

"Not the substance of the questions, no. She kept saying,

'It's private,' or 'That was between me and Paul,' or 'I can't think about that right now.' "

"Did you press her on this issue?"

"No, not really."

"Why not?"

"Because she was obviously distraught over the fire. She'd acted like she'd just learned that her father-in-law, her children's grandfather, was probably dead. She became very upset after a while. At the time, I thought she had a pretty good reason. I decided to let it go."

Hardy thought this was pretty good. Rosen letting Cuneo present himself as sensitive and empathetic. And now he was going on. "All right. Now, Inspector, did you have occasion to notice anything specific about the physical person of the defendant?"

"Of course. I'm supposed to notice things. It's my job. I checked out her clothes."

"And what was she wearing?"

Hardy squirmed in his chair. He wanted to break this up, object on relevance, but he knew that Braun would overrule him. Catherine had been wearing what she'd been wearing and there wasn't anything he could do about that now.

"A blue blouse under a leather jacket. And jeans."

"Would you please tell the jury why you particularly recall defendant's clothing that night?"

"Sure." Accommodating, Cuneo faced the panel. Hardy wondered if he might have taken a Valium or two during the lunch recess. There was little sign of the trademark jitteriness he'd exhibited before the break. "When we interviewed witnesses later, someone described a woman who had left Paul Hanover's house just before the fire wearing a blue blouse under a leather jacket and jeans."

"But you didn't know that on the night of the fire?"

"No."

Rosen wore his satisfaction on his sleeve. He paused for a drink of water, then came back to his witness. "Sergeant, we may as well address this question now. Did you make a comment to Inspector Becker about the defendant's attractiveness?"

Cuneo handled it well. They'd obviously rehearsed carefully. He shrugged with an almost theatrical eloquence. "I may have. I don't remember specifically, but if Inspector Becker said I said something of that nature, I probably did."

"Does a remark like that seem out of place to you in that context? At the scene of a fire and double murder?"

"I don't know. I don't even remember saying it or thinking about it. It was a nonevent."

"All right, Sergeant, moving along. On the day after the fire, did you see the defendant?"

"Yes. I went to her house."

"And what was your specific purpose on that visit?"

"I had two reasons. First, she'd mentioned the night before that the victims had been fighting, and I wanted to find out a little more about that. Second, I wanted to get some answers about the family issues she'd talked to him about."

"At that time, did you consider her a suspect?"

Here Cuneo showed a little humanity to the jury, another nice move. "That early on," he said with a smile, "everybody's a suspect." Then he got serious. "But no, the defendant wasn't particularly a suspect at that time."

"Okay, and did you get to ask your questions?"

"No."

"Why not?"

"Because right after she asked me inside and offered me some coffee, she told me that she'd been talking to Deputy Chief Glitsky."

"For the record, you mean Abe Glitsky, San Francisco's Deputy Chief of Inspectors?"

"That's right."

"How did he know the defendant?"

"I don't know."

Rosen threw a perplexed glance at the jury. He came back to his witness.

"Inspector, is it unusual to have a deputy chief personally interview witnesses in a homicide investigation assigned to another inspector?"

"I've never seen it happen before."

"Never before? Not once?"

Hardy raised a hand. "Your Honor. Asked and answered."

"Sustained."

"All right," Rosen said. "We may come back to the involvement of Deputy Chief Glitsky in a little while, but meanwhile you were with the defendant in her kitchen?"

"That's right."

"Can you describe for the jury what happened next?"

"Sure. She was in the middle of making homemade pasta noodles and she asked me if I liked them. Her husband, she said, was out of town . . ."

Catherine grabbed at Hardy's arm and started to whisper something to him. He couldn't let the jury see her react badly, and he all but jumped up, raising his voice. "Objection, Your Honor!"

Braun's voice was mild, merely inquisitive. "Grounds, Counselor?"

Hardy's thoughts churned. He had gotten to his feet to shut Catherine up and to challenge Cuneo out of pure rage because he knew the man was lying, but these weren't grounds for objection. "Relevance?"

Braun didn't have to think about it. "Are you guessing, Counselor? I believe you've made a point about this topic yourself in your opening statement. Objection overruled."

The gallery behind Hardy stirred at the promise of more fireworks. Rosen smiled up at Braun. "Thank you, Your Honor." He went back to Cuneo, all business. "Now, Inspector . . ."

But Hardy whispered quickly to his client and was again out of his seat, cutting off the question. "Your Honor!"

Making no effort to hide her exasperation, Braun pulled her glasses down and peered over them. "Yes, Mr. Hardy?"

"Defendant would like to request a short recess at this time."

"Request denied. Mr. Rosen, go ahead."

But Hardy wouldn't be denied. "Your Honor, may I approach?"

Her endurance all but used up, Braun rolled her eyes, then folded her palm upward, beckoning Hardy forward with a warning look. He left the desk, came to the base of the podium, spoke in a low voice. "I'm sorry, but my client urgently needs to use the restroom, Your Honor."

"Urgently. That's a nice touch," she whispered. Furious, the judge paused for several more seconds. "This is beneath you, Counselor." Finally she lifted her gavel and brought it down with a snap. "Court will recess for fifteen minutes."

"I can't believe he's just lying like that."

"Actually, it's worse than that. He's not saying anything you can deny."

"But I didn't . . ."

"You did. You told him Will was gone. You asked him if he liked homemade pasta. You've told me this."

"Then I'll lie and say I didn't."

Hardy moved his hands up beside his ears. "Don't even privately say that to me, please. We have got to stick with the truth here. It's all we have."

They were in the holding cell, five minutes to go in the recess.

"But they're going to think I wanted to get him close to me so he wouldn't keep investigating around me."

"That's right. That's what they're going to think."

"So how are we going to fight that?"

"I don't know that yet, Catherine. I don't know. But the most important thing right now, the *only* thing right now, is that you can't react in front of the jury. Don't let them see you do more than look disgusted."

In the end, Hardy couldn't keep it from the jury. Cuneo's testimony was that Catherine had offered him at least dinner and maybe more. He'd certainly gotten that impression, anyway. He'd had to rebuff her, reminding her that she was a suspect in a murder investigation. She did not take the rejection well and, scorned, had refused to answer any more of his questions. After a while, he'd decided to leave. For the first time, he began to regard her as a possible suspect.

And then, the damage done on that front, Rosen brought it back to Glitsky. "I'm curious, Inspector, did Deputy Chief Glitsky give you any explanation of why he, too, would be investigating the death of Paul Hanover?"

Hardy stood up. "Objection. Hearsay and irrelevant."

"Mr. Rosen?"

"Your Honor, this goes to Deputy Chief Glitsky's bias

and motive to skew testimony in this case. If he perceives he's under political pressure to obtain a certain result in this case, his recollection, conduct and testimony are all highly suspect."

"Your Honor," Hardy countered, "the deputy chief hasn't testified—he's not a witness so far, so there is nothing to impeach. This testimony, if relevant at all, only comes in after the witness says something that makes it relevant. If that happens later, then it happens, but it's premature right now." Hardy knew he was going to have to face this sooner or later, but he wanted Abe to bring it up first. Have him explain his status in the case in his own terms first, and not take the stand already burdened with the jury's preconception that he was somehow suspect. Hardy knew he was right—that Braun should have waited until there was a foundation to admit the testimony. But she wasn't having any.

The judge took a breath. "Counsel, given what I've heard so far, I'm going to let this in now, subject to a motion to strike. But you're on a short leash here, Mr. Rosen. Keep this very focused."

Hardy didn't like it, but the order of testimony was something within the court's discretion. Rosen had the recorder read the question back to Cuneo—the gist of which was whether or not Glitsky had tried to explain why he would be investigating Hanover's death.

"Yes, he did. He said that Mayor West asked him to become involved."

Mention of San Francisco's mayor brought a pronounced buzz to the gallery, but it died quickly. No one wanted to miss the next question. "Did he tell you why?"

"No, sir. He was my superior. It was a fait accompli. I just assumed it was something political and didn't worry too much about it."

Hardy objected—speculation—and Braun sustained him. But it was a small and insignificant victory amid a string of setbacks. And more to come. "Sergeant, how did Deputy Chief Glitsky's involvement affect your investigation?"

"Well, the most immediate effect was that he warned me off talking to the defendant."

"Warned you off?" Rosen displayed his shock and amazement to the jury. "What do you mean, warned you off?"

"He said that she was threatening to file a sexual harassment lawsuit against me and if I knew what was good for me, I should leave her alone."

"And how did Deputy Chief Glitsky tell you he found out about this?"

"She called him."

"Did he say why she called him?"

Hardy was up again, this time citing speculation and hearsay. He was sustained again, and he took a breath of relief and sat down.

But Rosen never skipped a beat. "Inspector Cuneo, did the defendant in fact file a sexual harassment complaint against you?"

This, of course, had been something Catherine and Hardy had discussed from the beginning. In the end, they'd decided that to bring the complaint after she'd been charged with the murders would only be seen as frankly cynical and duplicitous. So they'd opted against it. Now, of course, it looked like that might have been the wrong decision.

Cuneo actually broke a tolerant smile. He shook his head. "Of course not," he said.

"She did not?"

"No, sir. She did not."

Treya and Zachary still slept.

Glitsky had no luck running down the car. It had not been reported stolen, and it was not listed among the city's towed vehicles. He had called around to nearby public garages, where she might have leased a parking space. Nothing. This, in itself, Glitsky thought, was provocative. Where was the darn thing? He placed a call to traffic and ran a check on the booted vehicles, and struck out there, too. Odd. Although he knew it was entirely possible that someone had boosted the car one fine day and then decided—hey, a Mercedes—to keep it. D'Amiens, being dead and all, wouldn't be likely to report it stolen.

But what Glitsky did get was an address where

D'Amiens had lived at one time, when she registered her car. Embarrassed for not having discovered it earlier, when it had always been as close as a computer check with the DMV, he reminded himself that the French woman had never really assumed any prominence in his investigations. She was the invisible victim, an adjunct to Paul Hanover, nobody in her own right.

That's probably what she still was, he thought, but at least here was a trail he hadn't been down. It might take him somewhere. Or maybe it would lead him to 235 Eleventh Avenue and stop there. With something of a start, he realized that the place wasn't four blocks from where he sat at his kitchen table. In five minutes, he'd written a note to Treya, should she wake up. He was just taking a walk around the block. He'd be back in twenty minutes.

Outside, the day hadn't gotten any nicer. A thick cloud cover hung low over the city, and the fine drizzle of an hour before held visibility to a quarter mile or so. Glitsky wore his favorite weathered, brown-leather flight jacket with the faux-fur collar. He walked with his hands in his pockets, taking long strides, his shoulders hunched against the cold.

Like most of the other buildings in the neighborhood— indeed, like Glitsky's own—the place was an upper-lower duplex, with D'Amiens's address as the street-level unit. He went to the small covered entryway and rang the doorbell, its gong reverberating. After no one answered, he peered through one of the small glass panes in the door, and could make out some furniture, a rug and a bookshelf in a home that seemed to be very much like his own.

"Hello?" An old woman's tremulous voice with a Brooklyn accent echoed down from above and behind him. "They're not home. They're working. Can I help you?"

Looking up into the stairway that led to the upper unit, he stayed below on the bottom step. As a large black man, Glitsky knew that the welcome mat wasn't automatically out for him. He got out his wallet, opened it to his badge, and said, "I'm with the police department. Do you mind if I come up?"

"They're not in trouble, are they? They seem like such nice people." Then, with another thought. "Or dead, are they? Oy, tell me they're not dead. God, not again."

Glitsky stopped on the fifth step. "Again?"

"My last tenant, Missy. Such a nice girl. An officer comes . . ." She made a hopeless gesture. "And just like that, he tells me she's gone. Lost in a fire."

Until this moment, Glitsky had been under the impression that Hanover's fiancée had been residing at the house on Alamo Square. But apparently she had kept this address as well. Still, he wanted to be sure. "Missy D'Amiens, you're talking about?"

"God rest her soul."

"Yes." He touched the mezuzah on the doorpost. "You're Jewish, I see. So am I."

She squinted at him, not at all sure she believed him.

"Abraham Glitsky." He extended his hand, which she gingerly took.

"Ruth Guthrie."

"And actually, I was hoping to talk to somebody about Missy D'Amiens."

She was squinting at him. "You're really Jewish?"

"Baruch atah Adonai . . ." he said. Glitsky had had his bar mitzvah many years before, and he attended synagogue with his father several times a year, the High Holy Days. He could still spout liturgical Hebrew when the occasion demanded. His scarred and weathered face worked its way to a smile.

"Well, come in then out of this soup," Mrs. Guthrie said. "Can I get you something warm? Some coffee, maybe, tea?"

"Tea sounds good, thank you."

"Go in. Sit, sit. I'm right behind you."

Taking a seat in one of the slipcovered chairs in the living room, he heard her running water in the kitchen, then the "click click click" of the gas starter on the stove. In less than a minute she appeared with empty cups and saucers, sugar and cream, and some cookies on a tray. "When the kettle whistles, you'll excuse me." She sat down.

"So you own this place?" he asked.

"Since 1970, if you can believe. My Nat bought it as an investment."

"Nat," Glitsky said. "My father's name is Nat, too."

She pointed at him. "Now you are teasing me."

He held up his right hand. "I swear to you."

After a second or two, she decided to believe him. She sat back on the couch. "All right, Abraham son of Nathaniel, how can I help you?"

It didn't take him three minutes to acquaint her with where he was. This wasn't really official. She might have even seen something about the case in the newspapers over the past months, but there were some other issues about Paul Hanover's estate that related to Missy D'Amiens. Unfortunately, all efforts to contact her next of kin had been in vain.

"I know. Some of your police colleagues came and asked me about that right after it happened. But I didn't know anybody else who knew her."

"When she moved in here, did she fill out any paperwork?"

"Sure. Nat always said trust everybody, but make sure they sign the papers."

"So she had references?"

Mrs. Guthrie gave a sad little laugh. "For all the good."

"What do you mean?"

"Well, they were all in French. She read them to me in English, translated, but you know, she could just as well have made them all up. What am I going to do, call and check references? Anyway, Nat was gone and she seemed nice and she had the money. Ahh, there's the whistle."

She went again to the kitchen. Glitsky got up and followed her. "So she had a job?"

"Yes. Where was it now?" She poured the water into a kettle. "Lipton okay?"

"Fine," he said. "Her job?"

"Just a minute. It's coming." She turned and led him back to the living room. "Ah ha! Here it is," she exclaimed. "What's the name of that place? Arrgh. Ah. Beds and Linens and Things, something like that. You know the one. Almost downtown."

Glitsky did know it. It was a huge warehouse store for household goods, with perhaps hundreds of employees. Glitsky, thinking that this would be the next step in this trail, found himself asking if she paid her rent with checks.

Mrs. Guthrie thought, sipped tea, and said yes.

"You wouldn't have kept any of the stubs, would you? She might have had something left in the bank when she died."

She nodded. "Another thing Nat said. You don't throw it away. You store it. God bless him, he was right. Those tax bastards. But wait, it was just last year, right? Her folder would still be right here, in my files."

In the courtroom, Cuneo was still on the stand as Rosen's witness. The fireworks from his earlier testimony were mere prologue. They hadn't even gotten to any of the evidence. But after another recess, that was about to change.

"Inspector Cuneo, were you specifically looking for something when you made your search of the defendant's home?"

"Of course. You can't get a warrant without a list of specific items you're looking for." Cuneo and the jury were already on familiar terms. Now, the helpful instructor, he turned to face the panel. "The list of items you're looking for, it's part of the search warrant."

"Okay," Rosen said, "and what did you list on the warrant for your first search?"

"The clothes she'd been wearing on the night of the fire."

"And you found such clothing?"

"Yes. In the closet and also the hamper in the master bedroom. The tennis shoes she'd been wearing, along with the pants and the blue shirt."

Rosen had the clothing in the courtroom, separated into three plastic bags. After Cuneo had identified each of them, Rosen had them entered as the next People's Exhibits after the gun, the casings, one of the bullet slugs they'd recovered—they'd now gotten to numbers 5, 6 and 7. Then he came back to his witness. "And what did you do with these items?"

"Delivered them to the police lab to look for gunshot residue, bloodstains or gasoline."

"And was the lab successful in this search?"

"Partially," Cuneo said. "There were traces of gasoline on the pants and the shoes."

"Gasoline. Thank you." Rosen didn't pause, but walked back to his table, picked up a small book and crossed back to the witness box.

Hardy knew what was coming next—the diary. He *really* hated anew Catherine's insistence that Heather be excused from testifying. It might have caused her some temporary pain, true, but on the other hand, Hardy could have made Rosen look especially heartless and perhaps even nasty, forcing the poor girl to testify against her own mother. Jury sympathy for Catherine and her daughter would have flowed.

But there was nothing for all that now. It was going to play out. "Sergeant," Rosen continued in a neutral tone. "Do you recognize this item?"

Cuneo examined it briefly, flipped it open, closed it back up. "I do."

"And would you please tell the jury what it is?"

"Sure. This is Heather Hanover's diary. Heather is the defendant's youngest daughter."

While Rosen had the diary marked as People's 8, the gallery came sharply alive with the realization that this was the defendant's own daughter's diary. Part of *the people's* case?

"Inspector," Rosen asked, "when did you first see this diary?"

"The Monday after the fire. I was by now considering the defendant my chief suspect, and I obtained a second search warrant for documents in her house."

"What kind of documents?"

"I wanted to look at her financial records especially, but also downloads on the computers, telephone bills, credit card receipts, even Post-its with shopping lists. Anything written, which of course included diaries like this one, that could verify or refute her alibi for the day of the murders. The defendant had said her children were away. We wanted to check records to substantiate that."

"And what did you learn from this diary? Heather's diary?"

Cuneo turned his head slightly and brought his testimony directly to the jury. "Heather unexpectedly decided to come home after school and was home all that afternoon and night."

"And what had the defendant told you?"

"She told me that she came home after her afternoon talk with Paul Hanover and had stayed there all night until she'd seen the news of the fire on television."

"Inspector," Rosen said, "would you please read from the relevant portion of Heather Hanover's diary on the day that her grandfather was killed?"

Hardy stole a rapid glance at the jury. Every person on it seemed to be sitting forward in anticipation. As he'd known it would be, this was a damning moment for his defense; and doubly so now that he had just ascertained to his own satisfaction that Will Hanover had in fact been having an affair with his secretary. If he could at least demonstrate the truth of that assertion, it might lend credence to Catherine's actions on the night of the fire, even if she had originally lied about them. As it was, though, he only had Catherine's lie, no corroboration of the affair, and her own daughter's handwritten refutation.

Cuneo had opened the little book and now cleared his throat. ". . . for some reason Mom wanted us all out for the night and told us to stay out and get a pizza or something. But the homework this week is awesome—two tests tomorrow!!—so I told Saul to just drop me off here so I could study. Had to scrounge food since Mom was gone again which is, like, getting to be the norm lately."

Cuneo paused, got a nod from the prosecutor and closed the book.

"And did you later talk to the defendant's daughter about the entry?" Rosen asked.

"I did."

"And what did she tell you?"

"She said she was home alone that night. Her mother was not home." Cuneo skipped a beat and added, gratuitously, "The defendant had lied to us."

Hardy didn't bother to object.

22

Cuneo's testimony took up most of the afternoon, and Braun asked Hardy if he would prefer to adjourn for the day rather than begin his cross-examination and have to pick up tomorrow where he'd left off today after only a few questions. Like everything else about a trial, there were pros and cons to the decision. Should he take his first opportunity—right now—to attack the facts and impressions of Cuneo's testimony so that the jury wouldn't go home and get to sleep on it? Or would it be better to subject the inspector to an uninterrupted cross-examination that might wear him down and get him back to his usual nervous self again? In the end, and partly because he got the sense that Braun would be happier if he chose to adjourn, and he wanted to make the judge happy, Hardy chose the latter.

So it was only a few minutes past four when he and Catherine got to the holding cell behind the courtroom. They both sat on the concrete bench, Hardy hunched over with his head down, elbows on his knees.

"What are you thinking?" she asked.

"I'm thinking that I wish you'd have gone home after you talked to your father-in-law."

"I know."

He looked sideways at her. "So how did you hear about the fire?"

"What do you mean?"

"I mean, if you weren't home, watching the news on television, and you weren't, what made you go back to Paul's?"

The question stopped her cold. "I don't know. I must have heard it on the radio. Maybe I had the radio on. . . ."

"Must have!" Hardy suddenly was sitting up straight and snapped out the words. *"Maybe* you had the radio on! What kind of shit is that?"

"It's not . . ."

"You went to the fire, Catherine. You were there, talking to Becker and Cuneo. What made you decide to go there?"

"I . . . I'm not sure. I mean, I *knew* about it, of course. You can hear something and not remember exactly where you've heard it, can't you? I was parked outside Karyn's for I don't know how long that night, then I drove all the way out to Will's office, and nobody was there that late, and after that I was just driving around, not knowing where to go. I'm sure the radio was on then, in the car. I must have had it on, and when they announced the fire . . ." She ran out of words.

"You told both of the inspectors and me that you heard about it on *television.*"

"I did. I mean I remember . . ."

"You remember what? What you told them? Or what really happened?"

"No, both. Dismas," she ventured to touch his arm, "don't be this way."

He pulled away from her, got to his feet. "I'm not being any way, Catherine."

"Yes, but you're scaring me."

"*I'm* scaring *you*? I must tell you, you're scaring me." He sat down again and lowered his voice. "Maybe you don't understand, but we're looking at something like five *hours* between when you left Paul's the first time and when you came back for the fire. You've told me all this time that you went to Karyn's house and sat outside and waited and waited for her to come home, just hoping that she'd come home, which meant she wasn't with Will. Now I'm hearing you drove out to God knows where, maybe—*maybe*, I love that—with the radio on . . . Jesus Christ!"

Standing again, turning away from her, he walked over to the bars of the cell and grabbed and held on to them. It took a minute, but finally he got himself under control, came back and sat beside his client. "You know, Catherine, a lot of this—everything we've been through together on this, it's all felt like the right thing because I've taken so much of what you are, who you are, as a matter of faith. You're the first woman I ever loved and I don't want to believe, and have never been able to believe, that you're capable of what you're charged with here."

She started to say something, but he cut her off. "No, let me finish, please. I believed you before when you lied to me about this alibi and said you didn't want me to think you were the kind of person who would spy on her husband. Now I know you are that kind of person and I can accept it and you know what? It didn't even really change how I felt about you. It was okay. Lots of us aren't perfect, you'd be surprised. But more lies are something else again. Lies are the worst. Lies tear the fabric. I'd rather you just tell me you killed them. Because then I know who you are, and we'd work with that."

Catherine's hands were clasped in her lap and her tears were falling on them. "You know who I am."

"An hour ago I would have said that was true. Now I'm going to sit here until you tell me something I can believe."

The silence gained weight as the seconds ticked. Hardy's whole body felt the gravity of it, pulling him toward despair. He turned his head to see her. She hadn't moved. Her cheeks ran with tears. Without looking back at him, she spoke in a barely audible monotone. "I did see it on the television."

He waited.

"I went to a bar. They had a TV over the bar."

"What bar?"

"Harry's on Fillmore. I stayed parked outside at Karyn's until it was dark, and when she didn't come home, I knew she was someplace with Will and I just decided . . . it just seemed that I ought to go cheat on him, too. Pay him back that way. My kids, my girls especially, they can't know I did this. I don't act that way, Dismas, I never had before. But I was in a panic. The life I'd had for twenty years was over. I know you see that."

"I don't know what I see," Hardy said. "Who picked you up?"

"That's just it. I chickened out. I had a margarita and talked to some guy for an hour or so, but . . . anyway . . . the fire saved me."

"On TV?"

"Yes."

"You had to go see the fire because it was your father-in-law's house?"

"Right. And only a few blocks away. I had to go." She touched his arm again, this time leaving it there. "Dismas, that's really what happened. It's what I was doing. It's why I couldn't say. You have to believe me. It's the truth."

More tears, this time Frannie's.

Her face was streaked with them as she sat holding Zachary, Treya on one side of her and two-year-old Rachel on the other, all of them on the couch in the Glitskys' living room. Treya, still wiped out, had nevertheless gotten dressed. Rachel was uncharacteristically silent, picking up the strained atmosphere from the serious adults. She sat pressed up against Frannie, holding her little brother's bootied foot in her own tiny hand.

As soon as Frannie had heard the news, she wanted to know what she could do to help. At the very least, she was bringing dinner over tonight. She called her husband at work, telling him to meet her at the Glitskys' as soon as he could get away—something was wrong with their new baby's heart. They might be taking Rachel to live with them for a while if that was needed.

"But he looks so perfect," she said, sniffling.

"I know," Treya said. "It's just that they don't really know very much yet."

"They know it's not aortic stenosis," Glitsky said, but his voice wasn't argumentative. He and the guys—his father, Nat, and Dismas Hardy—were arranged on chairs on the other side of the small room. Glitsky gave everybody a short course on the cardiologist's initial visit, the two possibilities he'd described for Zachary's condition, with the VSD being the best outcome they could have hoped for. "So we're choosing to believe that we're lucky, although at the moment I can't say that it feels like it."

"But they're sure it's a hole in his heart?" Hardy asked.

"Yes," Treya said. "As of this morning."

"But it could change?" Frannie wanted to know.

"Well, not from being a hole," Treya said. "It's not going

to turn into aortic stenosis, if that's what you mean. They don't think," she added.

"Trey." Glitsky trying to keep her accurate. "They're sure of that. It's not aortic stenosis. Right now it looks like a benign murmur. That's what they're saying."

"The hard thing," Treya said, "is that they can't predict anything yet. He could turn blue tomorrow, or today, or in the next five minutes . . ."

"Or never," Glitsky said, "maybe."

His wife agreed. "Or maybe never, right."

Nat Glitsky, in his eighties, got up and shuffled across the room. "Time to let the kid get to know his grandpa," he said, "if one of you lovelies would scoot over and give an old man some room."

"Who you calling old?" Frannie said, making room.

Hardy gave Glitsky a sign and the two of them went into the kitchen, out of earshot of the rest of them as long as they spoke quietly. Hardy took the large casserole they'd brought out of its brown paper shopping bag, then took the foil off the top. Frannie had made her world-famous white macaroni and cheese with sausages. It was still warm. Hardy slipped it into the oven, then pulled a head of lettuce out of another bag. "Salad bowl?" he asked. Then, when Glitsky got it out of the cupboard and handed it to him. "How you holding up?"

"A little rocky." Glitsky let out a long breath. "It comes and goes. The hospital was pretty bad. When the doc said I should hope it's only a hole in the heart, I wanted to kill him."

Hardy was silent. He'd lost a child once. He knew.

Glitsky was going on. "I just keep telling myself it's good news, it's good news." The scar through his lips was getting a workout, dealing with the emotion. "We go in for some more tests tomorrow. Then we'll see."

"Tomorrow?"

Glitsky nodded. "The first days, they like to keep a close watch."

"But they let you go home?"

"He's fine at home, except if things change. I had a few minutes today when I managed not to think about it at all." He went on to tell Hardy about his unsuccessful efforts to locate Missy's car, but getting her address, his talk with Ruth Guthrie.

All the while, Hardy was silently washing the lettuce, rinsing it, tearing it into bite-size pieces and dropping them into the large wooden bowl. After Glitsky had gotten through where Missy had lived, where she'd worked, and that she had paid her rent from her checking account, Hardy dropped the last piece of lettuce in the bowl. "Do you have premade salad dressing or should I whip up a batch?"

"Maybe you didn't hear me," Glitsky said.

"I heard you. I'm glad it gave you something to do and got your mind off all this stuff here, but Missy D'Amiens isn't going to matter."

"Why not?"

"Partly because she never has mattered, but mostly because Catherine changed her alibi today. Again."

"At the trial?"

"No, thank God. Privately, with me." He met his friend's eyes.

"You think she did it?"

"I don't think it's impossible anymore. Let's go with that." He went over and grabbed a dish towel off the handle of the refrigerator. Drying his hands, he said, "So now letting her testify looks like it could be a huge mistake. . . ."

"Why is that?"

"Because they'll ask her about her alibi—they'll have to, since they've already got that she lied about it originally. And to answer them, she'll either perjure herself or change her story again. Either way, a disaster. But if she doesn't testify, there goes the sexual harassment, which was always my theory of why Cuneo got on her in the first place. And more than that, it's one the jury might have believed."

"You don't think they'll believe me?"

"Oh, sure. They'll believe Catherine told you about it. But so what? If I don't have her take the stand and say it herself, then you have nothing to corroborate. Your account is just plain hearsay and inadmissible . . . you know as well as me. To say nothing of the fact that we've already made a big deal about this and we're committed. So no chance if she doesn't testify. And if she does, we're screwed."

Glitsky was leaning back against the counter, arms crossed, a deep frown in place. "I don't want to believe Cuneo's been right on this all along."

"I don't either. But Rosen's got his eyewitnesses coming up next after my cross on Cuneo, and that's not going to be pretty, either. They all say they saw Catherine, and I'm beginning to think they're saying that because they did."

Glitsky remained quiet for a second or two, then asked, "So you think she's got the ring after all?"

"The ring?"

"Yeah. Missy's ring." At Hardy's questioning look, he explained. "Ruth Guthrie mentioned it today again before I left, and I remembered I'd heard about it way back at the beginning of this thing. And I know it's never showed up in evidence."

"I was going to call Strout about that. You're sure? It wasn't on the body?"

"No possibility. I saw the body, Diz. No ring. No fingers, in fact."

"Okay, but why would I think *Catherine's* got it?"

"Because if . . . well, if she's in fact guilty, whoever did it most likely took it off the body. The thing's supposed to be worth, what, a hundred grand? And it hasn't showed up? What's that leave? Somebody took it."

"Or it fell off in the fire."

"Okay, then it would have been in the sweep."

"And maybe Becker or one of his men kept it."

Glitsky didn't like that. "Unlikely," he said. "I've been at some of these things and the arson guys log everything. So why do you think Catherine didn't take it?"

Hardy didn't answer right away. It was a good question. "Mostly," he said, "because she asked about it only yesterday at the trial. I don't think she would have brought it up if she had stolen it. But mostly, it just occurred to her and she blurted it out. That's what it really seemed like. I'm positive it wasn't rehearsed. It was like, 'Where's the ring?' "

"Okay," Glitsky said. "So how bad is her new alibi?"

"No worse than the last one. It's just that it's *different*. Why?"

"I mean is it plausible? Could it be true? Do you think it's true?"

Hardy brought his hands up to his forehead.

"'Cause if it's true," Glitsky continued, "even if it's different, she still didn't do it."

Hardy looked up at the ceiling, shook his head, uttered an expletive.

"You need to find the ring," Glitsky said.

Hardy put the little disagreement he'd had with his wife out of his mind. Of course she'd been disappointed that he wasn't coming home after their dinner with the Glitskys, but she knew what trial time was like. She'd get over it, and so would he. But the reality now was that he had to try to talk to Mary Rodman, Catherine's sister-in-law. She'd been in the gallery today, and he'd wanted to get together with her for a few words, but the billing talk with Will had trumped that and taken all of Hardy's time.

But the unusually rapid pace of the actual trial—as opposed to the glacially slow movement of the endless pre-trial motions and accretion of evidence over the past months—was outstripping his efforts to keep a step ahead of the proceedings. Now, merely to keep up, he had to effectively utilize every single possible working second in this and the coming days. Even under that pressure, he'd felt he needed to see Abe and Treya tonight, to be there if they needed his support. But now that mission had been accomplished, that message delivered, and he was back on the clock, on his client's time.

He'd made the original appointment, for seven thirty, from his office as soon as he'd come in from his day in court, before he'd even checked his messages. When he got the call from Frannie about meeting at Abe's for dinner, he'd called Mary again and asked if he could change the time to nine o'clock, and at precisely that hour, he rang her doorbell.

The Rodmans lived in a well-kept, brick-fronted house on upper Masonic. Hanover's youngest daughter, Mary, like seemingly every other woman involved in this case, was gourmet arm-candy of a high order. Over the course of his involvement in this case, Hardy had come to realize that Hanover was one of those men who had an enviable penchant for pulchritude. His first wife, Theresa—Catherine's mother-in-law—although in her early sixties and with the personality of a domineering tyrant, was still very easy on the eyes, a latter-day Nefertiti. Both of Paul's daughters, Beth and Mary, had carried those genes into the next generation. Catherine, perhaps the best-looking of all of them, had married into the family. And Missy D'Amiens had been about to join it. Beauty everywhere you looked.

After introducing Hardy, again, to her husband, Carlos, and her son, Pablo, she led him back out to a tiny sunken living room, hardly the size of Glitsky's. But what the room, and the house for that matter, lacked in size, it made up for in charm. Comfortable burgundy leather wing chairs and highly placed narrow windows bracketed a functional and working fireplace. In front of it, a dark wine Persian rug covered parquet floors. They'd artfully framed and tastefully hung several original watercolors.

Mary indicated the couch at the far end of the room from the fireplace and sat at the opposite end of it from Hardy. Like the other Hanover women, she wore her dark hair long, a few inches below her shoulders. Unlike Theresa, her mother, though—and Catherine, for that matter—Mary was physically petite, fragile-looking, with somber eyes. She wore the same sweater and slacks that she'd had on in the courtroom today, and little makeup. Catherine had told Hardy that she was the most emotional of the siblings, and the most sympathetic. Somewhat to his surprise, she spoke first. "I have to say, you managed to upset my brother pretty badly at lunch. Is that your approach now that you're in trial? To get everybody all worked up?"

Hardy asked with a mild curiosity. "Who else is worked up? Are you?"

"Well . . . no. But Will was."

"Will wasn't paying me, Mary. I didn't want to have to abandon Catherine, so I . . ."

"You wouldn't have done that!"

"Maybe not, but let's let that be our secret, all right?"

She flashed a weary smile. "I think he's being horrible—Will, I mean—playing the kids off her. She was always a good mother." She shook her head. "I don't know what to think anymore. I never thought they would arrest her, and then when they did, it just didn't seem real that she would . . . I mean that it would get to a trial. With all this incredibly weak evidence against her . . . it just doesn't seem like Catherine could have done . . ." She trailed off.

Though depressing, it was good for Hardy to hear this from someone who'd been at the trial the whole time. If she was thinking this way, it was a litmus for the jury. "The evidence seems bad to you, then, does it?"

"Well, I know you said that there wasn't any physical evidence, and maybe there isn't too much of that, but the rest of it . . ."

"The circumstantial evidence?"

"That's it. I mean, that might seem to some people that it points to her, doesn't it?"

"But it doesn't to you." Not a question. "You know Catherine better than that, don't you? She says the two of you are pretty close."

"Why else do you think I'm there in court every day? She's got to know that the whole family hasn't abandoned her." She bit her lip. "I mean, Will and my mother . . . it just seems so cruel. I don't know why he's doing that."

"Their marriage was on the rocks before," he said. "Now, with this, with her accusations against him, it's a war."

"I don't know why Catherine said all that about Will's secretary and him. She could have just, I don't know, kept it between them. That's one of the reasons Mom is so mad."

"So you don't think Will was having the affair?"

"I don't know. It's just all so sordid, don't you think? I don't want to believe he'd lie to his kids, though. I mean, people have affairs and get divorced all the time."

"Sure, but he doesn't want his kids to think he's the reason for it. He'd rather they think it's her. And especially with this thing now at trial this morning, Cuneo saying she came on to him."

Now the dark eyes flashed. "That was horrible! That man's creepy. You see the way he's always moving, bouncing, jittering, like he's on drugs or something? There's *no way* Catherine is going to . . . I mean, just no. But with all these accusations flying, I can see where people might not know what to think anymore."

"Do you believe Catherine?"

"Yes, but I believe Will, too. He's my brother. He's my blood. Thicker than water, you know." She sighed deeply. "It's like this terrible nightmare. I just wish we could all wake up."

"It is like that. I know." Hardy took his opening. "But listen, I've taken enough of your time. I've got a specific question I wanted to ask you if you don't mind."

"No, of course, I don't. I mean, if it will help Catherine . . ."

"Great." Hardy didn't want to let her think about it. "Do you remember back on the afternoon of the fire, after Catherine had gone to see your dad and found out his plans about Missy and the family? I was reviewing all of my talks with her the other day, all the details she'd told me, and I came upon the fact that right after she'd left your dad's house—this was long before the fire—she said she called you. Do you remember that?"

Mary nodded. "Sure, I remember that very well. She was really upset."

"And what about you?"

"I was upset, too, I suppose, but we're doing okay here, Carlos and I. I mean, I didn't like what Dad was doing, but didn't see any way that we could stop it." Then, perhaps realizing what she'd said, she put her hand to her mouth. "I didn't mean that the way it sounded. Nobody was going to try to stop anybody. It was just a shame, that's all. Dad being so gullible."

"With Missy, you mean?"

Nodding, she said, "But he'd made his own money and I guess he could spend it however he wanted. The minority opinion in the family."

"But you didn't believe Missy loved your father?"

"Not for a minute."

"Okay, let's go back to the phone call for a minute. Why did Catherine call you?"

"Well, I guess because we're friends. We talked all the time. Our boys are about the same age, too, so there's that. And after she left Dad's, she wanted everybody to know, the whole family, so we could decide what we were going to do. But she and Beth aren't all that close—Beth's really serious and not much of a chatterer, like me—and there was no way Catherine was going to call Mom."

"So did you call them then?"

"Yeah. Mom right away, I remember, but not Beth. She hates being bothered at work. I should have called Catherine back, too, I realize now, and maybe invited her to come out to Pablo's soccer game and we could have just talked and gotten everything calmed down. If I'd have done that . . ." She shook her head. "Anyway, I didn't. Is that all you wanted to ask me about? That phone call?"

"Pretty much," he said. "It's part of Catherine's alibi and I wanted to make sure I had the chronology straight before I put her on the stand." This was not even close to true, but it sounded plausible and, more important, Mary bought it. "There is one other thing, though."

"Sure."

"What can you tell me about the ring?"

She shook her head. "That stupid ring. What do you want to know?"

"Anything you can think of."

She thought a minute. "Well, it was the dumbest thing Dad ever did, buying that for her. Then telling us, of course, what he paid for it. Six figures, he said, like he'd finally gotten into some exclusive club. But that's really what started all the . . . I mean that's when everybody started taking Missy seriously. And Mom! I thought she'd die. *'He spent over a hundred thousand dollars on a rock for her finger?'* He never even gave her, my mom I mean, an engagement ring at all. They could only afford a couple of gold bands in those days. But then, when Dad got this, this monstrosity for her . . ." She shook her head at the memory, blew out a sharp breath. "Anyway, that's the ring. Why?"

"It's come up a couple of times lately. No one seems to know where it's gone to."

The fact seemed to strike Mary as odd, and her face clouded briefly, but by then Hardy was getting to his feet.

Two minutes later, the two of them shook hands outside in the cold night at her front door, she closed it behind him, and Hardy jogged down to where he'd parked.

In his living room, at his reading chair, the lone light in the house on over his shoulder, Hardy reviewed his notes on talks he'd had long ago with Catherine's family. He was happy to see that his memory hadn't completely deserted him. From the outset of this case, he'd realized that every member of the Hanover family had the same motive to kill the patriarch, so he'd questioned Mary, Beth and Will as to their whereabouts at the time of the fire.

Will, of course, had been out on the ocean somewhere off the coast of California, with or without Karyn Harris. Beth, a consultant with an environmental insurance firm, stayed at her office crunching numbers with a team of four other colleagues until nearly eight thirty. Mary worked in investment banking downtown, where she'd taken Catherine's call. She'd checked her calendar and found that her husband had picked her up from work at quarter past five, and the two of them had gone together out to Golden Gate Park to take in their son's six o'clock soccer game.

At the time he'd done these interviews—early in the process, late last summer—Hardy hadn't fully appreciated the degree to which Theresa remained involved with her offspring and with the lives and futures of their kids, her grandchildren. Still, to date, he hadn't ever talked to Theresa about what she'd been doing on the night of May 12. Among the various other dudes he'd considered, she'd somehow never made the list. She was merely Paul Hanover's ex-wife, long estranged from him. But evidently still connected enough, either to him or to his memory, to become enraged about the size and expense of his new fiancée's engagement ring. And what Hardy did finally know, now, again thanks to his conversation with Mary tonight, was that Mary had called her mother right after she'd heard from Catherine, in the late afternoon of the day Paul and Missy had been killed, about three hours before the fire started.

Hardy closed up his notes binder, turned off the back

light and walked to his little tool room behind the kitchen where he kept his maps. There, he looked up Theresa Hanover's address, which was on Washington Street at Scott, in Pacific Heights.

Fifteen blocks in a straight line from Alamo Square.

23

Hardy was up at five o'clock, showered, shaved and dressed in a half hour. Opening the door to his upstairs bedroom, he was surprised to see light from the kitchen, more surprised to see his daughter, Rebecca, up and dressed for school. She sat writing at the dining room table with her schoolbooks spread around her. Looking up at him, she smiled. "Howdy, stranger."

"Not you, too."

"What?"

"You know what. I'm in trial. It's how I support us financially, and unfortunately it involves putting in long hours once in a while, which is not something I enjoy as much as everyone here at home seems to believe. Have you eaten?"

"No."

"Plan to?"

She shrugged.

"I could make you something."

"What are you having?"

"Just some coffee."

"I'll have that, too."

"No food? You know, protein to see you through those grueling school hours."

She stopped writing, smiled up at him again. "Are you having any?"

"I'm an adult," he said. "I have no needs."

"Well, I'm eighteen."

"I'm vaguely aware of that. I was there for your birth. But what's your point?"

"Just that I'm an adult, too. In many states."

"But here, as a full-time student with energy needs, you still need food."

"But not breakfast."

"It's the most important meal of the day."

"That's what everybody says, but if I eat it every morning, I'll get fat."

"You'll never get fat. You work out every day."

"I might stop."

"When you do, you can stop eating."

A pause. "Okay, I'll have something if you do."

Hardy felt his shoulders relax. He walked over and planted a kiss on the top of his daughter's head. "The way you argue, you ought to be a lawyer. I'd hate to face you in court."

Abstractedly, she reached an arm up and put it around his neck. "I love you, you know, even when you're gone a lot. But I do miss you."

"I love and miss you, too. But it can't be helped. I'm going to make hash and eggs."

She gave him her arch look, held up three fingers, then turned her hand sideways. Still three fingers out.

Hardy, translating the sign language, effortlessly picked up the "W" and the "E" and, proud of himself, said, "What*ever*."

An approving glance. "Not bad," she said.

Hardy shrugged. "For an adult."

While breakfast cooked in his black pan, he went out to the front porch, down the front steps and out into a steady dark rain. He picked up the *Chronicle* out by the gate, then hurried to get back inside. In the kitchen, he shook the paper out of its plastic wrap and checked under the lid of his pan, where the eggs hadn't quite set.

Thinking he'd give them another minute or two, he dropped the paper on the counter and opened it up. Though the trial had provided a great deal of sleazoid fodder for the tabloid press, as well as a steady if less-than-sensational flow of ink as local hard news, it hadn't been getting front-page play to date in the local newspaper, so the headline on the front page stopped him cold: CONSPIRACY ALLEGED IN HANOVER TRIAL. Then, in smaller but still bold type: MAYOR'S TIES TO DEFENSE TEAM QUESTIONED.

Leaning on the counter with his hands on either side of

the paper, Hardy read: "The double homicide trial of Catherine Hanover took an unexpected turn yesterday when one of the prosecution's chief witnesses and the lead inspector on the case, homicide sergeant Dan Cuneo, testified that Mayor Kathy West personally enlisted the aid of Deputy Chief of Inspectors Abraham Glitsky to direct and perhaps obstruct the police department's investigation of the murders of lobbyist/socialite Paul Hanover and his fiancée, Missy D'Amiens.

"Questioned after his appearance in the courtroom yesterday, Sergeant Cuneo expanded on the conspiracy theme, saying that Glitsky and, by extension, Mayor West herself had repeatedly undermined his efforts to apprehend his chief suspect, Catherine Hanover, in the slayings last May. 'They cooked up sexual harassment charges against me, they told me to keep away from her, told me not to do any more interviews, tried to direct me to other potential suspects. It was a full-court press.'

"Several groups in the city have already expressed outrage over the allegation, although the mayor herself has thus far declined to comment. Marvin Allred, spokesperson for the Urban Justice Project, a police watchdog group, has called for a full-scale investigation into the mayor's relations with senior police officials. 'The mayor's arrogance and sense of entitlement undermine the very basis of our system of justice. This peddling and trading of influence in our political leaders is a cancer on the body politic of this city and has to stop,' he said." Another half-dozen quotes spun the story the same way. It wasn't just an accusation anymore. Strongly implied was proof of a conspiracy.

"Cuneo's allegations also implicate Catherine Hanover's defense attorney Dismas Hardy, whose cozy relationship with top cop Glitsky and the mayor has long been a subject of conjecture and discussion among Hall of Justice regulars. Cuneo went on to say that 'Everybody knows that he dated Catherine Hanover when they were both in high school. They've been friends since they were kids. When it was obvious that she would be my chief suspect, he went to his friend the mayor and asked her and their friend Glitsky to use all of her influence to keep me away from her. Luckily, it didn't work.'

"Deputy Chief Glitsky has not been at work for two days and did not return calls to his office, and Hardy, likewise, could not be reached for comment."

"Dad? Are you all right?"

Still leaning on his hands, the paper spread open under him, Hardy stood immobile. "If any of the jury saw this or heard about it, we're going to ask for a mistrial. I've got to or I'm incompetent." Now he straightened up, pressed a hand to his eyes. "I'm going to have to do this all over again. And Catherine in jail all that time. Lord."

His daughter moved up next to him, put an arm around his waist. He turned back to the front page so she could read the article from the top. When she finished, she rested her head against him. "But none of it is remotely true."

"No. What makes it so effective is that most of it *is* true. The mayor and Abe and I are friends. She asked Abe to look into the investigation. I used to date Catherine. The facts are fine. It's just all twisted. I especially love where it says that Abe hasn't been in the office for two days, implying that he's ducking questions, when in fact he had a baby born with a hole in his heart. You think that might account for it?"

"How about your relationship with Uncle Abe being a source of discussion . . ."

"My *cozy* relationship. And it's discussion and conjecture. Don't forget conjecture."

"I never would. But what's *that* supposed to mean?"

"It means we're somehow up to no good."

They both stood over the paper, staring down at it. "So what are you going to do?" Rebecca finally asked.

"Well, first, let's see if I can get the judge to ask if any of the jurors saw this or heard about it."

"Do you really want that?"

"I don't have a choice. It's too big to ignore. I think I can convince Braun."

"To declare a mistrial?"

He nodded. "If any of the jurors read this, and I'm almost certain at least three of them can read, then it's extremely prejudicial. They get kicked off just for ignoring Braun's instructions. If they discussed it with the other jurors, the whole panel goes." Suddenly, he let out a little yelp of alarm and reached over to uncover his black pan and flick the heat off under it.

"I like a nice crust on hash." Rebecca squeezed his waist. "Don't worry about that."

But Hardy's lapse in timing bothered him. "I've never ruined anything I cooked in this pan before," he said miserably.

"And still haven't," his daughter responded. "Besides, it's not ruined. It's well done."

"Same thing. It's got to be an omen."

"No, it's a sign. Besides, I hate runny eggs."

Hardy stuck the corner of his spatula into one of the hard yolks. "Well, they're not that. And what would it be a sign of?"

She gave it a second. "Perseverance. Staying in the frying pan even when it's too hot."

The lighthearted, feel-good words resonated on some level, although Hardy couldn't put his finger on it. "You think?" he asked.

"Positive," she said.

In the "Passion Pit" two hours later, the attorney and his client sat on either end of the library table that served as the room's only furnishing. "This is unbelievable," Catherine said as she put down the paper. "What's it going to mean?"

"It means we might be able to start over if you want."

She threw a terrified glance across at him. "You don't mean from the beginning?"

"Pretty close."

"I can't do that, Dismas. I couldn't live here that long."

Hardy wasn't so sure that she was exaggerating. He'd known a lot of people who'd gone to jail—including some who more or less called it home—and most of them went through the original denial of their situation, hating every second of the experience, but then came to accept the surroundings as the reality of their life. Over these eight months, if anything, Catherine had come to hate her incarceration more and more each day. She'd lost the weight because she'd all but stopped eating. Another eight months, or more, preparing and waiting for another trial, might in fact kill her. If she didn't kill herself first. The year before Hardy had had another client try to do that very thing.

"Well, Catherine, after we find out if any of the jury has seen this, and they have, then if I don't move for a mistrial—regardless what Braun rules—it's damn close to malpractice."

"I'd never sue you for that."

"No. But an appellate court might find me incompetent."

She couldn't argue with that. "I don't want to stop, though. I think we're doing okay."

"That's heartening."

"You don't?"

"Honestly, Catherine, I don't know. Cuneo has . . ." He stopped.

"What?"

An idea had occurred to him, but he didn't inadvertently want to give Catherine any false hope. "Nothing. I'm just thinking we've still got some rocky ground ahead of us. You testifying, for example." He explained his problem with her old and brand-new alibi, how the discrepancy would sound to the jurors.

"But I have to testify if I'm going to talk about Cuneo. Isn't that our whole theory about why he kept coming after me?"

"Yes. Initially, anyway."

"Would a second trial be any different?"

"Maybe. Slightly. I don't know. A venue change might make a difference."

"Are you still mad at me?"

The question took him by surprise—talk about irrelevant—but he nodded. "Yep."

"I didn't kill anybody, Dismas. I know you don't like to talk about that. You've told me not to go on about it, but it's the truth. It really is. And I can't stay in here too much longer. I've got to see the end in sight."

"Don't do anything stupid, Catherine."

"I won't. But I can't start all this over again."

Hardy boosted himself from the table and walked across to the glass-block walls of the jail's attorney-client visiting room. He couldn't remember the last time he'd let a trial get so far away from him, and now he wasn't sure how to proceed. Most defense attorneys spend a great deal of their time trying to get delays for their clients—to put off the eventual day of reckoning and the finality of the sentence. But Catherine didn't want delay, couldn't accept it. She wanted resolution. But if he'd tried to deliver on that at the expense of a winnable strategy, a shortchange on the evidence issues, or a blunder in his refusal to press for an obvious mistrial, he stood the very real risk of condemning her to life in prison.

But maybe, he was beginning to think, there was another approach—legal but rarely invoked—that could change everything. If he could get Braun to rule that Cuneo's statements to the press were a result of deliberate misconduct on the part of the prosecution—i.e., Rosen—she might give him a mistrial for prosecutorial misconduct. In this case, Catherine—having once been placed in jeopardy by the state—would under the theory of double jeopardy walk out of the courtroom a free woman. They couldn't try her again for the same crimes, even if they were capital murder. But of course, this made it a potentially huge decision for the judge, since it would undo the efforts of the grand jury that had issued the indictments, as well as those of the district attorney and the police department. And there would be an immediate uproar from the conspiracy buffs that somehow the fix was in.

But Catherine cut him off mid-thought. "Can I ask you something?" she said from behind him.

He turned.

"Is this true, what Cuneo says? That the mayor asked Glitsky to intervene?"

"Yes."

"Why did she do that?"

"Because she was afraid of your father-in-law's enemies. She thought it might have been about business somehow. The city's towing contract."

"And Glitsky followed that up?"

" 'Til it ended with nothing."

"And all the other leads?"

"Every one he could find, yes."

"How about the political one?"

"You mean with the mayor?"

"No, with the president. You know, the cabinet thing."

In the endless reams of newsprint leading up to the trial, the nascent potential cabinet appointment naturally got its fifteen minutes of spin and conjecture. But no one—reporters, private investigators or administration officials—had uncovered or revealed anything remotely approaching a connection to Hanover's murder. Many people, including Hardy's investigator, had looked, and all had concluded that Hanover hadn't been involved in anything controversial on the national scene. Beyond that, the nomination process itself had not even formally begun—Hanover's vetting by the FBI was still at least weeks away when he'd been shot.

Hardy shook his head. "I don't know if Glitsky has looked at that specifically. Why? Has something occurred to you?"

Hardy was more than willing to take anything she could give him. A little ripple of concern ran through him. Here he was, nearly a year into his defense of this woman, on the third day of her actual trial, and in the past two days she'd given him not one, but two, potentially important facts—the ring and the nomination—which he'd previously given short shrift. It brought him up short.

Were his own personal demons—his concern over Cuneo's conspiracy theory, allowing the personal element inevitably to creep into his representation of his old girlfriend, the media madness, Abe's personal and professional issues—were these concerns threatening his ability to conduct a competent defense, blinding him to other critical facts? The basic rule of trial strategy is that you didn't want to be surprised by *anything* once you got to the courtroom, and now in two successive days he realized he'd been vulnerable to broadsides twice! Luckily, it had not yet happened in the courtroom, but he'd obviously been so sloppy in his preparation that it would only be a matter of time.

It was unconscionable—he ought to go in to Braun and get a mistrial declared today and then bow out entirely. In waves of self-loathing, he realized that he'd failed Catherine and even failed himself. He was unprepared. She would go down.

But Catherine was still on the nomination. "That's what they were fighting about, you know. The nomination."

"I'm sorry," Hardy said. "Who was fighting?"

"Missy and Paul."

"When?" Hardy, all but babbling.

"Dismas. That day. Don't you remember I said they'd been arguing?" Though it didn't eradicate the disgust Hardy was feeling with himself, he did realize that he'd reread this bit of information, the arguing, while reviewing his binders last night. Though he hadn't recognized its relevance, if any. And didn't even now.

But Catherine was going on. "That's why Missy wasn't there when I was. She'd left all upset that morning."

"Why was she upset?"

"Because she didn't want Paul to go for the nomination."

"Why not?"

"I think mostly it was the house. She'd just spent over a year redecorating the place. The thought of moving to Washington, D.C.? I don't really blame her."

"Is that what Paul told you?"

"What? That she didn't want to move? No. He said she was paranoid about the government and their background check, which he thought was ridiculous. She didn't even want them to start. She thought they'd be prejudiced somehow because she was foreign. She just didn't want to be involved. It scared her, he said."

"But Paul wanted it? The nomination."

"Did he want it? Did Paul Hanover want national recognition for a lifetime of public and private service? Does the pope shit in the woods? Of course he wanted it. Missy would come around, he said. They weren't going to break up over it. They loved each other. She'd see there wouldn't be anything to worry about. He told her that morning that he was going ahead anyway, and that's when they'd fought and she'd walked out."

"And then come back," Hardy said, "in time to get shot."

This sobered Catherine right up. "I know. Great timing, huh?"

In the end, though, Hardy thought with some relief, this at least was an example of a fact to be filed under interesting, even fascinating, but irrelevant. Paul and Missy's argument on the day of their deaths didn't lead either one of them to kill the other. Someone else had killed them both. Which left Hardy only with the ring, and the question of Theresa Hanover's alibi for the night of the fire.

But the bailiff now knocked at the door and announced that it was time to go over to the Hall. Hardy, in a dangerous emotional state in any event, had to bite his tongue to keep from telling the bailiff not to cuff his client, that she didn't need that indignity.

But he knew that this would have been wasted breath.

The cuffs clicked into place.

24

Marian Braun was a Superior Court judge when Barry Bonds was still playing baseball for Serra High School down in San Mateo. Her chambers reflected that longevity with an unusual sense of homeyness. She'd had built-in wooden bookshelves installed all across the back wall, put down a couple of nice large rugs to cover the institutional linoleum floor, hung several pleasant California landscapes here and there. Drapes under sconces softened the two window areas, and the upholstered furniture for her visitors marked a significant departure from the typical judge's chamber setting of a few metal chairs in front of an often imposing and distancing desk.

But the comfortable physical setting wasn't making anybody in the room more relaxed at the moment. To no one's surprise, Braun had summoned Cuneo and counsel for both sides here as soon as her bailiff told her they were all in the courtroom. At the same time, she'd had the bailiffs bring in a copy of the morning's *Chronicle* and told them to instruct the jurors not to speak with each other, even casually, until she came out into open court.

Now Hardy leaned against the bookshelf, hands in his pockets, and Chris Rosen held up the wall next to him. Jan Saunders had pulled in her portable chair from the courtroom and was setting up her machine on the coffee table in front of the couch. Braun, silent as a stone Buddha, sat at her desk sipping coffee and pointedly ignoring everyone's entrance as she turned the pages of the morning's paper. She was waiting for Saunders to be ready to record the discussion, and didn't seem inclined to make small talk to cut the tension until that moment arrived. In fact, to Hardy, the gathering tension seemed to be her point.

Saunders hit a few keys, then cleared her throat—a pre-arranged signal—and Braun glanced at her, took a sip of coffee, put down her newspaper. She looked first at Rosen, then over to Hardy, then over to Cuneo and finally back to the prosecutor. "Mr. Rosen, do you remember a couple of weeks ago when we were starting with jury selection and I said I didn't want anybody talking to the press about this case?"

Rosen pried himself off the wall into a respectful stance. "Yes, Your Honor. Of course."

"Here in the legal world, we call that a gag order. Does that phrase ring a bell?"

"Yes, Your Honor."

"And since Inspector Cuneo has been in the courtroom, sitting next to you at the prosecution table since the formal start of these proceedings, do you think it's unreasonable of me to assume that he is part of the prosecutorial team? And that therefore the gag order would apply to him as well?"

"Yes, Your Honor, but . . ."

Braun held up a hand, stopping his reply, and turned to Cuneo. "Inspector," she began, "what do you have to say for yourself?"

But Rosen rushed to his inspector's protection before Cuneo could say a word. "I don't think Inspector Cuneo quite recognized the sensational nature of his comments, Your Honor. Or how they would be taken."

"Oh? Since when does a gag order mean say whatever you want as long as it's not sensational? And just by the way . . ." She turned to Cuneo. "Inspector, you didn't realize that naming the mayor as a co-conspirator to obstruct justice in the case before this court would hit the news cycle?"

Cuneo had both hands in his pockets, patting his legs inside them. "Judge," he said, "I'm sorry if it's caused a problem, but nobody ever told me not to talk to reporters."

"No, but I'll wager that no one ever told you to wear your trousers here to court today either, and yet you did. How long have you been a cop? Two weeks? You were sitting there when I imposed the gag order. Did you figure I was talking to myself? The gag order told you not to talk to reporters about this trial while it was going on."

"But Judge . . ."

"How about 'Your Honor'?"

"Okay, Your Honor. But in this case, there's reporters all over this trial."

"Thank you," Braun said, "I've noticed. Which was the point of the order." She shifted her gaze to the prosecutor, came back to Cuneo, shook her head.

Into the pause, Rosen ventured an excuse. "You didn't formally call it a gag order at the time, Your Honor, if you recall, and I'm sure Mr. Hardy would agree with me. You said in the interests of fairness, you'd like to see us refrain from discussing the case with the media."

Braun stared for a second in frank disbelief. "That's what a gag order *is*, Mr. Rosen. And in any case, as soon as we go back outside, assuming we proceed with this trial at all, which is not at all certain, I'm issuing a formal gag order and sequestering the jury, which I'd very much hoped to avoid."

Shifting at her desk, she brought her steely gaze to Hardy. "If we hear what I expect we will hear, Mr. Hardy, I'm assuming you're going to request a mistrial. Perhaps review your change-of-venue motion."

Like Rosen, Hardy came to attention when the judge addressed him. "That was my intention, yes, Your Honor. Originally."

Braun narrowed her eyes, a question.

"But my client is opposed to simply beginning again. She doesn't want to spend more time in jail."

Cocking her head, Braun frowned. "Is that some kind of a joke?"

"No, Your Honor."

"Did you explain to her the prejudicial nature of Inspector Cuneo's remarks? How they could affect the jury, even if I query each of them individually, which I will do, and they deny they read the papers?"

"I think I did. Yes, Your Honor."

The judge couldn't seem to get her mind wrapped around Catherine's objection. "Does she know what prejudicial means? That, to some perhaps quantifiable degree, these comments make it *more* likely that she'll spend the rest of her life, and not just a few more months, in jail?"

"Yes, Your Honor."

"And yet she still might want to proceed?"

"It depends, Your Honor."

Before things went much further, Braun wanted to poll the jury, see where they stood. Out in the courtroom, Hardy learned that he was one off on his estimate of the jury's literacy—not three, but four of them had read the article. One claimed to have read only the headline. A second said he'd only read a couple of lines. Incredibly, two others admitted that they'd read half of the article before realizing that it was about this case. No one admitted talking to anyone else about it. There were four potentially excludable jurors. And only three alternates.

Now they were back in chambers, Braun talking. "So it's down to you, Mr. Hardy. What are you asking the court to do?"

"We're asking for a mistrial, Your Honor, with a finding of deliberate prosecutorial misconduct that will bar any further trial because of double jeopardy."

Rosen exploded in true wrath. *"Get out of here!"* Turning to Hardy, "That's the most outrageous . . ."

"Mr. Rosen!" The judge's voice cracked in the room. *"You will address the court only! Any more of this arguing with opposing counsel and I'll hold you in contempt."* She pointed a shaking index finger at him. "And don't think I won't." Without waiting for any response from Rosen, she whipsawed back to Hardy. "If memory serves, that provision only applies if the prosecution did this on purpose to cause a mistrial. Is that your contention?"

"Yes, Your Honor." Hardy knew what she was going to ask next—why would *Rosen* deliberately screw up the case at this point so he could get a mistrial?—and he rushed ahead to tell her. "Mr. Rosen obviously wasn't sufficiently prepared. The real story of Inspector Cuneo's sexual advances to my client, which is going to have a huge impact on the jury, comes out in my cross-examination today. And suddenly his case, weak to begin with . . ."

But Rosen interrupted. "Your Honor, this is absurd. I've got eyewitnesses."

Braun nodded with some impatience. "Which is the main reason why I denied Mr. Hardy's nine-nine-five. Don't get me started." But she wanted to see where Hardy was going with this, and turned back to him. "And so because Mr. Rosen's case may become potentially more difficult, you contend he's trying to . . . ?"

"To get *me* to ask for a mistrial. Yes, Your Honor."

"And why would he want to do that? So he can start again fresh, more aware of your strategy? That's a reach, Counselor."

"That's not exactly what I'm saying, Your Honor. He wants a mistrial because he can't take the chance of a not guilty verdict in a case this big. Not if he wants to be DA someday."

"My God, Your Honor! I don't believe . . ."

Braun held up her hand, stopping Rosen without saying a word. "Mr. Hardy?"

"What I'm proposing," Hardy said, "is a hearing on the issue. The court needs to know who talked to whom and when. Particularly Mr. Rosen and Inspector Cuneo, but possibly other witnesses and maybe some reporters as well. At the end of that hearing, defense may ask for a mistrial, but I don't want to do that until I've heard the evidence on prosecutorial misconduct."

"And what would this misconduct be specifically?"

"Breaking the gag order, Your Honor, and perjury."

Rosen was beyond fury, Cuneo looked ready to take a swing at Hardy. Braun hated the whole thing.

Hardy kept talking. "There is no mention anywhere in the record going all the way back to Inspector Cuneo's grand jury testimony—not in any of his reports, nowhere—that my client made any inappropriate advances to him. I think the court needs to see whether he mentioned these alleged advances to any of his colleagues, or anyone else, previous to the other day, or whether, perhaps after a discussion with Mr. Rosen, he just made up a new story. And then got encouraged to speak to the media to further discredit Deputy Chief Glitsky . . ."

"Your Honor," Rosen cut Hardy off. "This is an obscene accusation that will be impossible to prove one way or the other anyway. It's up to Mr. Hardy to ask for a mistrial. If he doesn't choose to do that, fine, perhaps we replace some jurors who might have read today's articles, but then we take our chances out in the courtroom. That's what trials are about."

But Braun was mulling, sullen. "I don't need you to remind me how to conduct this case, Mr. Rosen." Now she bit out her words. "It's *your* witness who's caused us this problem because *you* obviously failed to keep his enthusiasm in check. Meanwhile, on an issue of this magnitude, I won't be ready to make any kind of ruling on Mr. Hardy's question until tonight or tomorrow. I'd like to keep this ship afloat if I can, but I'll be damned if I'll let it go on and get reversed on appeal. And while we're talking about appeal, Mr. Hardy, perhaps you'd best tell us the tactical reasons why you will only accept a mistrial with a finding of deliberate misconduct. Seems to me that even without that, you've got ample grounds."

"That may be, Your Honor," Hardy said, "but it may also be that Inspector Cuneo's intemperate comments will work in my client's favor."

This was the crux, and for a second, Braun's fuse blew. "They shouldn't work at all, goddamn it." She whipped on Saunders like a snake. "Strike that last." Then back to Hardy. "Cuneo's comments to the press weren't made in the courtroom under oath. They should have no bearing on this case. None. That's the issue."

"Yes, Your Honor."

Braun sat back in her chair, stared into the middle distance for a beat, came back to Hardy. "I'm curious. How might these allegations help Mrs. Hanover?"

"She thinks the conspiracy idea is too far-fetched to believe on the face of it. The jury's going to think Cuneo's a press-hungry hot dog." He brought both other men into his vision. "Which, by the way, he is."

Cuneo took a threatening step toward Hardy while Rosen snorted and said, "We'll see about that."

"Yes, we will."

But this small exchange riled Braun even further. She straightened her back and raised her voice to a crisp, schoolmarmish rebuke. "You gentlemen will not address each other on the record, but only the court. Is that clear?"

Coming forward in her chair, she said, "Just so we're completely unambiguous here, Mr. Hardy, the defense isn't requesting a mistrial without a finding of misconduct?"

"That's correct, Your Honor."

"Meanwhile, you're both prepared to proceed today?"

Both counsels nodded. The judge nodded, drew in a deep breath and released it. "All right," she said, rising and walking to where her robes hung. "Time to go back to work."

Braun herself had a very tough morning, and it didn't measurably improve her already charming disposition. After reiterating her gag order to the participants on the record in front of the disgruntled media assembled in the gallery, she then nearly set off a riot among several members of the jury when she announced her decision that they would be sequestered for the remainder of the trial until they had reached a verdict or announced they were unable to do so. Hardy had to like the suggestion that a hung jury was a possibility. Every little bit helps. She wound up dismissing three of them—those who had admitted reading any part of the article, though she retained the juror who had only read the headline—and substituted them with two men and one woman, none of whom had read the article, thus exhausting all the alternate jurors.

Braun didn't want to inadvertently inform the remaining jurors who hadn't read the article what it was about, but she cautioned them again that the deliberations and conclusions they would eventually reach in this case must be based only on statements given under oath in the courtroom and evidence submitted to the court. They must disregard anything they heard on the news or read in the newspaper before, and must not read or listen to anything new. And to that end, she would be allowing neither television access nor newspaper delivery to the jurors for the duration.

And this really nearly sparked a mutiny among the panel. Several days without a television! What would they do? How could they live? One panel member, DeWayne Podesta, even asked for and received permission to speak to the court as a representative of the whole jury, and he argued that the jurors were good citizens doing their civic duty, and didn't the Constitution forbid cruel and unusual punishment? And if so—Podesta really thought it did—certainly deprivation of television qualified.

Eventually, Braun restored order to the courtroom. But the machinations, cautions, pronouncements and simple business consumed the whole wretched morning. When they resumed in the afternoon, Braun announced, they would begin with Hardy's cross-examination of Sergeant Cuneo.

Until then—she slammed her gavel—court was adjourned.

Glitsky and Treya were having opposite reactions to the boulder that had settled on each of their respective hearts with the concern over their baby's life. In Treya's case, it might have had something to do with the physical exertions of the birth itself. She had been sleeping nearly around the clock since they'd brought Zachary home, only waking up to feed him and for a couple of hours last night when the Hardys and Nat had been by. Glitsky, on the other hand, hadn't slept for more than a few hours.

Now it was nearly ten o'clock on a Wednesday morning, and he'd been awake since first light, finally having dozed off sometime a little after 2:20, or at least that was the last time he remembered looking at the bedroom clock. Rita, their nanny/house-sitter, God bless her, had made herself available and was back with Rachel now, and the two of them were watching the television down the kids' hallway, the sound a barely audible drone. Their cardiology appointment with Zachary was in three hours, and sitting at the kitchen table, a cold mug of tea untouched in front of him, Glitsky stared at the clock and wondered how long he should let his wife sleep. If she needed another hour, maybe more, he was inclined to let her take it.

In the four or so hours since he'd gotten out of bed, Glitsky had of course read the morning paper and made calls to Jeff Elliot at the *Chronicle*, to the mayor, to Hardy at his office and to his own office. The first three had not yet called him back at his private home number. His voice mail at work was clogged with reporters and even a few colleagues—including, he was happy to see, Chief of Police Frank Batiste offering his encouragement and support. But for the most part, nothing that happened outside the walls of his home was having much of an impact on him. Nothing was as important, even remotely as important, as the immediate health of his son.

The stark and terrible reality from his perspective, all the hopeful talk of "best-case scenario" notwithstanding, was that the boy likely faced open-heart surgery in the next few days or weeks, as soon as he was old and stable enough to possibly survive it. That possibility hung over him and Treya like a thick cloud of dread.

They might still lose their baby.

The thought was paralyzing and at the same time acted like a narcotic, a numbing agent that worked as a barrier to whatever reaction the events in the real world might otherwise have caused—whether anger or hurt or betrayal. Clearly, the city was getting itself worked up over this alleged conspiracy between himself, Kathy West, Dismas Hardy and Catherine Hanover, but Glitsky felt no sense of urgency to refute any of it, or even to respond to the half-dozen requests from reporters in various media. It was as if it were all happening somewhere else, already on television perhaps. Just another story that would fade when all the facts had come out because it simply wasn't true.

What was true was that they were taking Zachary to the doctor's at one o'clock to check his progress, or lack thereof. That, as far as Glitsky was concerned, was the whole world.

He went to the darkened bedroom for the fifth or sixth time this morning. Zachary was still swaddled, sleeping peacefully. Treya, completely covered in blankets, didn't so much as stir. Coming back into the light, he went out to the living room and stood at the windows, looking down at the street. He was wearing the same clothes he'd worn all day yesterday.

Hands in his pockets, he stood and listened to the faraway drone of the children's channel on the television down the hall, and watched the rain fall and fall.

When Glitsky first pulled the piece of paper out of his pocket, its origin and significance eluded him for a second or two. On it was a woman's handwriting, in pencil, barely legible. Then it came back to him. Ruth Guthrie. She'd written down the name of the store where Missy D'Amiens had worked, and her bank and account number. Last night, Hardy had said that he doubted that Missy D'Amiens was going to matter in the trial, and with this morning's blowup in the paper over the conspiracy nonsense, it appeared that the case was moving in an entirely new direction, one that would further remove either of the victims from the center of attention. To say nothing of the missing ring, which seemed a much more promising avenue of inquiry.

Still, Glitsky had discovered something they hadn't known before yesterday, and after all the time he'd spent on the investigation so far, that was provocative in its own right. He could follow it up in five minutes and get the last niggling tidbit off his plate, at least to his own satisfaction. God knew, he'd worked every other angle of this case trying to break Cuneo's lock on the apparent facts and he'd come up empty. A quick phone call or two would close the circle on D'Amiens, and then at least he would have been thorough, even if, as Hardy said and Glitsky believed, it was probably unimportant.

So he sat on the couch, picked up the phone and punched up information. Not identifying himself as a police officer, he finally got to the human resources office at the housing goods warehouse store and said he was an employer checking the reference of a woman who'd applied to work for him.

Replying that she was only allowed to verify the dates of employment, the woman went on to explain that she wasn't allowed to comment on the quality of the previous employee's work, or attendance, or anything else. "We have to be very aware of the potential for lawsuits," she said. "If we say anything, you wouldn't believe, it comes back to bite us."

"That's all right," Glitsky said. "I understand that. I'm just verifying the dates of employment."

"All right. The name please."

"Michelle D'Amiens. It says on her résumé that she calls herself Missy."

There was a short silence, then the woman spoke again. "Did she say she worked at this store? This location?"

"Yes." Glitsky read off the address. "Why do you ask?"

"Because I have personally approved the hiring of everybody who's worked here for the past six years, and I don't recognize that name. I'll check my files, of course, if you'll hold on. But does she say she worked here for a long while?"

Glitsky knew roughly when she'd moved into Ruth Guthrie's duplex, and he took a stab. "A couple of years, starting three years ago."

"So she just left, like a year ago?" Now the officious voice reeked with skepticism. "Just one moment please."

"Yes."

A minute later she was back. "I'm afraid it's not good news," she said. "Nobody by the name of Michelle or Missy D'Amiens has ever worked here."

Some part of Hardy thought it was the stuff of comedy—Podesta's notion that asking someone to live without a television for a few days was cruel and unusual punishment would stick with him for a while—but somehow he failed to find any of it amusing. Too much was at stake. He had too little time.

Abandoning Catherine to the holding cell and another jailhouse lunch, he ducked out the back door of the Hall and took a cab to his office on Sutter Street. On the ride over, he'd considered calling Glitsky—he'd even punched in the first few numbers of his pager—but then stopped when he remembered that his friend was bringing his son in to the doctor for tests today. He wasn't going to be available to do legwork, and legwork was what Hardy needed.

He got out of the cab in front of his office, stood still a moment, then abruptly turned and entered the garage. Next to the managing partner's spot, the elevator allowed him to bypass the main lobby. And Phyllis. And Norma, his office manager. And any and everyone else who would clamor for his attention or, in the wake of the article, for simple news of what was going on. Instead, he could ride straight to the third floor, where his partner Wes Farrell had his office.

"I'm afraid I can't, Diz. I'm busy, I really am."

Farrell didn't look busy. When Hardy had barged into his office after a perfunctory single knock at the door, Wes was in one of his milder trademark T-shirts—"Don't Use No Negatives"—and shooting a yellow Nerf ball at the basket he'd mounted on his wall.

"What are you busy doing? That's a fair question under the circumstances."

"Some people shoot darts to meditate. Your humble servant here shoots hoops."

"You're meditating?"

"Fiercely. I'm surprised you have to ask."

"Wes, listen to me." Hardy sat down on the overstuffed sofa. "I need to know what Catherine Hanover's mother-in-law—her name's Theresa—was doing on the day and night Paul got killed."

"Why don't you just call and ask her?"

"I don't want anybody to ask her directly. I'd prefer she didn't know I was interested in that. She's a prosecution witness and . . ."

"Wait a minute, your client's mother-in-law is testifying for the *prosecution*?"

Hardy nodded. "Sweet, isn't it? I don't know if Rosen actually plans to call her, but she's on his list."

"Against somebody in her own family?"

"Just the hated daughter-in-law."

"Jesus. And I thought my mother-in-law was bad."

"You don't have a mother-in-law, Wes. You and Sam aren't married."

"No, my first one. We weren't exactly close, but even so, I don't think she would have testified against me to put me in the slammer for life. What's she going to say, this Theresa?"

"Well, that's the thing. I haven't talked to her personally. When I saw her name on the list, I asked Catherine and she said Theresa and she just never got along about anything. She wasn't good enough for Will. She ought to get a job and help support the family. She was too strict with the kids. You name it."

"Wait a minute. Whose kids are we talking about?"

"Catherine's. Her own kids."

"What did Theresa have to do with them?"

"Evidently a lot. She expected to be a hands-on grandma. If you can believe it, she came close to suing them over grandparents' visitation rights."

"One of those, huh?"

"At least. The woman's a piece of work. And of course she's pretending to be a reluctant witness. Rosen or Cuneo just happened to ask her if she'd ever heard Catherine threaten Missy or Paul, and it just so happened she did. It was the truth. So what could she say? If they called her as a witness, she had to tell the truth, didn't she?"

"It's a sacred thing," Wes said.

"I couldn't agree more," Hardy replied. "But the real truth is that Theresa wants Catherine out of her life, out of her son's life, out of her grandkids' lives. And if a few words about Catherine's motive in front of a jury can help get that done, she's on board for it."

Farrell plopped into one of his stuffed chairs. "Okay, where would I come in? If I did, not saying I will."

"You make an appointment to see her as my representative. You're helping me out with the trial and wanted to get some sense of her testimony before she got to the stand."

"I thought you said you knew what she was going to say."

"I do. But tell her you want to hear it from her, and maybe coach her a little. Maybe we can throw the prosecution a curve ball. You know that she needs to tell the truth, of course, but if there's any way she can somehow help Catherine's defense, she'd want to do that, too, wouldn't she?"

"And why exactly, when she asks, didn't you get around to talking to her before this?"

"Tell her I really didn't think she'd get called. And still don't, but Rosen had talked about some motive witnesses, and I thought just to be safe . . . you get the idea."

"So what are you really trying to get at?"

Hardy broke a grin. "I thought you'd never ask."

25

"Sergeant Cuneo, you testified in front of the grand jury before this, did you not?"

"Yes, sir."

"And you were under oath?"

"Yes, sir."

"And where was that?"

"Upstairs in the grand jury room."

"How long did that testimony last?"

Cuneo was bouncing already, slight but visible tremors erupting through his shoulders every three to five seconds. "I don't know exactly. I'd guess something like three hours."

"Now, Sergeant, in this three-hour testimony, did you talk about your initial visit to Catherine Hanover's house?"

"Yes."

"Did you make any mention of Catherine making it clear to you that she wanted you to stay for dinner?"

"No. I don't believe I did."

"No, you don't believe you did." Hardy went back to the defense table, gave a confident nod to Catherine, and picked up some sheets of paper that had been stapled together. Walking back up to the witness box, he handed the stack to Cuneo. "Do you recognize these documents, Sergeant?"

He flipped quickly through the pages. "These are copies of my reports on this case."

"Of your interviews with Catherine Hanover and others, is that correct?"

"Yes."

"All right. Now, Sergeant, how long have you been a policeman?"

Hardy's change in direction caused Cuneo a moment's pause. His eyes flicked over to Rosen, then back to Hardy. "Sixteen years."

"So you've written reports such as the ones you now hold in your hand many times, yes?"

"Yes, of course."

"And the purpose of these reports is to memorialize evidence, is that right?"

"Yes."

"Good. Now, when you write up these reports, you try not to leave out important facts, isn't that true?"

Cuneo's shoulders seemed to be closing in around him, his neck sinking down into them. He was closing down defensively. His next answer came as a brusque nod.

"I'm sorry, Sergeant," Hardy said. "Was that a yes? You would never knowingly leave an important fact out of one of your formal police reports?"

Another nod.

This time Braun leaned over from the podium. "Answer the questions with words, Sergeant. Do you need the question read back again?"

"No, Your Honor." He leveled a malevolent glare at Hardy. "Yes, I try to make my reports accurate."

To keep the press on, Hardy ignored the answer. Instead, he repeated his exact question, using the precise same rhythm, tone and level of voice. It highlighted the fact that Cuneo had not answered the question the first time. "You would never knowingly leave an important fact out of one of your formal police reports?"

"No."

"Thank you. Now. Did you know that you were going to testify in this case?"

"Of course."

"And did you know that you would be asked about the reports you submitted?"

"Yes."

"And that others would rely upon the accuracy of these reports?"

"Yes."

"So, as you've testified was your habit and inclination, you tried to make your reports both accurate and complete, is that right?" Cuneo continued to wilt. If Hardy wasn't having such a good time, he might have let a little sympathy creep into him and let up a bit. But the thought never occurred to him. "Accurate and complete," he said, "and never more so than in the case of a homicide, correct?"

"Yes."

Pulling a page from Rosen's book, Hardy went to his table and drank some water. Returning to his position in front of Cuneo, he started in again. "Sergeant, when you conducted your interview with my client, did you tape-record it?"

"No, I did not."

"So the only record of your conversation with my client is in these reports? These complete and accurate reports, is that so?"

"Yes, I suppose it is."

"All right. Then, please point out for the jury where in your report you state that Catherine asked you to dinner, or came on to you in any way."

Cuneo's shoulders twitched. He stretched his neck, flicked his eyes to Rosen's table, cleared his throat. "I did not include it in the report."

"No, sir," Hardy said. "No, you did not."

Hardy went back to his desk, returned to the witness stand with another bunch of papers—Cuneo's grand jury testimony. Same questions, same answers. No, Cuneo hadn't mentioned anything about Catherine Hanover coming on to him, asking him to dinner, making inappropriate small talk. Hardy allowed surprise to play about his face for the jury to see. He hoped that by now that the word had spread to the panel that this witness was the reason that they wouldn't be watching any television for the next few days, why they would be locked up in their hotel rooms. He hoped they were primed to hate him. And he was going to give them more.

"Detective Cuneo," he said, "when Deputy Chief Glitsky conveyed to you my client's complaint about your conduct, you denied that any such exchange ever took place, didn't you?"

"Yes, I did. I didn't want to . . ."

"Thank you. In fact, Sergeant, the very first time you ever claimed that my client made an improper sexual advance to you was after she made her complaint to Glitsky, isn't that a fact?"

"I don't know. I'm not sure of the exact timing."

"All right, then, how about the first time on the record that you mentioned her invitation to dinner? Wasn't it when you were on the stand here just before this cross-examination?"

"It may have been."

"Yes or no, Sergeant."

"I believe so."

"I'll take that as a yes. When you were on the stand under oath. Like you were under oath at the grand jury."

"Your Honor. Objection! Badgering the witness."

Braun nodded. "All right. Sustained. Mr. Hardy, I'm sure Sergeant Cuneo realizes when he is under oath."

"Thank you, Your Honor. I just wanted to make sure."

"Your Honor!" Rosen again.

"Sustained." Braun glared down from the bench. "Don't get cute, Mr. Hardy. I'm warning you."

Hardy, straight-faced. "I apologize, Your Honor." He came back to the witness. "So, Sergeant, did you remember the alleged invitation before you took the stand?"

"Of course I remembered it."

"And yet you did not mention it? Why was that?"

"I didn't think it mattered."

"You didn't think it mattered?"

"I didn't think it would be part of the case. Besides, nobody asked me about it."

"That might explain why it didn't come up in your three-hour testimony. By the way, there was no defense lawyer at the grand jury, was there?"

"No."

"No one to ask you the sort of questions I'm asking now?" Hardy didn't wait for the answer. "No one to challenge your account of what took place?"

"No."

"Would it be fair to say, Sergeant, that you could talk about anything you wanted to the grand jury and no one would hear the other side of the story? Could it be, Sergeant, that you never brought up the incident because Catherine Hanover did not, in fact, extend any such invitation?"

"No. She did."

"She did? Can you recall her exact wording?"

"I don't think so. It was almost a year ago. She asked me if I liked homemade pasta and said her husband wasn't going to be home."

"Ah. Her husband. Since he was the son of the deceased, weren't you interested in his whereabouts?"

"Yes, of course."

"Since you've told the jury that *everyone* was a suspect at the time, was Will Hanover a potential suspect as well?"

"Yes."

"And did you ask his wife where he was?"

The questions were flying fast now, in a rhythm, and Cuneo answered without any forethought. "Yes."

"And wasn't it this, Sergeant," Hardy continued, "your question about her husband's whereabouts, and not an improper advance, that prompted Catherine's admission that her husband was gone and wouldn't be home for a few more days?"

Suddenly Cuneo straightened up in the witness box. "I took it as an improper advance."

"Obviously you did. Was that because this kind of thing had happened to you before?"

Rosen must have been waiting for his chance to break it up, and this was it. "Objection!" His voice had taken on some heat. "Irrelevant."

But Hardy wasn't going to let this go without a fight. "Not at all, Your Honor," he jumped in. "This jury needs to hear if other female witnesses have found Sergeant Cuneo irresistible."

"Your Honor!" Rosen was frankly booming now, outraged anew. "I object!"

Bam! Bam! Bam! Braun's gavel crashed down again and again. "Counsel! Counsel, come to order! Both of you approach the bench." When they were before her, she fixed them with a frozen gaze. "That's it from both of you. Last warning. Clear?"

It might be clear, but that wasn't the point to Rosen. "Your Honor," he began, "this line of questioning . . ."

"I heard you, Mr. Rosen. I'm going to sustain your objection and instruct the jury to disregard any innuendo contained in the question. Mr. Hardy, this is my second warning to you in the last ten minutes. There won't be a third. Now we're going to take a short break and let everybody calm down." She looked over the lawyers' heads to the gallery, slammed down her gavel again. "Five-minute recess," she said.

Hardy hated to leave off on the sexual harassment, but he knew he'd be able to come back to it. Meanwhile, he'd soon be talking to eyewitnesses who'd identified Catherine, and the jury needed to understand how Cuneo's methods in securing those identifications had been flawed. So he walked back to his table and picked up a small manila folder.

It looked like the kind you could get in any office-supply store, but one side had six holes cut in it. Through the holes you could see six color photos, three on top, three on the bottom. Each was a front mug shot–style color likeness of a young woman's face. The women were all brunette, all of a similar age and hairstyle. None wore jewelry, none were smiling or had their mouths open. There was no writing. Nothing distinguished one photo from the others except the facial features of the women depicted. One of the women was Catherine.

"Now, Inspector," he began, "I'd like you to take a look at what I'm about to present to you and describe it for the jury." Taking the folder in his hand, Cuneo opened it, glanced at the plastic pages inside, then closed it up and faced the jury. "It's a folder used to hold photographs."

"Have you ever used something like this in your work, Inspector?"

"Sure. All the time."

"In fact, this sort of display is used so commonly that it has a nickname, doesn't it?"

"We call it a six-pack."

"Why is that?"

"Because each page holds six pictures in the slots."

"Not just six pictures, Inspector, but six photos as similar as possible to one another, right?"

"Yes."

"Sergeant, in your career as a homicide inspector, in roughly what percentage of your cases have you employed the use of a six-pack to assist you in obtaining identifications?"

Cuneo again looked at Rosen, but this time there was no help. "I don't know exactly," he said.

"Roughly," Hardy repeated. "Fifty percent, sixty percent?"

"Maybe that much, yeah."

"More than that? Eighty percent?"

"Your Honor! The witness says he doesn't know."

But Braun shook her head. "Overruled. Give us an estimate, Inspector."

"All right. Say eight out of ten."

"So a great majority of the time. And a hundred percent of the time when the ID is in doubt, correct?"

"Yes."

"Now, Inspector, can you explain to the jury why, in the great majority of cases, you would use six photographs of similar-looking individuals to positively identify a suspect, as opposed to simply showing the eyewitness a picture of that suspect and asking if it's the same person they saw commit the crime?"

Cuneo hated it and was stalling, trying to frame some kind of response. Hardy jumped him. "It's to be sure the witness can really make an ID, right? That he can pick out the suspect from similar individuals."

"That would be one reason."

"And another would be to protect against the witness feeling pressured by police to agree that the one photograph they're shown is, in fact, the suspect?"

"That might be one reason."

"Can you give us another, Inspector?"

Cuneo rolled his shoulders, crossed his legs. "Not off the top of my head."

"So at least one good reason that the police, and you yourself, commonly use a six-pack is to avoid the witness feeling pressure from police to identify their suspect?"

"I guess so."

"So an eyewitness who identifies a suspect from a six-pack would be more reliable than one who was only shown one picture and asked to verify its identification?"

This time Rosen stood. "Objection. Speculation. Calls for conclusion."

Hardy didn't wait for a ruling. "Let me ask it this way, Inspector. You've had lots of training, including preparation for the examination to become an inspector, that taught you that this is precisely the function of the six-pack, to avoid mistaken identification, right?"

Cuneo hesitated. Hardy pressed on. "That's a yes or no, Inspector. Haven't you had literally hours of classes about the identification of suspects, where you learned that the six-pack is one way to avoid mistaken identification?"

Cuneo ducked. "I've had hours of training on IDs, yeah. I don't recall how many involved six-packs specifically."

Hardy felt the lame answer made his point better than either yes or no, and sailed on. "Inspector Cuneo, at any time in your investigation of Catherine Hanover, did you use a six-pack to assist eyewitnesses in their identifications?"

Cuneo didn't answer. Braun looked down at him. "Inspector?"

"Should I repeat the question?" Hardy asked, all innocence.

This earned him a glare from the judge, who repeated, "Inspector?"

"No, I did not."

Cuneo just couldn't let it go, so he made it worse. "We use this to confirm an ID when the witness doesn't know the person. When you know somebody, we might use a single photo just to be sure that we're talking about the same person. I mean, if you say you saw your cousin, we might show you a photo of your cousin just to be sure we got the right guy." Shoulders twitching, Cuneo tried an evasion. "It's pretty obvious."

"I'm sorry, Inspector. What's obvious? That witnesses can make mistakes, or that you shouldn't coach them to make an identification?"

Rosen was up in a second, objection sustained. Hardy didn't even slow down.

"When there is a question, Inspector, you use a six-pack to be sure there is no mistake. Correct?"

"Yes."

"And you never, ever tell a witness ahead of time who you think should be ID'd, or even give vague hints of what they look like, correct?"

"Yes."

Just a hint of sarcasm entered Hardy's voice—too little to object to, but just enough for the jury to discern. "And you, as a professional, intent on making sure that the wrong person doesn't get accused, you would always do what you could to make sure an ID was correct, wouldn't you?"

Cuneo got a bit heated now. "Yes, I would."

"So your failure to use a six-pack was not designed to bolster your preconception of who was coming out of Mr. Hanover's house, was it?"

"No! It was not."

"But the first time you showed a photo, you thought the person coming out was Missy D'Amiens, right? So you showed the witnesses a single photo and got your ID, right? And then, when you decided it must have been Catherine coming out of the house, you went to the same witnesses and used another single photo, and again got the ID you wanted, right?

"It wasn't a question of what I wanted, it was what the witnesses said."

Cuneo's eyes went to Rosen for an instant, but the prosecutor could do nothing to help him. Just this side of surly, he turned to face the jury box. "No, I didn't use a six-pack for these IDs. These witnesses all said they had seen this woman before."

"Which woman was that, Inspector? Missy D'Amiens? You remember her? The first woman they ID'd for you? Or Catherine, the second woman whose single photo got you an ID, too? In both cases, you told the witnesses who you thought they had seen, then showed them a single photo, and surprise! You got the ID you wanted, right?" Hardy, on a roll of adrenaline and anger, kept piling it on. "You said that you use a six-pack when the ID is in question, didn't you, Inspector? Can you think of anything that might put an ID in question *more than a previous ID of someone else's photo*?"

Another shrug, another glance at Rosen—*Do something!* Rosen tried to help. "Your Honor, objection. Vague."

"Not vague, but compound and argumentative. Do it a piece at a time, Mr. Hardy, and perhaps a bit less . . ."

"Sure, Your Honor." Then, with a slow and thoughtful cadence, he began again. "Inspector, you showed a single photo of Missy D'Amiens and got IDs, right?"

Cuneo couldn't disagree. "Correct."

"And after that, Catherine accused you of harassment, right?"

"I don't know what she said."

"Inspector, after you got the ID on Missy, and before you got the ID on my client, Deputy Chief Glitsky told you Catherine had complained of harassment, right?"

"Yes, that's what he told me."

"And with this information in mind, you took a single photo of Catherine, went back to those same witnesses, and said words to the effect of 'You made a mistake last time. Here's the woman you really saw.' Correct?"

"That's not what I said."

"The bottom line, Inspector, is that knowing these witnesses had already identified somebody else, you took a single photo of my client, showed it to them, and asked if this was the person they saw, not the other person they had ID'd, right?"

Cuneo had nowhere to go. "Yes."

"Tell me, Inspector, in all your hours of training, has anyone even hinted to you that this was a proper way to make an ID?"

"Not that I recall."

Hardy bowed from the waist. "Thank you."

But even after all this, there was one more nail to be driven into the inspector's coffin. He pressed ahead. "Sergeant Cuneo, during your visit to Catherine Hanover's house for your first interview, did you touch her?"

"No, I did not."

"Did you shake hands?"

"I may have done that. I don't remember."

"But to the best of your recollection, you did not touch her otherwise?"

"No."

"In passing perhaps?"

"Your Honor. Asked and answered."

"Cross-examination, Mr. Rosen. I'll allow it."

Cuneo: "No."

"Aside from the handshake, did any part of your hand come into contact with any part of Catherine Hanover's body at any time?"

"Objection."

"Overruled."

Cuneo: "No."

"Were you standing close enough to Catherine Hanover to touch her during any part of your discussion?"

"Objection."

This time Braun, obviously irritated by the needless interruptions, paused briefly. Hardy hoped the jury caught the signal. "Overruled. Sergeant, you may answer the question."

Cuneo obviously didn't want to, but he couldn't refuse, although first he looked at Rosen for a cue. By now he had the whole imaginary drum kit going, his eyes slits at Hardy. "Maybe."

"Maybe? You were or you weren't close enough, Sergeant. Which is it?"

"Yes, then, I was."

"Standing close enough to touch her?"

"Yes."

"But in fact you touched neither her arm nor her shoulder?"

Rosen, from his table. "Your Honor!"

But Cuneo, thoroughly worn down, replied before the judge could rule. "I don't know." Behind him, the gallery, which had obviously been closely following the testimony, made itself heard even through the security screen, as Cuneo mumbled. "Maybe I touched her once or twice by mistake."

Hardy stood stock still, then delivered the coup de grâce. "I'm sorry, Your Honor, I missed that. Could I have it read back?"

Jan Saunders read Cuneo's words again, playing it straight. "I don't know," she said. "Maybe I touched her once or twice by mistake."

* * *

Glitsky and Treya kept getting what they were told was good news, but it didn't seem to give them much relief. The great news was that the echocardiogram ruled out aortic stenosis. Today's X-rays on Zachary's heart also showed no abnormality or sudden growth in size. The EKG—wires and leads stuck all over the infant's body while he lay exposed and cold on the gurney sheet—also indicated that the heartbeat was regular. Through it all, the baby didn't cry, but endured it with a stoicism that would have done his father proud.

All the tests took the better part of an hour. In his office when they were done, Dr. Trueblood walked a careful line between optimism and realism. "I have to tell you that Zachary's condition as of today is the best that we could possibly have hoped for just a couple of days ago. Of all the children that I see in here, he's in the top one percent. And this is really terrific, terrific news."

These wonderful tidings were delivered, however, in a funereal tone. The old hunched man sat behind his desk with his shirt undone, his tie askew and his mottled hands linked in front of him. The light in the office itself was muted, the shades drawn against the dreary wetness outside, while the pitter of the constant rain provided the only soundtrack. "All that said, I feel I need to caution you that, though this is far better than aortic stenosis, it's still something to take very seriously. Sometimes a VSD can change quickly, especially in the early months. We'll want to keep a very close eye on Zachary."

"What does that mean?" Treya asked.

"Well, first I mean just watch him. If he shows any marked or dramatic change in color, breathing, feeding or energy level, you can call me at any time, day or night. You've got all my numbers, right? But then beyond that, it would be a good idea to bring him in here every week for the next four to six weeks for the same kind of tests. . . ."

Treya interrupted. "Every week?"

"Yes. For the next month or month and a half. Then, if there's no change, we'll go to once a month and see how that works out."

"What then?" Holding his wife's hand, Glitsky didn't want to betray his own fear. Treya needed him to be calm and even optimistic, and his voice reflected that. He wasn't relaxed, but they were moving into a routine, one they'd grown used to. He just wanted to know where they were now.

"Then," Trueblood said, "say, when he's a year old, we'll go to once every six months, and then once a year."

"For how long?" The Glitskys asked it simultaneously.

"Well, assuming the hole doesn't close up by itself—and it may do that because it's so small—but assuming that it doesn't, once a year certainly until he's a young adult. Maybe longer."

"Forever," Glitsky said.

Trueblood nodded. "Possibly, yes. But remember, they've found these VSDs in autopsies of ninety-year-olds."

"So you're saying Zachary could have a normal life?" Treya asked, barely daring to hope.

"He could. You'll have to be aware of his situation, of course. He'll have to be premedicated for any dental work or surgery, but other than that it's possible that it may never affect him at all. Maybe he'll be able to run, play sports, do anything. Maybe he'll need heart work in the short term, or in five years. We just don't know yet at this stage." Reading the agony in their faces, Trueblood broke out of his professional voice. "I realize that it's difficult not knowing," he said, "but please try to remember that it's better than almost any alternative we had just a day ago. It's entirely possible that Zachary's going to grow up to be a fine, normal, healthy child."

Treya squeezed Glitsky's hand, forced a smile of sorts. He knew her, knew that she didn't want to hear any false or possibly false cheer. She wanted to know what to do so that they could be prepared for it and do it right. "So I guess we'd better set up an appointment for next week, then. That's the next step?"

They got home by three o'clock, and Treya said she didn't want the two of them moping around together until it got dark, so Glitsky called his driver, Paganucci, thinking he would go check in at work for a few hours, maybe catch up on his mail, answer some of the more legitimate urgent calls, perhaps even talk to Batiste or Kathy West about the conspiracy and the various issues it raised.

But the normally taciturn driver hadn't taken him a block when he said, "Excuse me, sir."

He'd been looking at the slow continuous rain, his mind on his wife and new son, wondering how long it would take for this oppressive weight to lift, for life to begin to feel real again. In the backseat, arms crossed, he cleared his throat. "What is it, Tom?"

"Well, sir, it's the Hall. You know they're having the Hanover trial there, and the place is a circus, way worse than usual. Even going through the jail door, you're going to have to break through a line of 'em to get in. And then upstairs, there's probably a dozen in the hall just outside your office. They've been there all day since the morning, waiting for you to show up." Paganucci, depleted after the lengthy string of words, glanced into the rearview. "Knowing what you've been going through at home, I didn't know if you were really feeling up for that."

Glitsky was silent for a beat. "That bad, huh?"

"A zoo. Plus, look at the time, the trial's going to be getting out about when we get there or a little later, and then we're talking maybe three times as many of the vultures. I wouldn't normally say anything, you know, sir, but I just thought you ought to get a heads-up."

"I appreciate it, Tom. Thanks." They were moving east on Geary. "Why don't we take a detour and think about it?"

"You got it." Paganucci hung a right onto Fillmore Street. "Anyplace in particular?"

"I don't know. My wife doesn't want me home. Says I'm too morose. You think I'm morose, Tom?"

"No, sir."

"Me, neither. It's just most people don't have my sense of humor. Not that I've had a lot to laugh about lately."

"No, sir."

"We're close enough. Why don't we swing by the Painted Ladies? See how they're doing."

"The Painted Ladies, sir."

"Let's kick it up, Tom. Lights and sirens."

"Sir?"

"Joke."

"Ah." Then, "Good one."

"There you go."

*   *   *

Hanover's old place was now a gaping hole, still shocking even after most of a year. Especially since its sisters—cousins? daughters?—had been resuscitated and now preened with all or more of their former glory on the 700 block of Steiner. Paganucci, back to his habitual silence, drove the long way around Alamo Square and pulled over to the curb in front of the empty lot.

Hat on, in full uniform, Glitsky opened the door and let himself out into the steady drizzle. Walking up the steps to the front landing, he stepped over onto the earth in the footprint of the old building. Though soaked with the constant rain, the site still crackled with broken glass and the remnants of cinders. Glitsky thought he could still detect a slight burned odor. Walking through the vacant space, he got to the back of the lot and turned around due west to face the park across the street—a grassy knoll topped by windswept cypresses—deserted now in the awful weather. Crunching back the way he'd come, he made it back to Steiner, turned and looked at the row of lovely houses one more time.

He had no idea why he had come here. Could it have been as random as Paganucci's suggestion that he might want to avoid his office downtown today? He didn't think that was it.

Something nagged at him.

The house next door had a small sign in the front window that read: ANOTHER QUALITY REMODEL BY LEYMAR CONSTRUCTION. The health issues with his son had buried any other thoughts for the better part of the past few hours, but now suddenly he found that the loam had heaved as an idea mushrooming to the surface of his consciousness. No, not one idea exactly. More an accumulation of related inconsistencies.

What did it mean that Jim Leymar of Leymar Construction said he hadn't charged Hanover anything near a million dollars?

Why did Missy D'Amiens, apparently, lie to her landlady about where she worked?

For that matter, what had happened to her car? Or to the ring?

At the outset, Glitsky had of course considered from several angles the possibility that Missy D'Amiens, and not Paul Hanover, might have been the primary intended victim. But she had never assumed a prominence. Always cast into semi-obscurity by Paul's huge shadow, and then lost in the swirling maelstrom of events and media insanity that had seen Catherine charged and arrested, Missy's death came to feel to Glitsky like a kind of unfortunate footnote in an unsung and unknowable life. In some ways, she had become to him just another one of San Francisco's homeless, albeit a wealthy one, who one day merely disappeared, never to be mourned or missed.

But even the homeless, he knew, were sometimes—in fact, depressingly often—killed for their meager possessions, for their shopping carts, for their prime begging turf, for half a bottle of Thunderbird. As a more or less random human being walking around in San Francisco, Glitsky suddenly began to appreciate how tempting a target she might have been on her own, without reference to the Hanovers and their politics or money.

She wore a very visible diamond worth a hundred thousand dollars or more, and drove a Mercedes with a hefty price tag as well. Anyone could have seen her, an apparently defenseless woman alone, followed her home and broken in (or simply knocked at the door on some pretense). Many people who kept guns for their personal protection kept them in the headboard of their beds, and this might simply have been a bonus for the burglar and thief. After he'd killed them both, he removed the ring from her finger, probably rifled the house for other valuables. There might have been gasoline in a container in the garage, and he'd used that to torch the place, then drove off in D'Amiens's car.

On its own terms, it wasn't impossible. But it didn't explain the other discrepancies in Missy's story—the construction business, the false employment.

Back in his car, Glitsky sat with his arms folded over his chest. Paganucci saw him reflected in the rearview mirror and decided not to ask him where he wanted to go. Glitsky's natural authority was forbidding enough. When he scowled as he did now, his jaw muscle working and the scar through his lips pronounced, he was truly fearsome.

After a few moments, he shifted in his seat, searched in his wallet, then in the little book he kept. "There's a Bank of America branch at Twelfth and Clement, Tom. Let's go see if they're still open."

26

With full darkness outside and the rain still falling, Hardy stood at the window of his office looking down on Sutter Street and spun around at the knock on his open door.

"Anybody here?"

"I am, Wes."

"What are you doing standing around in the dark?"

"Thinking. You can turn the lights on if you want."

"*Fiat lux.*" The room lit up. "You know that Theresa was at the fire?"

"You talked to her." Hardy got to his desk, sat in his chair.

"At length. I think she developed a little bit of a crush on me."

"From what I hear, she's not exactly the crush type."

"Well, as the song says, Diz, 'There's someone for each of us they say.'"

"What song is that?"

"I think a bunch of 'em say it. You ought to listen to more country music, you know that? I mean it. Sam got me into it and now I don't listen to anything else."

"I'll put it on my list," Hardy said. "She was at the fire?"

Farrell plopped himself into one of the upholstered chairs in front of Hardy's desk. "This is going to sound familiar, but she saw it on TV and drove over. Got her name and address taken by one of the arson guys and everything. She didn't see Catherine, but that's not really surprising given the number of spectators. She said there were probably a couple of hundred people out there that night, maybe more."

"Okay."

"What?"

"I'm wondering if it means anything. Did you ask her what she was doing before that?"

"Watching television."

"Wes . . ." Hardy's patience, sorely tried throughout the long day, was all used up.

Farrell held up a placating hand. "I'm getting there, I promise. She works in real estate, you knew that, right? And she does okay, pays the bills, goes on a vacation every couple of years. But not much extra. Anyway, the point is she was home, alone. She remembers specifically because . . . well, it was that day, mostly, but also because . . . I think you'll like this . . . she remembers the call from Mary."

Hardy was, in fact, glad to hear this. For Theresa to be any kind of a convincing alternate suspect—for the jury's benefit if not in actual fact—he had to be able to establish that she had found out on the same day as Catherine that Paul was going ahead with his marriage to Missy, and that he was possibly changing his will in the very near future, perhaps the next week. She had to be strongly motivated to stop him immediately, and without the phone call from Mary to spur her to act, the theory would have had no traction.

"So she was home, got the call from Mary, then what?"

"Then nothing. She and Mary talked about it for a while, and she was extremely pissed off and upset, enough so that she canceled a date for dinner."

"That night?"

Farrell nodded, pleased with Hardy's enthusiastic reception. "I know. It's almost too good to be true, but there it is. She got a stomachache."

"Who was she going out with?"

"One of her girlfriends. I've got the name and we can talk to her if we need to."

"We might. But meanwhile, Theresa's so sick she can't go out to dinner, but a couple of hours later she's at the fire?"

"Right. But I mean, remember, this is her ex-husband's house burning down, maybe with him in it. Of course she's going to go."

"All right, I know. But still . . ."

"Still, no alibi. I get it."

Hardy scratched at his desk blotter. His partner often took a humorous and low-key approach, but he didn't miss much, which was why Hardy had thought to send him on this errand. "Anybody ever question her about it? Her alibi?"

"I didn't get that impression. Cuneo glommed onto her over Catherine, but he never thought about her as a suspect. And you're right, by the way, that they're not close, Catherine and Theresa. She should have stood up against her when Will said he was going to marry her."

"But she didn't?"

"And he's been paying for it ever since."

"Did she say that?"

"More or less verbatim." Farrell paused. "If you haven't gathered by now, Diz, she doesn't particularly want to help us out on the defense. She's finally got Catherine out of the family and wants to keep it that way. Will's happier."

"Will's a jerk," Hardy said.

"Well, at least he's a happier jerk."

"Four million dollars'll do that. Did she say anything about the money?"

"I believe the subject came up." Farrell stood up and walked over to the wet bar, opened the refrigerator and took out a bottled water. "You drinking?"

"No."

"Probably smart." He closed the refrigerator and turned. "Okay, money," he said. "She seemed slightly bitter about the whole Missy thing, to put it mildly. She and Paul split up before he got super rich, and after the kids had moved out, so she fell into the crack there between alimony and child support."

"Yeah, but the community property . . ."

"Peace, my friend, I'm ahead of you. So she took away about three hundred grand from the marriage, grew it up to a million some, all invested in guess what?"

"I bet I can. High-tech?"

A nod. "So now it's considerably less, the exact figure not forthcoming. But the smart guess is a lot, lot less."

"So she needed the money for herself, too. Not just the grandkids."

"It wouldn't kill her. Hasn't, in fact. Each of the kids has already cut her in, again no exact figures."

Hardy whistled. "So she's made out like a bandit here."

"She's better off than she was. Let's go that far."

"And no alibi?"

Farrell nodded. "No alibi. And one other interesting tidbit."

"I'm listening."

"She bought a new car."

Hardy cocked his head to one side. "With the estate money?"

"Uh-uh, before that. Early last summer."

"How did that come up?"

"I told you. She likes me. I have my ways. But the fact is, she traded in her . . . you're going to love this . . . her black C-type Mercedes . . ."

". . . for a red Lexus convertible, and paid cash for the difference," Hardy said.

Frannie brought her wineglass to her lips. It was Wednesday—trial or no trial, the traditional Date Night—and they were at Zarzuela waiting for their paella and sharing a plate of incredible hors d'oeuvres—baby octopus and sausages, anchovies, olives and cheese. "How much are we talking about?"

"Maybe as much as forty, fifty thousand dollars."

"And this means?"

"It means she got a lot of cash from somewhere late last May or early June."

"How about from her savings?"

"Maybe. But also, maybe, from pawning a ring."

Frannie looked carefully at a baby octopus she'd picked up with her fork. She put it back down on the plate and went for an olive instead. For his part, Hardy didn't appear to see or taste any of it, which didn't mean he wasn't putting away his share.

"You're seeing how this plays for me, aren't you?" she asked.

He smiled, nodded, reached across the tiny table and touched her hand. "A little bit."

"You think she might have done it?"

"No idea. But she could get the jury thinking it might not have been Catherine. Reasonable doubt."

"But what do you really think?"

"I think she had motive to spare. She hated Paul and Missy. She has no alibi."

"What about the eyewitnesses who say it was Catherine?"

Hardy hesitated for a long moment, then broke a rueful grin. "I'm hoping they die of natural causes before they testify."

All at once the bantering quality went out of Frannie's voice. She put down her fork and looked squarely at her husband. "Let me ask you something, really," she said. "How do *you* handle them?"

"What do you mean?"

"I mean the eyewitnesses. What do you tell yourself?"

His wineglass stopped halfway to his mouth. He set it back on the table. "I think they must have made a mistake."

"All three of them? The same mistake?"

He scratched the side of his neck. "I know."

"You think they mistook Theresa for Catherine?"

"No. Though the Hanover men seem to go for the same basic physical type. But Theresa's got fifteen years or more on Catherine. I can't really see it."

"How about Missy, then?"

"That's a better call if she wasn't dead."

"Except she is."

Again. "I know."

"So who's that leave?"

One last time. He twirled the stem of his glass, met her eyes. "I know. I know."

Glitsky entered his duplex dripping. He hung his wet raincoat on the peg by the front door, then his hat over it. In the little alcove, the light was dim and the house quiet. There was a light on in the living room to his right, but assuming that everyone else was asleep—it was nearly nine o'clock—Glitsky turned left into the dark kitchen and opened the refrigerator.

Nothing appealed.

He decided he'd go check in on Treya and Zachary and then come back out and fix himself something to eat when he heard a suppressed giggle from the living room. In a couple of steps, he was in the doorway, and Rachel jumped from the couch, finally yelled "Da!" and broke into a true, delighted laugh, running across the rug at him to be gathered up. But the real cause of the baby girl's hilarity and surprise was Glitsky's son Orel, a sophomore now at San Jose State about fifty miles south of the city, sitting on the couch next to Treya and holding his little half-brother easily in his arms. "Hey, Dad." The boy was beaming. "I'd get up, but . . ."

"We thought you'd never wander in here," Treya said. "What were you doing in there?"

"Foraging."

Treya seemed transformed—whether by the reasonably good news of the afternoon about Zachary or by Orel's appearance Glitsky couldn't say—but the change was dramatic. She'd put on some makeup, brushed her hair back, donned a nice maroon blouse tucked into some pre-pregnancy jeans. Most important, there was life in her eyes again.

Glitsky went down on a knee in front of her, shared a kiss with her and Rachel, patted Orel on the leg. "It is so good to see you," he said. "How did you . . . ?"

"Nat," he said. "What, you weren't going to tell me I had a brother?"

"No. I mean, yes, of course. We just . . . we didn't think you could get up midweek anyway," Glitsky said.

"*To see my new brother?* Are you kidding me?"

"Plus, there was . . ." He looked to Treya for help.

But Orel, obviously, had heard. "Chill, Dad," he said, "it's all right."

"All wight," Rachel echoed.

And Glitsky kissed her again and said, "I know it is."

Frannie and Hardy had just gotten back from their dinner when he got the call from Braun's clerk at ten fifteen. Apologizing for the late hour, she informed him that her honor had denied his motion for a hearing on deliberate prosecutorial misconduct, but that she would reconsider a motion for a mistrial if Hardy cared to renew it. Might that be his intention now?

He told her no.

Well, in either case, the judge wanted him to know that she would entertain such a motion until nine thirty the following morning, when court went into session. After that, a mistrial would be off the table and the trial would continue with the eyewitness testimony.

Now, at Glitsky's, the two babies were asleep, and the two adults and one near-adult sat at the kitchen table with cups of tea sweetened with honey. The pizza carton still covered most of the table in the middle of them, but none of them paid any mind. The mood was still far from euphoric—in the circumstances, how could it be otherwise?— but the sense of imminent doom was gone.

They were catching up, family news and gossip. Treya's daughter, Raney, had just been back home for winter break from Johns Hopkins in December, along with all of Abe's boys—Isaac from L.A., Jacob all the way from Milan, and Orel from San Jose. And of course Nat and Rachel. A full reunion. By now a large extended family, the Glitskys had celebrated both Hanukkah and Christmas before the diaspora had flung people to the far corners again.

"I'm just glad Nat got to see everyone one last time," Glitsky commented, "especially."

"What do you mean, one last time?" Leaning back on two rear legs of his kitchen chair, Orel's face clouded over. "Nat's okay, isn't he?"

"I think so. Why do you ask?"

"Because you just made it sound like he's dying of something."

"Not that I know of. But he's in his mid-eighties, Orel. He's not going to live forever, you know."

Orel brought his chair down, leaned into the table. "Jeez, Dad. You kill me."

"What?"

"What. Things don't always turn out bad. That's what."

"I don't think they do."

"Yes you do. Look at me. Remember when I was thirteen or fourteen after Mom died and I started to stutter and you thought I wasn't ever going to stop?"

"Okay. So? Nobody else really thought you were going to stop, either."

"Yeah, but I did, didn't I? And then you weren't ever going to meet anybody else good enough again after Mom, were you?" He turned to his stepmother. "And look right here at this very table. Voilà. Good enough, and that's saying something."

Treya inclined her head with a small smile. "Thank you."

"Yes, but . . ."

"But then, if you remember, you had a heart attack and somehow got completely better enough to be walking around and actually get shot a year later. Oh, after having your great little baby girl who's sleeping down the hall even as we speak."

"Wait, wait. Time out." Glitsky made the signal. "In all fairness, let's acknowledge what really happened over that time, aside from my miraculous recoveries. All right, you got over your stuttering. But your mom did die. I did have a heart attack, and then got shot and then had a few minor complications after that for a year or so, if *you* remember."

"I do remember, Dad. But here's the deal. You got better after the complications. You didn't die."

But Glitsky wasn't going to give up his worldview without a fight. "Yeah, I got better in time for them to demote me down to payroll."

"From which, I might point out, you got promoted over half the guys with your seniority and now you're deputy chief. Way farther than you ever thought you'd go."

"Or wanted to."

Orel, shaking his head, turned to Treya. "Am I the only one who sees this?" Then, back to his father. "Sometimes—I really do think and you might consider—sometimes it's half full, Dad. On the way to full. You know? Not half empty."

Glitsky took a breath, sipped at his tea. "Everybody does die, Orel. That's a fact."

"I'll grant you that, but they *live* first. That's the part that counts. The living part. You can't wait around doing nothing because everybody's going to die. I mean, in a hundred years, we're all dead, right?"

"Do we have to talk about dying?" Treya asked.

Orel sighed. "I'm not talking about dying. I'm talking about living." He seemed at a loss for words for a moment, twirling his mug on the table. "Guys, look. I know it's been a tough few days . . ."

"You don't know," Abe said.

"Okay, right. Not as much as you, I admit. But didn't you tell me that already the kid's beaten the odds you heard at first? I mean, wiped them out? Top one percent of heart irregularities, right?"

He looked at the two parents, who looked with heavy-lidded eyes at one another.

Orel lowered his voice. He didn't want to browbeat. "Didn't your doctor even say he could have a normal life?"

"But might not," Glitsky said.

"Yeah, but I might not, either. You might not. Okay, so maybe the odds are slightly less for Zachary right now . . ."

Glitsky interrupted, putting his hand across the table over his son's. "O," he said gently, "you don't know what you're talking about. It's not all roses with the prognosis, believe me."

"I do believe you. Obviously, it's hard. Obviously, I don't feel it as much as both of you. But my question is what does it get you to always keep expecting the worst? That Nat's going to die before the next time we're all together. That Zachary won't get a chance to live? Look at what you've got right now, Dad. Look where you are. In spite of it all, things have worked out pretty good, haven't they? I mean, doesn't that count?"

In their bedroom, later. Glitsky getting out of bed, leaning over the bassinet, picking up Zachary for basically the first time.

"What are you doing?" Treya asked.

"Just holding him."

He sat on the side of the bed, the baby in his lap. Behind him, Treya shifted closer to him. Her hand rubbed his back, came to rest on his leg.

"I'm thinking Orel's right," he whispered. "I never believe things are going to work out, and then they do, and I still don't believe it."

"I wouldn't beat myself up over that. You're fine the way you are."

"No, I miss things. I haven't held this guy yet—I don't know if you've noticed. . . ."

"I noticed, sure."

"Well, that's because I thought he'd die and then if I'd never held him, it wouldn't be as bad. I wouldn't feel it as much. Of course, then I also wouldn't have felt this while he's here."

"Right. I know."

A small night-light glowed dimly near floor level at the door and provided the only light in the room. But it was enough to see by. Glitsky moved the blankets out from around his baby's face. "He's got your eyes," he said.

"I think so. Your nose."

"Poor kid." Glitsky scooched himself up and around so he was leaning up against the bed's headboard. Then, after a while, "I'd better enjoy every minute."

"I think so. Both of us."

The night settled heavily around them, Glitsky still holding the boy in his lap. "Out of the mouths of babes, huh?" he said.

"Orel's a good boy," she said. "Reminds me of his dad."

"Except for that rogue positive streak."

"Not a bad thing, maybe."

"No."

Another extended stretch of time in the shadowy dark. "Trey?"

"Yeah, hon."

"The reason I got home so late. I found something out today. Completely off topic."

"Off topic's okay. What was it?"

"Hardy's case. This Missy D'Amiens. The dead woman."

"What about her?"

"She had a bank account—our branch of Bank of America, if you can believe it. You know Patti, the manager?"

"Uh-huh."

"I asked her if I could look it up. The account. Completely illegal, of course. I need a subpoena. I need to go through their legal department. But she knows me. . . ."

"Okay." Treya, now up on an elbow, interested. Even

cloistered as she'd been, she'd been aware of the latest news stories, the conspiracy theory. The Hanover case, like it or not, was part of their lives, and probably would be for some time. "What?"

"She had a checking account and a safe-deposit box, a big one." He drew a breath. "She closed the account and the box on May seventh, five days before she was killed."

"What does that mean?"

"I don't know." He looked over at her. "Eighty-eight hundred dollars, plus whatever was in the box."

27

Hardy was in his kitchen with Glitsky. The overhead light was on—it was still black out through the window over the sink, though the rain seemed to have stopped. The clock on the stove read 6:24. From the back of the ground floor came the muted sounds of Hardy's children knocking around, using the bathroom, getting ready for school. From upstairs, the shower. The house waking up.

Hardy, awakened by Glitsky's call forty-five minutes earlier, was in one of his dark gray courtroom suits, white shirt, muted tie. He blew over his mug of coffee, took a sip. "Missy signed it out herself?" he asked.

"There's no other way to get it."

"Wire transfer."

"She'd still have to sign something."

"Yeah, but she could have done that months ago."

"But somebody would have had to place the order, right? Either way, it doesn't matter. She signed the withdrawal form, took it in cash. They had the hard copies still there."

"How'd you get a look at them without a subpoena?"

Glitsky considered, hesitated for a second. "That's a state secret that could get the manager fired. I know her. But forget the logistics for a minute. She got her hands on more than eight grand. Maybe a lot more. No way to tell. Five days before she got killed."

Hardy put his mug on the counter, boosted himself up next to it and picked it up again. "Where'd she get that much money?"

"Hanover. She inflated the remodel costs and skimmed. I'm thinking she might have had as much as a few hundred thousand dollars in her safe-deposit box."

"A few *hundred* thousand? You've got to be kidding."

"No."

"If that's true, she was leaving him." Not a question.

"Had to be."

"He didn't have a clue, though."

"You know that?"

"According to Catherine. They'd evidently been arguing about this cabinet appointment, and that's why she was gone during that last day, but Paul told Catherine it would blow over. Missy wasn't leaving him. No way."

Glitsky's frown was pronounced. "So he didn't know."

"I hope it's true and he didn't just lie to Catherine to rile up the family. That might have been what got them both killed." Suddenly Hardy brought himself up short, a palm against his forehead. "Lord, what am I thinking? I'm sorry, Abe, trial time. The focus is a little narrow. How's your boy?"

"He's all right," Glitsky said evenly. "Top one percent of kids in his boat."

"There's a relief."

"A bit." But Glitsky didn't trust himself with optimism too long if they kept talking about Zachary's health, so he went right back to business. "I thought I'd do it legal today. Get your sorry signature on a subpoena so we can have copies of the records by next week."

"You mean Missy's bank records?"

Glitsky nodded. "I thought you could help me get 'em as essential to this case. Tie it into Hanover's estate and missing money. You sign a subpoena, the records just come to court. Rosen won't care that we've got them."

"I've got one for you," Hardy said. "How'd you get on this in the first place? Missy."

"*You* got me on it," Glitsky said. "The car." Mirroring Hardy, boosting himself on the counter by the stove, he told him about the series of unusual findings he'd happened upon as he had followed up leads on Missy, from the address he'd gotten at the DMV site, to Ruth Guthrie her landlady, to the bed and bath store where she hadn't worked, which had led to the checking and other accounts and the bank.

"Wait a minute," Hardy said when Glitsky had finished.

"So you're telling me that before she showed up here in San Francisco when? Three years ago? You still don't know anything about where she came from?"

"No. She came from somewhere they speak French, apparently. But how she got here? She dropped out of the sky. Although there's a social"—a Social Security number—"on her Bank of America accounts, and I was going to run that, too. If you'll sign off on the subpoenas." In fact, it was no big deal for Hardy to request Missy's bank records, and both men knew it. Preparing the subpoena wouldn't take Hardy five minutes. "I'm just saying it might help, Diz."

Hardy felt a wash of fatigue—the coffee wasn't kicking in quickly enough. He brought his hands to his eyes, then grabbed his mug and tipped it up. "I know it might," he said. "Sorry. I'm thinking about eyewitnesses. If I could just see how I can use this D'Amiens thing. If she had all that cash on her, plus the ring, and Catherine knew about it . . . but if anything that only strengthens her motive."

"I'm not guaranteeing any of this is going to help your case," Glitsky said. "I'd just like to know more."

"So would I," Hardy said, "perennially. Sometimes it's just not in the cards."

"True, but it'd be dumb not to look."

"Not if it doesn't help my client, which is pretty much all I'm thinking about right now."

Glitsky shrugged. "Your call. I'm going to do what I can anyway."

Hardy threw a veiled and vaguely malevolent glance over his coffee mug. "There's a surprise," he said.

When Hardy came around the corner in the hallway and saw Catherine in the holding cell behind the courtroom, she was sitting hunched over almost as if she'd been beaten, as though huddled against further blows. When he got to the cell door, she looked over quickly but, smoothing her hands down over her face, didn't get up, didn't change position. When the bailiff let Hardy in, he went and sat beside her. Her face hadn't completely dried. Putting an arm around her, he drew her in next to him, and she broke down.

He let it go on until it ended, just allowing her to lean against him until she'd sobbed it all out. When her breathing finally slowed, he gave her the handkerchief he'd learned always to have with him, then gave her a last buck-up squeeze with his arm and stood up. He walked over and stood by the bars, giving her some space while she got herself back together. He consulted his watch. They weren't due in court for another twenty minutes, plenty of time. Finally, he went back to her and sat.

"I'm so sorry," she said. "I don't know what . . ."

"It's all right."

She nodded. "I've been trying to keep myself from thinking about my kids, but today's Polly's birthday." She took a shaky breath. "Now I've missed every one of them since I've been in here."

"I know."

"I still don't know where to put any of this. How this can be happening to me." She gestured at the surroundings. "None of this is in my life, Dismas. Even after all this time, I can't understand how I've gotten here. I keep telling myself to just be strong and bear up and don't give them anything they can use. But then I think, so what? It's already been too long. I'm not their mom anymore."

"You're still their mom, Catherine. They visit here every chance they get."

"But I can't . . . I mean . . ." Again, she bowed her head, shaking it slowly side to side, side to side. "This isn't getting us anywhere. I'm sorry."

"First, one more apology and I start pulling out your fingernails. You've got every right to be miserable and lonely and afraid and have all of this get to you. Second, we don't always have to be getting anywhere. That's for in there." He indicated the courtroom. "Here we can just sit if we want."

She nodded again, then reached over and took his hand. "Can we do this for a minute?"

"I'm timing it," he said.

Seconds ticked by. At last her shoulders settled in a long sigh. "I've been wondering if I could have seen the seeds of all this back when Will and I first started, if that wasn't my original mistake. And everything followed from that."

"You got your kids out of it," Hardy said, "so maybe it wasn't all a mistake."

"I know. That's true. But I also knew it was a different thing with him than I had with you. You know what I'm saying?"

Hardy nodded. He knew.

"But I'd finished college and worked almost ten years and pretty much given up on dating because of all the losers, and then suddenly here was this kind of cute guy who could be fun in those days. But I knew, *I knew*, Diz, in my heart, that it wasn't . . . well, the same as I'd always wanted. But I also thought there wouldn't ever be anything better. So I settled. I settled. So, so stupid."

"You did what you did, Catherine. You made a life that worked for almost twenty years. That's not failing."

A bitter chuckle. "Look around you. Getting to here isn't failing?"

"It's not over yet."

"It isn't? It feels like it is. Even if they let me go. That's what I'm saying."

"I understand what you're saying. But I can't have you bail on me now. The first job is to get you acquitted. After that, when you're back outside . . ."

She was shaking her head and let go of his hand. "Dismas. Don't."

"Don't what?"

"Don't give me the standard pep talk. We both know I might not get back outside."

"I don't know that!" Hardy's tone was firm, nearly harsh. He turned on the bench to face her directly. "Listen to me." Taking her hand back almost angrily, holding it tight with both of his. "I believe you're innocent, and because of that the jury will not convict you. I'll make them see it. And you need to hold on to that thought. I need you to do that for me."

She closed her eyes, took a deep breath and let it out all at once. "All right," she whispered, nodding her head. "All right. I can try."

Moving on to news and strategy, he told her of Farrell's interview with her mother-in-law, the remote but arguable possibilities presented by the missing ring, combined with Theresa's purchase of a new car for cash. While acknowledging without much enthusiasm that it might be something Hardy could introduce to the jury, she really didn't show much interest until he got to what Glitsky had told him about this morning. "You mean Missy was stealing from Paul? When she was going to get all the money anyway?"

On the slab concrete bench, the two of them might have been coaches huddled on the sidelines, conferring in intimate tones. "She wouldn't have gotten any if she left him," Hardy said.

"No, I know. But that much . . . I mean, if that's true, she must have been planning to leave for quite a while, and I don't understand that at all. They only got formally engaged six months or so before they died, and the remodel had already been going on long before that."

Hardy's shoulders went up an inch. "Maybe she wasn't sure they'd ever really get married and she wanted to make sure she got something out of him for the time invested. Then, by the time they actually started making plans, she'd already socked all this money away."

"Maybe. But I don't know what it means. Why did she take it out?"

"You said it. They were arguing. Paul might have thought it wasn't a major issue, but maybe she didn't agree. She was leaving him."

Catherine sat straight up. "Maybe I'm stupid, Dismas, but that doesn't make any sense. She wasn't going to leave him over some possible minor sub-cabinet appointment. Paul told me. That day. Remember? That's what the fight was about. He was going to tell them to go ahead and start the vetting process. But beyond that, there were other candidates. He might not have even gotten the nomination, and if he had, he still would have had to be confirmed. The whole thing was months away at least, if it happened at all. I can't see Missy deciding to leave last May over it."

"I'm not arguing with you. But the fact remains that she did take out the money. If she wasn't leaving him, what was she doing?"

"Maybe giving it back to him?"

Hardy tossed her a get-real look. "Maybe not." In the hallway in front of them, two bailiffs led eight jailhouse residents in their orange jumpsuits to another holding cell down the long corridor. The chains that bound them together rattled and echoed, then died, and Hardy said, "Now if somebody was blackmailing her . . ."

"What for?"

"I don't know. But that's kind of been the mantra around Missy, hasn't it? Nobody knows anything about her. Even the tabloid guys never printed any dirt, and if they couldn't find anything, I've got to believe that if something was there, it was well hidden. But now I wonder if somebody found some nasty secret of Missy's and threatened to tell Paul. So Missy would have had to pay to keep it quiet."

Catherine barely dared say the words. "Are you thinking Theresa?"

"She's the ex-wife," Hardy said. "She hated Missy more than anybody. She'd be motivated to look for dirt on her." He didn't add, though they both knew, that Theresa had no alibi, that she'd paid cash for a new car soon after Missy had withdrawn the money. Hardy didn't want to overplay it, but the suddenly very real possibility that Theresa might have killed Paul and Missy was there in the cell between them. "Did anybody else in the family ever talk to Missy about her life?" Hardy asked. "Even when you all were first introduced to her?"

"It wasn't like we all got together and played parlor games, Diz. She and Paul ran in different circles than all of us. We'd see them both at holidays or sometimes at some social thing, but we weren't doing sleepovers and trading intimate secrets, I promise you."

Out of the corner of his eye, Hardy saw the bailiff appear in the small, wired-glass window to the courtroom door. They heard the keys, and the door swung open.

Showtime.

They were just back from the first morning recess, and so far Hardy felt he was doing very well on the eyewitness front. He was delighted with Rosen's decision to call Jeffrey (Jeffie) Siddon, since the young gas station attendant's demeanor was unsympathetic, to say the least. Flat of effect and subtly hostile to if not bored by the entire pro-

ceeding, his mumbling responses surely didn't inspire any
confidence in the jury.

Further, his identification of Catherine was not exactly
emphatic. Yes, he'd picked her out of a photograph, then
out of her booking mug shot. Hardy had already made his
point about IDs from a single photo, but the fact is that
other people were saying they recognized Catherine, and
this guy would be just one more. But facing her in person,
he seemed to hesitate. Rosen had to ask him twice if he
recognized in the courtroom the person who had bought
the gasoline in the container from his station. Could he
point out that person to the jury? Jeffie had raised his hand
an inch or two, nodded, and pointed briefly at Catherine.
Hardy thought, from the performance, that it was almost as
if he had pantomimed the words "I think" afterward.

Even beyond all that, though, and far more important,
was the legal nicety that even if every word Siddon said were
completely true in all respects, and if his identification of
Catherine had been firm and convincing—even given all of
that, his testimony did not put her at the crime scene at any
time. There was simply no connection.

Hardy had argued in a motion to exclude this testimony
before the trial, but Braun had allowed it for God knew
what reason. The inference that because Catherine may
have bought gasoline in a container somehow implicated
her in the arson was, Hardy thought, absurd. He could tell
that the judge and most of the jury thought the same
thing. Still, he rammed the point on cross-examination,
reestablishing that Jeffie hadn't picked Catherine out of a
six-pack of photographs—Cuneo had only shown him one
at a time; he hadn't even seen Hardy's client leave the station, hadn't noticed the direction she'd driven in when she
left, hadn't ever seen her again afterward. And then Hardy
had completely destroyed him on the question of what
day, even what *week*, he had noticed the woman in the blue
shirt. The station records showed that *someone* had purchased two gallons of gasoline on that Wednesday afternoon, and Jeffie had finally admitted—in his defensive
manner—that he figured it *must have been* her. He remembered her, and therefore she was the one who had come
by that day.

Maxine Willis would be rougher, but still, Hardy thought, manageable.

Unlike Jeffie Siddon, she had no trouble pointing out Catherine as the woman she'd seen leave the Hanover home a half hour before the discovery of the fire. Fortunately, though, Hardy had interviewed both her and her husband at some length. In the course of these talks, he had discovered a foothold from which he was confident he might pick his way through cross-examination.

"Mrs. Willis," he began. "Your initial identification of the woman who left the Hanover home a few houses down from yours on the night of the fire was made to an arson inspector on the night of the fire, is that right?"

"Yes."

"Could you tell the jury about that?"

Cooperative, she turned to face the panel. "There really isn't much to tell. My husband and I live three houses down from Mr. Hanover's house and were evacuated the night of the fire when it looked as though our place might catch fire as well. We were all standing outside when a gentleman came up and identified himself as being an arson inspector with the fire department. He got our names and address and asked if we had anything we'd like to report about the fire."

"Did the man have identification?"

"Yes."

"And did that identification say that his name was Sid Bosio?"

"That was it, yes."

Hardy went back to his desk, pulled a sheet of paper from his open binder. He showed it to Rosen and the judge and had the clerk enter it as the next defense exhibit, then came back to the witness. "Mrs. Willis, do you recognize this document?"

"I do."

"Would you tell the jury what it is, please?"

"It's a statement I wrote for the arson inspector after he talked to me on the night of the fire."

"All right. And is this your name and address on the top of the paper and your signature on the bottom of this piece of paper?"

"Yes it is."

"Indicating that the statements are true and correct?"

"That's right. As I knew them at the time."

No surprise, Mrs. Willis had been coached since the last time Hardy had spoken to her. Now she looked out into the courtroom, over to Rosen, finally back to Hardy. She knew what was coming, even gave him a confident smile.

"Mrs. Willis, will you please read for the jury what you signed off on?"

"Sure. The whole thing?"

Hardy smiled back at her. "After your name and address. The highlighted area."

"All right." She studied the document for a minute. " 'Saw occupant of house, Miss Damien, exit structure shortly before fire.' "

"And by 'Miss Damien,' you actually meant one of the victims in this case, Missy D'Amiens, isn't that right?"

"Yes. I got her name a little bit wrong."

"Thank you. That's fine." Hardy took the paper back from her, placed it back on the evidence. "So, Mrs. Willis, just to make this absolutely clear, you gave this statement to arson inspector Bosio on the night of the fire?"

"Yes."

"All right, then, moving along. The next time you had an opportunity to identify the person leaving the Hanover home a short while before the outbreak of the fire, it was by photograph, was it not?"

"That's right."

"A photograph shown to you by Inspector Cuneo, correct?"

"That's right."

"Now, did you pick the photograph of the person you saw leaving the Hanover home that night out of a group of photographs?"

"No, there was just the one."

"Inspector Cuneo showed you only one photograph and asked you to identify who it was, is that right?"

"Correct."

Nodding amiably, Hardy cast a casual eye over to the jury. He strolled easily back to his table and took from it both the newspaper picture of Missy D'Amiens and the original he'd subpoenaed from the *Chronicle*'s files. After having them marked as the next defense exhibits, he showed the glossy of it to the witness. "Do you recognize this photograph?"

"I sure do. That's the picture I saw the first time Inspector Cuneo came by."

"All right. So Inspector Cuneo showed you this picture. Now Mrs. Willis, do you know who this is a picture of?"

"That's my ex-neighbor, Missy."

"The same Missy D'Amiens who is one of the victims in this case, is that right?"

"Yes."

"And the same Missy D'Amiens you identified to arson inspector Bosio as the woman who'd left the Hanover house just before the fire, is that right?"

"Yes, but . . ."

"And you identified her to Inspector Cuneo as well, is that correct?"

She hesitated. "Well, that was before . . ."

"Mrs. Willis, I'm sorry." Hardy cut her off in his most respectful tone. "Is it correct that on this first occasion with Inspector Cuneo, you identified the woman in that picture, Defense Exhibit F, as Missy D'Amiens? Yes or no."

"Yes, but . . ."

Hardy held up a palm. "And it was only later that you ID'd the photo of Catherine, is that right?"

"Yes."

"And each time you were shown—Sergeant Cuneo showed you—a single photo, correct?"

"Yes."

"Just to be clear, he never showed you a variety of photos from which to choose, correct?"

"Right."

"And when Sergeant Cuneo showed you the first photograph, Exhibit F, you had already said it was Missy coming out of the house, right?"

"Right."

"And so he clearly expected you to ID the person he named?"

"Yes."

"And you did identify the woman in Exhibit F as Missy D'Amiens on that occasion, did you not?"

"Yes, I did."

Hardy took a breath. "All right," he said. "Now let's talk for a minute about the next time Sergeant Cuneo asked you to identify the person who'd left the Hanover home that afternoon. On that second occasion, did he also show you one photograph of a single person?"

"Yes."

"And he told you that you must have been wrong the first time, since Missy D'Amiens was dead?"

"Yes, that's right."

"So it couldn't have been Missy that you saw?"

"Right."

"Okay. And next he told you, did he not, that he thought the person whose photo he now showed you was the person you must have seen?" Hardy didn't give her a chance to answer. "And again, you ID'd the person whom Inspector Cuneo clearly expected you to ID, isn't that right?"

"Yes, I suppose that's true, but that doesn't mean . . ."

"Let me ask you this, Mrs. Willis. Did Sergeant Cuneo ever give you an opportunity to view several photos of different people?"

"Well, no, he . . ."

"Did he ever ask you to consider the possibility of a third person?"

"No."

"Thank you, Mrs. Willis. That'll be all." He spun on his heel and took a step toward his table.

"But . . ." She started again.

He whirled on her. "Thank you," he repeated with slightly more emphasis. "No more questions."

But Rosen was already on his feet, moving forward. "Redirect, Your Honor." A nod from Braun. "Mrs. Willis, did you know Missy D'Amiens well?"

"No. Hardly at all."

"Hardly at all. Had you ever had a conversation with her?"

"No."

"Spoken to her at all?"

"No. Never."

"All right. So you could easily have been mistaken in identifying her?"

"Your Honor!" Hardy said. "Speculation."

But Braun was already ahead of him. "Sustained."

Rosen stood in the center of the courtroom for a moment, then came at it another way. "Mrs. Willis, did you have occasion to change your mind about the identity of the woman whom you'd earlier identified as Missy D'Amiens?"

"Yes, I did."

"And when was that?"

"When Inspector Cuneo brought a picture of another woman and I realized it wasn't who I'd first said."

"And that is the picture of the defendant, Catherine Hanover, People's Exhibit 12, that you identified earlier, is that correct?"

"Yes, it is."

"And did you subsequently identify the defendant as the woman who'd left the Hanover home minutes before the fire from the booking photograph, People's 11?"

"Yes."

"Did you also identify the woman who'd left the Hanover home minutes before the fire from a police lineup held on or about July eleventh of last year? A lineup that included five other women?"

"Yes, I did."

"And would you please tell the members of the jury once again if you see the woman you saw leaving the Hanover home minutes before the fire in this courtroom today?"

"Yes, I do."

"You have already pointed her out to the court, but may I ask you to please do so once again?" She pointed and Rosen said, "Let the record show that the witness has once again identified the defendant, Catherine Hanover. Mrs. Willis, thank you. No further questions." He turned to Hardy. "Recross."

Hardy was in front of her before Rosen had sat down. "Mrs. Willis, when you ID'd the first photo of Missy D'Amiens, you were telling the truth, were you not?"

"Of course I was."

"Of course. And you were as sure of that first ID as you later were of the second, true?"

"Well, at the time . . ."

"Let me rephrase. Did you express any hesitation or reservation with that first ID?"

"No."

"And that's because you were sure. Correct?"

She didn't like it, but she had to admit it. "At the time, yes, but . . ."

"So you were sure. As sure as you are now that it was Catherine, correct?"

She didn't answer, and Hardy didn't wait. "But of course you were wrong."

28

Glitsky wasn't going to deal with any part of the media. He was laying low on this mission. He hadn't done much more than check into his office early in the morning, then disappeared to move on these D'Amiens questions. He wasn't carrying his cell phone and had turned his pager to vibrate.

In the Bank of America's eponymous polished granite building downtown, he now sat in an enclosed cubicle office in the legal department on the eleventh floor. Outside his windows, an immovable cloud blocked any view. Five attorneys and their secretaries worked in the space just outside—the lawyers in their own cubicles about the size of the one Glitsky was using, their slaves at desks against the opposite wall.

Glitsky's guide for his tour of the D'Amiens financials was a serious young woman with mousy brown hair, in a beige suit and Coke-bottle eyeglasses. Probably not yet thirty, her name was Lisa Ravel and she was the right person to sit with him while they searched. Diligent, knowledgeable about the bank's systems, enthusiastic for the work. She had already printed out the final statement that Glitsky had gotten a look at yesterday at his local branch (they only kept physical records in the branches for two years). Now she suggested that they review deposits over the nearly three-year course of the entire account, moving toward the present.

Glitsky remembered that he wanted to run Missy's Social Security number—find out something more about her—and he called back to his office and asked Melissa to get on it, to page him when she had something. Then he and Ravel began in earnest.

The opening deposit had been in cash for exactly $9,900. Glitsky, who by now was disposed to see a sinister pattern emerging, found that interesting if only because banks were mandated to report any cash transactions of over ten thousand dollars, and this was just under that threshold. At the beginning, now more than four years ago, there'd been very few checks and all of them predictable—to Ruth Guthrie every month for rent, for phone, utilities and the like. Over the next five months, the account had almost gotten down to zero when regular deposits in the thousand-dollar range began turning up. Glitsky, who'd given Ravel an overview of the situation at the outset, said, "I think by now this must be when she's seeing Hanover."

After a while, the deposits started averaging—again, that threshold figure—around nine thousand dollars per month. D'Amiens started making monthly payments on the Mercedes in February of the year before she'd died. Regular deposits and checks started turning up—one every month for twenty months in the six- to eight-thousand-dollar range, but three of them greater than a hundred thousand dollars—to Leymar Construction. Then more standard-size monthly payments to a Macy's credit card, a Nordstrom card. She got a Visa card and started making regular payments on it. Here was a check for $885 made out to the offices of Dr. Yamashiru. Another similar check for $1,435.

Glitsky pointed to the screen. "This guy. He was her dentist," he said. "She must have had teeth problems."

"Looks like bad ones," Ravel said. "And no insurance."

This struck Glitsky. No insurance?

They kept scrolling. "I ought to go get a subpoena for Hanover's accounts while I'm at this," he said. "Compare the construction bills. I think she was taking cash out of her deposits and putting them in her safe-deposit box."

"Well, wait a minute," Ravel said. She hit a few buttons on the keyboard. "There you go." The screen revealed that Glitsky's theory, at least insofar as the deposits went, was correct. The backup record of several of the more normal deposits indicated the cash disbursements from the amount of the checks she'd cashed and deposited. Hanover evidently had written her regular monthly checks to cover both her living expenses (these perhaps unwittingly) and Leymar's contracting fees. The three that were over a hundred thousand dollars were neatly paired with checks she'd written to Leymar in the same amounts less that critical nineteen thousand dollars. The other Leymar checks, though, came in at nineteen thousand dollars per month. Glitsky surmised that she took this money, deposited half in her checking account and the other half—ninety-five hundred dollars a month—into her safe-deposit box. Over the twenty or so months of Hanover's regular payouts to her, this would have come to roughly two hundred thousand dollars.

"So he was supporting her, too," Ravel said.

"Look at what she was stealing," he said. "She wouldn't have needed him to."

"I can't believe the IRS didn't get wind of this somehow."

"I don't know. She kept everything under ten thousand dollars, you notice."

"Okay, but the income."

"Maybe she didn't file."

Ravel shook her head. "Playing with fire."

"She wasn't American. Maybe she didn't get it."

"Well, she may not have been an American," she pointed at the screen, "but that's a real Social Security number."

"Which reminds me."

Glitsky called back to his office, where Melissa had gone to lunch. Leaving another message, he got back to their computer.

Finally, at it for almost two hours now—printing out pages as they went, the two of them getting along, theorizing—they got to the last month's closing statement again. At his belt, he felt his buzzer. "That's my secretary." But checking the number, it wasn't. It was Hardy.

Glitsky called him right back.

"I just thought of something you said this morning," Hardy said. "You know the car?"

"I know the car."

"We still don't know where it is."

"Yes we do. Somebody stole it."

Disappointment sounded through the line. "You know that for sure?"

"No. I deduced it since it's nowhere else. Somebody must have taken it, and there wasn't anybody to complain."

"So it's not been reported stolen?"

"Good, Diz. I think I just said that. What's your point?"

"My point is where did you look?"

Glitsky fought the rise of impatience. "You want a list? I looked. Traffic and parking, warrants, booted vehicles, towed vehicles . . ."

"Where? What towed vehicles?"

"At the tow lots."

"Yeah, but for both companies?"

A hint of anger leaking through now, Glitsky began, "What do you . . . ?" Then stopped, realizing in a flash that if the car had been towed in the first few weeks after the fire, it would have naturally gone to the Tow/Hold lot. But less than six weeks later, Bayshore AutoTow had taken over, and since that's where the city now towed its cars, that's where Glitsky had checked. The transition after the contract change to the city's new towing company had gone anything but smoothly, with records lost or mislaid, cars dismantled or stolen. With Tow/Hold dragging its feet supplying anything that would help Bayshore become efficient and productive, the city's computer hadn't come close to catching up and didn't look like it would for a while. "Tow/Hold," Glitsky said.

"Just a thought," Hardy said.

Joseph Willis was the last eyewitness, and presented the most significant challenge, which was of course at the same time a golden opportunity.

Erudite, soft-spoken, nattily dressed in a soft camel-hair sport coat, light blue dress shirt and red bow tie, Maxine's husband didn't have any uncertainty whatsoever surrounding his identification of Catherine. Rosen had walked him through his testimony, which was unambiguous and delivered with great confidence. Unlike his wife, on the night of the fire he had never told arson inspector Bosio that it had been Missy leaving the house. He'd only ventured that it had been a woman. He hadn't been home for Inspector Cuneo's first visit when he'd brought around the newspaper photo of Missy, either, and so he hadn't tentatively identified her first. He, too, had picked Catherine first from Cuneo's photo, next from her booking mug shot, and finally from the July lineup.

Hardy, rising to cross-examine, knew that he had his work cut out.

"Mr. Willis, I'd like to go over your testimony about the woman you saw leaving the Hanover home on the night of the fire, and whom you've identified as Catherine Hanover."

"Certainly." Like his wife, Joseph knew he was key to the prosecution's case, and he, too—and with more justification—seemed to revel in the role. "I thought you might."

This brought a titter to the gallery, and Hardy let himself appear to smile. He was a swell guy able to take a little good-natured ribbing.

"Splendid," he said. "Then we're in accord." He paused for an instant. "Would you mind telling me about what time you saw the woman leave the Hanover home on that night?"

"I don't know exactly. I didn't check my watch."

"Could you hazard a guess?"

"Well, our friends had come by and we'd made cocktails. The show we hoped to attend started at nine and we wanted to get there by eight thirty, which meant we'd have to leave by eight. So I'd say we were in the living room between seven fifteen and seven forty-five."

"And what kind of evening was it?"

"As I recall, it was cool with a breeze, and then got foggy later." He looked over to the jury, and added, "As usual in May and June." Meaning to be casual and friendly but coming across to the jury, Hardy hoped, as pedantic and even condescending.

"All right. Cool with a breeze. And you've testified that you noticed the woman's dark blue shirt because it was shiny, some kind of silklike material, is that right?"

"Yes?" Joseph Willis shifted in the witness box, crossed one leg over the other. From his expression, he didn't understand where this line of questioning was headed.

"Was that a question, Mr. Willis? Or an answer."

"I'm sorry. Yes. The shirt was shiny."

"And so are we to assume that the sun was out?"

"Your Honor!" Rosen spoke from his table. "Calls for speculation."

Braun looked down over her podium. "Mr. Hardy?"

"Let me rephrase." He came back to the witness. "I'd ask you to close your eyes if it would help you to remember, sir. When you first saw the woman leaving the Hanover home, was the sun shining?"

Much to Hardy's surprise, Willis actually complied. When he opened his eyes again after a couple of seconds, he nodded. "I believe it was, yes."

"Good. Now when did you first notice the woman?"

"Coming down the steps at Hanover's."

"Three houses up the street from your own?"

"That's right."

"About a hundred feet, would you say?"

"About that."

"And at that time, the very first look you got, you told Mr. Rosen that you thought the woman was Missy D'Amiens?"

"I did."

"And why was that?"

"Well, primarily I think because it was her house. She lived there. I'd seen her in similar clothing. I would have expected it to be her."

"All right. And where were you standing in your own home?"

"By the front window."

"A jutting bay window, is that right?"

"Yes."

"All right. Now, after this woman came down the steps, you said she crossed the street, is that right?"

"Yes."

"On a diagonal, or directly across?"

"I wasn't really watching that closely. I couldn't say."

"You weren't watching her?"

"No, not specifically. I was having cocktails with friends, as I said . . ."

"That's right. How many cocktails had you had by this time, by the way?"

For the first time, Willis's affable manner slipped.

Clearly affronted, he flashed an angry look at Hardy. "One," he answered with no expression.

"In other words, you were on your first cocktail? Or you'd already had one and were on your second?"

"Your Honor." Rosen trying to come to the rescue. "Argumentative."

"Not at all, Mr. Rosen," Braun said. "Overruled. Mr. Willis, you may answer the question. Janet."

Jan Saunders read it back and Willis straightened his shoulders. "I don't recall exactly. I believe it was my first one."

"All right," Hardy said. "And for the record, what kind of cocktail was it?"

"Your Honor!" This time Rosen stood up with the scraping of his chair.

But before he could even state his grounds, Braun overruled him.

"It was a Manhattan," Willis said.

Hardy gave him a cold grin. The men were enemies now, punctiliously courteous in direct proportion to their growing hatred for one another. "That's two shots of good bourbon and a shot of sweet vermouth, is that right?"

"That's right."

"All right, now let's go back to the woman, who is now across the street, correct?"

"Yes."

"The woman you initially thought was Missy D'Amiens?"

"I thought she *must have been* Missy D'Amiens. I didn't think she *was.*"

"Ah." Hardy brought in the jury with a look, then went back to the witness. "What made you change your mind?"

"She walked differently."

"She walked differently? How do you mean?"

"I mean, she had a different walk. I think it's rather clear. She didn't walk the same."

"So you'd studied Ms. D'Amiens's walk?"

This brought another rolling round of laughter to the gallery, and Willis glared out at it with nearly the same intensity as Braun.

"I noticed it. As one notices things. I didn't study it."

"All right, then. So this evening you simply noticed Ms. D'Amiens's walk?"

"Yes."

Hardy heard a sound behind him, a dull thud. He guessed it was Rosen letting his hand fall in frustration to the table, but he didn't dare slow down enough to turn and look. He didn't know if Willis realized what he'd just said, but he was certain some members of the jury had.

"All right," he said. "But let me ask you this. If you were looking at Ms. D'Amiens's walk, how did you see her face?"

"I just," he stammered. "I just saw it."

"As she came abreast of where you stood in your bay window?"

"Yes."

"Directly across the street?"

"Yes."

"So you only saw her in profile?"

This stopped Willis for an instant. "Yes," he said with a resurging bravado. "Yes, I guess I must have, mustn't I?"

"I believe so," said Hardy. He wasn't going to push on Willis any harder now. He'd already wounded him badly and the jury would resent him for it. Instead, he took a beat, a breath, then asked quietly. "Mr. Willis, your bay window is on Steiner Street, facing due west, is that true?"

"Yes."

"So it faces the sun as it sets, right?"

"Yes."

"And the sun was out on the day of the fire, correct?"

"Yes."

"Low in the sky, since it must have been at least seven fifteen and possibly as late as seven forty-five when the woman came out of Hanover's house? Mr. Willis," Hardy continued, "to review for the jury, you saw a woman whom you initially took to be Missy D'Amiens leave the Hanover home at around seven thirty. You saw her again in profile only across the street from your bay window, looking directly into a setting sun, in the course of which you were in the middle of an alcoholic beverage made with two shots of spirits and one of fortified wine. Is all of this correct?"

"Yes," Willis said. "As far as it goes."

"I think it goes pretty far, sir," Hardy said. He turned

and walked back to his table and sat down next to Catherine, who reached over and gripped his arm.

"Redirect, Mr. Rosen," Braun intoned. "No? All right, Mr. Willis, you're excused."

In Farrell's office, Hardy was prepared to beg if need be. "Wes, I need this."

"You needed her missing alibi, too, Diz. Which I dutifully provided, if you recall. But even assuming the lovely Theresa Hanover would see me again . . ."

"I thought she had a crush on you."

"I may have overstated that slightly. But as I say, even if she would see me again, Sam and I have a date tonight."

"You have no children. You can have dates every night."

"We do, in fact. And every one a treasure. But this one is actually planned. We've got reservations with some pals at Farallon."

Hardy grimaced. And Farrell, horizontal with a legal brief open on his chest up until now, straightened up on the couch with a deep, theatrical sigh. "For informational purposes only, what do you want to know this time?"

"How much she knew about Missy D'Amiens. If she ever dug to find any dirt on her. If she might have been blackmailing her."

Farrell nodded. "Just the kind of stuff I might easily work into a casual conversation. You realize she'll understand pretty quick what's going on? Didn't the cops ask her any of this?"

"Cuneo didn't, no."

"And you expect me to find this out in a couple of hours?"

"Sooner if you want to make your dinner."

"How do I do that?"

"Your usual, Wes. Charm, brains, psychology. Whatever it takes."

"You really think she did this?"

"I really think it's not impossible. I'd like to have some kind of song I can get the jury to dance to."

Farrell threw his abandoned brief down onto the floor at his feet. He swore in resignation, then looked up at Hardy. "All right, I'll give her a call."

"Thank you. And do me one other favor, would you?"

"Of course. It goes without saying. I live to perform favors for all and sundry. What is it?"

"Be careful."

29

The money got Glitsky nowhere. The Social Security number, or SSN, turned out to be valid, although inactive because of the death of the person to whom it was issued. Glitsky's only hint beyond that lay in the first three digits of the SSN, which reflects the ZIP code in the mailing address on the application. Missy had applied for and received her card and number in Washington, D.C. Not much help.

He'd spent three hours with Lisa Ravel and learned that Missy D'Amiens was a careful and perhaps sophisticated money mover—over a twenty-odd-month period, and with the exception of the straight pass-throughs of large sums to Leymar Construction, she had never moved a sum of money, either to cash or to another account, greater than ten thousand dollars. Occasionally, when the balance in her checking account wouldn't be completely depleted before the next deposit was due, she would withdraw all the cash down to a few hundred dollars, and sometimes this would be as much as four thousand more dollars destined for her safe-deposit box. In all, Glitsky's rudimentary math revealed that she might have squirreled away nearly four hundred thousand dollars.

And that meant that, for at least a few days before she died, she'd had access to that much money in cash. Maybe she'd even carried it with her, on her person, somewhere—in a backpack, a briefcase, a shopping bag. If the wrong person even caught a glimpse, then this, Glitsky knew, was plenty to get yourself killed over. What he didn't know and couldn't figure out was why, other than Hardy's theory that she had been planning to leave Paul Hanover, she'd withdrawn it just when she had. He was beginning to think it had to be some sort of blackmail. A payoff had gone wrong in the Hanover home, and the witnesses/victims hadn't survived.

Coincidence, he believed, was not an option.

But there was something he'd clearly overlooked and that now beckoned as the next, maybe the only, logical step left for him to take, although the specific destination remained murky. Why did he care so much about Missy D'Amiens? Was it just a desire to prove that Cuneo had been wrong all along? Or was it that his gene for justice wasn't being served? He kept discovering more facts about her, only to learn that in some ways he seemed to know less. But he couldn't stop himself. All of this money, her sophistication, the duplicity about where and whether she worked, her exotic and unknown background—all of these factors contributed to the fascination. She was the key to something significant; he was certain of that. Maybe it wasn't the key to her own murder as well, but her story begged for a resolution, and Glitsky felt that if he could provide one, it might help to close a circle for him as well.

And, not incidentally, though he couldn't predict exactly how, he believed it might have an impact on Hardy's trial.

He called Paganucci while he waited for Lisa Ravel to finish her xeroxing, then thanked her for her time and expertise. When he exited the building, his driver was waiting on the Kearny Street side, heading downtown. Even with the late-afternoon rush hour, it didn't take them fifteen minutes to get back to the Tow/Hold headquarters a few blocks south of the Hall of Justice on Townshend.

A large, brownish brick warehouse that now screamed desertion—from the street the place looked as though it hadn't seen any sign of life in a decade. The large auto bay doors were closed at both the front and sides. Several windows, high up, on all three visible sides, were broken black, jagged holes, and the others, covered with cobwebs, dust and soot, were opaque. Paganucci pulled up in front of the entrance with its peeling white paint and faded logo and lettering. He put the car in park, turned it off, got out and opened Glitsky's door to the gritty and wet wind.

Much to Glitsky's surprise, the door was open. He entered and turned into the administrative office that had been drywalled into the semblance of a planned room. A dozen or so gray metal desks squatted in the bullpen behind the counter. The tops of each of them were bare except for a computer terminal, a telephone, a blotter and a two-tiered, metallic in/out basket. He saw no one, but heard a radio somewhere, and walked by the counter, then behind it, following the sound. Within the larger office, a smaller unit sulked in one corner, and here Glitsky found two slightly beyond-middle-aged men playing cards—it looked like gin rummy—on another desktop, this one completely bare.

"Who's winning?" he asked.

The fat man facing him raised his eyes and showed no surprise at the sight of a large uniformed black police officer filling his doorway. "Glen," he said, his breath rasping with the exertion. "But not for long."

"Ha!" Glen didn't even turn around to look.

Glitsky stepped into the room. "I'm trying to locate a car."

"Got a license for it?"

"Yes."

"Welp." The fat man put a "p" on the end of his "well," punctuating it further with a little pop of breath, as though the syllable had nearly exhausted him. He placed his cards facedown in front of him. Wheezing, he lifted himself out of his chair, squeezed his way out from behind the desk. He extended a hand as he passed, said, "Horace" and kept going into the outer office. "Stay here, you don't mind. Watch him he don't cheat," he said.

"Ha!" Glen said again.

Horace got himself situated behind one of the outer desks, fiddled with the mouse, waited for the screen to brighten. "What's the number?"

Glitsky gave it to him. 4MDC433.

Horace's fingers moved. He waited, staring at the screen, each labored breath the sigh of a bellows. After a bit, he nodded. "Yep. Mercedes C-130?"

"That's it."

"Your lucky day," he said. "They took it here. Space N-49. Your car?"

"No. A crime victim's."

Horace made a sympathetic, clucking sound through the

rasping. He leaned in closer and squinted at the screen. "Mitchell Damien? He okay?"

"She," Glitsky said. "And she's dead."

From the other room. "Hey Horace! You playing or what?"

"I'm *what* is what. Keep your pants on." He shook his head in displeasure at his opponent's impatience, then came back to Glitsky. "Welp," a deep breath, "so what do you want with the car?"

"I just want to look at it. See if she left anything in it that might identify her killer." He left the doorway of the smaller room and got close enough to Horace where he could see the screen. "Does it say where you picked it up?"

"Sure. Two hundred block of Eleventh Avenue."

"That's where she lived."

"There you go." Horace leaned back, ran a hand around his florid face. "There's nothing in it, that don't mean nobody stole nothin'. Means there wasn't nothing in it when it got here."

"Okay," Glitsky said. "Could I trouble you to print out a copy of the record for me?"

"Sure. Take two seconds."

For whatever good it would do, Glitsky thought. Already today, he had added sixty-some pages of Bank of America records to the D'Amiens folder he'd been developing. Just being thorough. But it would be foolish to abandon the practice now.

Horace pulled the page from the printer by the counter and handed it over. Taking Glitsky's measure one last time and seemingly satisfied, he walked with great effort all the way back across the outer office, to a large white panel, about six feet on a side, that swung out to reveal a numbered grid of eye-hooks, most of which held sets of keys. He picked the one off of N-49, walked back and handed it to Glitsky.

"You've got the keys?" Glitsky asked. "She left her keys in the car?"

"No. Car sits in the lot this long unclaimed, generally it's going to auction, so we need keys. We used to have a couple of locksmiths on staff, even, but those days are gone now. Still," he pointed, "those ought to open the thing up.

It's inside, about two-thirds of the way back. They're numbered. You can't miss it. I'll flick on the lights for you. Bring the key back when you're done. I'm off at five thirty, so before then. Or come back tomorrow."

Glitsky looked at his watch. He had forty-five minutes. "Today ought to do it," he said. "Thanks."

"What if he doesn't call her as a witness?" Glitsky, referring to Theresa Hanover, was in Hardy's office throwing his darts. Hardy, weary but still rushing with adrenaline and elation—he thought he'd basically kicked ass with all of the eyewitnesses—sat crossways on the love seat perpendicular to his desk.

"He's got to call her. She's the motive. The jury's got to hear how badly Catherine wanted the money, and from her own sweet reluctant mother-in-law. It ought to break hearts."

"And then what?"

"And then I introduce our alternate theory on cross. Theresa's own motive, every bit as good as Catherine's, her own lack of alibi, her attendance at the fire itself, the ring and paying the cash for the car, plus whatever Wes might be finding out even as we speak."

"And the judge will let you do all that?"

"Maybe not the cash for the car. But the rest, maybe, at least the beginning of it. I'll be subtle. Besides, I think her honor is beginning to thaw. The eyewitness testimony was Rosen's case and, if I do say so myself, it took a pretty good hit today. I'd hate to jinx my good fortune, but if I'm Rosen, I'm a worried man about now."

"And Theresa's his last witness?"

"She might be. Close to it, anyway. Which is why I'm going to need you around. You're next up after I call Catherine."

"For the defense. I love it." Glitsky threw the last dart in his round and was walking to the board. Halfway there, he stopped and faced his friend, his expression black. "Starting tomorrow? All day?"

Hardy nodded. "Most of it, anyway. But look at the bright side, like you always do. I ask you questions and the answers eviscerate Cuneo."

But Glitsky was shaking his head. "I don't like him any more than you do. More than that, between you and me, this whole conspiracy thing he's on about terrifies me. He's too close, and maybe he's got other people thinking. I go up on the stand against him, it's going to look personal, and he's going to itch to pay us both back personally if he can. Tell me you haven't considered this."

"Of course. As things now stand, he's a threat, I grant you."

"A big threat. And I'm not just talking careers."

"I get it, Abe, really. But what's the option? I've already creamed him on cross. He can't hate me worse than he already does. Or you, probably."

"But above all, he's a cop, Diz. Cops don't testify against cops, maybe you've heard. So you think Theresa's a reluctant witness? Wait'll you get me up there."

"You really don't want to go on? Get the son of a bitch."

"I'd rather get the murderer."

"And that's not Catherine."

Glitsky wasn't going to fight him on that. "All right," he said, "but I hope you're real aware that my friends in uniform are not going to double their love for me after I snitch out a cop on sexual harassment." Glitsky got to the dartboard and slowly, pensively, pulled his round from it.

Reading the body language, Hardy came around square on the love seat, sitting up. He spoke quietly, with some urgency. "All you'll be talking about is what Catherine said to you, Abe. That's not *you* accusing Cuneo of anything. Catherine will say what happened. You'll simply say she reported it before she got arrested."

Glitsky barked a bitter little laugh. "That distinction might not sing to the troops."

"It'll have to. I need the testimony."

"I know. I know. I just wish . . ."

"You'd found something else?"

A nod. "Almost anything. God knows I looked. I thought between the banking and the car something would have popped, but nothing."

"Really nothing? At all?"

Glitsky indicated the folder of D'Amiens's stuff he'd brought up with him. "You're welcome to look at all the fascinating detail, but I wouldn't get my hopes up."

"I won't. But if it's any consolation, maybe I won't need it."

"For your client, maybe not. But there's still the murders. And whoever did them is still walking around on the street."

"Yeah, but there's a lot of that, Abe. It happens."

"Granted, but that's no reason to accept it." The words came out perhaps more harshly than he'd intended. "I don't mean ..." Glitsky let the phrase hang, then laid Hardy's three darts on the polished surface of the desk. "I'm going home," he said. "I'm done in."

Hardy knew lawyers who couldn't get to sleep until nearly dawn for the duration of their trials, others who crashed after dinner and woke up at 3:30 in the morning. The one constant seemed to be the disruption of sleep patterns. For his own edification and amusement, Hardy played it both ways, which tended to wreak havoc on his life and psyche. Two days ago, up at 5:00 A.M., asleep at 1:00 A.M. Then, this morning, Glitsky's call again around five. Now here he was at his office, no dinner inside him, 8:00 P.M. He'd called home an hour ago and told them it would be late. Don't wait up.

Hardy had been going through the D'Amiens folder Glitsky had delivered. The precise relevance of all this continued to be elusive, although Hardy couldn't escape the same conclusion that Glitsky had reached. It may not have been what killed D'Amiens and Hanover, but some other intrigue was definitely going on in her life. Blackmail, extortion, money laundering. Something. He'd been surprised enough to learn about the siphoned money, but even the smaller details rankled. He hadn't known that she'd kept up her rent on the place on Eleventh Avenue, for example. Not that it mattered, but still ... or why she would have lied about her employment. The fact that she'd written the Leymar checks out of her own account.

If any kind of significance came to attach itself to these details, and so far none did, he'd have to try to find out from Catherine. Maybe she knew how Missy and Paul had specifically connected. There had to have been a mutual friend or acquaintance. Hardy didn't believe Paul had just picked Missy up somewhere, although, of course, that was also a possibility. Maybe Missy had in fact set her sights on Paul, just as his ex-wife and children suspected, for his wealth and standing.

The galling thing was that he didn't even know why he was continuing with the exercise. Studying numbers, going over the monthly statements page by agonizing page. Deposits, withdrawals, deposits, withdrawals. At one point he looked up and said aloud, "Who cares?" But he kept up the routine. Halfway through, he made himself a double shot of espresso and brought it back to his desk.

No word at all yet from Wes Farrell.

When he finished he checked his watch again and saw that it was nearly 9:00. He stood and closed the folder, leaving it on the center of his blotter. All that work, like so much of trial preparation, to no avail. The worst thing about it, he thought, was that you very rarely knew what you'd need, so you had to know everything.

Cricking his back, he brought his coffee cup over to the sink, then crossed to the door and opened it. He vaguely remembered a knock on that door in the past hour or so, one of the associates telling him she was leaving, he was the last one left in the building if he wanted to set the alarm on the way out.

In the lobby, dim pinpoints of ceiling lights kept the place from being completely dark, but it was still a far cry from the bright bustling business environment it assumed during the day. Off to his right, through its immense windows, the Solarium's plants and ferns and trees cast strange, shape-shifting shadows that seemed to move, which made no sense in the empty space. Hardy had once had some bad luck in the supposedly empty office and now curious, he walked over and opened the door to the room. A small bird—sparrows got in through the side door from time to time—swooped down out of one of the trees and landed in the center of the conference table, where it eyed him with a distant curiosity.

Hardy flicked on the lights and walked around the outside of the room. At the door that led out to the small patch of ground that held the memorial bench they'd installed in honor of David Freeman, he stopped and turned.

The sparrow was still watching him, too. Hardy opened the door all the way and went outside.

The sides of buildings rose on three sides around him. The "memorial garden" existed thirty-six feet above the Sutter Street sidewalk, with a grilled fence along the parapet on the open side. Hardy sat himself down on the Freeman bench. It was very still here, and quite dark, with only the barest of muffled sounds coming up from the city below.

He let his burning eyes go closed. His breathing slowed. The passage of time ceased.

And then, suddenly, wide awake, he sat up straight, hyperaware of the silence and emptiness around him. He brought his right hand up to his forehead, whispering "Wait." Staring unseeing for another several seconds into the open space in front of him, his head pitched slightly to the side, he sat as if turned to stone. He dared not move, afraid that the still-evanescent thought might vanish with as little warning as it had arrived. He looked at it from one angle, then another, trying to dislodge the force of it. There was the fact itself, and then, far more important, there was what it meant. What it had to mean.

What it could mean nothing else but.

When it appeared that the idea had set—unnoticed by Hardy, the sparrow had flown out to the bench, then off into the night—he went back inside, closing the door behind him. Back at his desk, he hesitated one more moment before opening the folder again.

It was still there, the fact that had finally penetrated. The only significant detail in the mass of minutiae. Just where it had been before, and not a mirage at all.

30

"It's not a trick question, Your Honor." Hardy was in Braun's chamber first thing in the morning, on three hours of sleep, and was aware that a bit of testiness had found its way into his voice. It didn't bother him too much. "I'm trying to accommodate my witnesses, some of whom, Mr. Rosen might admit, have lives outside of the courtroom. If they are not going to be needed until tomorrow or even next week, I'd like to let them go home or back to their jobs."

"Reasonable enough, Mr. Rosen," Braun said. "Let's answer Mr. Hardy's question, shall we? Is Theresa Hanover your last witness?"

"I don't know how long she'll be on the stand, Your Honor," Rosen said.

"Then it'll be a surprise for all of us. What's your problem here?"

"No problem, Your Honor. I like to keep my options open."

Hardy knew that Braun was not a fan of sarcasm, and so tried with some success to keep the irony in his tone to an acceptable level. "If he changes his mind and calls another witness, Your Honor, you have my word I won't appeal."

Braun's reaction showed that he'd come close, but after the quick squint at him, she directed her words to Rosen. "Defense counsel will not hold you to your statement here, all right? Now, barring last-minute decisions that you'll have every right to make, do the people currently plan to rest after Theresa Hanover's testimony is complete?"

"Yes, Your Honor."

"Thank you. That wasn't so hard, now, was it?" But she didn't wait for him to answer. Instead, she said, "Mr. Hardy, you've got your witnesses here, I take it."

"Yes, Your Honor."

"Good, then . . ." She started to rise from her couch, pulling her robes around her.

But Hardy interrupted. "There is one other small point we need to discuss, though."

With a frown and a grunt of disapproval, the judge lowered herself back onto the cushions. "And that is?"

"Before I begin my case in chief, I'd like to recall one of the state's witnesses for further cross-examination."

Rosen didn't want any part of this, and shaking his head in disbelief at his opponent's gall, he immediately spoke up in both outrage and indignation. "*Your Honor!* Mr. Hardy has had his fair chance to cross-examine every one of my witnesses, and now because perhaps he's remembered something that he's overlooked or should have asked the first time, he shouldn't be allowed a second chance. He can just call the witness during his case."

Hardy simply stood at ease, a bland expression on his face, his eyes on the judge. "Your Honor," he said, "further cross-examination of this witness may materially change the way I present my defense."

Rosen didn't believe it. "Sure it will. So first we're supposed to let you know who I'm calling today so you can accommodate your witnesses, and then I tell you and you're stalling anyway." Though he'd addressed Hardy directly, and not the court, Braun didn't seem to notice this morning. "I don't have any other witnesses in court today except Theresa and Sergeant Cuneo. Anybody else we'll have to subpoena again. It could take weeks. Is it one of them?" Rosen asked.

"Do you want to play twenty questions?" Hardy asked. He turned to the judge. "This is ridiculous, Your Honor. I've already spoken to the witness just last night and he told me he'd be happy to come down and talk on the record. He is in fact in this building right now. I didn't need a subpoena to get him to do it. He's interested in the truth."

This brought a guffaw from Rosen. "I bet."

Braun turned on him. "Now that will be enough, Mr. Rosen. Mr. Hardy, who is this witness?"

"Dr. Yamashiru."

"And you say he's here now?"

"Outside in the hallway, Your Honor. I talked to him just before we came in here. There will be no delay at all."

"And your cross-examination will focus on what he's already testified to?"

"Yes, Your Honor. In light of these new facts. His testimony is of course central to the people's case, and I believe these new facts will be critical if the jury is to reach a just verdict."

"Would you care to share these facts with the court back here?"

"If it please the court, Dr. Yamashiru's testimony will speak for itself."

Rosen couldn't hold back from addressing Hardy directly. "So now you're withholding discovery?" Turning to the judge, "Your Honor, this is both blatant and outrageous."

"But," Braun countered, "legal. If he calls his own witness he has to give you his statements, as you know. If he recalls one of yours, it's just further cross and he doesn't." She turned to Hardy. "This had better be further cross, Counselor, and not new material."

Braun wasn't sure that she liked it, but Hardy's motion specifically excluded questions that he might have neglected to ask through oversight or error the first time Yamashiru had testified. She knew that new facts sometimes did get discovered in the middle of a trial, and when they were legitimate, should be admitted. Braun let out a heavy sigh, gathered her robes around her again, and this time stood all the way up. "How much time are we talking about, Mr. Hardy?"

"A half hour, I'd say, at the most."

"Mr. Rosen, any objection if he goes first? Get it out of the way."

At last Rosen seemed to understand the way the wind was blowing. "If it's really a half hour, Your Honor, I have no objection."

It didn't even take half of a half an hour.

Braun succinctly explained the situation to the jury, and then Hardy called back up to the stand the forensic odontologist who'd identified Missy D'Amiens by her dental records.

The clerk reminded Yamashiru that he was still under oath, and he said he understood that and sat erect in the witness box. He was a medium-sized, wiry man in his early fifties, well dressed in a dark gray suit and a modern-looking, multicolored tie. His attitude was of expectancy, even eagerness. Recognizing his patient Catherine Hanover at the defense table, he gave her a friendly, though discreet, nod.

Hardy noticed it and hoped some of the jurors had seen it as well. Anything to humanize the defendant. He held some loose papers in his hand—the "dailies" from the day earlier that Yamashiru had been on the stand testifying for nearly two hours. He'd studied them this morning at his dining room table just after he'd gotten up an hour before dawn. Now, in the courtroom, he stood six feet in front of his witness and bowed slightly. "Dr. Yamashiru, since it's been a while since you gave your testimony, I wanted to review for a moment the thrust of what you said the last time you were here. It is true that Missy D'Amiens had dental work done at your office on several occasions between . . ."

Keeping it concise but detailed enough to jog the memories of the jurors who, like Hardy, had possibly slept through parts of Yamashiru's earlier testimony, he brought the witness up to the present. "And you concluded, did you not, Doctor, based on your expertise and experience, that the dental records identified in your office as those of Missy D'Amiens correlated exactly with those of the female victim of the fire in this case?"

"Yes, I did."

"Exactly?"

"Exactly. There was no doubt whatever."

"Thank you, Doctor." Hardy took a surreptitious deep breath as he walked back to the defense table where Catherine sat staring at him with a laserlike intensity, a mixture of fear and faith. He hadn't had time to meet with her before they got to the courtroom today, and even if he'd found the time to talk to her in the holding cell, he wasn't completely sure he would have told her his plans. Until it was done, it wasn't done, and he was loath to raise her hopes.

Walking back to his place in front of the witness, he said, "Doctor, did you yourself do any dental work on Missy D'Amiens?"

"No."

Even through the security doors, Hardy was aware of the expectant buzz in the gallery. But he dared not pause. "No, you were not her dentist?"

"Not personally. She came to my office, but the work was done by my associate, Dr. Kevin Lee."

"And is Dr. Lee still with your practice, Doctor?"

"No. He opened his own shop in San Mateo about a year ago."

"Think back carefully, Doctor. Do you recall if you ever actually met Missy D'Amiens yourself?"

It took Yamashiru twenty seconds, an eternity in a courtroom. "No, I can't say that I did."

"And yet you identified her records?"

"Yes, well, I had the records. I examined the records. They were in her name."

"Thank you, Doctor." Back at the defense table, Hardy reached over and squeezed Catherine's hand, and then straightened up and turned back around. He walked to the table off to the right of the jury box that held the prosecution and defense numbered and lettered exhibits. There he picked up the eight-by-ten original photograph of Missy D'Amiens that he'd introduced for his cross-examination of Maxine Willis as Defense Exhibit A. Turning again, he faced the judge. "May it please the court," he said, "I am holding in my hand a photograph earlier designated as Defense Exhibit A. I'd like to pass it around the jury if I may."

Hardy waited in suspended tension as the photograph made its silent way down the front row of six, then to the back row—man, woman, man, man. And at last it was back in his hand.

Taking another breath to calm his nerves, now jangling, he advanced right up to the jury box. "Dr. Yamashiru," he said, "would you please take a careful look at this picture and tell the members of the jury who it is a picture of?"

"Yes, it's Missy D'Amiens."

"Doctor, if you never met her, how do you know that?"

"Well, I guess first because Inspector Cuneo told me it was her when he showed me the picture, and then of course I saw her picture in the papers, too."

"Please think back, Doctor. When Inspector Cuneo showed you this photo, it was a single photo, wasn't it?"

"Yes, I'm sure it was."

"And he didn't ask you if it was Missy D'Amiens. He told you it was, didn't he?"

"Yes."

"So, Doctor, you merely confirmed what the inspector already knew, correct?"

"Yes."

"Doctor, if I told you that your former associate, Dr. Lee, who actually worked on the patient, told me just last night that this was *not* the person whom he knew as Missy D'Amiens, would you have any reason to doubt him?"

Yamashiru paused again. "No."

Behind Hardy, an audible gasp rippled through the courtroom. He heard Catherine's restrained "Oh, God," and one of the jurors swore under his breath. Up on the bench, Braun looked for a moment almost as though she'd been struck.

But Hardy didn't savor the moment. He needed to nail it down for the record. "Dr. Yamashiru," he said, "I'd ask you to please take another moment to look at this picture. And once again I'd ask you, outside of what you've read or been told, do you know who this woman is?"

"No."

"Have you ever seen her before?"

"I don't think so."

"Has she ever personally been a patient of yours?"

"No."

Suddenly, Hardy felt the strain go out of his shoulders. He drew a breath, let it out, and addressed the judge. "Your Honor, the defense will be adding Dr. Kevin Lee to our witness list."

Catherine gripped his hand as he came back to the defense table. "How can that be?" she asked. "What does it mean?" She brought his hand up to her mouth and kissed it. "Oh, thank you, thank you." Hardy brought both of their hands back down to the table, covered hers with both of his, firmly. "Easy," he said. "Easy. It's not over."

All around them, in the gallery as well as the jury box, pandemonium had broken loose and Braun was gaveling to get her courtroom back under control. To Hardy's left, Rosen was on his feet as though he were going to ask some questions of Dr. Yamashiru, but he hadn't yet moved from the prosecution's table. Beside him, Cuneo slumped, head in his hands. Their case was suddenly in shambles and everyone in the courtroom knew it.

Rosen threw a look over to Hardy, then brought his eyes back front. Gradually, as order was restored, Braun seemed to remember that she still had a witness on the stand. "Mr. Rosen," she intoned, almost gently, "redirect?"

Shell-shocked, Rosen opened his mouth to speak, but couldn't manage a syllable.

Hardy saw his opening and decided to take it. Normally, in a largely pro forma gesture, the defense would make an oral pitch for a directed verdict of acquittal at the close of the prosecution's case in chief. This 1118.1 motion asked the judge to rule that as a matter of law the prosecution hadn't presented a sufficient weight of evidence to satisfy its burden of proof. Therefore, without the defense even having to present its case, the defendant should be released. In practice, the release of a defendant in this manner was a rare event indeed.

But it did happen on occasion. There was ample precedent, and Hardy thought that if ever a directed verdict were called for, it would be now. After all, Catherine was charged with killing Missy D'Amiens. If she wasn't the victim in this case, if Missy wasn't in fact even dead for certain, and that now appeared to be the case, then that charge against Catherine became moot. Even more satisfyingly, the botched identification of one of the victims underscored the ineptness and even prejudice of the original police investigation. If they couldn't even get the victim right, how was the jury going to believe anything else they proposed?

So Hardy was standing now and the judge was nodding, indicating with her hand that counsel should approach the bench.

*   *   *

In the relative calm of Lou the Greek's, Hardy and Glitsky sat in a darkened back booth about a half hour before the lunch crowd would arrive in earnest. Hardy was dipping pita bread into the Lou's version of *tsatsiki*, which incorporated soy sauce and hot chili oil into the standard yogurt, garlic and cucumber mix, and somehow the resulting glop managed to work.

"I blame you," Hardy said. "If you hadn't whined so much about having to testify . . ."

"I wasn't whining."

Hardy put on a voice. "If I testify against a cop, the other uniforms won't like me anymore." He popped some bread. "So if I wanted to save you all the embarrassment and worse, I figured I had to come up with something."

"All right, but how did you get it?"

"The car."

"The car?"

He nodded. "I always said that was the key. Now if you'd only have found it earlier . . . but I guess better late than never, huh? I'm sure you did the best you could."

Glitsky wasn't going to rise to the bait. "What about the car, though?"

"It was towed from in front of Missy's apartment."

"Yes it was. So?"

"So she drove it there."

"Right. And?"

"And if she died in the Steiner Street house, it would have still been somewhere near Alamo Square, where she had parked it, where the Willises had seen her get into it."

"No. They said it was Catherine."

"That's what they said, but they were wrong. It was Missy all right. At least I assumed it had to be. It couldn't have been anybody else, really. But I wasn't completely sure until I talked to Yamashiru, then found Dr. Lee and went by his place last night and showed him the picture. Actually, I had some more family snapshots of Missy, too, and Yamashiru didn't recognize any of them. I just wanted to pin Yamashiru down before Cuneo got him to 'remember' seeing Missy around the office."

"And if she wasn't the one in the fire," Glitsky said, "she

couldn't have been the one he identified from the dental records."

"Exactly right."

"So she did it. Missy."

"That's the money bet," Hardy said. "Then she split with the money."

"You have any idea why?"

"I thought I'd leave something for you to figure out. That's police work. As you are no doubt aware, I deal only in the realm of exalted and abstract thought."

Glitsky couldn't fault him for crowing a little. He figured he'd earned the right. "So where's it at now?" he asked. "The directed verdict?"

"Braun's deciding. Technically, she shouldn't grant it. The motion only goes to the people's case, and whether that evidence alone could support a verdict. Yamashiru has only said he doesn't really know if the photo belongs with the records in his office. Those records are in the alleged victim's name and Dr. Lee hasn't testified yet. But everybody knows what's coming, and Braun's so pissed at Rosen and Cuneo she might just pull the trigger. And whether she grants the motion or not, the jury's got to believe the police investigation was totally inept if not completely contrived."

City Talk
BY JEFFREY ELLIOT

The big news around the Hall of Justice this week was the bombshell dropped by forensic odontologist (read "dentist") Toshio Yamashiru in the double-murder trial of Catherine Hanover. Dr. Yamashiru had previously testified about the identity of the female victim in the case, whose body had been discovered burned beyond recognition with that of Paul Hanover at his Alamo Square mansion last May. Hanover's girlfriend, Missy D'Amiens, had been one of the patients in Dr. Yamashiru's practice, and he compared D'Amiens's dental records with those of the deceased woman and pronounced them identical.

On Thursday morning, however, defense attorney Dismas Hardy recalled the dentist to the witness stand for cross-examination. During the questioning, Hardy showed him a *Chronicle* file photograph of Missy D'Amiens and inquired if Dr. Yamashiru could identify the woman in the picture. He could not, stating that he'd had no real contact with the woman. His patient, who had called herself Missy D'Amiens as well, was still clearly the deceased, but evidently she was not the person who'd been engaged to Mr. Hanover.

Dental records are often the only way to identify a body that is otherwise unidentifiable. Outside the courtroom after the stunning testimony, Dr. Yamashiru emphasized, however, that the forensic odontologist only verifies that the teeth of the victim match those of his sample dental records. "The actual identification of the individual is left to the detective in charge of the case," Yamashiru explained, "Sergeant Dan Cuneo. And he got it wrong."

Judge Marian Braun called a halt to further proceedings today while she mulls over her ruling on Mr. Hardy's motion to dismiss all charges against his client, who—because a double murder mandates the charge of special circumstances—is facing life imprisonment without the possibility of parole.

Which of course leaves two related questions: assuming Hardy is right and the dead woman is not Missy D'Amiens, who is the dead woman? And where is Missy D'Amiens?

In the end, the district attorney himself—Clarence Jackman—appeared before Braun could rule on the 1118.1 motion. "Your Honor," he said, "in light of the new evidence we've seen in this case, the people move . . ."

For Catherine, the ordeal was over.

PART
THREE

31

On a fogbound, windswept and blustery Thursday in early March, six weeks to the day after Jackman dismissed the charges against Catherine Hanover and Braun ordered her released from jail, Glitsky was doing his own driving. He was not in uniform. Instead he wore a pair of dark, heavy slacks and a blue dress shirt and his new Glock .40 automatic in his shoulder holster. When he got out of the car, he'd cover the weapon with his all-weather jacket.

The night before, he'd checked out another city-issued Taurus, and this morning he'd gone against the traffic over the bridge to the East Bay and taken Interstate 80 east. Now, just beyond American Canyon Road outside of Vallejo, he encountered a blanket of some of California's Central Valley fog—he'd heard of "tule fog" but hadn't before experienced it. For his money, the stuff put its more notorious San Francisco counterpart to shame.

Never mind the fog that rolled in over the city for six months out of the year off the Pacific. *This*, he thought, was the real deal. Every year, he knew, it was responsible for multivehicle wrecks and double-digit fatalities from Redding to Bakersfield, Fairfield to Auburn. Visibility was under a hundred yards, and Glitsky got into the slow lane and decreased his speed to thirty-five, which still felt too fast. But on his left, cars continued to fly by at twice his speed, each on the tail of the vehicle in front of it. Three times people *in the slow lane* had come up on him hell-bent for leather from nowhere out of the whiteness, disappearing back into it as they swerved to avoid him, honking all the way, flipping him off.

Idiots.

Glitsky wasn't in a hurry and even if he was, this wasn't

the time or the place. He'd get where he was going when he got there, and that would be soon enough.

The reason for his reluctance was that he wasn't completely certain of the wisdom of his intended actions, and the more time he took before they became irrevocable, the more comfortable he'd remain. He might even give himself enough time to change his plan entirely. But he didn't think so.

On the D'Amiens matter, and the Hanover murder—they were one and the same—he'd decided to stay on in the role of prime mover in whatever events unfolded. The smart move, the professional approach, he knew, would take him out of the loop. He should leave it to the local jurisdiction in the valley now, or to the FBI. Each had an equally strong claim to supervise and carry out the apprehension of Missy D'Amiens.

But almost a year ago Kathy West had asked him to take a watchdog role in the case. He'd been unable to prevent Cuneo from end-running around him, getting an indictment on a woman who was almost undoubtedly innocent. Then the trial—with all of its tabloid stupidity, vulgarity and waste—had led to the renewed currency of the conspiracy theory. Cranks came out of the woodwork and insisted on involving him, Hardy and his client, the mayor, possibly even Chief Batiste and District Attorney Clarence Jackman as players in every problem plaguing the city, from potholes to a rise in the rate of auto theft. And for every one of his good "co-conspirators," the charges and innuendoes had been, and in some cases remained, a huge burden—always personally, always politically and sometimes in business terms as well.

But for Glitsky and Hardy, specifically, the charge held an even greater threat. For they both *had* conspired. Yes, there had been defensible reasons, even compelling ones. But they *were* conspirators, and while the word was bruited about, they were both in constant, if not to say imminent, danger of being discovered. Even at this remove in time.

And all of it, Glitsky believed, on some level, was his fault. He'd been intimidated by Cuneo, who'd unwittingly played on Glitsky's own deepest fear that someone would discover his role in the shoot-out that had killed a police lieutenant. He'd been outmaneuvered by both the inspector and Rosen, then during his investigation while the trial went on he'd been plain outthought by his best friend. At every turn of this case, at every opportunity to make a difference, Glitsky had failed.

A murderer had killed in the jurisdiction for which he held the ultimate responsibility. And that person was still at large.

After a lifetime of service, Glitsky was finally in a position of real authority as the Deputy Chief of Inspectors. But the entire Hanover affair had destroyed much of his own self-esteem. Far more importantly, he knew that it had sullied his reputation among the Police Department's rank and file, and perhaps also at higher levels. He felt it every day in many ways large and small—a silence when he entered a room, a failure to meet his eyes, invitations for anniversaries and retirements that somehow never got delivered to him.

He was afraid now that his ascension to upper management had turned him into what he swore he'd never become—a functionary, a bureaucrat, Peter-principled out at his position. If he didn't get back the respect of his people—from below and from above—his tenure at the top would remain in a hollow holding pattern. He would achieve nothing great—neither revolutionary change for the better nor even simple efficiency. His earlier promise would forever be perceived as a chimera; his promotion a function of the conspiracy, nepotism and cronyism. His future only a slow slide into retirement, when he would become a forgotten and pitiful full-pensioner, a father of grandfather age, unable to keep up with his young children, or even his wife.

The fog thinned somewhat and he punched it up to fifty, passing Vacaville now—enormous malls and outlet stores lining the freeway for miles on both sides. Housing developments all on top of each other. He didn't get out here to the valley very often, but the growth seemed all out of proportion somehow. When his first set of kids had been younger, he'd driven this road many times on the way up to ski the Sierra, and it had all been farmland back then, really not too long ago. Fifteen, twenty years? And all of it gone now? Isn't this where California was supposed to

grow its crops? What were they going to use for land when
the rest of it was all covered up and built over?

Keeping his mind from confronting the real issue. Missy
D'Amiens.

The first glimpse. The Tuesday after the dismissal.

Hardy picks him up at the Hall.

Glitsky putting on his seat belt, Hardy greeting him. "You
said we're going somewhere?"

"We are. Glide Memorial. I wouldn't have bothered you except it's Hanover and you might have questions of your own."

"I'm all over it. You gotta love a field trip."

"You will."

*The soup-kitchen dinner was over by 5:30 most nights, but
some people stay around making sandwiches to give out for the
next day. Glitsky stands at the door a minute until an older
gray-haired black man looks up, puts down his knife, wipes his
hands and comes over.*

"Lieutenant Glitsky?" *Using the civil service rank Glitsky
had given him. He sticks out his hand.* "Jesse Stuart."

"Rev. Stuart, thanks for meeting with me. This is Dismas
Hardy. He's interested because he defended the woman
charged with killing Missy."

*Rev. Stuart doesn't much care—his life is feeding starving
homeless people. White men in suits don't figure much in the
picture. But he's polite.* "So what can I do for you?"

"I'd like to go over a little of what we talked about earlier
today. About Missy."

"Sure. I looked it up in the meanwhile, and it was like I said.
She started coming in to help out about four years ago now. She
was a regular, couple of nights a week, for most of a year, then
slowed down. Eventually stopped altogether. Some do."

"And Dorris? No last name?

The minister smiles. "None I ever knew. She was just Dorris."

"I'm sorry," *Hardy says,* "but who's she?"

"A regular here 'til last year."

"Last May, right?" *Glitsky says, throwing Hardy a pregnant
look.*

"Right. I remember because she came in on my birthday and
brought me a flower. So Dorris stopped on May tenth. Didn't
never come again."

"Did you report her missing?" Hardy asks.

Stuart doesn't try to show that he thinks this is a dumb question, but a hint of it leaks out. *"No, sir. We try to feed as many as we can, but we don't keep tabs on 'em."*

"But you didn't think it a little strange that she just stopped?"

"No. Happens all the time. People come and go."

Glitsky steps in. *"Did you know anything about her? Where she lived? Who with?"*

"She didn't live anywhere, or she lived anywhere. Say it any way you want. She usually came in alone, though. Sat by herself if she could. But didn't make nothin' out of it. She was friendly enough to me, and a good talker if you got her going. Actually pretty educated. Did some college one time."

"How old was she?" Glitsky asks.

Stuart shrugs. *"Thirty, fifty, somewhere in there. Mostly she was hungry."*

"And she and Missy became friends?" Glitsky, getting to it.

"I wouldn't say that exactly. Sometimes they'd sit together, that's all. Then one day she comes in, I'm talking Dorris now, and she's all smiling, showing off her teeth all clean and fixed up. You know the clinics don't generally do dental, so somebody asked and she said she had an angel. That was all. That's really all I remember about it. Nothing connected to Missy herself. It was just another little miracle like happens all the time here."

Hardy's is all game face. He's got his own teeth clenched hard in his mouth, his lips set. Glitsky thanks the reverend and they walk outside together.

"She paid Dorris to establish the dental records," Hardy says. *"She knew she was going to kill her."*

"Maybe not when she made the deal to get Dorris's teeth fixed," Glitsky says. *"Maybe just setting it up in case she ever needed to."*

Glitsky knew that Davis, California, was the home of one of the campuses of the University of California, but that was about all he knew of it. He'd never before stopped in the more or less upscale college town, which was located about ten miles southwest of Sacramento. The fog had lifted and now a drizzle surrounded the car, steady enough to keep his windshield wipers on intermittent swipe.

Leaving the freeway, deep in thought, he made an inadvertent wrong turn until a sign for a surgery clinic next to a sushi place struck him as so incongruous that it shook him out of his reverie, and he realized he'd come the wrong way and turned around. Heading back toward downtown, he waited in a surprisingly slow and lengthy line of traffic. Ten minutes later, the reason for the delay became clear. Some genius of a small-town city planner had evidently decided it would be a good idea to have the five lanes of the freeway overpass funnel down into a narrow, two-lane tunnel/underpass beneath an old railway line. But Glitsky was a longtime resident of San Francisco to whom traffic delays were an everyday fact of life. If he let traffic bother him, he would have had a nervous breakdown or psychotic episode years ago. There was a light at an intersection up ahead of him, just in front of the tunnel, that had already cycled through red twice. It wouldn't be long, another few minutes at most. He'd just wait it out.

It's one week after the dismissal, five weeks ago to the day, and FBI Special Agent Bill Schuyler sits with Glitsky downstairs in one of the half-hidden back booths across from the Hall at Lou the Greek's. It's way after hours, going on nine at night, and Glitsky hasn't yet been home. Everything he is doing with the Hanover matter, and all week he's been at it, has been transpiring outside the realm of his daily work.

The two men have had a professional relationship for more than six years. But it's never easy with overlapping jurisdictions, different procedures and priorities. Feds and locals weren't like oil and water. More like oil and oranges. This is about to become clearer than ever. Schuyler says, "Yeah."

Glitsky, hands around his mug of hot tea, nods. He's not surprised by the admission so much as by the sudden current of anger that courses through him. "You're telling me you knew?"

"I didn't know, personally, myself, but yeah, somebody in the bureau knew."

"And whoever it was didn't think it might be worth mentioning, say to the cops investigating a double murder?"

Schuyler isn't going to fight about it. "Nope. She was dead. We checked ourselves and she was gone. What difference would it make?"

"It might have made a small difference to the woman who spent eight months in jail accused of killing her."

"Not my problem. Neither is this. I inquired into it as a favor to you and got what you wanted. I don't see what's your beef, tell you the truth. She was connected into witness protection, okay. That's what you asked. Then somebody else apparently killed her. So?"

"So maybe the killer was who she was being protected against."

"It was determined that wasn't the case."

Glitsky presses the skin at his temples, runs his finger over the scar through his lips. *"It was determined . . ."*

"That's what they told me." Schuyler doesn't move a muscle. His hands are clasped on the table in front of him. He may know Glitsky somewhat as an individual, but this is not a personal conversation on any level. It is bureau business.

"So what was the protection about?"

"That's 'need to know.' " Then, softening somewhat. *"So I don't know."*

"Any way to find out?"

A shrug.

"And what about now, when it appears she's alive?"

"That I did ask. Seems she fooled us, too."

"So she's really gone?"

"That's what I heard."

"Why would she do that? Shake your protection if it was working?"

Schuyler shakes his head. *"No idea."*

Glitsky wills himself to speak calmly. *"Let me ask you this, Bill. Your personal opinion. Would somebody in the bureau have helped her with this?"*

"With what?"

"Getting away."

After a minute, he nods. *"It's barely possible, I suppose, but not if it involved killing Hanover and another citizen and then torching the house."*

"But you do agree that it must have been her?"

"It's possible. I don't have an opinion. Officially, she's still dead."

"She's not dead. There's no body."

"Okay, you've only known that for a week. Before that, she'd been dead for ten months. In the system, she's still dead."

This isn't Glitsky's war. Besides, dead or missing, the official call doesn't matter to him. "Do you know who her connection was?"

A flare goes off in Schuyler's eyes. He does a favor for Glitsky and the guy wants to go around him, higher up? "Negative," he says. "And they wouldn't tell me if I asked."

"Need to know again?"

"That's how we do it." *Schuyler, truly pissed off now, starts to slide out of the booth.*

Glitsky reaches out a hand, touches his arm, stops him. "She's alive, Bill. I intend to find her, but I need something to work with. I need to know who she is."

"Put in a request." *He gets out of the booth.* "If anybody wants to talk, they'll call you."

Glitsky came to believe that the only realistic possibility of tracing Missy D'Amiens had to be through the very large sum of money she'd stolen. She wouldn't want to carry it around in cash. She would have to put it somewhere, if only for safekeeping. So on the day after his meeting with Schuyler, he had made some inquiries with the local branch of the Department of Homeland Security and had finally been put in contact with the Treasury Department's Financial Crimes Enforcement Network, known as Fin-CEN. He didn't hold out much hope that the financial search would yield any results, since he'd already learned that Missy's Social Security number was inactive due to her apparent death. But he had nothing else to pursue.

As a law enforcement officer, Glitsky had the authority to initiate what they called a Section 314(a) request, under that numbered provision of the Patriot Act. At the same time, he petitioned the attorney general of the United States, indicating that the person he was investigating in the Witness Protection Program had been charged, according to 18 U.S.C. Section 3521 et seq., with "an offense that is punishable by more than one year in prison or that is a crime of violence."

The 314(a) request, originally intended to monitor the financial dealings of suspected terrorist groups, had in fact become primarily a tool to identify money laundering. There was, Glitsky knew, a host of problems with this approach—

privacy issues, First Amendment questions, the basic problem of government interference with the lives of private citizens—but they were not his problems. Not now. And beyond that, the approach seemed somewhat backward. But to his astonishment his research turned up the fact that banks and most other financial institutions—even in post-9/11 America—didn't try very hard to verify the identity of their customers.

In California and several other western states, banks hire a private company to validate addresses and maintain databases on driver's license information, for example. But these verifications only concern themselves with whether the information is properly formatted. That dates of birth are made up of a month, a day and a year, for example. Or that residence addresses are not, in fact, business addresses. Or that there are nine digits in the SSN, broken in the right places—although inactive SSNs due to death are flagged.

Most unbelievably to Glitsky, banks did not even have to try to verify whether a given Social Security number matched a name. Instead, they would open an account with a valid SSN or business tax ID number and accept an accompanying driver's license or other form of ID. If the driver's license had your picture on it, with the name Joe Smith, and it seemed like a valid license, then the bank would take your SSN and list the account under Joe Smith. There was no system in place to identify fraudulent or fictitious names by comparing them to SSNs, or for tying all of this various identification information together.

The 314(a) procedure is straightforward, simple, low-tech. Every two weeks the government compiles a hardcopy list, usually with between fifty and two hundred names, of the government and law enforcement requests and sends it by fax or e-mail to every financial institution in the country. Each one of these institutions, within two more weeks, then must provide information on whether it maintains or has maintained accounts for, or engaged in transactions with, any individual, entity or organization listed in the request. If a match is found, the bank must notify FinCEN with a "Subject Information Form."

And when Glitsky had gotten that form forwarded to

him as the requesting party, submitted to FinCEN by Putah Creek Community Bank in Davis, California, he had gone to District Attorney Clarence Jackman in great secrecy. Only Jackman, the judge who'd signed the warrant and Glitsky's wife knew that he had obtained a search warrant for the records referenced in the report.

32

Downtown Davis was arranged in a grid with lettered streets running north/south and numbered ones east/west, and Glitsky had no trouble finding the Putah Creek Community Bank at Third and C. It was a small corner building, about half the size of Glitsky's BofA branch in San Francisco. He drove by it, continued on to Fifth and turned right. About a mile farther on, outside the downtown section, he navigated an unexpected roundabout and pulled into the parking lot of a low-rise building that looked new. As an armed on-duty officer from another jurisdiction, he needed to check in with the local police not only as a courtesy, but to try to avoid any of those complicated misunderstandings that sometimes cropped up when dark-skinned men carrying concealed weapons encounter uniformed patrolmen. Glitsky didn't expect anybody to hold a parade in his honor, but it couldn't hurt to have the locals know that he was in town. He knew that he might also need to make arrangements for support and logistics.

The chief, Matt Wessin, came out and greeted him in the lobby. Ten or more years Glitsky's junior, Wessin exuded health, competence and vigor. The shape of his body indicated that he worked out for a couple of hours every day. His hair bore not a streak of gray either on top or in the clipped military mustache. The face itself was as smooth and unlined as a boy's. But he was every inch a professional cop, first talking privately to Glitsky about the situation in his office, then bringing him into a small conference room to brief a small team of detectives and a couple of patrolmen who he assigned to temporary detail.

"Ladies and gentlemen," he began. There were two women in the room, a lieutenant and a sergeant. He made the introductions, then continued. "By now, you've all had a chance to look over the fax pages that Deputy Chief Glitsky sent down yesterday. He's got some more show-and-tell today, mostly a couple more pictures of the woman he's hoping to locate here in town, although she may already be gone. As these pages indicate, it appears that she's closed up her post office box. She may also have simply abandoned her safe-deposit box, which is down at Putah Creek Community Bank, but the upshot is that her address, if any, is a mystery. I'm going to pass these new pictures around and invite you all to look at them and then review for a minute who we're actually talking about. This isn't something we hear every day, I know, but in this case, I'd take it to heart. She should be considered armed and extremely dangerous.

"She got the deposit box under the name Monica Breque, although she has previous aliases, which include Michelle, or Missy, D'Amiens. If you'll open the files in front of you, you'll see . . ."

It's two and a half weeks ago, just after lunch on a Monday afternoon.

Glitsky made his 314(a) request more than three weeks ago and hasn't gotten any response yet. An hour ago, Zachary was cleared for a month without the need for more testing, and the dour and cautious Dr. Trueblood even allowed himself what looked like a genuine and even optimistic smile.

Glitsky gets back to his office at the Hall of Justice in the early afternoon. He greets Melissa, spends a minute giving her the good news about Zachary, then turns left out of the reception area, passes through the small conference room adjacent to it and into the short hallway that leads to his office, where he stops.

His door is closed.

When he left for the doctor's appointment three hours ago, he'd left it open. He almost goes back to ask Melissa if she'd locked up for him while he was gone, but then realizes that it's probably nothing. Maybe some cleaning staff, somebody leaving a note, not an issue.

So he opens the door.

Inside, on one of the upholstered chairs in front of Glitsky's desk, in a relaxed posture, slumped even, with his legs crossed, is a man he's never seen before. He's wearing a business suit and looks over at Glitsky's entrance. "You might want to get the door," he says.

Glitsky doesn't move. "Who are you?"

"A friend of Bill Schuyler's." There's no threat in the soft-spoken voice. He points. "You mind? The door?"

Never taking his eyes off him, Glitsky complies. The man returns the gaze for a second, then stands up. He is probably in his forties, tall, slim and pale, half bald with a well-trimmed tonsure of blond hair. He's already got his wallet in his hand and opens it up, flashes some kind of official-looking identification. "Scott Thomas," he says. "You've been making inquiries about Missy D'Amiens. Do you really believe she's still alive?"

"I do. I don't think there's any doubt of it. Are you FBI?"

A small, tidy, almost prim chuckle. "No, I'm sorry. CIA."

Glitsky takes a beat. "I understood she was in witness protection."

"She was. We put her in it, farmed it out to the bureau." Another ironic smile. "The company isn't allowed to operate domestically."

"All right," Glitsky says. "How can I help you?"

"Maybe we should sit down."

"I'm okay on my feet."

Thomas's mouth gives a little twitch. The man clearly isn't used to being gainsaid. His orders, even his suggestions, get followed. His eyes, the pupils as black as a snake's, show nothing resembling emotion. "It might take a minute," he says in a pleasant tone. "We'll be more comfortable." He sits again, back in the easy chair, and waits until Glitsky finally gives up, crosses behind his desk and lowers himself into his chair.

"I want to tell you a story," Thomas says.

In the next hour, Glitsky hears about a young woman, born Monique Souliez in 1966 in Algiers. The sixth child and youngest daughter of a very successful French-trained surgeon, she, too, was schooled in France. Linguistically talented, she traveled widely during her vacations—within Europe over several summers, Singapore another, San Francisco, Sydney, Rio. But she came from a well-established and very closely knit family, and when her formal education was completed in 1989, she returned to Algeria, where she took a job in junior management at the local branch of the Banque National de Paris and soon fell in love with a young doctor, Philippe Rouget.

In 1991, she and Philippe got married in a highly visible society wedding. This was also the year in which a party of some moderate but mostly radical Islamists called the Islamic Salvation Front, or FIS, won a round of parliamentary elections for the first time. This victory prompted Algeria's ruling party, the National Liberation Front (FLN) to outlaw the FIS, and this in turn led to the first violent confrontations between the FLN and the FIS, confrontations that within a year had grown into a full-scale civil war.

Monique and Philippe were not particularly political. True, they both came from the upper classes and socialized almost exclusively within that circle. But mostly they kept to themselves and to the strong Souliez extended family of doctors, engineers, professional people and their educated, sophisticated, well-traveled relatives. The young couple themselves were contented newlyweds doing work that they felt was important and that would go on regardless of who was in power. After Monique became pregnant, their personal world became even more insular, even as the civil war escalated throughout the country and all around them.

Idealistic and unaffiliated with any of the warring factions, Philippe volunteered when he could at both emergency rooms and makeshift clinics that treated both sides. Sometimes these weren't clinics at all, but calls in the night, wounded and dying young men at their doors.

The slaughter, meanwhile, continued unabated until the government finally took the conflict to another level. Anyone suspected of FIS sympathies would simply disappear amid rumors of mass graves and torture. The government issued weapons to previously noncombatant civilians, and this led to a further breakdown in order, with neighbors killing neighbors, with armed bands of simple thieves creating further confusion and havoc. On the rebel side, a splinter organization that called itself the Armed Islamic Group, or GIA, began a campaign of horrific retaliatory massacre, sometimes wiping out entire villages, killing tens of thousands of civilians. Favoring techniques such as assassinations, car bombings, and kidnapping—and then slitting their victims' throats—they brought a new definition of terror to the conflict.

Philippe and Monique considered leaving the country, of course. They had a baby, Jean-Paul, to protect now. The rest of the family would understand. But the rest of the family wasn't fleeing. This was their home. They and their civilized counterparts in similar predicaments believed it their duty to stay. And Philippe and Monique came to feel the same way. They would be the only hope for the country when the fighting stopped, as they believed it eventually would.

But it didn't stop in time for Philippe and Jean-Paul.

Pounding on their door in the middle of the night, a twenty-man squadron of government security forces broke into their home. Informants had told authorities that they'd seen Philippe working on the GIA wounded. He was, therefore, with the GIA. They dragged him from the house, knocking Monique unconscious with rifle butts in the street as she screamed and fought and tried to get them to stop. When she came to, Philippe was gone, the door to her house was open and nearly everything in it was destroyed. Jean-Paul's broken body lay in a corner of his bedroom with his dismantled toys and slashed stuffed animals littering the floor around him.

Here Glitsky holds up a hand. "I get the picture." He pauses, explains. "I'm not in a good place to hear stories about dead babies right now."

Thomas, jarred out of his narrative, narrows his obsidian eyes in impatience or even anger. Then he checks himself. Glitsky suddenly gets the impression that he knows about Zachary. It's unnerving.

"Sure," Thomas says. "No problem."

He gathers himself, picks up where he left off.

After the government thugs killed her husband and her son, Monique became transformed both by her need for vengeance and for her passionate hatred for the government, and particularly its so-called security units. Within a month of the twin tragedies she'd endured, she went underground and joined one of the revolutionary brigades.

At this time, the rebels still lacked a strong organizational structure or even a cohesive political platform. They were united in seeking to overthrow the current administration and replace it with an Islamic state, but there was no central command, or even a consensus on what type of Islamic structure the country would eventually embrace if they were victorious. The typical cell consisted of a loosely confederated group of between ten and twenty-five individuals. Most of these were Islamic, of course, but many Christians and even some Europeans were drawn to the cause in the way Monique had been—by the government's brutality or by simple hatred of individuals in power. Many, too, joined the rebels because they hated France, which supported the FLN and its military-dominated regime.

The details of Monique's next couple of years were sketchy, but it was clear that she had become affiliated with one of the cells. She may or may not have actually participated in many raids and ambushes—the accounts varied—but she certainly became comfortable with a variety of weapons and took part in planning and funding operations, especially against security details such as those that had killed her family.

But as the government's ongoing campaign continued to decimate the rebels' numbers, the individual cells were forced to congeal into more cohesive and ever more secretive units. The GIA, effectively beaten as an army, had to abandon the pitched street battles that had marked the civil war stage of the conflict, although they continued to assassinate, to bomb and to kidnap. The government, for its part, waged what began as a successful torture campaign against captured prisoners who were suspected of GIA affiliation. Increasingly marginalized, the rebels countered with an effective tool to guarantee the silence of its captured operatives. If a captive talked, his or her entire family would be killed. Not just husbands and wives and children, but fathers, mothers, grandfathers and grandmothers, uncles, aunts and cousins, to the third degree.

The most celebrated of these slaughters occurred in 1997. The government arrested a nineteen-year-old boy named Antar Rachid on suspicion of taking part in the carjacking and assassination of a minor Algiers municipal official. Three days after Rachid's arrest, government security forces raided the downtown café out of which Rachid had operated, in the process killing three other GIA soldiers and confiscating a large cache of automatic weapons, cash and ammunition from the hidden room in the café's cellar. Obviously, they broke Rachid with torture and he talked.

Here Glitsky speaks again. "How many of his relatives did they kill?"

"I was getting there." The number seems to slow down even the phlegmatic Thomas. He takes a breath, tries to sound matter-of-fact. "One hundred and sixty-three. Raids in Algiers itself and in thirteen villages over the next couple of days. Gone before they knew what hit 'em. After that," Thomas says, *"captured suspects stopped talking and started dying in jail."*

In 1999, Algeria finally got a new civilian president, Abdelaziz Bouteflika, and he offered amnesty to rebels who hadn't been convicted of rape or murder or other heinous crimes. Along with about eighty-five percent of the rest of them, Monique returned to civilian life, moving back in with her father and mother, going back to work at the bank. But she'd proven herself a valuable organizer and strategist to the GIA, and they weren't ready to abandon her. It wasn't the kind of organization where you simply walked out—Rachid's experience, and many others similar to it, made that crystal clear. It was like the mob. It doesn't matter if you were arrested, or if you tried to leave on your own . . . you are never out.

"But by now, I'm talking 1999," Thomas continues, *"things have really begun to change over there. A new faction called the GSPC splits off of the GIA, and though they're still hitting government and military targets, they swear off civilian attacks within the country. After all the killing of the past years, this has a lot of grassroots appeal. The GIA leadership doesn't see it that way, but they're losing influence and, more importantly, members. And funding. They need to do something dramatic to call the faithful to them. This is jihad now, not just revolution. The will of Allah will be done, and even if fellow Muslims are killed, it is acceptable because they all become martyrs."* Thomas pauses again. *"The GIA decides they are going to blow up the biggest elementary school in Algiers. Six hundred kids."*

"Lord, the world." Glitsky's elbow is on his desk. His hand supports his head.

"But Monique won't help them. She can't go there. It's too much."

Glitsky snorts a note of derisive laughter. *"A saint, huh?"*

"In some ways, she was, actually." Thomas shifts in his chair. *"But now she's got an even bigger problem. On the one hand, she hates the government and what it stands for. But on the other, she can't let the GIA go ahead with this bombing. But if she tells anybody, if she betrays her cell, she knows what hap-*

pens next. Her family disappears, all of it. She's seen it happen not just to Antar Rachid and his family, but maybe half a dozen other times.

"She's got four brothers and a sister, all of them married with kids. Her mother and father, both still young enough to be working. Her mother comes from a family of five, her father's the oldest of four. She's got about forty-five cousins." Thomas comes forward, finally showing a hint of urgency. "They're all dead if she talks. There's no doubt about it. Meanwhile, she's in on the planning. If she refuses, she's with the enemy. She can't show a thing."

Glitsky, nodding, appreciates her problem. "So she comes to you guys."

"She comes to me, personally. I'm stationed over there at the time. My cover is I'm with the visa section at the embassy, but she's been underground for four years and she's figured that out. I do some banking at her branch and she approaches me one day, tells me her story.

"The only way she figures she can do it is if she appears to be killed in the raid on the planners. If I'd help her appear to die, she's got information on a major planned terrorist attack. Remember, this is pre-9/11, but the Cole had already happened, the African embassies. It might have been a trap, but the bottom line is, I believed her. And it turned out it was all true. They raided the cell and found the explosives, and the government announced that Monique Souliez was one of the rebels killed in the raid."

"And Monique became Missy D'Amiens?"

"That's right."

Glitsky sits in silence for a minute. "So why are you here now, with me?"

"I thought you needed to hear the story."

"Why is that?"

"Maybe so you'll understand where she's coming from. She's a quality person. Maybe the best thing would be to leave her alone, wherever she is. More than anything else, she's a hero."

But Glitsky doesn't even begin to accept this. "More than anything else, she killed two people in my town. I can't leave her alone."

"That might not have been her."

"No? I'll entertain other suggestions if you've got them."

"It could have been GIA."

Glitsky snorts. "Here? They found her here?"

But Thomas keeps on with it. "It's not impossible. You know the guy they arrested at the Canadian border with explosives bound for LAX? He was GIA. They're still very much active. They're not going away."

"Maybe so," Glitsky says, "but they didn't befriend some homeless woman so they could establish phony dental records for her."

Thomas takes in the truth of that. It costs him some. But he tries another tack. "If she's exposed, they kill her family, even now."

"I would hope they wouldn't do that."

The words say it all. Thomas hears them clearly. This, his personal mission, has failed. But he tries one more argument. "I'd ask you to think of what she's been through. It's so different over there. She hasn't lived in the same world as most of us do. If she did kill these two people, I know it was to save her family. Two deaths against sixty. That's the kind of choice she had to make all the time back home. It must have seemed like the only option she had."

"Maybe it did," Glitsky says.

But he doesn't give him any more. After a last moment of silence, poor lovesick Scott Thomas gets up out of his chair, walks to the door, opens it and, like the spook he is, vanishes.

33

Inside the Putah Creek Community Bank, three tellers sat ready to work the windows, but there weren't any customers. A couple of other employees were huddled over a desk behind the screened work area—muffled voices that seemed to be talking gossip, not banking. Out front, a matronly-looking middle-aged woman raised her head at the entrance of Glitsky and Matt Wessin. With a nervous smile, she rose from her seat behind a shiny, empty desk.

Glitsky, in his all-weather jacket with a gun in his armpit, hung back a few steps while the chief extended his hand to the woman. Obviously, the two were acquainted—small town. "Traci," he said, "this is Deputy Chief Glitsky from San Francisco police."

"Yes, we talked a couple of days ago." More handshakes.

And Wessin went on. "He's told you, I believe, that he's got a warrant to view the records of one of your accounts, and also the contents of a safe-deposit box linked to the same account. Do you remember a match in a 314(a) form you sent in a couple of weeks ago? Monica Breque?"

"I do. I think it's the first one we've had out of this branch, but I'm afraid I don't remember her. When I saw the name on the 314 form," she turned to Glitsky, "and then when we talked the other day, I tried to remember something about her, but nothing came to me."

Wessin said, "Maybe one of these will help." He produced from the folder he carried several likenesses that Glitsky had brought up with him, including not only the glossy of the *Chronicle* photo, but also several of Hardy's snapshots from the Hanover family albums. Now Traci examined the pictures slowly, one by one. When she'd gone through them all, she shook her head. "I'm afraid I don't know her at all. And we pride ourselves on personal service, knowing our customers on sight by name."

"She might have had a bit of a French accent, if that's any help," Glitsky offered.

She stopped shaking her head. "A French accent? Now that rings a bell. And she started here last May, we said? That would have been me if it was a new account, too. I'm sorry." Traci looked back down at the pictures. "I just don't have any memory of someone who looked like this. I do remember the accent, though. Is it all right if I show these to the staff?"

Five minutes later, one of the tellers admitted that, like Traci, maybe she'd seen the woman, or someone who looked like her. If it was the same person, though, the hair was certainly different, and she doubted if she'd been wearing the same kind of tailored, high-end city clothes she fancied in the pictures. "But all the same, I'd bet it's her. Great face."

"So she still comes in here?" Glitsky asked.

"I don't know," Carla said. "I wouldn't call her a regular."

"Can you think of what was different about the hair?"

The teller closed her eyes and gave it a try. "Maybe it was short, and not so dark, but I can't really be sure." She checked the picture again. "But I've seen her. Definitely."

This was reasonably good news, but didn't get them any where, so Glitsky and Wessin went back to the manager's desk and got to the account records themselves. Missy, or Monique, or Monica, did not use her checking account to write checks. She had deposited a hundred dollars to open the account on May 17, and hadn't touched it since.

This gave Glitsky a sense of foreboding that he tried to ignore. "Let's take a look at the safe-deposit box," he said.

They all walked into an old-fashioned vault with a heavily reinforced door, its inner workings and tumblers open to the lobby. Traci had a set of the bank's master keys for one of the locks and she'd called in a locksmith to drill out the other one, which needed the customer's key. In short order, she was taking the box from its space in the wall. She placed it on a table in the center of the vault. It was one of the larger boxes—a foot wide, eighteen inches long, four inches in depth. It only took another few seconds to get it open.

Unwittingly, Wessin whistled under his breath.

The stacks of money—fifty- and hundred-dollar bills—was what caught the eye first, but then Glitsky noticed what looked to be a rogue bit of tissue paper stuck against one side of the box. He picked that up first and opened it in his hand. It was, of course, the ring, with the stone actually larger than he'd pictured it. Wrapping it back up rather more neatly than it had been, he put it on the table next to the box. "I guess we ought to count this next," he said.

Tuesday, two days ago, early afternoon in Jackman's office with the door closed behind him and thick, rare slabs of sunshine streaking the floor over by the windows, the wind screaming outside. Jackman is in his oversize leather chair behind his desk, his fingers templed at his mouth. Treya, on the second day of her first week back at work after Zachary's birth, stands guard with her back against the door.

Glitsky is looking on while the DA reads the 314(a) form. "I just got this thing and wanted to run it by you."

"I don't understand how this can be," Jackman says. "Didn't you tell me her Social Security number came up deceased?"

"When I checked six weeks ago, yes. But if she opened this account within a few weeks of the Hanover fire, say, or even sooner than that, the computer wouldn't have caught up with her yet."

Treya says, "She's a banker, sir. She knew it wouldn't."

Glitsky adds. "She's done this before, remember. Established an identity in a new town with ginned-up docs. Undoubtedly she knew they don't check names against socials. If nobody ever thought to ask, and nobody has now for ten months, she's golden. What she didn't know about were the changes since 9/11."

Jackman asks, "So what name is she using now?"

"Monica Breque."

"I bet people call her Missy," Treya says.

"I wouldn't be surprised."

Jackman straightens up in his chair. "We need to get her in custody. Have you talked to the Davis people? Police."

"Yes, sir, a little. And there is still a problem—I talked to the manager at the bank and got a local address that seems not to be hers. It's not fictitious. It's just not where she lives. They sent

some officers around to check right away, and it was somebody else's house entirely. So we don't know where she is."

Jackman isn't too fazed by this. "It's a small town. Somebody'll know where she lives."

"I'll be following up on that."

"I thought you might be." Jackman hesitates. "Abe." He talks quietly, but he's firm. "Why not have them *work on the follow-up, the Davis police? Have them bring in the FBI if they want. It's a banking matter, so it's federal. And she's a protected witness. And when they find her and surround her and place her under arrest, then have* them *bring her down here for her trial when they're done with her. You've found her. You don't physically have to bring her in."*

Glitsky is standing in the at-ease position between his wife and the DA. He wouldn't be at all surprised if they both had the same opinion of what he should do now, but he is not going to be drawn into this discussion. Instead, he nods in apparent assent. "Good point," he says.

Three hundred and fifteen thousand, four hundred dollars even.

It took them nearly an hour to count it twice and be sure. Traci left the two policemen to the work. Toward the end of it, Wessin seemed to become a bit impatient, checking his watch several times, and Glitsky learned that he was to be the speaker at a Rotary event at noon. Glitsky had loosened up by now and had become nearly voluble. He told Wessin he should have known that the chief would have some public event he needed to attend—half of Glitsky's own life was administrative stupidity and public relations. Both men agreed that if people knew, they'd never want to move up through the ranks. Even so, they both understood the importance of Wessin's speaking gig and picked up their speed. When they finally finished, Wessin still had fifteen minutes.

They called Traci back in to lock up the box again and insert it into its proper location. A next-to-worst-case scenario for Glitsky—after the possibility of her escaping again altogether—would be if they could not locate the woman in a day or two of canvassing shopkeepers and neighborhoods and had to assign a full-time person to keep watch in case she went to the bank for some cash.

But he had hopes that it wouldn't come to that. Already this morning, Wessin's task force had gone out into the town and onto the university campus, armed with their photographs. Two officers were going to the post office—they had what they hoped was a current alias, and if she'd ever gotten so much as a gas bill under that name, they could find where she lived. The French accent would stand out, as would the face. All talk of small town aside, though, the population of the greater area during the school year when college was in session was something in the order of a hundred thousand souls. If she were consciously laying low—and her years as a rebel in Algeria had certainly prepared her for that—they could miss her for a very long time, perhaps forever. And that's if she were still here at all.

Although the money argued that she was.

Glitsky and Wessin—by now they were Abe and Matt—were standing on the sidewalk outside the bank. The drizzle had let up along with most of the wind, and though the streets were wet and it was still overcast, patches of blue were showing in the sky above them. "People will be checking back in at the station after lunch, Abe. I could drop you back there now if you'd like. Or you could grab a bite downtown here. It's not San Francisco, but there's a couple of places to eat."

"I'll find 'em. You don't have a Jewish deli, do you?"

"No, but if you want deli, Zia's is pretty damn good Italian. It's on the next block, on the way to where I'm going to talk. You want, I'll show you."

It was a sad but true fact of Glitsky's life that since his heart attack and the never-ending battle with cholesterol, he rarely ate sandwiches anymore, especially freshly sliced mortadella and salami and all those great nitrates with cheese and vinegar and oil on a just-out-of-the-oven sourdough roll. But he was having one now, enjoying it immensely, washing it down with San Pellegrino water, thinking he liked this low-rise, not-quite-yuppified town, even as he wondered where the black people were.

With the improving weather, a steady stream of mostly young people—students, he surmised—passed in front of him where he sat outside on the sidewalk. He saw as many per-capita Asians as there were in San Francisco, and Hispanics, and from the evidence a thriving lesbian community—in fact, ethnicities and minorities of every stripe seemed well represented here, but there was nary a black person. What, he wondered, was that about? More than anything else, he found it odd, out of sync with the world he inhabited.

It was clouding up again as he was finishing his sandwich and his drink, and he went back inside the crowded little deli to discard his bottle and napkins. He looked at his watch. He wasn't due to meet Wessin for another twenty minutes, so he stopped for a moment to look at the display of imported Italian goods around the shelves. Maybe he'd pick up some eggplant caponata for Treya, or roasted red peppers, and surprise her. They hadn't had much romance in their lives since Zachary's birth, and now she was already back at work after the maternity leave. He should really get her something. He never thought to surprise her. He ought to change that. In fact, he should bring her presents more often, he was thinking, let her know how much she was appreciated.

Appreciated? He silently berated himself for the understatement. He way more than appreciated her. In four years, she had become the center of his life. Some days he felt she had given him the gift of feeling again, when it had for so long been dormant.

Maybe some chocolate? A box of Baci, or "little kisses"? Too romantic? What was *too* romantic? What kind of concept was that?

Carefully replacing the roasted red peppers and the little jar of relish so they wouldn't fall, he went over to the cash register where they kept the boxes of candy and was reaching out to pick one up when the woman behind the counter waved and cheerily called out, "Au revoir, madame."

An answering chirp of "au revoir" came from the doorway and Glitsky whirled to catch a glimpse of female profile as she walked out the door and turned left up the street. The candy forgotten now, his mind completely blank, he stood for a long instant frozen in his steps.

He wasn't completely sure. Whoever she was had become blond now, hair cropped so short that it nearly appeared crew cut. He'd only glimpsed her briefly, and the first impression—after the shock of recognition itself—was her youth. This could not be a thirty-nine-year-old former terrorist and killer. This was an anonymous student, possibly in graduate school, wearing very little if any makeup and sporting maybe a piercing through her eyebrow.

He didn't exactly have to fight his way out of the little shop, but if he didn't want to push people over and cause a scene, he had to be careful. By the time he'd come out onto the sidewalk, she was already at the corner crossing, walking away from him.

His mind racing, he fell in behind her. He had his pager on his belt, but had left his cell phone in his car back at police headquarters—they were only going down to the bank and then back on a quick errand, and he'd had no reason to think he'd need it. He did have his gun, but the sidewalk was, if not packed solid with humanity, at least well traveled—twenty or more people shuffled and strolled and simply walked in the space that separated them.

Reluctant to close too much of the space between them, he overruled his early inclination to try to make an arrest alone in the midst of these people. He knew nothing about her own preparations or readiness in case of trouble. She herself might well be the embodiment of that old cliché—armed and extremely dangerous. He could not risk provoking anything like a hostage situation. He also had no idea how she would react if he tried to place her under arrest by himself. The sight of a black man with a gun in a strange, curiously white-bread town might cause the citizenry to react unpredictably. Even if he flashed a badge, there might be enough craziness to allow a young screaming woman to get away in the startled crowd.

He had to get a plan. He had to get a plan.

Half a block further on, she stopped to look in a shopwindow and it gave him a chance to close the gap. Already he was within the same block, close enough to study her. He had lived with the photographs of her now for six weeks, that face from any number of angles, that face with a wide range of expressions. A car honked on the street behind him and she turned to look, and any doubt melted away.

He had found her!

She wore oversize tan overalls and sandals with no socks. On top, an overlong sweater in a washed-out green hid any intimation of the form beneath. She was any dowdy, even slovenly student, unconcerned about her appearance. Without the casually overheard French good-bye, Glitsky might have stood next to her in the deli—probably had been standing next to her—and he would have missed her entirely.

She brought a hand to her mouth. Biting into some kind of pastry, perhaps a cannoli, from the deli, she leaned over slightly to keep the crumbs from falling on her. Then she began walking again. Glitsky stepped into the doorway of the magazine store where she had slowed down and watched as she crossed over diagonally in the middle of the block. A few raindrops hit the pavement and she looked skyward, threw her pastry into a corner trash can and picked up her pace.

He was going to lose her if he didn't move.

But when he crossed behind her and got to the corner, she was still within the block. Stopping under the shelter of a building's overhang, she seemed to be checking her reflection in the bank's window, then brushing crumbs or the rain from her clothes. With another glance at the sky, she started up again, walking away from downtown.

They crossed what Glitsky recognized as Fifth Street and after that entered a residential neighborhood with small stand-alone houses on tiny lots. The foot traffic, here only three blocks from downtown, was nonexistent, which obliged him to extend the distance between them. He ran the slight risk of losing her, but he didn't think he would.

In any case, he had the feeling that this was her general neighborhood. She had come out for a snack or for lunch and now was walking home.

He could, of course, rush her now. With no other pedestrians about, he could put her on the ground if need be and place her under arrest. But he was most of a full block behind her, and there would be very little possibility of surprise. And if she did notice him coming up on her, and was in fact armed, it could become needlessly ugly very fast. Better, and it looked as if the opportunity would soon present itself, would be to remain unseen and unnoticed behind her and let her get home. Then he would have her address, after which he would immediately get to a phone and call for backup.

And the arrest would be done according to Hoyle.

She crossed another larger street—Eighth—then turned right and left and into the driveway of a parking lot in front of a two-story stucco apartment building. Jogging, Glitsky managed to reach the driveway in time to see her disappear into the next to last downstairs unit.

He checked his watch. Wessin would have finished his talk and would be waiting by his car, wondering where Glitsky was, but he could do nothing about that now. All he needed was the unit number, and he didn't even, strictly speaking, need that. He knew it was the second from the end unit on the ground floor. But he wanted to know for certain when he called it in. It would be bad luck to get it wrong and have a bunch of eager patrolmen, guns drawn, come crashing through the door of some piano teacher.

He stood now in a steady light rain at the outer entrance to the open asphalt parking lot. It was a small enough area, with hash lines marking spaces for each of the eight apartment units, and occupied at the moment by three well-used cars, none of them models from the current millennium.

In number three, where she'd gone, a light came on in the window. He took a few steps into the lot, getting some relief from the rain under a tree.

He still had the option to take her now, by himself. Under any pretense or none at all, he could simply knock at her door and wait until she opened it. Why would she suspect anything? She'd been living here, apparently unmolested, for ten months now, and her life must have settled into some kind of a routine.

But he would be wise not to take her too lightly. She'd had years of experience in the terrorist underground of Algeria, and in that time had learned who could say how many tricks to elude capture or incapacitate authorities when capture was a synonym for death. And truth be told, though it galled him, he was not sufficiently prepared for an arrest. Even if she had no weapon at her disposal, he had no handcuffs, and no way to restrain her except at the point of a gun, which might turn out to be a limited option if he wasn't prepared to shoot her out of hand.

He had to get to a phone. He thought it unlikely that having just returned home, she would leave again, especially in the rain. He wondered if one of the cars in the lot was hers. Maybe the apartment belonged to a friend and she was visiting, not living there.

He had to move. He could lose her if he waited until every possible contingency had been covered.

But she was right here! He stood under the tree, torn by indecision, mesmerized by the light in her window. Had a shadow just moved in the room? He moved a few steps to his left to get a better view. The rain fell in slow, steady vertical drops. A little harder now in front of him, suddenly audible above him in the leaves of his sheltering tree.

He had to move.

The familiar *snick* semi-automatic's round being chambered sounded very close to his ear. The woman's voice from behind him was quiet and assured, with no trace of panic or even unusual concern. "I have a gun pointed at the back of your head. Don't turn around. Don't make any sudden movements. Keep your hands out in front of you where I can see them. The only reason you're still alive is that I need to know who you're with."

"San Francisco police."

"Walk toward the apartment house, second door from the left."

"Are you going to shoot me?"

"If you don't walk, yes."

Glitsky moved forward, out into the rain. He heard her footsteps now behind him and marveled that she could have come up behind him so quickly without a sound or a warning.

"Stop," she said when he reached the door. "Turn the knob and kick the door all the way so it swings open." Following her instructions to the letter, Glitsky stood in the threshold. "Now walk into the middle of the room and link your hands on the top of your head."

He did as he was told, heard her come in behind him and close the door. "Now turn around." The orders continued, specific and organized. "Take your right hand only—slowly, very slowly—and unzip your jacket all the way. Thank you. Get it off, easy, slowly, and drop it to the floor behind you. Step away from it. *Now!*"

She held the gun steadily in one hand. Glitsky noted how comfortable she looked with it and, at the same time, how nearly unrecognizable she'd made herself. The haircut was not so much short as chopped unevenly. With no lipstick or other facial makeup, and with the silver post through her bleached white eyebrows, she had adopted the look of an all but marginal figure, anonymous. By looks alone, she was a kind of lost-looking older and pathetic waif, a spare-change artist from whom people would naturally tend to avert their eyes.

But she never took her eyes from him. "Hold your left arm straight out like I'm doing. Okay, now with your right, thumb and first finger only, lift the gun out of the holster and put it on the floor. Stand." She raised her own gun to his chest and Glitsky thought she was going to execute him. But she extended her arm instead and said, "Back up. More."

The backs of Glitsky's knees hit the couch and he heavily, awkwardly, went down to a sit on the piece of furniture. She got to his gun, picked it up, put it into the pocket of her overalls. "Pull both of your pant legs up to your knees. All right, you can let them back down. Now hands back on your head. Link them." Neither eyes nor gun ever leaving him, she went to the open kitchen area, six feet away, and pulled a metal chair over onto the rug in the center of the room. She sat on it, facing him. "What's your name?"

"Abe Glitsky."

"You're with the San Francisco police?"

"Yes, I am."

"You need training in how to follow people. You're no good at it."

"I'll keep it in mind next time," he said.

But she didn't follow up on that, a conversation line that he thought might humanize him, which in turn could perhaps give her pause as she was deciding whether or not to kill him. Although to protect her identity and her family, he knew that she would have to.

But she simply said, "It's about Paul, then. "

"And Dorris." Glitsky would keep her talking if he could, even if he had to bait her. "You remember Dorris?"

She moved her shoulders in a kind of shrug. "Dorris had to be. In the world, there are millions of Dorrises who have uses and then become expendable. I wish it hadn't been necessary." Almost as an afterthought, she added. "I thought I was done with killing. But no one will ever miss her. She didn't matter."

"And what about Paul?"

"We won't talk about Paul. In fact, there is nothing more to say." Her eyes went to the gun in her hand.

"But there is " He was staring at the gun's barrel. If it moved, he would try to jump her, and probably die trying. But maybe they weren't quite to that point yet. "I don't understand what happened," he said. "You had a life together. You were going to get married."

Shaking her head as though to ward off the thought, she snapped out the words. *"I loved him."* Then, matter-of-fact. "I loved him."

"But you killed him?"

"I killed him. That's what I do. I betray people and then kill them. Or someone else does."

Glitsky risked unlinking his hands, lowering them slowly onto his lap. "Why?"

"Because I have no choice. He gave me no choice. I begged him please."

"Please what?"

"Please not to let them . . . how do you say? It's not exactly the right word. Investigate him."

"For what?"

"For the nomination."

Glitsky's every nerve pulsed with urgency. He knew that if he was to have a chance at life, he would have a split second to recognize his moment and seize it. But part of him settled to a stillness with this information. "You mean the cabinet post?"

"With the government, yes."

"And they needed a background check?"

"The FBI, yes. But don't you see, he didn't need it, the post. He had position and power and money and love. He didn't need it. I begged him not to let them even start."

"Because once they started on him, they'd get to you."

She nodded. "They would have to. I was his fiancée, soon his wife. They would have to background me, too."

"You could have left him. Wouldn't that have been better?"

"Of course, if it would have been possible. You think I would not have done that? But it wouldn't have done any good. I was too close to Paul. They would still have needed to check me."

"But the FBI already knew about you. You were in witness protection."

"Yes? So? The people checking me and Paul were a different department." She hacked in disgust. "They could do nothing. I asked them. They would not. They said they could contain it."

"Did you try to tell them it was life and death?"

"Ha! Of course. The CIA in Algeria knew that, but the FBI didn't believe it, or didn't care. I didn't matter. It's *government*, don't you understand? Where—how do you say?—the left doesn't know what the right hand is doing, and doesn't wash the other even if they could. And the FBI doesn't answer to the CIA."

"So they would have found out who you were and gone public with it?"

"That's what they do. Not on purpose, certainly. Very discreetly, of course. Need to know, high security. Like every junior congressman and tabloid journalist in Washington. And their wives. And their whores. And anyone who would trade the information for something they wanted."

"And you believe that word would have gotten back to Algeria that you were still alive?"

"Don't you understand? There is no way that it wouldn't have. It was too valuable a secret to keep. Who could have a million dollars and not spend any of it?"

Suddenly her expression changed. Glitsky tensed on the couch, focused on the gun, ready to spring. But she didn't move the gun. Canting her head to one side, she went still, eyed him inquisitively. "How do you know about that?"

"Because I know who you are, Missy. Or Monique."

She stared at him, hung her head for a heartbeat, but not long enough to give him an opening. When she looked back up, her face had set into a mask of conviction. "Then that is your death warrant," she said, and started to move the gun.

Glitsky put his hands up in front of his face, but didn't make another move. "It's too late," he said. "I've told the police here. It's already public."

"You're lying! If you worked with the police here, they'd be with you now."

"Call your bank then. Ask them if I was there this morning with your police chief."

She rested the gun on her knee. "You've been to the bank?"

"To your box, Missy. Three hundred thousand dollars and Paul's ring. I told your story to the district attorney in San Francisco and got a warrant. The affidavit's under seal, but it's only a matter of time. Everyone will know it by tomorrow. If you kill me, they may know it by tonight."

Outside, they heard the rain suddenly falling with a vengeance.

Monique, Michelle, Monica, Missy put a hand up to her forehead and pulled nervously at the stud over her left eye. "They will murder my family. Don't you understand that?"

"I'm sorry," he said, and he meant it. "But it can't be undone."

The two of them sat about eight feet apart. The one light by the front window flickered with the freshening wind, the power of the deluge. The gun was on her leg, but she was no longer pointing it at him. "What is your name again?" she asked.

"Abraham."

"My parents. I cannot let . . ." She choked on the rest.

"Maybe we can contact the CIA . . ."

"And what? What do they do in Algeria? Ask their Muslim brothers for mercy for someone who betrayed them? Don't you see? There is no mercy so long as I am alive."

Glitsky had come to the front of the couch and was now sitting slightly forward, in a relaxed posture, with his elbows on his knees and his hands clasped in front of him. "Missy," he said. "I'm going to stand up now."

She immediately gripped the gun in both of her hands and pointed it at the center of his chest.

His eyes locked on hers. "You've had enough of killing to protect your secret. That's over now. The secret is out."

"It isn't. You're lying."

His voice was calm and reasonable. "I'm not lying. You know that."

A long pause. Then a longer pause. "You said you were tired of killing, but that you had to do it. But killing me now will accomplish nothing. So I'm giving you another minute to think it over, then I'm leaving. Shoot me or not, run or stay, it's over. You know that."

He gave her the promised moment to think. Then he stood.

"Don't come any closer!"

"Now I'm going to walk around you."

"No! Don't you move! I'll kill you, I swear to God I will."

"I don't think you will," he said. "It wouldn't accomplish anything."

He was moving up to where she sat, giving her a wide berth. She stood up, too, and took a step back. Going slowly and smoothly, never stopping, he leaned over to pick up his jacket, then putting it on, he continued past her, feeling the gun trained on him at every step, until his back was to her now and there was nothing to do but reach for the doorknob and pray that he was right.

Never looking over his shoulder, he closed his hand around the metallic orb and gave a yank, then stepped out into the downpour and pulled the door closed behind him.

Half an hour later, eight Davis city police cars were parked in the streets surrounding and in the parking lot in front of the apartment building. The rain had resumed its regular steady drifting. The police switchboard had received three calls from the immediate neighborhood in the past twenty minutes reporting what sounded like a gunshot.

But no one was disposed to take unnecessary chances. The policemen had gone door-to-door in the apartment building, rousting the six students who lived there, getting them out of harm's way. Matt Wessin used the bullhorn and informed Missy that she was surrounded by police and had sixty seconds to throw out her weapons and give herself up.

When the minute was up and there had been no response, Abe Glitsky held up a hand to Wessin and his men and, all alone, walked across the few open feet of parking lot to the front door. He stopped for an instant, drew a breath and gathered himself before he pushed.

Slumped over to her right, the terrorist, the killer, the lover, the martyr was on the couch where he'd been sitting not so long before. Glitsky took a step into the room. His chin fell down over his chest. Always professional, still and always an exception to the rule, Missy D'Amiens had shot herself in the head.

In a moment, Glitsky would turn and nod to Wessin and the routines would begin. He tried to imagine some other way it could have gone, something he might have done differently.

But it had all been ordained and set in motion long before he'd been involved. He was lucky to have escaped with his life, when so many others had not.

That was going to have to be enough.

34

On a sunny Saturday evening a couple of weeks into April, Hardy was driving with his wife, top down on the convertible, on the way to Glitsky's. A week before, he'd come across a CD of Perry Como's greatest hits, and since then had been alienating everyone close to him—especially his children—with his spontaneous outbursts into renditions of "Papa Loves Mambo" and "Round and Round" and others that were, to him, classics from his earliest youth, when his parents used to watch the crooner's show every Sunday night. Now, as his last notes from "Hot Diggity (Dog Ziggity Boom)" faded to silence along with the CD track, Frannie reached over and ejected the disc.

"You really like that guy, don't you?"

"What's not to like?"

"I know there's something, but I can't quite put my finger on it. Maybe it's just that he's before my time."

"Perry? He's eternal. Besides, you don't hear polkas often enough nowadays. If you did, the world would be a happier place. I'm thinking of trying to find an Oktoberfest record so we can have more of them on hand at the house."

"The kids might kill you. On second thought, I might kill you."

"No. You'd all get used to it. Pretty soon all their friends are coming over for polka parties. You're the hostess wearing one of those cute Frau outfits. I can see it as the next big new thing." He broke into a snatch of the song again.

"Dismas."

He stopped. After a moment, driving along, he turned to his wife. "Okay, if polka isn't going to be your thing, do you want to hear an interesting fact?"

"I live for them."

"Okay, how about this? The 'zip' in ZIP code? It stands for 'zone improvement plan.' Did you know that?"

She cast him a sideways glance. "You've been reading that miscellany book again."

"True. Actually, my new life goal is to memorize it."

"Why?"

"So I'll know more stuff."

"You already know too much stuff."

"Impossible. I mean, the 'zip' fact, for example. Zone improvement plan." He looked over for her response.

"Wow," she said.

"Come on, Frannie. Did you know that? Don't you think that's neat to know?"

"No, I do. I said 'wow,' even. Didn't you hear me?"

"It sounded like a sarcastic 'wow.' "

"Never."

"Okay, then." They drove on in silence for a moment.

"Zone improvement plan," Frannie suddenly said after half a block. "Imagine that."

Hardy looked over at her, a tolerant smile in place. "Okay, we'll drop it. But only because there's yet another unusual and interesting fact you may not know, and probably want to."

"More than I want to know about what 'zip' stands for? I can't believe that."

"This dinner tonight at Abe's? He asked me what kind of champagne to buy."

"Abe's drinking champagne?"

"I got the impression he intended to."

"Wow. Not sarcastic," she added. "When's the last time you saw him drink anything with alcohol in it?"

"Somewhere far back in the mists of time. Certainly not in the past few years."

"So what's the occasion?"

"I don't know. But it's got to be a good one."

Hardy found a spot to park within a block of Glitsky's house, and figuring he'd won the lottery, pulled his convertible to the curb. Setting the brake, he brought the top back up, turned off the engine and reached for the door handle. Frannie put a hand on his leg and said, "Do you mind if we just sit here a minute?"

He stopped and looked questioningly over at her. "Whatever you want." He took her hand. "Is everything all right?"

"That's what I wanted to ask you."

"If everything was all right with me?"

"Yes."

"You mean with us?"

"Us. You. Everything."

He stared for a moment out through the windshield. He squeezed her hand, turned toward her. "Look at us right now. Look at where we are. It's a good place."

"Not if you're unhappy in it."

"I'm not unhappy. I wouldn't trade this, what I've got with you, for anything. What's got you thinking this?"

"It just seems you've been ... distant, especially since the trial, now that you've stopped seeing her every day."

He said nothing.

"It makes me wonder if what we have isn't enough for you."

"Enough what?"

"Enough anything. Excitement, maybe. Fun. It's all kid stuff and routines and bickering sometimes."

"And you think Catherine was more fun? That it was fun at all?"

"You want me to be honest? I think you loved every minute you spent with her."

This was close to the bone. Hardy chose his words with some care. "That's not the same as wanting to be with her now. It seems to me that the way this marriage thing works is you keep making a choice to be in it every day."

"Even if it makes you unhappy?"

"But it doesn't make me unhappy, not at all. To the contrary, in fact. And here's an unfashionable thought: Unhappiness is a choice. And it's one I don't choose to make." He raised her hand to his lips and kissed it. "What I want is what we've already got. But I guess I'm not communicating that too well, am I? For which I apologize. Really. Maybe you ought to leave me for making you worry."

"I would never leave you. I don't even think about it."

"Well, you know, I never think about leaving you. Ever. We're together, period. The topic's not open for discussion. We've got our family and our life together, and nobody has as much fun together as we do ninety-nine percent of the time. I wouldn't trade it for anything."

A silence gathered in the closed-in space and finally Frannie sighed. "I'm sorry I need reassurance once in a while."

"That's acceptable. I'm sorry if I've been distant."

"I'm sorry you're sorry." She squeezed his hand. "Between us, we are two sorry campers, aren't we?"

"Apparently." He caught her eye, broke a trace of a grin. "Two sorry campers on their way to break bread with People Not Laughing."

"Sounds like a good time. Should we go on up?"

As one, they opened the doors of the car and stepped out into the warm evening. The neighborhood in early dusk smelled of orange blossoms, coffee and the ocean.

People Not Laughing was in his kitchen with a cold bottle of Dom Perignon held awkwardly in his hands. He'd already struggled first with the foil wrapper, then with the wire, and now he was looking at the cork as though it was one of life's profound mysteries.

"Don't point it at your face!" Hardy said. "They've been known to just blow off and take out the random eyeball."

"He's not used to this," Treya said, somewhat unnecessarily.

"So how do you get it off?" Glitsky asked.

Hardy reached for the bottle. "Why don't you just let a professional handle it? My partner will attend the window."

"The window?"

Frannie bowed graciously, crossed to the window over the sink and threw it open. Hardy turned to face the opening. "Now, one carefully turns the bottle, not the cork, and . . ." With a satisfying pop, the cork flew out the window into the warm evening. "Voilà."

And then the glasses were poured and the four adults stood together in the tiny kitchen. "If I might ask," Hardy said, "what's the occasion? Frannie's guess is you're pregnant again."

Glitsky let out a mock scream.

"Read that as a no," Treya said simply. "But I'll propose the toast, okay? Here's to former homicide inspector Dan Cuneo. May his new position bring him happiness and success."

Hardy looked at Glitsky. "What new position?"

"He just got named head of security for Bayshore Autotow. Marcel called me this morning and thought I'd want to know. Cuneo's out of the department with a big raise and great benefits."

"How did that happen?" Hardy asked.

"Well, you might not be surprised to hear that his stock in homicide fell a bit after Hanover, Diz. He felt that people were starting to look over his shoulder when he picked up new cases. They even made him take a new partner whose main job seemed to be to keep him in line. I guess he saw the writing on the wall."

"Yeah, but I'd heard he was up for the Tow/Hold gig way back when, not Bayshore."

"Right, but it's the same job. If he's qualified for one, he can do it for anybody."

"It's the qualified thing I'm thinking about. If he was known to be in such low standing in homicide . . ."

Glitsky's face was a mask. "I heard Harlan Fisk might have put in a good word to Bayshore on his behalf."

"But Harlan . . ."

"Kathy West's nephew Harlan, remember."

"Okay, but why would he . . . ?" Hardy asked.

Treya jumped in. "You can't blame Cuneo for wanting out of homicide. They obviously didn't want him anymore. Now this new job gets him off the force and everybody's happy."

"So it's over," Hardy said.

Glitsky nodded. "He was essentially through when you finished with him in court, Diz. But now he's not just through. He's really, truly gone."

"That really does call for a toast," Frannie said.

But Hardy had a last question. "I'm just wondering how it happened. I can see Kathy passing the information along to Harlan, but how would she have heard about an opening like that?"

A glint showed in Glitsky's eyes. He shrugged with an exaggerated nonchalance. "Somebody must have told her," he said. Without further ado, he raised his glass. "Well, dear and true friends, here's to life. *L'chaim!*"

ACKNOWLEDGMENTS

This book was born in fire.

I knew it would begin with a blaze in a San Francisco residence. I also knew next to nothing about the workings of fire departments or arson inspectors. So I asked my friend Josh Marone, a Santa Rosa fireman, if he could introduce me to some of his colleagues, which he was kind enough to do—thank you, Josh, for getting the ball rolling. Also in Santa Rosa, thanks to Paul Lowenthal and to Mark Pedroia, senior fire inspector, and especially to Charles J. Hanley, division chief, Santa Rosa Fire Department. Chas in turn introduced me to Thomas A. Siragusa, assistant deputy chief, San Francisco Fire Department; and Brendan O'Leary, fire investigator, Arson Task Force, San Francisco Fire Department. Thanks to all of these gentlemen for the fun and informative sessions.

Other technical advice came from forensic odontologist James Wood, DDS; from Curtis Ripley, for the critical ceramics instruction that too many of us neglect; on banking matters, from Kelly Binger and John DiMichele of Yolo Community Bank in Woodland, California; on general legal and other really cool stuff, from Peter J. Diedrich. Additionally, Peter S. Dietrich, MD, MPH, provided some very fine libations over the course of the past year and still found the time and energy to correct medical errors in the first draft. Thank you to one and all. If any of the technical details in this book are wrong, it's entirely the fault of the author.

Throughout this entire series of San Francisco books, and this one is no exception, my collaborator, Al Giannini, has been a terrific source and inspiration on all matters related to criminal law and the justice system. His judgment and expertise in these areas are second to none, and I'm blessed to count him among my closest friends.

At Dutton, Carole Baron continues to set the standard for great publishers/editors. Her wonderful personality, intelligence, sensitivity and taste make her an absolute pleasure to work with, and my great hope is that I continue to write books that she considers worthy of her time and commitment. On a more day-to-day level, Mitch Hoffman is a talented editor who endures regular doses of author angst without apparent ill effects. A careful and disciplined reader, Mitch brings a clear focus and passion to the editing process, and this finished book is vastly superior to its first draft in large part because of his insight and suggestions. I'd also like to acknowledge some of the terrific backstage folks at Dutton: the publicity team of Lisa Johnson, Kathleen Matthews-Schmidt and Betsy DeJesu; webmaster Robert Kempe; and Richard Hasselberger for another great book jacket.

Out in the real world, many friends and colleagues play more or less continuing roles in my career and my life. My incredible assistant, Anita Boone, goes a long way toward making every workday productive, efficient and fun. She's also a mind reader (which helps, believe me), an unparalleled genius of an organizer and a tireless and cheerful detail person, who bears no resemblance whatever to Dismas Hardy's Phyllis, and that is high praise indeed. My great friend, the talented novelist Max Byrd, is a much-cherished regular source of both inspiration and motivation. Don Matheson, perennial best man, remains just that. Frank Seidl, besides keeping me up on my wine knowledge, has a knack for joy that is infectious and much appreciated. Karen Hlavacek is a fantastic proofreader whom I can't thank enough. On general principles, I'd just like to acknowledge my brothers, Michael and Emmett; Kathryn and Mark Detzer; Rick Montgomery; Glenn Nedwin; Andy Jalakas; Tom Hedtke; Tom Stienstra ("Men love him. Fish fear him."); and Bob Zaro.

Several characters in this book owe their names (although no physical or personality traits, which are all fictional) to individuals whose contributions to various charities have been especially generous. These people (and their respective charities) include Lisa Ravel (Sutter Medical Center Foundation); Mary Monroe-Rodman (Court Appointed Special Advocates—"CASA"—of Yolo County); and Jan Saunders (Monterey County Library Foundation).

My children, Justine and Jack, inform and enrich every moment of my life and my writing with their great selves. I love you both immensely.

Last, but by no means least, I'd like to thank my agent, Barney Karpfinger, for all of his continuing efforts on on my behalf. I am forever in your debt, my friend, and remain delighted to work with you every day.

Read on for a preview
of John Lescroart's
riveting new novel

The Hunt Club

Coming in January 2006
from Dutton

Although he was now considered an official hero, Inspector Devin Juhle was coming off a very bad time. Six months ago, he and his partner, Shane Manning, were on their way to talk to a witness in one of their investigations at two in the afternoon, when they'd picked up an emergency call from dispatch—a report that somebody was shooting up a homeless encampment under the Cesar Chavez Street freeway overpass. As it happened, they were six blocks away and were the first cops on the scene.

Manning was driving, and no sooner than he had pulled their unmarked city-issue Plymouth into the no-man's-land beneath the overpass, a man stepped out from behind a concrete pillar about sixty feet away and leveled a shotgun at the car.

"Down! Down!" Juhle had screamed as Manning was jamming into park, slamming on the brakes. One hand was unsnapping his holster and the other already on the door's handle, and Juhle ducked and hurled his body against the door, swinging it open and getting below the dash just as he heard the blast of the scattergun and the simultaneous explosion of the windshield above him, which covered him with pebbles of safety glass. Another shotgun blast, and then Juhle was out of the car on the asphalt, rolling, trying to get behind a tire for shelter.

"Shane!" he yelled for his partner. "Shane!"

Nothing.

Peering under the car's chassis—he remembered all of it as one picture, though the images were in different directions, so it couldn't have been—he saw two bodies down on the ground by a cardboard structure and behind them a half dozen or so people crouched in the lee of one of the concrete buttresses that supported the overpass, penned in so they couldn't escape. At the same time, the man with the gun had retreated behind the pillar again. To the extent that Juhle was thinking at all and not just reacting, he thought the killer was reloading. But it was his only chance to get an angle and save himself and maybe these other people as well.

He bolted for the low stump of a tree that sat in the middle of the asphalt. It shouldn't have been there—Caltrans should have uprooted the thing before they poured, but they hadn't. Now there it was and he'd reach it if he could. Running low, then diving and rolling, he got to it in two or three seconds, enough time for the shooter, who had come out in the open again, to fire his next round, which pocked into the stump in front of him and sprayed him with wood chips and pulp.

Juhle, on his stomach and with the side of his face and body pressed flat to the ground, knew that the stump didn't give him six inches of clearance and that the man was advancing now, sensing his advantage. He was still probably sixty or seventy feet away—and coming on fast. Once he got to forty feet or so, the shooter's height would give him the angle he needed. The next shotgun blast and Juhle would be history.

There wasn't any time for thought. Juhle rolled a full rotation, extended his gun gripped in both hands out in front of him, drew a bead, and squeezed off two shots. The man stumbled, crumbled, dropped like a bag of cement, and did not move.

Juhle called out for his partner again and again got no reply. Still in a daze, his adrenaline surging, he eventually got to his feet, his gun never leaving the downed man. In half steps, he warily crab-walked sideways toward him, with his gun extended across his body in a two-handed stance. When he got to his target, he saw that he had made the luckiest shot of his life. One bullet had hit the man between the eyes.

Which should have been the end of it. After all, Juhle had six witnesses to everything. Manning was dead, killed by the first blast. The car was a shot-up mess. It was clearly self-defense at the very least and heroism by any standard.

But not necessarily.

Not in San Francisco, where every police shooting is suspect. One of the homeless in the encampment, a highly intoxicated diagnosed schizophrenic, insisted that police had run up to the deceased and executed him for no reason. The fact that he claimed there had been five such officers and that he maintained that the man had not had a shotgun—in spite of Manning's death by shotgun blast—didn't even slow down the right-minded public nuisances of the antipolice crowd.

Beyond that, Juhle's shot was so perfect that it led Byron Diehl, one of the city's supervisors, to opine that perhaps the killing had, in fact, been an overreaction by an overzealous and enraged cop. Perhaps it had, in point of fact, been an execution. Nobody could hit a moving man with a pistol between the eyes at fifty or sixty feet. That just wasn't a possible shot. The man with the gun might have already surrendered, laid his gun down, and Juhle—out of control because of the murder of his partner—had walked up and shot him point-blank.

The other witnesses? Please. Most of them wanted the shooter dead, anyway. Plus, they were naturally afraid of the police. If Juhle told them they'd better back up his story or else, they'd say anything he wanted. They were simply unreliable and their testimonies worthless. Except for the schizophrenic, of course, who was struggling with his substance abuse issues. The idiocy was so palpable that it may have been fun to watch but not to be part of.

So Juhle spent the next three months on administrative leave, under the shadow of a murder charge. He testified four times before different city and police commissions, not including a formal session defending his actions and confronting Diehl in the chamber of the board of supervisors. He was asked to demonstrate his prowess with a handgun on various police ranges in San Francisco, Alameda, and San Mateo counties, where they had pop-up targets that demanded speed as well as accuracy.

Finally, a couple of months ago, he'd been cleared of any wrongdoing. Returning to his place in homicide, though—Manning was of course gone forever—he found himself newly partnered with an obviously political hire, Gumqui

Shiu, whose ten-year career didn't seem to have included much real police work. He'd been an instructor at the Academy, worked in the photo lab, and been assigned to various other details, where his progress had been rapid but unmarked by any real accomplishment. He clearly had juice somewhere, but nobody seemed to know where it came from.

This morning, Juhle was at his desk. Insult to injury, he still had his right arm in the sling from arthroscopic rotator cuff surgery—three little holes. His doctor had told him it was an in-and-out-in-the-same-day procedure, little more than an office visit. He'd be pitching Little League practice again in no time.

Not.

Like he ever wanted to do that again, anyway. Little League was pretty much the reason he'd thrown out the damn arm in the first place, letting his macho devils con him into a little mano a mano with Doug Malinoff—perfect baseball name—the manager of Devin's son Eric's team, the Hornets. Doug was a good guy, really, if maybe slightly more competitive than your typical major-leaguer during the playoffs, talking Assistant Coach Devin into playing a game of "burnout" for the enjoyment of the kids. Give them a taste of what it's like to *really* want to win.

Burnout's a simple game for simple adults and pre-adolescent boys: You throw a baseball as hard as you can starting from, say, sixty feet. You use regular gloves, no extrapadded catcher's mitts allowed, and you move a step closer after each round. First one to give up loses. Devin was no slouch as an athlete, having played baseball through college. He still had a pretty good gun of an arm. Nevertheless, he gave up, conceding defeat, after seven rounds, his opponent nearly knocking him down on his last throw from thirty-five feet. Malinoff had played shortstop in minor-league ball, made it to double-A. He could throw a baseball through a plywood fence.

Juhle caught the sixth toss not in the webbing but in the palm of the mitt. He never mentioned to a living soul and never would that on top of ruining his shoulder through his own stupidity on that cold and misty March day, he also allowed Malinoff's major-league fastball to break two bones in his *catching hand*.

Since then, Juhle had been having confidence issues. He found it hard to convince himself that he was among the most brilliant homicide inspectors on the planet when at the same time he considered himself a certified idiot for going at it with Malinoff.

It was Tuesday morning, May 31, nine fifteen. June, just a day away, is synonymous with fog in San Francisco, and today Juhle couldn't see the elevated freeway sixty yards to his left out the window. Awaiting the arrival of his partner, he was at his desk in the crowded, cramped, and yet wide-open room without interior walls that was the homicide detail on the fourth floor of San Francisco's Hall of Justice. He was sipping his third cup of coffee this morning, his right arm and still untreated opposite hand—damned if he was going to let anybody know—both throbbing in spite of six hundred milligrams of Motrin every four hours for the past ten days. He turned to the second page of the transcription of a witness's testimony in one of his cases that he was checking against the tape and suddenly took off his headphones, stood up, and made his way past the shoulder-high, battered green-and-gray metal files that served as room dividers, and stopped at the door of his lieutenant, Marcel Lanier, who looked up from his own paperwork.

"What's up, Dev?"

"We gotta do something about the quality of people they hire, Marcel."

Lanier, only fifty-some and yet still a hundred years with the department, scratched around his mouth. "That's a song I've been singing for years. What kind of people this time?"

For an answer, Juhle handed him the printout he'd been reading. "You'll see it," he said.

Five seconds into his reading, Lanier barked out a one-note toneless laugh, then read aloud. " 'And what is your relationship with Ms. Dorset?' "

Juhle nodded. "That's it. You don't see a relationship like that every day."

"He was her power mower?"

"Must have been, since it's right there in black and white."

"Her power mower?"

"Yeah, except maybe instead of *power mower,* what he actually said was that he was her 'paramour.' " Juhle leaned against the doorpost. "And this is, like, mistake ten on one page, Marcel, not counting the big chunks that she has marked 'unintelligible' on the transcript, but that *I* can hear perfectly on the tape. Do they give an IQ test before we start paying these people? Of course, I've got to correct the transcript, anyway, but now it's going to take me two days instead of an hour. It'd be quicker to write the whole goddamn thing out in longhand."

Shiu floated up behind Juhle into the space left in the doorway. "What's going to take two days?"

Lanier ignored both the arrival and the question. His phone rang and he picked it up. "Homicide, Lanier." Frowning, suddenly all serious, he pulled over his yellow pad and started jotting. "Okay, got it. We're moving." Looking up at his two inspectors, he said into the phone, "Juhle and Shiu." When he hung up, there was no sign that he'd ever laughed or thought anything in the world had been funny ever. "Either of you already signed out on a car?"

The inspectors shared a glance. "No, sir. Paperwork day," Juhle said.

"Not anymore it isn't. Grab a ride in a black-and-white downstairs," he said, "and have 'em light it up out to Clay at"—he shot a quick look at his notes— "Lyon. Don't pass go, guys. I'll get word to the techs. I want a presence there yesterday. Somebody just killed a federal judge."